# This Is Where I Came In

## Mike Robertson

# This Is Where I Came In

## Mike Robertson

MIKEY'S IMAGINATION PUBLISHING

Austin

A Division of Shadownoze, Inc.,
A completely imaginary company
www.whereicamein.blogspot.com

Mike Robertson
PO BOX 606
Dripping Springs TX 78620

email: WhereICameIn@yahoo.com

Copyright 2010 by Mike Robertson. All rights reserved.

ISBN: 1453884912
EAN-13: 9781453884911

This book is also available as an ebook on Amazon.com and BarnesAndNoble.com.

This is a work of fiction. Characters and events in this book are fictitious. Any similarity to real persons, living or dead, is coincidental and not intended by the author.

For more information about this book, visit www.whereicamein.blogspot.com.

*Before the Fall, when they wrote it on the wall,*
*When there wasn't even any Hollywood.*
*They heard the call and they wrote it on the wall.*
*And you and me, we understood.*

— Steely Dan, *Caves of Altamira*

*Movies is magic.*
*Real life is tragic.*

— Van Dyke Parks, *Movies Is Magic*

## CHAPTER ONE

I made movies. And movies made me.

Of course, they weren't called movies back then. The first ones I ever saw lasted about thirty seconds each. And they had no actors! There might be a scene of a horse eating hay — or waves crashing on the beach. That was the whole film.

Do you remember when you saw your first motion picture? I do. I've had a lot of time to remember it. October 10, 1896. Right here in Austin, Texas.

It was a different time…a different world. I had never seen an automobile, and of course there was no such thing as an airplane — or a radio. I lived in a house without electricity or running water. I had never used a flush toilet before. You couldn't buy a bottle of Coca-Cola, although the fountain version was just becoming popular. Women couldn't vote or show their ankles… and that was true in all forty-five states. Forty-five states, ha!

I suppose I'm just trying to tell you that it was a time when new miracles were happening all the time. But to me, there was something special about this one. Somebody had figured out how to make pictures move.

As I sat in that opera house, I realized something. Movies could capture life.

I just didn't realize they would capture mine.

## REEL ONE

## 1896

*Mike Robertson*

## CHAPTER TWO

I lived with my family on a farm outside of Blanco, Texas, a small town west of Austin, north of San Antonio and far from excitement. Father was a Baptist preacher and had occupied the pulpit in Blanco for my entire life. He was a kind and gentle man; oh, he could call down fire and brimstone with the best of them, but he was not the sour, judgmental prophet of doom found in so many pulpits. His name was Jesse Joseph Wilkinson, but most of the folks around Blanco called him Brother Jess.

While at the seminary in Fort Worth, he met and married Inella Lou Stuckey, the daughter of Baptist missionaries to China. She had been born in Mississippi, but spent most of her formative years in China. She was soft-spoken, though with an iron determination. Music could make her cry, as could many of Father's sermons. She played the pump organ for services and it was sometimes quite a toss-up as to whether she could play the offertory through her tears.

The first child born to my parents was a girl named Hannah, who arrived in 1878. She was followed two years later by a son, named Aaron, but Aaron only lived for four months, falling prey to pneumonia. I was the third child, followed by two more girls — Mary and Martha — and another boy, Paul. We were by no means the largest family in Blanco County; in that day, big families were seen as a built-in community and I remember how folks talked about that poor, poor Minton family, who only had one child. In addition, it was exceptional for a couple to raise a family without the specter of death claiming one or more of their children. Doctors were few and far between and much of their prescribing was based on guesswork. They were therefore viewed as a last resort for sick folk. We prayed; if healing resulted, hallelujahs were hoisted. We tried folk remedies; if they worked, wonderful! If they didn't, we would try to find a doctor, who would mix up a horrible-tasting batch of some sort of elixir which would either cure the patient or make him feel that death was an acceptable alternative.

All of us were given Biblical names. My father, having borne two Biblical names, decreed that we all should do the same. Mother was intent on giving me a musical head-start, and insisted that I should be named after a musician in the Bible. That narrows down the choices quite a bit. I would have preferred to be named after that lusty, charismatic harpist and future king, David — he of the giant-killing, battle-winning, song-writing and window peeping. Instead, I bear the name of the earliest musician in creation, mentioned way back in Genesis, chapter four — Jubal. Fortunately, Father got to pick my middle name and he chose one that he hoped would fill me with courage, faith, and the ability to withstand large, carnivorous beasts. Yea, verily, Jesse and Inella begat Jubal Daniel Wilkinson on February 23, 1881. And, behold, I was good…pretty good, anyway.

Mother usually called me Dan, although — when I was in trouble — I got the full scriptural weight of my Holy Trinity of names. "Jubal Daniel Wilkinson, you get in here right this minute!" When I started to school, the Jubal mantle caused me plenty of grief. I was sometimes called "Jew-balls" or "Jew-boy" by boys who had never seen a Jew in their lives (neither had I). Eventually and blessedly, I became "J.D."

In the late nineteenth century, preachers lived by the grace of God and the charity of their congregations. In a good month, Father might receive forty dollars via the offering plate; frequently it was less…sometimes much less. I had many times seen both parents look balefully at a near-empty collection plate after it had passed almost unscathed through the congregation. Both parents told me that God would always provide for our needs and I believed them. There were many instances in our family history to reinforce this belief, like the Christmas of 1892, when there was not a cent in the house and it looked as though there would be no presents, no tree, no special dinner.

Just after dark on Christmas Eve, there was a knock at the door of our two-room farmhouse. When Father opened the door, we all heard the voice of Harlan Whitson, who said, "Preacher, I been carrying this in my pocket for months, wondering what I was supposed to do with it. Just today, I felt like God was telling me to bring it to you. Merry Christmas and God bless you." I heard his footsteps clomping across the porch and he was gone. Father turned back to the fire-lit room with a stunned expression on his face as he stared at the twenty dollar gold piece in his hand, amazed that God had provided and embarrassed that he was amazed. It was too late for us to venture into town to buy gifts that night, so our Christmas arrived a day late, on the twenty-sixth. Mother and Hannah got material for new dresses, Father chose a new hat, I got new boots and a bag of candy, Mary got a storybook, Martha a doll and Paul got a top and a wooden locomotive. I knew already that Santa Claus was a myth, but I certainly was convinced that God himself had an eye trained on the Wilkinsons of Blanco County.

Beyond taking care of us when we were doing without, God must have had a pretty boring time watching us. For the country outside of Blanco was a quiet, lonely place, where even temptation was scarce. If sinning required something besides cedar trees and rocks, it would most likely go undone. Our house was devoid of playing cards or dominoes, since they could be seen as tools for gambling. We had the Bible and a few other books, but nothing which was likely to put impure thoughts into the head of a young man…although I did furtively peruse the Song of Solomon in the family Bible at times. Take a look, you'll be surprised.

Our only source of music was a pump organ which Mother had ordered out of the Montgomery Ward catalogue; it had cost more than forty dollars and thus represented quite a commitment of the family's resources. A small stack of sheet music and a hymnal sat atop the organ. The few songs that weren't overtly religious tended to be about babies dying and going to live in Heaven, or missing your Mother. I didn't have much chance to miss my own mother, who was regularly reduced to a sobbing wreck when she played and sang some of these weepers. I was usually drafted into harmonizing along with her and it was difficult to maintain a manly composure when her tears began to fall and her voice began to break. I didn't cry…usually.

Dancing was not only considered a sin, but I clearly recalled how Willy Perdue and his wife were driven out of the church after they dared to attend a dance in a house in Blanco. After they were "churched" — booted out of the fellowship — dancing was mentioned in the sermon several Sundays in a row.

And as for more serious sins, I really wasn't aware of them. There was no alcohol in our home, no tobacco, and, as far as I could tell — in spite of the presence of me and four siblings — no sex. I had a pretty good idea of how babies were made, due to growing up on a farm, but I was quite unclear as to how human plumbing corresponded with its bovine equivalent.

Father, by virtue of staying at one church for so long and being untarred by scandal, had acquired some standing in the Baptist Convention of Texas, so it was not a big surprise when he made plans to attend their annual convention in Austin. What was a big surprise was that he invited me to go along. His theory was that being around a couple hundred preachers would be a good experience for me, not to mention the salutary effect of observing the seat of Texas government in the state's capital.

You see, my parents both hoped that I would also receive that mysterious call and enter the ministry. I was in church from the time I was a week old — twice every Sunday and once every Wednesday night. My mother had begun teaching me to play the organ and sing about the time I learned to read, perhaps in the hope that I could be a triple threat preacher-singer-organist. Maybe even a traveling evangelist! I had a charming boy soprano voice, but by my fourteenth year, the soprano had vacated the premises, leaving a wandering goose behind. My voice was unsure of which way it was going, and the meanderings it took caused me no end of embarrassment. By fifteen, though, it looked like I was going to be a tenor.

Father assured me I would hear the absolute best preachers and singers at the convention and that I would also have time to explore Austin during the times he had committee meetings, prayer vigils or seminars in exegesis. I could scarcely sleep the night before we left, tossing and turning while I tried to picture the big city in my mind.

## CHAPTER THREE

Father and I set off in the buggy on Tuesday morning, October 7. It was still warm — Indian summer, I guess you'd call it. On the way to Austin we must have seen ten million little orange butterflies; they filled the air, drifting like fat snowflakes, and all heading south for some reason.

Father whistled as he drove, although he only seemed to know two tunes, both of them hymns, of course. When I got tired of both tunes, I would ask him a question about our family history or one of his most trying times as a pastor. He loved to tell stories and did so in a soft, expressive voice that was very different from his preaching tone. He told of showdowns with deacons who wanted to run the church, of the dramatic conversion experiences of some reprobate ranchers, of his assurance that he was exactly where God wanted him to be. He related how he'd met Mother, how Aaron died, how he and Mother had prayed for someone to help the church with music…and I had been born.

It was just getting dark as we came over the last hill and I was amazed at my first sight of the capital city. Father told me that, just a year before, in 1895, Austin had erected 31 "moonlight towers" around town. Each tower was 165 feet tall and was crested with six carbon arc lights that bathed the town in a beautiful glow. The contract for the lights specified that they had to provide sufficient illumination for a citizen to read his pocket watch — without squinting — at a distance of 1500 feet from the nearest tower. In a city with no paved streets and lots of hills, the moonlight towers were thought to be a more efficient lighting system than the later practice of putting a street lamp on each corner. The effect of a whole city illuminated by artificial moonlight was amazing to me.

After we crossed the bridge over the Colorado River, I could see the framework of the first tower. It was a smooth metal pole for the first fifteen feet, but then a triangular framework bloomed from this stem. Inside the framework, I could see a large pulley; Father informed me that each tower had a man-powered elevator and that Austin employed a man whose sole job was to go from tower to tower, crank himself up to the dizzying apex and trim the six carbon arcs. I looked up as we passed under the tower, but the bluish-white light was so bright I could not even see the top of the structure.

Our buggy proceeded down an extremely wide street. I guessed that it was Congress Avenue because I could see the pink granite Capitol building at the end. Texas had built a new Capitol just a couple of years before, after a fire had destroyed the old one. A special railroad line had been constructed to transport the granite from Marble Falls. The result was the tallest Capitol building in the United States — a fact much touted by Austinites and other Texans — and the sight was very inspiring to me. It's one thing to read about the government and lawmakers, but quite another to see the scene of the crime. It looked like a palace to me, with its massive dome topped by the silvery statue of Lady Liberty. There was not another building in Austin taller than three stories, so the contrast was even greater than it would be in just a few years.

We checked into a room in the Hotel Salge which contained a single electric light bulb hanging nakedly from the ceiling. Although the room was also fitted with the more familiar gas jets, this bulb was the harbinger of a new day and I flicked it on and off repeatedly until my father told me to stop before I wore it out. I couldn't help it, though! The town of Blanco had no electricity and our lighting came from gas, kerosene, coal-oil or wood fire. I fell asleep in the hotel's soft bed, listening to the mysterious sounds of a large city at night: the ringing of a trolley car bell, the galloping of horses, the tolling of a clock ringing the hours. This was in contrast to nights in the country, where nights were quiet unless a strong wind was blowing or it was raining.

On Wednesday morning, we attended the opening session of the convention, which was being held at the First Baptist Church of Austin, an imposing edifice which made our church in Blanco look like a clapboard shack, which is pretty much what it was. I had my fill of preaching by lunchtime, but there were hours more in the afternoon. In addition to the evangelical oration of the best preachers in Texas, there were political matters to settle, as well. Delegates had to be recognized, resolutions passed, motions made, nominations entered.

The convention in 1896 was consumed with the matter of Bro. Elmo Honeycutt, a minister from New Canaan, Texas, who had apparently been preaching the doctrines of "Martinism" and "Futunism" (no, I have no idea what either of those was). Articles had been written in all the Baptist newspapers and debate raged over how this thorn in the flesh should be addressed.

Thursday was full of more of the same and by Friday morning I was feeling about as sanctified as I was likely to get. I had been called to repentance, chastised for backsliding, exhorted to proclaim and given glimpses of Heaven until my eyes and ears were tired and my brain drifted out to the Avenue, where all sorts of wonders awaited.

Finally, on Friday afternoon, while my father was meeting with other pastors at the hotel, discussing whether Reverend Honeycutt might receive forgiveness or damnation, I was permitted some free time to explore the streets of Austin. As I passed through the heavy lobby door, I could see the Capitol building; it was ten blocks away, but it was still huge, the biggest building I had ever seen. Although there were no paved roads in Austin, an electric streetcar ran up and down Congress Avenue on tracks laid in the dirt. I thought about hopping on one to see how far it went, what adventures it might lead to.

Instead I headed north on foot, passing Scarborough's store with its windows full of finery: hats, suits, ladies' shirtwaists. I had an unfamiliar feeling. I had certainly heard plenty of sermons about temptation, but how much temptation was there on a farm in Blanco? Ah, but this! This was a city that held wonders I had only read about — and some I was sure had never appeared in the bowdlerized library of our home. I felt a curious rush of freedom at the thought of being in a big city, with big temptations. As I felt the weight of the new choices in my head, I was also conscious of another weight, the prize in my pocket — the silver Liberty dollar Nana had sent me on my birthday. Both my parents thought it was too extravagant for a fifteen-year-old, but I had squirreled it away in a cloth tobacco pouch that Thomas Clough had given me.

"Choose wisely," I thought. Chiles' Drug Store had a placard in the window proclaiming, "We Are Sole Agents for HUYLER'S CELEBRATED CANDIES. From 65 cents to $1 per pound." I loved candy and in my fifteen years I had never had the chance to eat all the candy I could stand. But this was an important decision and I didn't want to be hasty. J.A. Jackson's store had all manner of musical instruments, but for a dollar, I could only get a harmonica or a Jew's harp.

When I reached the corner of Congress and Sixth, I looked both ways to see what might catch my fancy. Half a block west on Sixth Street, I could see a building which was fronted by more electric lights than I had ever seen in one place. The arched front of the building bore gilt letters: HANCOCK OPERA HOUSE.

Several people were crowded around the glass-framed poster box. I couldn't imagine that an opera could hold their attention. When some of them moved away, I wormed my way close enough to read the large, inky letters:

>**This Afternoon — — —**
>**— — — and To-night.**
>**Edison's VITASCOPE**
>**Edison's greatest and latest marvel,**
>**which is baffling analysis and**
>**delighting immense audiences**

**because of its wonderful imitation
of human beings in action.
An instrument showing life-like
pictures in action and in natural colors.
Two hours of amusement and instruction.
ADMISSION, 25¢ AND 50¢.
Seats now on sale.**

"What is it?," said a woman behind me.

"No telling," spoke a man's voice. "But with Edison behind it, it ought to be worth a look!"

A boy about my age said, "I think it's a lantern show of some kind."

"But it says they move," I protested. "A lantern show doesn't move!"

"Aw, sure they do," the boy insisted. "They had a Fourth of July lantern show this summer that had fireworks goin' off and Uncle Sam wavin' and the flag sorta flappin' in the breeze and—."

"I don't believe it is a lantern show." The man again. "Mr. Edison would certainly not claim the magic lantern as one of his own creations."

"The paper today says it's like one a them Kinetoscopes, 'cept it shines on a canvas like a lantern slide." The older woman who added this detail waved her copy of the Austin Daily Statesman as though it gave her words added weight. I had to find out what was in there. This was the big city and I was wealthy!

"Twenty-five cents…or fifty cents," I pondered.

"You goin' in?" Now the boy wanted to be my best friend. "I ain't got but a nickel."

My thoughts were engaged in higher mathematics. If I only paid a quarter for a seat, I could still get over a pound of candy with the other six bits. And what the man said was true; Mr. Edison could do just about anything, it seemed. I might be the first person from Blanco,

Texas, to see this…this Vitascope. I stepped to the middle plate glass door and went inside. Inside was a tiled lobby, bathed in more electric light. While gawking a bit at the walls and frescoes of orange and terra cotta, I edged over to the box office on the left side of the lobby.

The moustachioed man in the booth took my Liberty dollar and slid three quarters and a yellow ticket back to me. "Welcome to the Hancock, sir. Balcony stairs are on either side of the lobby."

Clutching the ticket, I climbed the broad staircase, taking in the lush green and gold draperies and the gold-framed painting on the first landing. The balcony was almost empty and I had a good chance to look around. At the front of the balcony were fifteen loges with circular fronts, private boxes which could each accommodate four people. These were obviously for the fifty cent crowd. Behind these were rows of maroon plush theater seats. I snagged one on the left aisle and looked down toward the stage.

Inside the Opera House was more splendorous than I had imagined. Velvet curtains hung in front of the stage, while a gold brocade wallpaper made me feel like I was inside the Ark of the Covenant. And indeed, cherubs and seraphim decorated the arch above the stage and I began to feel that excitement in the pit of my stomach as I thought that Heaven was probably very much like this.

The auditorium was filling rapidly and it seemed there were several groups of school children present with their teachers. The boxes in front of me soon were almost completely filled with what I took to be businessmen and their wives. They were all well-dressed, impeccably groomed and lacking the dusty, somewhat rumpled look that I feared marked me as a bumpkin.

I noticed for the first time that the center loge of the balcony, just behind the rail, contained two odd-looking machines. From the distance at which I viewed them, I could only tell that they were made of metal; I could see the yellow glint of brass and the silvery sheen of polished steel. Each had a tube on the front, pointing toward the stage.

Finally, when it seemed that every seat must be full, a man stepped out onto the stage.

He was dressed in what I eventually came to know as a tuxedo, and had a carefully waxed moustache that made impressive loops upward.

"Ladies and gentlemen, boys and girls! It is with great pleasure that I welcome you to the opera house today for this historic event. You are privileged to be among the first people in the world to view the latest and most amazing device to spring from the mind of that great American, Mr. Thomas Edison!" Applause followed; Edison truly was a wizard. If the speaker had told us that Edison had grown a second head on his shoulders, we would have accepted it, nodded our heads and proclaimed that it was only a matter of time, of course.

"Mr. Edison, expanding on the promise of his earlier creation, the Kinetoscope, has asked me to journey here to the capital of the great state of Texas to share with you this most wonderful diversion which he calls… the Vitascope!" More applause, more for the mention of Texas than for the mention of the Vitascope.

"The Vitascope brings to life, before your very eyes, scenes from other places, other countries, in such vivid and vital detail that you will be amazed. In the same manner that Mr. Edison's phonograph brings the great music of other lands into the ears of the fortunate listener, the Vitascope may bring to your vision sights hereto unseen by all but the most intrepid explorers and world travelers."

"How, you may well ask, can such wonders be performed? Mr. Edison has perfected a system by which a great many photographs of a particular subject are taken in rapid sequence. How rapid? Well, ladies and gentlemen, if you will observe…"

The man clapped his hands twice. "Can you imagine that a device could make 60 photographs between the first time I clapped my hands and the second? Indeed it is true!"

Skeptical murmurs were heard around me, though the people in the boxes seemed unperturbed. But how could anyone possibly take sixty photographs in the space of a second?

"These pictures, when viewed in rapid succession, succeed in giving the illusion of movement, even though each individual photograph is of a captured moment in time. If you have seen the Kinetoscope, you are familiar with this amazing illusion."

I had no idea what a Kinetoscope was, though I later learned that it was Edison's first attempt to bring motion pictures to the public...one person at a time. The Kinetoscope was a wooden box with a metal viewer. When a coin was inserted, whirring gears inside propelled a filmstrip which showed a brief dance sequence or a single short round of a boxing match. For a few years after creating this device, Edison refused to believe there was any potential for large-scale commercial use. It was not until the Lumiere brothers devised a method of projecting celluloid film that he became convinced.

"This illusion, which scientists call 'persistence of vision' enables the human brain to experience a perfect simulation of the serial movements of people, animals, machinery and natural phenomena. And because these pictures are printed on a transparent material called celluloid, they may be projected by the application of a very bright light and an optical lens, the resulting image thrown upon a canvas to be seen by hundreds of people simultaneously."

There was more, but the audience was beginning to wonder if they had shelled out two bits (or even four) for a lecture. Just at the point when my attention was being drawn to the noisy University students in the upper balcony yelling, "Get on with it!", the tuxedoed man wrapped it up: "And without further ado, ladies and gentlemen, I give you Thomas Edison's Vitascope!"

The lights of the theater were dimmed and suddenly a bright beam of light struck the white canvas on the stage. It showed a photograph of a street scene in some large city. There were tall buildings on either side of the street, much taller than the ones in Austin. A horse-drawn wagon was at the left of the picture and various people were scattered along the street. After a couple of seconds of viewing this static scene, there was an audible groan from some members of the audience, who apparently suspected they had been sold a bill of goods.

But then, with a whirring clatter, the image began to flicker and the horse began to pull the wagon across the street. The small figures of people began to walk. A streetcar materialized from somewhere and sailed through the intersection.

And the audience cheered! After about thirty seconds, the horse and wagon suddenly appeared back at the left of the screen and the whole episode transpired again. When it began a third time, I began to notice smaller details. A puff of smoke from a man's cigar was clearly visible. A flag on a pole rippled with the breeze. The barrels in the horse's wagon tipped and swayed with the bumps in the street. Shadows of people, animals and vehicles were obvious and animated.

After the brief scenario had run six times, I realized my mouth was hanging open. I closed it and looked around, but the bright light went out completely and the theater was dark. Now the audience groaned again, louder this time, but the darkness only lasted for a few seconds.

Now another image filled the white canvas. At the bottom of the picture was a rocky beach. Above it, an ocean stretched to the horizon. A series of waves rolled in, directly toward the front rows of the audience! The first wave struck the rocks and a huge spray of water went up. Many women in the orchestra seats squealed and some actually stood up. But no water fell upon them and they all sat back down to watch more waves roll in and crash splendidly. Having never seen a body of water greater than the Blanco River, I was in awe of the vastness of the sea and the power of the waves. Again, the sequence repeated several times, long enough for me to glance at the two machines at the front of the balcony. A harried-looking man was fiddling with one of the machines, the one which was now dark. As I watched, he finished his task, straightened, and reached over to the other machine. He flipped a switch and the room again fell dark. Then he touched something on the machine he had been working on and a new beam of light flickered on the canvas.

I could no longer observe the man, for I was so curious to see what new wonders the Vitascope might produce. The audience was soon convulsed in laughter at the sight of two Negroes engaged in a sloppy watermelon-eating contest; their slobbering and seed-spitting was given additional comedic impetus by the ferocity of their attack on the melon wedges. The next hour and a half flew by, filled with images of dancing girls surrounded by swirls of bright color, boxing matches, military parades, Venetian gondolas, Niagara Falls and many others.

For sheer audience reaction, there were two views which stood out. In the first, a train chugged into a depot. Since the tracks began in the upper right of the canvas and ran off the lower left, extreme consternation arose in the boxes on the left side of the theater when the huge iron horse seemed destined to derail right where they sat. In the second view, a moustachioed man planted a kiss on a woman's lips. Our narrator informed us that these were the prominent actors John Rice and May Irwin, and that they were recreating the thrilling climax of The Widow Jones, a musical comedy. Reenactment or not, the kiss caused a stir in the theater, titillating some while scandalizing others. I had never even seen my father kiss my mother on the lips. Fortunately, this view ran eight or nine times, and I observed it closely in the name of research. It didn't seem that difficult, but I couldn't really see why it should be so appealing, either. In fact, repeated viewings showed that May Irwin was beginning to laugh after John Rice's lips met hers. When the kiss finally disappeared from the screen, the theater lights brightened again and the narrator, after a few more remarks about how the Vitascope would soon bring world events to the reach of every person, thanked us for coming.

The audience began to file out, but I remained glued to my seat. I felt as though I had seen a vision. Part of it, I suppose, was that I had never before experienced "entertainment," never traded money for some professional presentation of acting or dancing or boxing or feats of strength. My mind felt exhausted from the trip around the world I had just experienced. Yet, the people around me seemed inured to such wonders. I overheard one man remark that it was only "some kind of trick." There were many smiles, but no one except me seemed fundamentally changed by the experience of the previous two hours.

I sat in the soft plush seat, musing over the wonders I had seen. After a few minutes I looked around to see the entire balcony deserted, except for me…and the harried-looking man operating the two bizarre machines.

I descended the steps to the front of the balcony and mutely observed him for a moment. He was gathering up loose piles of the long celluloid strips, muttering to himself. He sensed my presence and glanced at me, nodded, then continued his work. He resembled pictures I had seen of Edgar Allen Poe, with the long, dark hair parted in the center, the high forehead, the thick moustache.

The tuxedoed narrator stepped out onto the stage and yelled, "Leo! The next show's at seven. When you're done up there, get yourself something to eat and be back here by 6:30." Without waiting for an answer, the narrator swatted at the curtain until he found the opening and then disappeared.

"Fine, don't help me, you oily bastard. I'll get everything ready all by myself." This inspirational thought escaped through Leo's clinched teeth in a half-whisper. I was fascinated by this casual profanity! My mother had once shoved a bar of homemade soap in my mouth for saying "Darn."

Then he remembered I was nearby and he glanced at me again. "Sorry, kid. Little busy here and I need a smoke."

"It's okay. Can't you smoke in here?"

"Yeah, I can smoke in here, but this stuff will burn like gasoline if I do."

"Oh. Well. Need any help?"

"Mmmmm…yeah, okay. Come here and hold your arms out straight." Leo began to drape the celluloid strips over my outstretched arms. Up close I could see the individual photographs that comprised each endless loop, but I still could not grasp how this flimsy strip of stuff could produce the animated pictures.

When Leo had untangled and separated all the loops, he began to lay them across the seats.

"Why do you do that?" I asked.

"Well, it's so's I can grab a new loop as soon as the old one finishes. I start up the second machine, pull the loop off it and drop it on the floor, thread up the new loop, check the arc and, if I'm lucky, have time to scratch my rump before I have to crank up this machine."

"I don't understand how they work."

Leo gave me a weary look. "Naw, neither do I kid. Thanks for the help."

I had obviously been dismissed.

I made my way down the carpeted steps, crossed the lobby and found myself again on Sixth Street. A gnawing in my stomach reminded me that I hadn't eaten since lunch. I did not feel confident about going into a restaurant on my own; I had no idea how much such a meal would cost and whether I would like the choices presented me. Instead I patronized a street vendor who gave me a bundle of tamales for a dime. They were something my mother had never served and the novelty of eating a new food in a new setting made them taste a lot like forbidden fruit.

I headed back up the Avenue and stood again at the window of Chiles's Drug Store, thinking of the pound of candy I could buy with my remaining sixty-five cents. As I stared at the glass, I noticed the reflection of a horse and wagon slowly passing and my mind was instantly back at the opera house, seeing that first moving picture of just such a conveyance. I knew I had to go back for a second look at the Vitascope. There would perhaps never be another chance, certainly not in Blanco. I turned out my pockets to see if my coins had mysteriously multiplied, but I knew I would only find two quarters, a dime and a nickel. I was determined to purchase one of the expensive seats this time, to better see the images and be even closer to the foreign worlds pictured.

I stepped into Chiles's and purchased fifteen cents worth of rock candy. It was fairly cheap and constituted a substantial bag full. I lodged a piece in my cheek and stuffed the bag in my pocket. Carefully rationed, the bag could last me several days, as long as I resisted the urge to chew up the crystalline nuggets, letting them instead dissolve slowly into a sweet sap.

It was forty minutes until the next showing began, so I looked in several more windows along Congress as I meandered back toward Sixth Street. I passed the front of Hancock's Opera House and continued walking east when I heard a hissing sound from the alley beside the theater.

"Psssst. Hey, kid!" There was Leo, leaning against the outside stairway which led to the second balcony. He was enjoying his much-anticipated smoke and looking considerably less harried. I entered the alley.

"Hey, thanks again for the help. I need three arms sometimes."

"Oh, I enjoyed it. That Vitascope is really something! I'm going to see it again."

"Yeah? Where's a kid like you get all this money?"

"Birthday present. My grandmother."

Leo grinned. "Your granny wouldn't want you to waste all your cash on this stuff. Tell ya what, this one's on me, kid. Since you helped me and all."

I couldn't believe my ears. Leo was going to let me in free? I felt euphoric, but when I grinned, the rock in my cheek suddenly reminded me I could have had those Huyler's Celebrated Candies after all.

"That would be great! Would you like some candy?" I dug the rumpled bag out of my pocket.

"Sure, thanks. Maybe it'll get the taste of those rancid tamales out of my mouth. I tell ya, kid, don't ever eat something that you don't know where it's from." Leo flipped the butt of his cigar across the alley and motioned for me to follow him up the outside stairs. "What's your name, kid?"

"J.D. Wilkinson."

"I'm Leopold Matula. Call me Leo. You live here?" He pulled open the door to the balcony.

"No, I'm visiting here with my father. He's a preacher, in town for the convention."

Leo looked a bit surprised as he followed me into the darkened balcony. I've found that lots of people treat you differently when they find out you're a PK. "Hmm, Benny the bartender over at the Iron Front told me all the Baptists were in town. He said they came to town with a ten dollar bill in one hand and the ten commandments in the other and would leave without breaking either one. Your pa know you're here?"

"No. I mean, he knows I'm looking around town, but he doesn't know particularly where I am." I hadn't really worried about what my father would say about how I had chosen to spend my money. But it suddenly dawned on me that he would be wondering where I was, since it was almost dark outside. "You know, Miste…I mean, Leo, I better go back to the hotel and let him know where I am. I'll come back if it's alright with him."

"Okay, kid. Get here before the show starts and come to the door on the alley back of the building. Tell the old man there that you're helping Leo run the Vitascope and he'll let you in."

"Fine, then! I'll see you!" I raced down the outside stairs and trotted back to the hotel, conscious of the impending darkness and the fact that the moonlight towers were once again alight.

Dashing through the lobby of the Salge, I went upstairs to our room, to find my father in an agitated state.

"Jubal Daniel Wilkinson! Where on earth have you been? Do you know what time it is? Don't you know you shouldn't be out in a big city like this after dark?"

"Yessir, but…"

"I have been waiting for you here for almost two hours. I missed dinner with the other pastors because I didn't know if you'd been hurt or killed or fallen into some sort of mischief. Where have you been?"

"Well, I went to this…this science demonstration at the Opera House. It's one of Mr. Edison's inventions, Father, and I thought it would be a good chance to learn something."

He was a bit dubious. "Was it this Vitascope I read about in the newspaper today?"

"Yes! It was so amazing, Father! It was like really going to, to Paris and New York and, and…other places."

"Well, I trust it wasn't objectionable?"

"No." I saw no need to mention the dancing girls or May Irwin's kiss. "It was very educational!"

"Very well, then. Let's go see if we can find something to eat."

"Oh, I've already eaten."

"Really? Where?"

"I got some…uh…tamales, I think they were called, from a man on the Avenue."

"J.D.! Your mother would have a fit! Do you feel alright?"

Upon reflection, I had to admit that I felt absolutely great.

"Did you spend all your birthday money?" said Father.

"Only half. I spent 25 cents at the opera house, a dime on the tamales…and fifteen cents on some candy." I pulled the rumpled bag from my pocket. Father peeked inside the bag and tried to make a stern face.

"Well, I can see why you're not hungry. I'm going downstairs to get something to eat."

"Father, can I go back to the opera house? I'd like to see the Vitascope again and this man there said I could get in free."

"I think you've had enough gallivanting today. It's not so safe on the streets of a city like this once the sun goes down."

"But with the moonlight towers it's —"

"Don't argue, J.D. I think it's best we stay in this evening."

"Yes, sir."

I have always had difficulty disconnecting my brain when it was taken by some new problem or interest. That night, I tossed and turned as flickering images flashed on the canvas in back of my eyes, images of trains, waves, dancing women and me kissing…someone.

## CHAPTER FOUR

On Saturday morning, we had breakfast at the hotel and then ventured up the Avenue to visit the Capitol building. I was in a good mood because Father had read the morning paper over breakfast and there was a small article endorsing the Vitascope exhibition as being of great value for all school children and a wonderful invention. I was hopeful that I could take in both the matinee and evening performance.

The Capitol was beautiful and we walked through the echoing halls to take in the Senate and House chambers. The sight of that much pink granite was truly impressive, but my mind was in a darkened balcony a few blocks south. We bought some postcards and went back to the hotel to write Mother before lunch.

In the afternoon, Father had more committee meetings; the fate of Bro. Honeycutt was still undecided. After a small cautionary sermon on the potential evils of a large city, I was again given free passage to explore Austin.

I ran to the opera house to see if Leo was hanging around outside, but he was not to be found. I still had a couple of hours to kill, so I wandered up and down Sixth Street, looking at the samples in the photographer's window, viewing a dead body in the furniture maker/ undertaker's front room, watching passengers disembark from the train after it steamed into the depot.

I went back to the opera house and still saw no sign of Leo, but I decided to take a chance and climb the outside stairs to the balcony door. I banged on the door and waited. Sure enough, Leo pushed open the heavy door with an annoyed look on his face. When he saw it was me, his features softened and he said, "Hey, kid, what happened last night? The preacher wouldn't let you out?" He motioned for me to come inside.

"Do you need any help?" I asked, ignoring the question about my father.

"Surely. Here, untangle these loops." He pulled a length of celluloid out of a wooden box, which was full of tangled film. I began pulling the stiff ribbons out of the box and I had a first good chance to look at one. At first, all the pictures seemed to be the same; when I looked more closely, I could see how a horse's leg moved a fraction of an inch from picture to picture. It was still amazing, though, that these individual photographs could so seamlessly imitate life when beamed upon the white canvas.

I watched Leo as he threaded the long loop of film through a series of pulleys and then through the metallic mechanism. I noticed that a gear or sprocket engaged the small holes in the side of the celluloid strip. He straightened from his task, flipped a switch and watched as the apparatus clattered to life. I could see the flickering image appear on the canvas once more, the street scene which had opened the program last night. Leo adjusted the glass lens on the machine, which made the pictures blur, then clear again.

"This is such a wonderful machine!" I enthused. "How did you come to operate this one?"

"Aw, I used to do lantern shows."

He threaded another piece of film in the second device and made similar adjustments. When both machines were ready for the show, he told me more about lantern shows.

The audience for the matinee was gradually filling the auditorium. A few minutes before two, the tuxedoed man materialized in the balcony. He eyed me suspiciously, then asked Leo if everything was in readiness for the show. Leo replied in the affirmative and then pointed me out as his helper. "This is Mister J. D. Wilkinson; he's very interested in moving pictures and he's been helping me get set up. J.D., this is Mr. Koog."

I tried to turn on what little charm I could muster. "Pleasure to meet you, Mr. Koog, I sure did enjoy hearing your talk last night. This is some machine!"

Koog's face softened a smidgen, but he was loathe to spend another second on me, turning back to Leo. "The manager thinks we should run the kiss a few more times, and maybe run it earlier in the order."

"It's better if we close with it. If we don't, it's all downhill from there. That's the picture that everyone talks about the most."

A reddish flush colored Koog's face. "We're leaving tomorrow. It doesn't matter what you think. We'll do it the way I say." He then turned on his heel and strode toward the stairs.

Leo looked at the departing tuxedo and his lips curled as if he needed to spit. "That son of a bitch wouldn't know how to do a good show if his life depended on it. I've half a mind to run it the way I want and let him look like a buffoon when his lecture doesn't match up with the pictures." He paused. "On the other hand," he said, looking at me, "I've grown rather attached to my weekly salary." With that, he turned back to the Vitascope machine and continued sorting out the loops of film. He could tell at a glance what subject was on each loop and as I watched him, I wanted more than anything else to have the power to flip a switch and make women dance — and make an audience ooh and ahh with pleasure.

During the matinee performance, I tried to watch Leo as much as I could, but it was so difficult not to look at the moving pictures as Mr. Koog described the wonders to be shown. Even though I had seen them all the day before, the wonder of their movement and detail still enthralled me. The performance was marred a few times by some of the University students or "gallery gods" who sat in the upper reaches of the balcony and made rude comments about the pictures and Mr. Koog's speech. At times, they tossed wadded-up programs toward the screen. Mr. Koog and Leo both seemed accustomed to such interruptions and did not let them distract them from their duties.

The show ended about four o'clock and there would be a three-hour delay before the evening performance. As the audience filed out, Mr. Koog yelled up to the balcony, "Six-thirty, Leo. And sober!"

Leo gritted his teeth as I helped him untangle the film loops. He glanced at me as though to judge my reaction to Mr. Koog's admonition, but I tried to appear oblivious. When the films were all straight and arranged on the backs of the theater seats, Leo asked if I wanted to go get something to eat before the next show.

"Well, I really ought to go back to the hotel and see if my father's planning on us having supper together."

"Okay, kid. If you decide to join me, I'll be at the chop house over on the east side of the Avenue. See you for the next show if you can get away. Thanks for the help."

I walked quickly back to the hotel and found my father seated with a group of pastors in the lobby. They all seemed in a jovial mood and were swapping stories and jokes. Father waved me over and asked me where I was heading.

"I came back to see if you were wanting to have supper or if I should do something on my own."

"I believe I'll eat with these fellows in the dining room. Do you want to join us?"

"Well, if it's alright with you, I'd like to get something to eat on the Avenue and go back to the seven o'clock sh— uh, lecture, at the Opera House. Mr. Matula allowed me to help him with the Vitascope machine." I had small hope that I could escape another meal with a passel of preachers, but Father's ebullient mood was in my favor. He reached into a vest pocket and gave me a quarter. "Be careful. And remember who you are and where you come from. What time will you be back?"

"The lecture ends about nine o'clock. I'll come straight back to the hotel. It's the last chance I'll have to hear it, because they're leaving tomorrow."

"All right, J.D. I'll see you upstairs."

## CHAPTER FIVE

I left the hotel, crossed to the east side of Congress, and started looking for the chop house. When I found it and rushed in, I was rather surprised to see Leo eating with a lady. But a lady unlike any I had ever seen in Blanco. Her clothing was a bright purplish-red and black and her hat bore a large white ostrich feather. Long reddish-brown curls spilled from the back of her hat halfway down her back and her face was all painted up with whitish powder and red cheeks and black circles around her eyes. I became aware that I was staring at her with my mouth open when Leo said, "What's wrong, kid, never met a lady before?" The lady looked amused and let out a cackling laugh.

"This is Mabel," said Leo. "We're old, old friends…of a day or two." Leo and Mabel both cackled at this.

I nodded my head and said, "Pleased to meet you, ma'am."

"Oh, you don't have to call me ma'am, honey. Mabel never met a boy she didn't like. Sit down, sit down!"

I took one of the empty chairs at the table. A man in a long white apron materialized beside me and recited a list of possible meal choices. I picked a fried beef chop with potatoes and carrots. While I waited for my food, I watched Leo and Mabel whisper, giggle, tease and flirt. Up close, I could see the pockmarks under Mabel's face powder and the makeup couldn't fully disguise the fact that she was a somewhat homely girl. But Leo seemed to enjoy her company. I was beginning to wonder why he had even invited me, since he spent almost all of his attention on Mabel. Occasionally he would look over at me and wink, or Mabel would give me a somewhat appraising look. Both of them were drinking beer with their meal and I again felt the hot flush on my face that I always felt when in the presence of some alien sinful vice.

My food arrived, and beside it the man in the apron set a glass of beer. I stared at it in disbelief, then asked if I might have a glass of water instead. The waiter reached to take away the beer, but Leo said, "Aw, leave it. Mabel gets awful dry sometimes." This set them off in new paroxysms of laughter.

I ate my supper, which was pretty good, although not the way my mother would have fixed it. But I felt like an intruder, sitting there with a couple of lovebirds. I finished as quickly as I could and paid my bill — all of ten cents. I told Leo I would see him at the Opera House and told Mabel it was nice to meet her, then I left the restaurant.

I was walking and thinking about my strange meal and that strange woman. At the first corner I came to, I turned west and continued walking. I had not been west of the Avenue before and I really took no notice of things around me until I began to notice loud music. I looked up to see a large Victorian two-story house. All the windows were open and someone in there was giving a piano a good working over. It sounded like what Mother called "ragged time" music. She couldn't or wouldn't play it, but I knew a little what it sounded like. As my eyes rose upward, I noticed a few women in white sitting in the upstairs windows. One of them waved and I looked around to see who she was waving to; there was no one there but me! I waved back and noticed the red lantern hanging on the front porch.

You may think me impossibly naive, but I still had no idea what sort of place I stood before. The music was novel and exciting, the woman in the window looked pretty, and I merely felt puzzled. The girl upstairs put her hands on the windowsill and leaned out, affording me a view that made me feel very strange. "Got any money, sugar?"

Forcing my gaze north of her gaping neckline, I stared at her face. She bore the same sort of paint that Mabel had worn and, in my addled state, I somehow figured there was some connection. "Are you a friend of Mabel's?" I asked.

Her smile turned to a look of puzzlement and then she smiled again. "I know Mabel, sure. Are you a friend of hers?"

"Well, I just had dinner with her, if that's what you mean."

"Ready for dessert, then?"

I remembered the bag of rock candy still in my pocket. "I've already got some, thanks."

"Strong young fella like you oughta be ready for seconds, I bet."

What in the world! I pondered this remark and then said, "Thanks, but I bought fifteen cents worth yesterday and it's lasting real good."

Now it was the painted woman's turn to look puzzled. I waved at her and resumed walking, but now paid more attention to where I was. This section of town bore little resemblance to Congress Avenue. The pedestrians seemed to be all male and the street rang with more ragged time piano, fiddle and occasional trumpet music. Several houses featured windows full of women like the one I had just encountered. I wasn't sure what went on here, but I definitely got a feeling that I should not be in this setting. I crossed the street and started back east, feeling a sense of relief at the now-familiar storefronts on Congress Avenue. I pulled a piece of rock candy from my pocket and let it dissolve slowly in my cheek as I wandered up and down the street. With the change from the quarter Father had given me, plus what was left of my birthday money, I still had sixty-five cents. I spent the next hour looking in shops, especially the bookstore, but I had suddenly become very possessive of my funds and ended up buying nothing.

At 6:15 I was back in the alley by the Hancock Opera House, waiting for Leo. I was still standing there twenty minutes later, when the upstairs door opened and the red face of Mr. Koog poked out. He looked up and down the alley, then recognized me. "Have you seen Leo, young man?"

"I saw him at the chop house earlier with a...with his supper."

He scowled and slammed the door shut.

Moments later, Leo came down the alley in what could only be called a swagger. "Hey, preacher-boy! You made it out after dark, hey?"

"Yes, sir. Mr. Koog was just looking for you. He didn't look very happy."

"Happy? Happy is not in the repertoire of that sourpuss. Come on, let's get ready to amaze the rubes."

As we climbed the fire escape, I could smell beer on Leo and also a trace of the scent of Mabel. Although my feelings were a bit hurt, I said, "Have a nice supper?"

"Woooo, yessir! Supper was fine, but dessert was a whoop-de-doo indeed!"

"What'd you have?"

Leo looked at me again. "Well, what do you think I had, P.K.? Some of the sweetest stuff on earth."

I was beginning to feel like a stupid country bumpkin again; did everyone in this city know something about dessert that I didn't? What could possibly be sweeter than rock candy, which was pretty near pure sugar as far as I could tell?

Thanks to the work we had done earlier, the film loops were ready for the show and there wasn't much preparation to be done. From the wings of the stage, Mr. Koog spied Leo and made a great show of pulling out his pocket watch to take a look at it. Leo just smiled and threaded the first two loops on the two Vitascope machines.

Since this was my third time to see the program, I was able to pay a bit more attention to Leo's actions and I studied how he threaded the loops of film over the system of rollers and sprockets and how he set the machine in motion. It didn't seem too hard. My attention was again diverted by the May Irwin kiss, which indeed fell earlier in the program than before. It suddenly reminded me that I had dreamed of touching my lips to someone's last night, but I could not recall the face of the lady. I wasn't aware of being especially attracted to anyone in Blanco, but who else could it be?

When the program ended, I helped gather up the film loops. This time, we rolled them up into small rounds like ribbon and placed them in small metal cans, which went into a wooden crate covered with railroad stickers on the outside. It suddenly struck me that I would probably never see the Vitascope or Leo — or May Irwin — again.

"Where do you go next, Leo?"

"We leave for San Antonio early in the morning, then on to Houston, Baton Rouge, and I don't know where-all. Why, you wanna come?"

Oh, my heart leaped! "I wish more than anything I could, but I have to go home with Father on Monday. I sure would like to work the Vitascope, though."

"Well, maybe you'll get a chance someday if it really catches on. Lots of traveling, though."

"I suppose so. Would…could you maybe write me and tell me what you do next?"

Leo stopped packing film and looked at me. "Kid… I mean, P.K. or whatever your name is…"

"J.D."

"Yeah, well, this is not much of a life for a clean young man like yourself. I got no family, no brothers or sisters, no wife. It doesn't matter to anyone where I am or how long I'm gone. I think your maw and paw would miss you something awful. This moving picture stuff is just a toy anyway; it's only gonna last another year or so and then something else will come along to take its place."

"But if you don't have any family, maybe you could write to me like I was your little brother or something. You know, send me articles out of the newspapers and such? You don't have to write big long letters. I just am really interested in the Vitascope and these moving pictures."

"Uh-oh, you feeling like you ought to be in the show business?"

"No, it's just interesting to me."

Leo stood silent for a minute, then began to fumble in his coat pockets. He pulled out a scrap of paper and then found the nubbin of a pencil in his vest and said, "Okay, then, write your address on here."

I tried to print neatly, but my hand was a little shaky. "There. J.D. Wilkinson, Blanco, Texas. That's all you need. We get our mail at the post office."

"Okay, kid." He nailed the lid on the box of film, and began to pack the Vitascope machines in their specially fitted boxes. In a few minutes, the boxes were sealed and we carried them downstairs to the lobby. Mr. Koog was talking to the manager of the opera house and seemed to be in a good mood. They shook hands and then Mr. Koog strode over to us and said, "The cart is outside. Load the crates and we'll take them to the depot."

I helped Leo carry the crates outside; Mr. Koog carried nothing except a brown envelope that apparently contained his and Leo's share of the ticket sales. We loaded the boxes on the horse-drawn cart in front of the theater. Mr. Koog started walking back toward the Avenue and his hotel, leaving Leo to deal with the driver of the cart.

"Thanks for the help, kid. I'll go along to the depot and make sure these get loaded on the train to San Antonio. So, I guess I'll see you sometime." He stuck out his hand and I gave it the firm shake that was my father's stock in trade.

"Thank you for letting me help you. And for letting me in the show for free. It was about the best thing I ever saw."

"Naw, thank you. It felt kind of good to have somebody actually appreciate what I do for a change. I'll try to write you sometime."

"Thanks, that'd be great. I'll…I'll pray for you."

Judging from Leo's expression, it had been a long time since anyone had offered to pray for him. His jaw worked for a few seconds and then he said, "Goodbye, J.D." He climbed upon the buckboard seat and the driver spoke gently to his horse and the wagon rolled off down the dirt street.

I watched until the cart turned the corner toward the train station, then I looked back at the front of the opera house. The poster advertising the Vitascope was already gone, replaced by one for a Bert Coote and Nick Long, "Aided by a COMPANY OF COMEDIANS Under the management of EDWARD C. WHITE, In a Screaming Comedy, Adapted from the French, THE OTHER MAN'S WIFE, To Be Preceded By JAMES A HERNE'S Delightful One Act Play, A Soldier Of France, Seats Now On Sale." As I stood there, the glorious electric lights all went out. For a second it seemed I was in darkness, but then my eyes got accustomed to the light coming from the moonlight towers. I walked back to the Hotel Salge and again fell asleep to flickering images in my head. This time, when the May Irwin Kiss began to play, her face blurred, then changed to that of Mabel and then to the face of the girl who had waved at me from the window. Regardless of which face I kissed, the woman giggled as my lips touched hers.

## CHAPTER SIX

The remainder of my time in Austin was routine. On Sunday, we attended services at the First Baptist Church, having lunch on the church grounds and singing in the afternoon before another worship service in the evening. I enjoyed the singing, but when the preaching started, my mind would drift away. I felt as though something fundamental in me had changed, as though I had had a lifelong need which I had only just now learned about. I had seen a wonder, maybe even a miracle. And just like people in the Bible who had miraculous encounters, I wanted to share it with someone. Father listened with polite interest to my report of the moving picture machine, but it was obvious that my story made no impact on him and that he was humoring me. And besides him, who could I tell? There was an auditorium full of preachers who would probably find something sinful in the fact that I had attended a theater at all, not to mention the dancing girls and the Kiss.

It was a long ride home on Monday. I was quiet much of the time. Father was talkative; he always was full of ideas for sermons and church activities after attending a conference. He often said it was the only time that a pastor could receive some spiritual food of his own.

Late in the afternoon, we pulled up in front of our house. Mother, Hannah, Mary, Martha and Paul came out on the porch to greet us with hugs and I was reminded of Leo's remark that he had no family to care about him. How blessed we were! Mother had a big meal prepared and supper that night was a fine time, with Father telling the best jokes, sermon illustrations and facts about Austin that he had gleaned during our stay. He had brought small gifts to all the children and Mother, although I had not been aware of his taking time to go buy them.

Eventually, Hannah asked, "And what was your favorite thing in the big city, J.D.?"

All eyes turned toward me, but before I could answer, Father said, "Oh, he got to see Mr. Edison's latest discovery!"

"What has he come up with now?" said Mother.

"It's called the Vitascope," I said. "The Vitascope brings to life, before your very eyes, scenes from other places, other countries, in such vivid and vital detail that you will be amazed. In the same manner that Mr. Edison's phonograph brings the great music of other lands into the ears of the fortunate listener, the Vitascope may bring to your vision sights hereto unseen by all but the most intrepid explorers and world travelers." The words rushed out of me in a torrent before I could even realize that I was spouting Mr. Koog's speech, word for word.

The rest of the family looked at me with expressions of surprise and amusement; I had never been a particularly talkative child and they were taken aback at my sudden verbosity. I continued to tell them all I could remember — and I remembered almost everything after hearing it three times — including the fact that the Vitascope showed sixty photographs in the space of one *CLAP* second. But my confident recreation of Mr. Koog's lecture ceased when I tried to describe the visual effect of the moving pictures.

"It was like a big photograph of a street, but the horses and carriages and people were all moving and walking along just as natural as could be and then the picture changed and there were these waves rolling in from the ocean and it looked so real, Mother, and a train looked like it was going to roll right into the theater and people screamed and…"

I stopped talking for two reasons. One, I was just about to describe the dancing girls and

*This Is Where I Came In*

the Kiss and that was probably unwise. Two, my father was staring at me as though I was the Vitascope; his eyebrows furrowed into an expression of fascinated study and I knew that he understood for the first time what this experience had meant to me.

My life returned to normal in the following months, although a few changes occurred. I began leading the singing in our church. Father showed me how to wave my hand in time to the music and I slowly gained confidence in being in front of the congregation. Initially, I would simply call out the hymn, wait for Mother to play the introduction and then wait again for Father to start singing, since I was shy about starting the singing myself. But after a few months I was singing solos before the sermon and was even able to look into the faces of the people while I sang. Mother continued to teach me to play the piano and organ. I was pretty good on the piano, but had a hard time playing the pedals on the organ at the same time I played the keys with my hands.

By the time I turned sixteen, in February of 1897, I was no longer afraid of being in front of a crowd of people. I had been called on to read scripture, sing solos and even give my testimony. This consisted of an impromptu telling of my own experiences in the Christian faith and it was something a lot of people could not do, standing up with no prepared text and sharing from the heart.

Father and Mother were extremely pleased at my growth in these areas and I believe they were beginning to hope that I would actually receive the "call" to preach. I wasn't sure, myself. Sometimes I thought it was something I could do easily; other times I thought about what I might miss in life if I surrendered to preach.

Apart from Sundays and Wednesdays, though, I was still a farm boy. There was always something to be done and I was now old enough and big enough to be of real help to Father. Farming keeps your body strong, but it also gives you much time for thinking. One day I was chopping wood east of the house. I looked up to see how high the sun was so that I could gauge how long it was until supper. When I looked up, the windmill was between me and the sun and the rotation of the windmill blades in front of the bright white light created a flickering vision which instantly put me back in the balcony of the Hancock Opera House. I stood there for a moment, wondering if I would ever again see anything as miraculous as the Vitascope, stopping only when I realized I was staring into the sun. It was many minutes before the colored dots cleared from my vision.

My vision.

What was my vision? What was my purpose? I thought of Moses' burning bush and how God spoke out of it to tell Moses what to do. I had heard Father preach so many sermons about people in the Bible and how they heard God's voice and responded to it. All I heard was the creaking of the windmill and the clattering of a moving picture machine.

Leo had written, but only three times in seven months. His letters were brief, usually just a page telling of whether the audience had been good or bad, how Mr. Koog was not worth a tinker's dam, and how lousy a hotel could be. There were usually a couple of clippings enclosed with reviews of the Vitascope's performance. I had never been able to write back to him, since he never thought to enclose a schedule or to let me know where mail might be sent; I would learn he had been to a particular city only after he left it.

I had kept the sixty-five cents I had left from the trip to Austin for several months. The cloth tobacco bag of coins reposed in a tin box under my bed in the room I shared with Paul. After I had acquired a few more cents, I ordered a magic lantern from the Sears catalogue:

> **No. 61000. The "Home" Magic Lantern for parlor entertainments; has metal body, handsomely japanned, with gilt decorations, and has kerosene lamp with six colored slides, with view 11/8 inches wide, magnifying picture to about one foot. Each.......75¢**

I had hoped that this machine might afford me some semblance of the pleasure I had derived from the Vitascope, but it proved to be a poor substitute. The kerosene lamp cast a rather feeble image on the wall, scarcely visible unless the room was pitch black. Mary and Martha and little Paul found it somewhat amusing, but I felt I had wasted my money on a cheap child's toy. At times I would flutter my fingers in front of the lens tube, in the vain hope that the flickering motion would coax movement out of the static drawings on the glass slides.

*This Is Where I Came In*

The Sears catalogue did come in handy for another attempt at recreating the magic of the moving picture machine. One day I looked in the index to find some item Mother wanted to order. As I riffled the lower edges of the pages with my thumb, watching the page numbers change, I was reminded of the changing frames of the moving picture film I had examined in Austin. I tried an experiment; in the upper margin of the odd-numbered pages of the thick catalogue, I drew a tiny stick figure in pencil. Remembering how each frame of film had differed only slightly from the frame before or after it, I drew the same stick figure in minutely different poses on subsequent pages. When I riffled the corners of the pages, I did indeed witness the illusion of movement as the stick-man waved his arms up and down. My initial effort took only about 25 pages out of the catalogue's 800, so I made other experiments in other parts of the book: a bouncing ball, a tree that grew from a tiny seed, even a series of our old windmill turning. Everyone in the family was interested in seeing these tiny amusements and I was gratified enough by their attention to continue drawing until I ran out of both ideas and empty page margins.

I continued my schooling at the one-room schoolhouse two miles from our house. A Miss Griggs was the schoolmarm and she loaned me books to take home and read; I had long since read everything in our house, even making two complete trips through the Holy Bible. Thanks to Miss Griggs, I discovered Horatio Alger, Mark Twain, James Fennimore Cooper, Daniel Defoe and Arthur Conan Doyle. Occasionally a visitor to our home or church would have a newspaper from some large city and I would look to see if the marvelous Vitascope was being exhibited there. I never saw it mentioned, but I did find mentions of other mysterious contraptions like the Pantoscope and the Cinematographe and, from the descriptions given, I deduced that they must be similar to the Edison machine.

These mentions fueled in me the hope that eventually someone would bring a moving picture machine to Blanco. Prospects seemed unlikely, though. When the county fair was held in April, I scoured the fairground, hoping to at least get a look at the Kinetoscope, but no one had gotten around to seeing that Blanco got to see moving pictures.

There was another new interest in my life that spring. At school, a girl named Bess

Endicott seemed to pay me more than just polite attention. She was also a voracious reader and we discovered we had read some of the same books, although she was much more partial to Louisa May Alcott than to Mark Twain. Bess's family had moved to Blanco just after New Year's and she quickly stood out from the few other girls my age in the school, due to her red hair, flawless complexion and air of mystery and sophistication; she had moved from Waco, after all. Her father had been a banker in Waco and had inherited some land in Blanco from an uncle. He built the Blanco State Bank and soon became a prominent citizen in our small town. Bess's mother had died from influenza and Bess helped take care of her younger brothers and sisters.

She and I would take walks together after school, discussing books, dreams, ambitions, religion and our families. I found myself looking forward each day to seeing her at school or at church and I once again began to have dreams in which the May Irwin Kiss played over and over and over, but now with Bess's pretty face in place of May Irwin's.

My mother was bemused but pleased at how my manners, hygiene and posture all improved when Bess was around. She said that I could invite her to have lunch with our family some Sunday afternoon. Early in May, when Miss Griggs dismissed school for the summer, I nervously asked Bess if she could join us on the following Sunday. She said she would have to ask her father. When he came to pick her up in a buggy, I extended the invitation from my mother and Mr. Endicott gave his permission with a smile.

That Sunday morning I was on my best behavior as I led the singing at church. I was scheduled to sing a solo and had selected The Holy City, a demanding anthem that showed off my upper range with some lengthy high notes. As I stood behind the pulpit and reached the climactic end of the song — "Hosanna in the HIIIIIIIIIIIIGHEST, Hosanna to our King!" — I glanced at the pew where Bess sat; her head was slightly bowed, but she was gazing at me from under her lovely eyebrows with an expression that nearly caused my voice to catch in my throat. I made it through the last high "G" without cracking and received many "Amens" from the congregation as I took my seat on the front pew. During the sermon, I could not look back at Bess, but as soon as Father called on Bro. Kelly to offer the closing prayer, I walked up the center aisle to the church entrance alongside Father. We shook hands with all the people as they exited and I received many compliments on my song, but when Bess shook my hand and told me she was very proud of me, I nearly ascended straight to the Pearly Gates.

Lunch was a lively experience; Bess was seated across the table from me and it seemed that we could neither look directly at each other nor keep from trying. When the meal was over, Father said I could drive the buggy to take Bess home. On the way, she sat very close to me and told me what a wonderful day it had been. She asked me if I was going to be a preacher or a singer.

"I'm not sure. I guess I haven't felt any real strong guidance to make a decision like that." Her red hair and creamy complexion in the outdoor light were mesmerizing me and I had to force myself to look back at the road now and then.

"I think you'd be real good at preaching. You sound so mature and sure of yourself when you stand up there."

"Hmmm. I'm not sure of much, Bess, least of all about myself. I sure do like spending time with you, though."

"Me, too. I think it would be just fine if you were a preacher. Preachers need someone to be a helper and stand beside them. I think that's just as real a calling as being called to preach."

"Yes, Mother says she always knew she was going to be a preacher's wife. Is that what you feel, too?"

Bess paused. "Yes. I think so. But I never really felt that way until recently."

The conversation had certainly taken an unexpected turn! Here I was with no idea what my future was and this charming girl was virtually telling me that God wanted her to marry me! I looked at Bess for a long moment and said, "I sure wish I could get some sort of clear sign from God about what I'm supposed to do. It'd be a shame to make a wrong decision that could ruin your whole life."

Her lips tightened as though I'd said something hurtful; that had not been my intention at all. But my father had always told me how sure he was of his calling and I just didn't feel any similar assurance.

The beautiful moment seemed to have slipped away and we rode the rest of the way in virtual silence.

During the summer, I spent more time helping Father on the farm. We had planted corn, potatoes, tomatoes, eggplant, cucumbers, squash, radishes, onions and okra in the spring, so there was always picking to do, as well as weeding, shucking (corn), snapping (beans) and canning (everything). We had two cows which I milked each day; Mother would churn fresh butter for us and make cottage cheese.

In my sixteenth summer I also began to make trips alone into town for flour, coffee, sugar and other items we could not produce on our own. I frequently saw classmates in town at the icehouse or the general store or sometimes having a cool swim in the Blanco River.

Bess had gone away to visit relatives in Waco for most of the summer, so there had been no chance to mend any bridges which might have been burned during our buggy ride on that Sunday in May. She had sent me a couple of newsy letters, but never mentioned my future career, her future husband or that fateful ride. I wanted her to broach the subject, but I must confess that my letters to her were much the same, full of tales of the dullness of a summer on the farm, broken only by the occasional swim in the creek or the July Fourth parade in town. I felt bad about the unacknowledged pall between us, and yet it was gratifying to know that I at least had someone to feel bad about.

One Tuesday afternoon in August, I was on my way back home with a buggy load of supplies, including canning supplies for our bumper crop of okra. It seemed that the more okra we picked, the more sprang up in the garden. We had eaten it stewed, boiled, fried and baked and now Mother was going to pickle many quarts of the fuzzy vegetable; the prospect of eating okra all through the fall and winter was not a joyous one.

At the general store, Mr. Hyden had said the temperature was 104 degrees. I was grateful to be driving the buggy instead of chopping weeds or cutting wood. I sipped from the canteen

I had filled in town and periodically removed my hat to mop my brow with a blue bandana. There wasn't a hint of a breeze and gnats buzzed around my face unless I coaxed the horse into a trot. I was thinking of Bess and wondering when she would be back home and what I would say to her that could recapture that moment when she thought I was pretty wonderful.

When I pulled up to the house, Mother and Father both came out on the porch, looking somewhat worried. Had I dawdled in town too long? I didn't think so. Was one of the children sick? Had someone died? Before I could think of any more questions to ask myself, the screen door opened again. And Leo Matula said, "Hiya, kid! Long time no see."

## CHAPTER SEVEN

I couldn't have been more surprised if the angel Gabriel had been standing on our porch waiting to give me a trumpet lesson. My mind raced, trying to figure some reason for Leo to be here…HERE…in Blanco!

I jumped to the ground and shook Leo's hand as he clapped me on the shoulder. "Bet you're surprised to see me, eh?" He leaned close and whispered, "Your ma and pa weren't real sure what to make of me, either."

"Well, what are you doing here? I haven't heard from you in months."

"Oh, and I guess I didn't get any mail at all from you, now did I?"

"You never told me where to send anything!" I protested.

"I know, I know. We'll talk about it. I got a business proposition for you."

In the hundred degree heat, a cold chill ran down my spine. We stepped up on the porch and I told Father, "This is the man I told you about, the one that let me help with the moving pictures in Austin."

"Yes, he told us," Father said, looking a bit relieved. "I've already invited Mr. Matula to stay for supper and to spend the night if he likes."

"Please, Reverend, call me Leo."

"I will, Leo, as long as you don't call me Reverend. Jess is fine. Or Brother Jess."

"Okay, Brother Jess, I appreciate your kind offer. I'd be pleased to share a meal with you folks if you're sure I won't be intruding."

"Not at all," said Mother. "We're always grateful for company. Supper should be ready in about an hour."

Leo helped Father and me unload the wagon and then Father went inside to help Mother. Leo and I walked down by the creek and I asked, "How did you ever find me?"

"Wasn't so hard. I knew you were in Blanco. We just did a show in Burnet and we've got one Thursday in Fredericksburg. So I caught a train down here and a man at the bank told me where your house was. Mr. Endicott, I believe?"

"Yes. But why? Why did you come here?"

Leo plopped down by the creek, removed his boots and socks and stuck his feet in the clear, running stream. "Ahhhhhhh, that's good, right there!"

I sat down and waited. Leo kicked his feet slowly back and forth awhile and then said, "J.D., I got a problem. You remember Old Man Koog?"

I nodded.

"He's in Burnet in awful bad shape. He's got an abscessed tooth that he's been nursing for weeks and it looks like it's decided to show him who's boss. The dentist there yanked it, but it was way too late and it looks like he's not going to make it."

"Not going to make the show in Fredericksburg?"

"No, not going to make it to another show anywhere. The doctor says he's gonna die." I knew it was not uncommon for people to die from dental problems, but it had never happened to any of my family. Mother had had several teeth pulled over the years, but never was brought so low that she was in danger of dying.

"Did you ask my Father to pray for him?" I wondered.

"Uh, no, I haven't done that yet, but it's a real good idea. Look here, kid, I mean, J.D., I need somebody to go with me to Fredericksburg. There's no way I can do the show by myself. And since you were so interested in the Vitascope and lived sorta on the way to Fredericksburg, I thought maybe you could come and run the machines. You saw how I thread 'em and everything, right? Then I can do the lecture part. I reckon I've heard Koog do it five hundred times. It's one show on Thursday, two on Friday, two on Saturday, and if it works out okay, we're scheduled to be in New Braunfels next week, and then on east toward Houston."

Leo began to speak faster and louder. "Kid, I got very little money saved from this job. Between the women and the whisky and stuff, I've just barely scraped by. And if I don't keep these bookings, I'm up the creek. I don't know nobody else in Texas that cares a tinker's dam about moving pictures but you. What do you think? I know you like the show business, I could spot that right off in you."

Well. No burning bush for me. No still, small voice from a whirlwind, no fiery letters on the wall. God had chosen Leo Matula to deliver a message, MY message. My head felt light and my throat was dry as I said, "It sounds like a dream come true, Leo. But we're going to have to talk to my Father and Mother about it. I'm not sure I can just up and leave so sudden."

"I know it's not the best situation, J.D., but how did I know that old Koog was gonna croak? How old are you now?"

"Sixteen."

"Old enough. It's time you leave the nest and fly on your own. Look, I don't know how much Koog was keeping of the take each week, but I can tell you we'll both make a lot more money if he's out of the picture."

"What if he gets better?"

"He won't."

"How do you know?"

"I just do. I just… He's already dead. Died yesterday morning."

"Oh, Leo! That's a shame."

"Yeah, well, I don't like to speak ill of the dead, but dying could be the only break that son of a bitch ever gave me. I've got the two Vitascopes and all the films and a tuxedo that I can maybe wear and a list of playdates from now through December. Come on, J.D.!"

The sound of my mother ringing the dinner bell halted any further discussion between us, but everything Leo had said was replaying in my mind like one of the endless loops of film in the Vitascope.

Supper was a bit awkward. Father and Mother still didn't know why Leo was there and they were too polite to ask. So the main topic of conversation during the meal was all the different places Leo had been. I learned that he had been hired by Mr. Koog in Chicago and that Mr. Koog had purchased the exclusive rights to exhibit the Vitascope in Texas and Louisiana. Leo confided that the field was getting more crowded, with competing machines like the animatographe, the animotiscope, the projectograph, the cineograph and many others. As a result of the overabundance of film machines, exhibitors were being forced to play smaller and smaller cities. It was only a matter of time, Leo said, before Blanco hosted a moving picture exhibition. He also shared some of the problems he had encountered in cities with electrical systems based on alternating current, instead of the direct current favored by Edison. At this time, there was no standardization of voltages or currents and Leo frequently had to adapt creatively to the prevailing local situation; on occasion, he had even tapped into the electric streetcar line for power.

Since Blanco had no electric system, Father postulated that it might be a while before we could witness the Vitascope after all. But Leo answered that he had run the machines off of battery power in a couple of instances and had heard that some exhibitors had even tried bicycle power to provide the necessary energy. My little brother Paul volunteered to pedal if this option proved necessary in Blanco, saying he always wanted a bicycle.

After supper, we retired to the front porch to watch the sun going down. Here at last, Leo got down to brass tacks. "Brother Jess, I'm here to offer your son a job in our traveling exhibition. I think he's got the interest and know-how to do the job and I'm prepared to offer him fifteen dollars a week to start off. Plus his travel expenses, meals and hotel room." I could see that Mother wanted badly to speak at this point, but she held her tongue, her lips forming a straight line. Father's brow furrowed, though whether at the thought of me leaving or the idea that I would be earning fifty percent more money than him, I could not tell.

"But…but… J.D., is this something you want to do? Your mother and I have been so pleased at your progress in your singing and playing and your speaking in church and all. Has this been a plan of yours all along?"

"No, Father," I said.

At the same time Leo jumped in, saying, "No sir, Brother Jess, he didn't know nothing about this until I showed up here today. I was just impressed when I met him in Austin last year. I could tell he was a good kid…er…young man who had been raised properly and could be trusted with responsibility." Leo was trying awfully hard.

"Well, my question still is, do you want to do this? Have you decided not to be a preacher or an evangelist?"

"I hadn't decided anything before today. I been asking and asking God for a sign of some kind, because I didn't know what I was supposed to do. And then here Leo shows up on our porch today. Couldn't that be a sign?"

Father looked at Mother. She said, "But you're only sixteen, J.D. Don't you want to finish your schooling? Don't you want to serve the Lord like your daddy?"

"How do I know…how do you know that this isn't what I'm supposed to do? Doesn't it seem like the timing of all this means something?"

"I'm not sure about God calling somebody into the moving picture business," said Father. "Being in a different town every day or two, no place to call home. Nobody to help you or watch over you."

"Now I'm gonna watch over him, Brother Jess. I'll make sure he stays out of trouble and

I'll see that he writes to you every day." Leo was sweating, although the air was cooling off as the sun sank behind the hill.

"No offense, Mr. Ma — Leo, but I don't know a thing about you. Are you a Christian? How can we know that J.D. will have some spiritual guidance?" Father leaned forward in his chair. "How do we know he'll go to church when he's in some far-off town?"

I don't know where it came from, but Leo had a doozy of a comeback. "Doesn't the Bible say, 'Train up a child in the way he should go, and when he is old he will not depart from it'?" Father was rocked back in his chair by that one, and Leo pressed on. "I'm not a saint, preacher, but I'm not the devil, either. If J.D. doesn't like the work or the traveling…or the company, I'll send him back here on the fastest train. I'm offering him a chance to do something exciting and something that I think he's very interested in. But he still hasn't really answered that question yet. Do you want to do this?"

I licked my lips. Of course I wanted to do it! But I didn't want to hurt these two people who had seen to my every need since I was born. "I think I do. It just seems like this is all happening for a reason."

"When would he have to leave?" asked Mother.

Leo inhaled deeply. "Well, we've got an engagement Thursday night in Fredericksburg. We would need to leave here in the morning to make it there in time."

"In the morning? Oh, my goodness, we can't make such a big decision so quickly," said Mother.

"Mother. Father. It's not your decision. I'm the one that has to decide. I'd like to think about it tonight and decide in the morning." This satisfied nobody, not even me. In fact, I had already made up my mind, but I couldn't face telling my parents I wanted to leave them.

"J.D., I know you're sixteen and just about a grown man," said Father. "But I want you to think very carefully about this. Pray about this. You'd be leaving your home. Leaving a lot of responsibilities. Leaving your family."

I knew this was true, mostly. But school would be starting soon and my share of the work on the farm would have decreased greatly anyway. Hannah, my oldest sister, was twenty and a great help to Mother. She had no real suitors and it didn't look as though she would be marrying anytime soon. Mary was fourteen, Martha thirteen and Paul eleven. They were becoming increasingly helpful with chores. I had no doubt that I would be missed, but it didn't seem insurmountable.

"I will pray about it, Father. In fact, I'm going to go say my prayers and turn in. Good night, Leo. 'Night, Mother. 'Night, Father." I went to my room and got undressed, then lay on top of the covers trying to stay cool. Paul had given up his bed for Leo and was already asleep on a pallet on the floor. I placed my hands behind my head and stared up at the ceiling. "Lord," I thought, "It sure seems like I oughta do this. But if I'm not supposed to… let there be a bolt of lightning outside."

Considering it was a clear, cloudless night, this would have been a pretty clear sign, but no more difficult than some of the ones in the Bible, I thought. I turned my head to the window and waited for a flash. I could hear my parents and Leo talking softly, but I knew the debate was over. It was up to me. After minutes passed without a bolt from above, I again turned my gaze to the white ceiling where I had watched the May Irwin Kiss so many nights. But this time I saw another film, the one with the train at the depot. The only difference was that the train was not arriving over and over. It was leaving, leaving, leaving.

## CHAPTER EIGHT

The next morning, I said my goodbyes. It had crossed my mind in the night to awaken Leo and slip away, but I simply couldn't do that to my family. When I entered the kitchen with my valise, Mother burst into tears. Father came in from the yard and took in the scene with a grim determination. Leo simply tried to make himself invisible, telling Mother he didn't need any breakfast and indicating to me that we should just leave. I hugged Paul and told him he could have my magic lantern, but that he must ask Father or Mother to light the wick for him. Mary and Martha kissed me, crying. Hannah hugged me somewhat coldly; as the oldest child, she felt it was her right to be the first to go out on her own and that I was usurping her birthright. Mother just sobbed, squeezing me so tightly I could scarcely breathe. She whispered to me, "Stay close to the Lord, Jubal Daniel Wilkinson. Remember what you've learned and who you represent."

I held out my right hand to Father; he took it, but pulled me close for an embrace and I saw the tears in his eyes. I was crying by this time as well, and it began to get quite noisy in the crowded little kitchen. Father didn't offer any last-minute advice, but simply said goodbye and pressed a double eagle into my palm. I stared dumbly at the twenty-dollar gold piece, half a month's salary for my Father. And twenty times as much as I'd had in my pocket last fall in Austin, when I had felt so prosperous. While I turned the coin over and over in my hand, Father pulled his gold watch from his pocket and held it out to me.

"Here, take this, too. You'll probably need a good watch."

"Father, I can't take your watch!"

"I want you to have it. Don't argue." I looked at the watch; it was the only ornamental item Father ever wore or carried and I had admired it since I was a tot. The gold case showed a majestic elk standing on a craggy mountain peak. On the gold chain attached to the timepiece was a little gold charm in the shape of a Bible. I fastened the chain to a shirt button and slid the watch into my pocket.

I looked around for Leo, but he had already gone out to the buggy. The whole family tromped out onto the porch as I swung my bag into the back of the wagon and then took my seat alongside Leo. He looked at me and said, "All right, then?" I nodded and he gave the reins a snap and the buggy began to roll. I looked back to see the six people I loved most, all waving at me.

I cried for miles, sure that I had made a terrible mistake. Leo looked panic-stricken, obviously thinking the same thing. After half an hour or so, I began to realize that I was on a trip now — on a journey I had wished, hoped and prayed for. I began to ask Leo questions about what I would have to do and soon my complete attention was on learning how to make moving pictures appear on a screen.

In Blanco, we turned in the rented wagon and waited at the depot for the train. I had never ridden on one before and I began to get very excited about it. We finally boarded and when the car began to move, the hot interior of the train began to cool off. Leo told me that in Fredericksburg we would have a schedule much like the one in Austin, with a matinee and evening show on Friday and Saturday. He and Mr. Koog had added a few new films since the previous fall, including some humorous ones that had been well received by audiences. He repeated to me several times the steps involved in starting one machine running, checking the focus, then taking the loop off the second machine, pulling out a new loop, threading it correctly through the machine and its multiple rollers, a process that took about two minutes. Since most off the films only lasted twenty to thirty seconds, the endless loops were allowed to repeat over and over; this was acceptable to the audience since the novelty of the projected image merited repeated viewings. But because of the endless loop format, exhibitors favored scenes without a narrative story, since the sharpest joke was bound to wear thin after seeing it six or eight times.

Leo's plan was to introduce the Vitascope as Mr. Koog had done. "I think I can cinch up the tuxedo pants in the back to work alright. I'll do the lecture, I know it by heart. You run the machines and we'll clean up!"

"Hey, Leo. Something I've been wondering about. How did you know that scripture you quoted to my father about bringing up a child in the way he should go?"

He grinned. "Easy, kid. Before I came out to the farm, I stopped by to see the Methodist preacher. Told him I was having trouble with my son and wasn't sure what to do about it. He gave me that verse and never knew what I was going to use it for."

## CHAPTER NINE

When we arrived in Fredericksburg, we picked up the crates containing the films and projecting machines at the depot, then hired a boy with a wagon to haul them and us to a small hotel. Leo and I would share a room and a bed. He unpacked the tuxedo of the dead Mr. Koog and began to brush it. I opened my valise and took out my two spare pairs of pants, two extra shirts, my other socks, my spare union suit and my black dress suit. I put all the clothes in a bureau drawer and hung up my suit. Leo said he had extra cuffs and collars that I could wear. I also unpacked my Sunday-go-to-meeting shoes and a nightshirt.

It was dark outside by the time we unpacked and we were hungry, having only eaten some fruit on the train. We went downstairs and the lady who ran the inn directed us to a small steakhouse up the street where we had a good meal. Leo was on best behavior, telling me what a great time we would have. He didn't drink during the meal, but afterwards he suggested that I must be tired and should probably go turn in. I was fatigued, but the excitement of my first trip away from my family and the anticipation of being part of "the show business" kept me tossing and turning for what seemed like hours in the iron bedstead.

Leo finally crept in, trying to be quiet, but banging clumsily about in the dark so much that I had to bite my lip to keep from laughing. He crawled into bed beside me and seemed to drop off to sleep immediately. It took me much longer.

Thursday morning dawned in Fredericksburg and I was not much rested, but still eager to meet the day. We had breakfast at the hotel, then wandered down the main street of town. Our show was to be in the Masonic Hall and we located it and hauled our equipment there. A Mr. Schulte met us there and told us that interest in the show had been brisk and the locals were eager to see the Vitascope. Upstairs in the Masonic Hall was a large meeting room where benches had been set up. There was no canvas or screen, but Leo said the bare white wall would serve just fine. We opened up the wooden crates and Leo showed me how to assemble the machines. Fredericksburg had no electrical system, but Mr. Schulte directed us to a box full of dry-cell batteries he had acquired for our use. I watched Leo hook up the batteries to one Vitascope and tried to imitate his actions, but I got several annoying shocks in the process.

"Okay, let's see if this is going to work," Leo said. He pulled a random film loop out of the box and threaded it up, checked the arc and flipped the switch. After adjusting the focus, I could see that this was a picture I had not seen before, in which an artist drew a rapid sketch of Thomas Edison on a large white board. It was delightful and seeing the Vitascope in action again after ten months felt comforting.

"See if you can thread up something on the other machine," Leo told me. I picked up a film loop and carefully threaded it on the little teeth of the advance mechanism and then around the roller system. "Pretty good, but you're going to have to do it faster than that. The audience is going to get bored otherwise." I practiced the routine at least a dozen times until Leo was satisfied.

We went to a general store and got some bread, cheese, pickles and summer sausage for lunch. After that, it was time to go back to the hotel to get dressed for the first matinee. Leo kept assuring me that everything was going to go smoothly, but he seemed to be the one who needed assuring. He got into the tuxedo and I put on my black suit and we strolled back to the Masonic Hall. On the back of a playbill for our presentation, Leo wrote out a schedule of what was to be shown:

1. Bicycle Parade
2. Venice Gondolas
3. Train Station
4. Rough Sea at Dover
5. German Emperor Reviews Troops
6. Umbrella Dance
7. May Irwin Kiss
8. Drawing of Edison
9. Passaic Falls
10. Trolley Cars
11. The Bad Boy
12. Cissy Fitzgerald Dance
13. Boxing Exhibition
14. Fourteenth Street & Broadway
15. Battery Park Steamer
16. Rockaway Bathers
17. Place de la Concorde
18. Eugene Sandow
19. Military Parade

About an hour before the show was to start, Leo began to pace, muttering the lines of Mr. Koog's lecture to himself. I busied myself laying out the film loops in the correct order so that the even-numbered ones would be near the left-hand projector and the odd-numbered ones would be near the right-hand projector. I flicked on the projector a couple times, practicing focusing the image on the white wall.

By 6:15, people were beginning to arrive. Many of them looked curiously at the equipment as they walked in, some bending to examine the strips of film. There were people from the age of five or six up to one gentleman who must have been close to 90.

The hall was full at least ten minutes before seven and Mr. Schulte, the man who had greeted us earlier, asked if we were ready to begin, even though it was a few minutes early, since it was already getting stuffy in the room. I looked at Leo to see his answer and was surprised to see him looking greenish and sweaty, his eyes darting here and there. He licked his lips and said he supposed the sooner the better.

Mr. Schulte and Leo walked up the side aisle and Mr. Schulte raised his hands for quiet. "I just want to thank everybody for coming out tonight. I'm sure many of us have read about moving pictures and the Masonic Lodge is happy to bring you the first look at them in our town. But I know you didn't come to listen to me, so let me get out of the way and introduce you to Mr. Leopold Matula and the Vitascope!"

There was great applause and Leo walked to the center of the room and looked over the audience with the expression of a prisoner facing the firing squad. There was a very long pause and then he finally began, "Layzengenmen… boys… girls… Mr. Edison… uh… has this… uh… Vitascope!" With that he pointed grotesquely at me! I was standing there, open-mouthed, expecting about fourteen and a half more minutes of lecture before the first film was shown. But I obediently fumbled for the switch and the Vitascope machine clattered to life. Only then did we realize that neither of us had instructed Mr. Schulte to lower the lights. The images of the bicycle parade were barely visible and people began squinting to make them out, hindered greatly by the fact that Leo was standing smack in the middle of the image, blinded by the beam. "Lights, lights!" shouted Leo. Mr. Schulte and another man quickly turned down the gas lights and Leo moved to the side of the hall and the bicycle parade came into view. I breathed a sigh of relief as I heard members of the audience exclaim, "Look at that!" and "Amazing!" The scene finished, started over again, finished, started over again. After six complete cycles, I wondered if Leo was ever going to introduce the second film. I tried waving at him, but he could not see me in the darkened hall, especially since I was standing next to the projector. Finally, after the film had run ten or eleven times and I could hear murmurs from the audience around me, I turned off the projector, plunging the room into pitch blackness. There were a couple of screams at the unexpected darkness as I fumbled around for the second machine, finally finding and flipping the switch. Venetian gondolas began to float down the canals as I began stripping the film off the first projector. If Leo was not going to speak between scenes, I had very little time to make the switch! I grabbed the next film loop and threaded it through the cogs and rollers. The pressure of time made me fumble a bit, but I think the gondola scene had only played about six times when I finished. I decided to flip the switch on the first projector before turning off the second one, so that there would be no dark interval. This proved to work well and the gondola scene was replaced by the one of the train coming into the station. This was always popular with the crowd, Leo had told me, and I watched some of the reaction until I realized I had to slap a new picture on machine two. I grabbed the next loop while trying to spot Leo; the film tangled with the other loops and fell from my grasp. I bent, snatched it up and began threading it. Now I could see Leo standing right beside the moving picture, trying to read his list by the light from the projector. He gave me a high sign and then yelled, "Here's one called Rough Sea at Dover!"

I flipped on the second projector and turned off the first and began to change the film when I head big laughs all around me. I looked up at the front of the hall to see that the waves were indeed rolling in, but the film was upside down, forming a most peculiar tableau, with waves at the top of the frame, above a cloudless sky below. It was a fascinating, hard-to-figure-out image and I stared at it like one entranced. Leo was again looking at his list, not at the picture, when I instinctively turned off the upside-down ocean, again sending the room into darkness, punctuated only by Leo's loud "God Dammit!"

The rest of the performance was calmer by comparison, but it was over in forty minutes, instead of the two hours it should have taken, since no information was given by the esteemed lecturer, Dr. Matula. The May Irwin Kiss was a big hit, as were the pictures of Sandow the strongman and the serpentine dance. Leo and I looked like whipped pups while Mr. Schulte dressed us down afterwards, telling us he was of a good mind to cancel the other shows and run us out of town. Leo managed to convincingly portray a man with a devastating illness which would probably go away by tomorrow and he assured the Mason that all subsequent shows would be as previously promised and that our technical difficulties would not be repeated. I felt like I had run ten miles. The strain of changing films as rapidly as I could possibly move while having no support from Leo had sapped me of every ounce of energy.

We returned to the hotel exhausted and crestfallen. "What on earth happened to you?" I asked accusingly.

"I dunno, kid. I got in front of all them people and suddenly could not remember a single stitch of Koog's talk. I thought it would be so easy! I know that spiel like I know my own name."

"Well, you nearly killed me, both from working me to death and embarrassment! I did my job pretty well except for turning that one film upside down and that wouldn't have happened if you could have scraped up a couple of sentences to give me enough time to check what I was doing."

"I know you're right, J.D. What am I going to do? I don't think I can pull off this speechifying."

There was silence in the room as we both got ready for bed. I tossed and turned all night, but Leo slept fine, thanks to a healthy dose of medication he produced from his bag.

## CHAPTER TEN

Next morning I was still very tired, after two nights of poor sleep. Leo was feeling poorly, too, apparently a side effect from his "medicine." We had breakfast and talked little. Back in our room, Leo was muttering about his options. "I can't afford to leave town without getting paid. But I don't believe I can say that speech in front of a bunch of people."

"Alright, Leo. Suppose I do the talking and you do the projecting?"

"You? You think you can speak in front of people any better than me? You think you're better than me?"

"I've been talking in front of people all year. Singing, too. Not as many people as we had last night, but I think I can do it."

"But how will you know what to say? You haven't heard the Koog talk since, when, last October?"

"Yes, but I've heard it in my head a hundred times since then. I used to run through the whole thing while I was chopping wood or driving the buggy into town. I can do it, Leo. What other choice do we have?"

We had a two o'clock matinee performance that day and I spent most of the day sitting quietly, reviewing the Koog speech in my mind. I donned my black suit; Leo loaned me the white tie from the tuxedo and I was obviously dressed up, but for what occasion no one could have discerned.

At the Masonic Hall, Mr. Schulte was waiting for us and informed us we would not be paid for the engagement if there was any repeat of last night's fiasco.

"Don't worry, sir," said Leo. "We were both a bit under the weather last night, but today we're feeling fine and we're going to go back to our original assignments."

"Original assignments? What do you mean?"

"Well, normally I run the machinery and, uh, Professor Wilkinson here does the talking." Mr. Schulte turned a skeptical eye at me as Leo continued, "But he was suffering from a little catarrh or something last night and could barely speak, so I tried to fill in for him, but he's right as rain today, sir!"

"Professor Wilkinson?"

"That's right, sir. He looks young, but he was actually a child prodigy and has already been to university and everything."

Mr. Schulte was unconvinced, but said, "I'll just remind you that you won't get a red cent if you don't do the show we were promised." With that, he strode off.

Leo straightened out the film loops and got the projectors ready. The afternoon audience seemed to be largely women's groups and quite a few school children. Apparently, word of mouth from last night's show had not killed off interest in the Vitascope.

Mr. Schulte called for quiet, thanked the audience for coming and introduced me as "Professor J.D. Wilkinson." There were a few snickers when I took my place at the left of the wall. But although I was nervous, I felt a hot surge through my body and I suddenly knew — knew! — that this was indeed my calling.

"Ladies and gentlemen, boys and girls! It is with great pleasure that I welcome you to the Masonic Hall today for this historic event. You are privileged to be among the first people in the world to view the latest and most amazing device to spring from the mind of that great American, Mr. Thomas Edison!"

"Mr. Edison, expanding on the promise of his earlier creation, the Kinetoscope, has asked me to journey here to this fair city of the great state of Texas to share with you this most wonderful diversion which he calls… the Vitascope!"

And so it went. My voice was strong and authoritative and even when I introduced the newer films for which I had never heard Mr. Koog's description, I discovered that florid speech flowed from my mind just as quickly as I could shovel it up.

"Eugene Sandow, ladies and gentlemen, the most perfect physical specimen ever to walk the earth, has developed every muscle in his body to an extent heretofore unknown. As you gaze upon his form, perhaps you will be compelled to compare his phenomenal physique to that of yourself… or your spouse, ladies!" I just made that up! And there were huge laughs from all the women in the crowd as they eyed Sandow, naked except for a small loincloth, flexing his muscles in a way they had never seen or dreamed.

I faltered a tiny bit when describing the May Irwin Kiss scene. I knew I had to sound worldly-wise and much more experienced than I actually was while describing the Broadway play from which this scene was taken. But my voice did crack the smallest bit when I tossed the word "osculation" into my description, mainly because I could see many women in the audience staring at me; I had won over their initial skepticism with my confident speaking and they hung on every word now, laughing at all the right places, oohing and ahhing at the impressive sights and nodding appreciatively at the facts I gave regarding each picture. I found it exhilarating to speak and not feel ashamed of being "showy." In church, every song and every testimony was delivered with a humble demeanor and an almost apologetic tone. But now, now I was the expert, the Professor, the close friend of Thomas Alva Edison!

So I was very aware of several dozen women, dressed to the nines, watching me as I described the kissing scene and there was an electrical energy in my voice which nearly got out of hand.

But the show went very smoothly, lasting one hour and fifty-five minutes. At the end, there was tumultuous applause and I had the unfamiliar pleasure of taking a bow, then another and another. Finally I raised my hands for silence and said, "I thank you for your kind reactions and your devoted attention. But I would be remiss if I did not introduce the engineer of this remarkable machine, the gentleman whose electrical knowledge and achievement has enabled you to see this wonder, Mr. Leopold Matula, the skilled operator of the Vitascope!" As I indicated Leo's location with my hand, the entire audience turned and continued to applaud wildly. Leo grinned the biggest smile I'd ever seen and took a bow himself.

After the crowd had left, he pounded me on the back and was giddy with excitement. "Kid, we are going to clean up! You were great! And the dames were eating you up with a spoon!"

"If I'm going to be the Professor, maybe you should quit calling me kid."

"You're absolutely, totally right. You're a natural! Old Schulte was nearly kissing my feet after the show. And thanks for the mention at the end. Koog never did that one single time. I appreciate it, ki—, Professor."

Mr. Schulte had indeed been effusive in his praise following the show, but I could scarcely pay attention to him due to the many women who felt compelled to express their enjoyment of the show personally to me. Some had asked me technical questions that I couldn't answer, but I bluffed my way out of anything I was unsure about. Others said they would be coming back to one of the other shows. I shook many a gloved and perfumed hand.

We went back to the hotel for a rest, then had an excellent supper at a German place. Leo could not get over how effective my lecture had been. "You can toss it with the best of 'em, J.D. I about died when you said all those women should compare Sandow to their old men. I believe we could be having supper in some gal's home right now if you played your cards right."

The evening performance was much the same; a packed house turned out to see the wonderful Vitascope and I stuck with the same lecture I had done earlier, changing only a line or two. The evening crowd had more men than the afternoon group, but they enjoyed Annabel's dancing as much as the women enjoyed (secretly) gazing at Sandow's physique.

After the evening performance, Mr. Schulte asked Leo if we could stay over another few days, but Leo took great pleasure in informing him that we were booked solid through the end of the year, but perhaps we could work him in next year sometime.

On Saturday morning, when I strolled the main street of Fredericksburg, I was amazed when several people stopped to compliment me on the previous night's performance. Some young women coming out of a dry goods store stopped short when they saw me. They whispered and giggled as I pretended to be studying the window display. Finally one of them — either the bravest or the one who lost the drawing of straws — stood at my elbow and said, "Excuse me, Professor. I wanted to tell you how much my friends and I enjoyed your presentation yesterday."

"Why, thank you, ma'am," I said, trying to sound mature. "What was your favorite part?"

She looked at the other girls and suppressed a smile, which only made her dimples appear more lovely. "Well, you were very interesting and we all learned so much! Especially from that May Irwin picture!" Gales of laughter washed over me from the four ladies and I could feel my face blushing, but I tried to maintain as much dignity as I could muster.

"Ah, yes. I'm surprised you ladies didn't already know all there was to know about that subject." More laughter and now it was the turn of the spokeswoman of the group to go crimson.

"We were all wondering… where did you learn to speak so well? Where are you from?"

Uh-oh. If I revealed that I was the preacher's kid from Blanco, the jig would be up. "I was trained by Mr. Edison himself in Menlo Park."

"Oh, what is Mr. Edison like? Do tell us!"

"He's a quite remarkable man. He rarely sleeps at night, but takes a brief nap whenever he feels the need. He's somewhat hard of hearing, but a delightful man and, of course, the greatest intellect in our country and possibly the world." I had read all of this in a newspaper article Leo had sent me during the previous winter.

"Will you be coming back to Fredericksburg again, Professor? Or do you have… obligations elsewhere?"

"Ladies, I must go where the Wizard sends me. But I have certainly been gratified by the reception and friendliness of your citizenry." Good Lord, where did this stuff come from? It seemed as though I could not stop it once I had started. I had the distinct feeling that the four ladies would happily have strolled with me or stopped for a phosphate, but I was unsure of how to proceed. Instead, I said, "Now, if you will excuse me, ladies, I must take leave of your pleasant company to write some letters. Good day."

The girls all said farewell, but said they would try to come to one of the two shows that afternoon or evening. I went back to the hotel and found Leo in the barber shop getting a shave and reading the newspaper. He gave me a wink and I sat down to wait until he was done. After he flipped the barber a quarter, we went upstairs to the room.

"J.D., read this. It's a review of our show yesterday. You'd think we brought the Lord himself to town." I read the extremely complimentary review, especially the part where the local scribe mentioned "Professor Wilkinson, who, though young in appearance, is wise and authoritative in matters pertaining to the new science of moving pictures. His presentation was easy to follow, yet entertaining and educational for all, from the many schoolchildren present to the oldest citizen in attendance."

"Gee whiz." I was unsure of how to feel. I had been taught to take pride in doing good, but not too much pride, to seek to point attention to God, not to myself.

"Why don't you tear that out and send it to your folks? Have you written them yet? You promised you would keep in touch, you know."

Leo was right. I had not written on Friday morning because the disgrace of Thursday night's fiasco was too shameful. But now I got a sheet of stationery from the desk and wrote Mother and Father, telling them how I enjoyed the train trip and how Leo and I had decided to switch roles. I did not tell them why. I explained that my experience in church had proven very helpful in preparing me for my newfound role of lecturer and how thankful I was that they had not stopped me from coming on this trip. I mentioned the sold-out shows and enclosed the newspaper article, adding that I imagined they would be surprised to learn their son was now a "Professor." I also wrote down the travel schedule that Leo had given me, so that they could write me back as we travelled.

After lunch, I walked to the post office and mailed the letter, again meeting a few people who had seen and liked the performance. That afternoon and evening were duplicates of the previous day; I recognized a few faces from earlier shows, but the majority were first-timers who responded wonderfully to our program.

Following the performance, Leo and I went downstairs to a small office with Mr. Schulte, who offered a bottle of whisky. Leo poured himself a drink; I, of course, abstained. Mr. Schulte opened a strongbox and began to count out bills. The five shows we had presented had taken in over 200 dollars, at twenty-five cents a seat. I was unaware of the agreement Leo (and Mr. Koog) had made with the Masonic Lodge, but Mr. Schulte counted out a hundred dollars and passed the stack to Leo.

"Can't say we ever had a better show here… or better response. You boys sure had me going on that first day, though."

"My apologies for that, sir," said Leo. "As I said, we were both under the weather. But we've enjoyed showing our pictures here and appreciate your hospitality." He knocked back the whisky, pocketed the bills and said, "Let's go box up the machinery, Professor."

By the time we had crated the projectors and films and taken them back to the hotel, I was dead tired. Leo handed me fifteen dollars, thought for a moment and then counted out five more. "There's a bonus, Professor. We're going to go great guns now and there's no limit to what we can make in time.

With the double eagle Father had given me, I now had forty dollars in my pocket — a month's salary for Father and forty times what I had been carrying in Austin when I felt so wealthy ten months before. I had no idea what forty dollars would buy or what I might use the money for. But I was sure of one thing: I had found my calling.

## CHAPTER ELEVEN

Over the next few weeks, we played New Braunfels, San Marcos and San Antonio, then had a long train ride to Houston. I continued to write Mother and Father regularly and got letters from them in most of the cities where we played. Father still sounded doubtful about my career choice and questioned the deceitfulness of passing myself off as some sort of professor. Mother wanted to make sure I was eating well and keeping myself neat and clean. She also mentioned that Bess Endicott had returned at the end of the summer and been very sad that I was gone. Bess was now back in school and, according to Mother, rarely came to church anymore. This caused me a twinge of regret, but I was not lacking for the attention of young ladies. Everywhere we played, I would find myself surrounded by a bevy of women, all intent on… something. I never sought to press my advantage with any of them, but some of them seemed to imply very clearly that they would welcome my company. For now, this felt like enough to me. I certainly wasn't looking to get married and saw no real point in forming any bonds in a town I would be leaving in a few days.

Until we reached Houston, I had done a good job of writing to my parents and I had dutifully tried to attend church in whatever town we found ourselves on the Sabbath. But the diversions of Houston ate up a great deal of my free time. We were in town for two weeks and I was again astonished at how much there was to do and see in a big city. By this time, I was carrying around over a hundred dollars and I decided to spend some of it on a more appropriate outfit for the show than my black marrying-and-burying suit. For twenty dollars I got a black wool tailcoat and pants with a gold brocade silk vest and white shirtfront with white tie. This made me feel even more confident in my professorial role and it only took a couple of days to recoup the cost. In a city the size of Houston, we were able to play three shows a day Monday through Saturday; this was hard on my voice, but I made ninety dollars each week we were there. Since Leo was paying for the hotel and meals, I was able to salt almost all of this away in a small leather bag I wore around my neck under my clothes.

One pastime I did spend some of my money on was entertainment. Houston was full of shows than ran the gamut from drawing room concerts to opera, minstrel shows to Gilbert and Sullivan, monologists to illustrated lectures. We were not the only moving pictures in town, either. One of the lecture halls featured a husband and wife team who had travelled to darkest Africa and made scenes of the natives engaging in their primitive rites. An opera company performing Carmen used film of a bullfight to strengthen the third act. I was also able to see the Kinetoscope which Mr. Koog had mentioned in passing — and which I had been mentioning in my own speech, despite my unfamiliarity with said machine. For a nickel, I could look through a metal slot as one round of the Corbett–Courtney boxing match was revealed. If I wanted more, I could move to the next Kinetoscope and insert another nickel; there were six machines in a row and for thirty cents I saw the whole fight. Boxing matches were illegal in every state of the Union and there was a certain aspect of the forbidden in watching the fighters ply their trade.

I also got a look at the Mutoscope, a variation on the moving picture idea. This machine was also a stand-alone, but — unlike the Kinetoscope — it was hand-cranked by the viewer, who thus controlled the speed of the scene. Instead of film, the Mutoscope contained several hundred cards, each printed from a frame of motion picture film. When cranked, the cards turned past a metal "finger" which held them in place for the fraction of a second it took to register upon the eye. Thus, it was similar to the tiny drawings I had made in the margin of the Sears catalogue, except it featured actual photographs, some of which were quite tantalizing. The first one I saw featured Little Egypt, a renowned (though not at my house) "hootchie-kootchie" dancer. Leo had seen many of these machines in his travels and said that some towns saw fit to censor the shocking gyrations of Egypt and her ilk. One belly dancing scene he saw in Waco featured a white picket fence painted or printed across the dancer's midsection, a diversion which only served to make the motions seem much more lascivious.

But the reason Houston had such a plethora of entertainment choices was due to its large population, and that guaranteed a ready audience for just about any sort of show.

It was a good thing we were drawing good crowds, because Leo was doing quite a bit of entertaining, wining and dining a different woman almost every night. Some nights he did not come back to the hotel room at all, but he assured me that I should not worry about him, but should concentrate on resting my voice and my body.

Somewhere during this time, I asked Leo how our performances were scheduled. He told me that Mr. Koog had arranged all the dates through December.

"What happens after that?" I wondered.

"I guess I need to get us a booking agent to start finding us dates for the new year. Koog always took care of that end of it, so I'm not too sure how to go about it. But I'll check around here in Houston; there's bound to be an agency here."

Some of our film loops were getting scratchy and brittle, and we were constantly having to patch sprocket holes and splice broken film. I didn't understand why we could not get new films from the Edison company, but Leo said they were having problems filling orders and that he could get new films elsewhere.

He left the hotel in Houston early one morning and didn't come back until almost noon, but he had two metal boxes of new film strips. These were not continuous loops, but we could splice them together at the ends. We walked over to the opera house we had been filling for nine days and went up to the balcony to view them. Some of these new films were amazing.

One scene featured a magician who made a woman completely disappear with a wave of his hands! Another showed a mischievous boy in a garden; when the gardener tried to water his flowers, the hose stopped flowing, due to the boy standing on the hose out of the gardener's sight. When the gardener looked into the end of the hose to see what was wrong, the boy jumped off and the gardener got a face full of water! I laughed and laughed over this one and Leo was delighted, saying, "Yeah, this one is going to knock 'em out! And some of these are by the Lumiere brothers in France. They're unlike anything we've showed before. See, kid (He always reverted to calling me "kid" when he was trying to explain something he thought I wouldn't or couldn't understand.), I found a fellow here that sold me these films at a great price. He makes duplicates of films from other companies and sells 'em for less."

Copyright was a vague concept in those days, to say the least. And in fact, no one had yet figured out a way to copyright films at all. It was standard operating procedure for one company to remake any film that was popular. And if it was too difficult to restage and film a copycat story, there was always someone willing to just dupe the film for a price. The print might not be quite as sharp, but that was a small concern in this era of flickering, jerky pictures.

Perhaps a word about the "flickers" might be in order here. Whatever else the moving pictures were called back then, "art" was not a term I ever heard proposed for them. The mechanics of making a picture were fairly straightforward: You decided what you wanted to photograph. The cameraman peeked through the camera lens — not through a viewfinder, but through the actual lens — and framed the shot. Then he closed the camera, loaded the film and began to crank. There was no moving the camera; how would you know what was in the frame? More than one film was developed only to find most of the action was off to the side or out of the picture entirely. So the stationary camera recorded a scene with no pans, no zooms, no cuts to closeup. Most commercial films were a single shot; the concept of editing together different shots to form a narrative was still in the future.

Showing a film was actually harder than photographing one. The projectionist had to guard against the film jumping out of the gate or getting jammed and burning up.

On the last Friday night we were in Houston, we worked the new films into the program with great success. We were accustomed to good audience reaction from our films, but the new "story" films brought forth peals of laughter that boosted our company's worth a notch or two higher. After the second show on Friday night, I went back to our hotel while Leo went a-wandering. We had one more night in the big city before we resumed our circuit of smaller towns. I fell asleep quickly, having grown accustomed to sleeping in hotels and having become acclimated to the thrill of performing. I woke up briefly when I heard Leo enter the room and noisily fall on the bed. But he began to snore directly and I went back to sleep.

Next morning, we were awakened by a loud pounding on the door and shouts of "Open up!" and "Come out of there, you!"

Leo sat straight up in bed; he was still in his clothes from last night and looked and smelled badly. He looked questioningly at me and I shrugged. He stumbled to the door and opened it, whereupon four burly policemen and a man in a tan suit barged in.

"What's this? What's the matter?" Leo shouted.

One of the policemen boomed, "We've got a warrant for the arrest of Leopold Matula. Is that you?"

Leo gulped, "What's the charge?"

"Possession of stolen property, namely a pair of motion picture machines and related photographic films," said the cop, reading from a yellow paper.

The man in the tan suit spoke up. "Those machines don't belong to you, they were leased by Elbert E. Koog."

"But Mr. Koog is dead! I was his assistant and when he died I had no idea what to do with his belongings. I would have been out of a job if I hadn't tried to continue playing the dates we were contracted for."

"You weren't contracted for any dates! Mr. Koog owned exclusive states rights for Texas, which he bought from Raff & Gammon."

"B-but, if Koog is dead, why can't I take over his territory?"

"Fine, if you've got thirty-five hundred dollars to spend for it."

Leo sagged between the two policemen holding his arms. "Thirty-five hun— look, I don't have anything like that kind of money. But I haven't stolen anything. Didn't Koog own the two Vitascopes outright?"

"No, indeed. Mr. Edison — or, rather, Mr. Raff and Mr. Gammon — do not allow private ownership of the Vitascope. It is only available on a lease basis and the lease on these two machines has expired. Mr. Koog's heirs have the right to renew the lease."

"Heirs? I didn't know he had any family. I saw him on his death bed and he never asked me to send for anyone or let anyone know he was ill. What heirs?"

"His wife in Fort Worth, a brother in Marlin, two grown sons and two daughters. That enough heirs for you? Now where are the machines?"

"Not here. They're at the theater. Let's go, I'll take you there."

An exodus began. No one had paid me the slightest attention, but my heart was pounding so hard I thought I was going to keel over and die. The police led Leo out, followed by the tan suit man, who slammed the door shut behind him. I sat there, still in bed, still in my nightshirt, without a clue of what to do. I felt like crying, but I knew that wouldn't help much, so I got up and hurriedly dressed. For reasons I could not define, I decided to pack my valise and then I went ahead and packed Leo's as well. I hauled the bags downstairs to the front desk and asked the clerk to please watch them.

I ran the four blocks to the theater and stood across the street, studying the scene. The front door stood open and one of the policemen strode back and forth in front of it. In a moment, another officer came to the door and spoke to the first, who nodded and then walked off down the street. I looked up and down the street, trying to think of something I could do to help Leo. Arrested! How could this be?

Inspiration was in absentia that day and I could only pace helplessly until I saw two of the policemen carrying the familiar wooden crates out into the sunlight. There were the two large crates which contained the Vitascopes and the smaller one which contained the original films, but they did not bring forth the metal boxes containing the new films. I supposed Leo had convinced them that he had purchased those in Houston and they were not part of Mr. Koog's property. Eventually, the tan-suited man came outside, followed by the ashen-looking Leo. I stepped inside a store on my side of the street and watched through the window. Momentarily, a wagon pulled up before the theater, driven by a small old man. Beside him was the policeman who had left sometime before. The four officers loaded the wooden crates on the wagon and then the tan suit man spoke to them and hopped aboard. The wagon rolled away, carrying our moving picture machines and much, much more. Leo stood with the officers, watching it merge into the crowd of traffic and then the group began to walk away in the opposite direction.

When they reached the corner and turned, I dashed across the street to the theater, where the door still stood open. Peering inside, I saw no one, so I skipped up the carpeted stairs to the balcony, where I found the two metal boxes of films. I carried them over to the fire escape door. Pausing to hear if anyone was in the theater, I opened the door and set the two boxes on the fire escape, closing the door quietly again. Then I went back down the main stairs and headed for the manager's office. He was in his shirtsleeves at his desk and looked up angrily when I entered. "A fine kettle of fish this is! Your partner in the pokey and me with no show for tonight, Saturday night!"

"Yes, sir, I'm sorry about that. We certainly didn't foresee this happening and I'm sure it's all just a misunderstanding."

"Hmmph. I've got to find something to put on the stage tonight. Get out of here and don't let me see you again."

"Yes, sir, but I'd like to collect for the shows we did do. That's only fair. We've been here two whole weeks and I believe you owe us a tidy sum of money."

This did not sit well with the manager. Although he was furious that he had no show for the night, his anger was somewhat assuaged by his hopes that he could keep the entire take from our previous performances. "Look, Professor," he said, his voice dripping sarcasm, "you've damaged my reputation in this town by cancelling my show tonight. That's worth something. I don't need some kid telling me I owe him money."

I felt an unfamiliar anger swell in me, but it was accompanied by that recently discovered bull-slinging ability. "No, you look! Who do you think will play your theater when I tell them you're not likely to pay them, that you can't be trusted to give an honest day's pay for an honest day's work. And how will you pay anybody when my father's law firm attaches your assets with a court order and your little stage remains dark, not for one night, but for a month OR A YEAR! Ever hear of Wilkinson, Endicott and McCormack?"

The manager shook his head.

"No? You never heard of Jesse Wilkinson? His law firm in Dallas? Well, you will, I can assure you. He's not crazy about me taking time out from Harvard to show these moving pictures, but he's certainly behind me when some glorified saloon owner tries to pilfer a few pennies out of my pocket, which I earned by filling your auditorium several times a day for the past two weeks. I may OWN this goddamn theater in a month or so!"

The manager was making halting motions with his hands now. "No, no, no, you misunderstood me. I was merely saying that I shouldn't have to pay you for tonight's shows if you're not able to do them, right?"

I was leaning on the front of his desk, out of breath from my tirade and from having uttered "goddamn" for the first time in my life, out loud anyway. "I see your point. We would not, of course, expect to be paid for shows we have not done. All we want is what is due us."

The manager turned to a heavy floor safe and began to spin the dial. He drew out a steel box that contained more money than I ever dreamed of and began to count bills, pausing now and then to consult sales figures for each of our performances. Finally he looked up at me and said, "I figure eleven hundred and forty-five dollars and fifty cents. That sound right to you?"

I steeled myself to keep my voice from cracking like it did when I first described the kissing film. Eleven hundred dollars! Good God Almighty! Did they print that much money?

I had no idea what Leo's arrangement (or, more likely, Mr. Koog's arrangement) was with each theater, what percentage we should receive. So I said, "Seems low to me. But we want to be fair and you will need to find someone for this evening, so… alright."

I left the theater with a fat roll in my pocket, ran around the corner and looked up, relieved to see the film boxes still on the fire escape. I climbed up and got them, then went back to the hotel and asked for our bags. The clerk inquired if we were leaving and when I said yes, he said, "Let me total up your bill. Just a moment."

I stood there impatiently, tapping my foot until he returned and quoted me a price of fifty-two dollars. I pulled out the huge wad of money in my pocket and his eyes gaped. I counted out fifty-two bucks and told him to call for a cab. In moments, a hansom pulled up in front and a bellman loaded our suitcases and the film boxes.

I climbed up in the back of the cab and said, "Police station."

## CHAPTER TWELVE

I was not allowed to see Leo for a couple of hours, until he had been charged. Then I was escorted to a small cell he shared with several other men. He seemed very glad to see me, but acted whipped.

"Can't believe this is happening, J. D. You know I didn't steal those projectors, don't you?"

"Sure, Leo. What happens now?"

"I don't know. I guess they'll get ahold of Koog's relatives and tell 'em I'm in the pokey. Then I guess I'll be put on trial."

"Who was the man in the tan suit?"

"His name's Sandifer. He's a detective hired by the Koogs to track down the Vitascopes. Must not be a very good one, though; it took him two months to find me."

"I can't figure out why Mr. Koog never told you he had family. Especially if he had any idea he was going to die."

"We didn't exactly socialize after the shows. But we did travel together a bunch of miles. He must have hated his old lady. I never even saw him write a letter or send a wire. Wonder if he was sending money back home."

We both pondered this and then I asked, "Did Mr. Koog have a bunch of money on him when he died?"

"Nope. When I saw him last at the doctor's office, he didn't mention anything about money or what I should do if he died. I asked him if he thought we would make the Fredericksburg dates and he said, 'Contracts must be honored.' I sorta took that to mean that if anything happened to him, I should try to carry on…until he got better or…worse. Then, I got word from the doctor that he had passed. They wanted to know about next of kin and burial and all that and I just told 'em I didn't know anything. So they said they would take care of funeral arrangements and call the undertaker. I sat around awhile thinking and then I headed for Blanco."

"Did you tell the detective all this? It seems to me you didn't do anything wrong. How were you supposed to know what to do with Mr. Koog?"

"I told him, but he just said he had to file his report with his clients and they would decide what to do."

"I checked out of the hotel, Leo, because I kind of thought we might be able to make some kind of escape. But I'll find a cheap place to stay until we can get you out."

"Thanks. I've got a couple hundred dollars, but they took it away from me when they booked me. Have you got anything to live on?"

"Oh, sure. I've been saving most of my pay from the beginning. And I went by the theater and got our new films and our money."

"Our money?"

"Yeah, I got real serious with the manager and he ended up giving me eleven hundred and forty-five dollars and fifty cents. Does that seem fair?"

Leo cackled like a chicken. "You are about the luckiest thing that ever happened to me!

When the cops carried me out of there, I didn't think we'd see a penny from that old skinflint."

"So when you get out of here, we can buy a new projector and use those new films and get back on the road. Right?"

Just then an officer strode up and informed us my time was up. I told Leo I'd see him the following day, then went back to the street and had the cab take me to a small boardinghouse where I could pay day by day. This wound up being a Victorian two-story owned by a widow named Maultsby. For a dollar a day, I got a bed and a washstand. For a quarter more, I got meals, too.

The next morning, Sunday, I asked Mrs. Maultsby if there was a Baptist church nearby and she directed me to the Olivet Baptist Church, where I sat through my first worship service in several weeks. After lunch, I thought about writing Mother and Father, but I couldn't see any way to describe my present situation that wouldn't alarm them. I visited Leo again, taking him a sandwich and some tobacco. Nothing had changed and he was getting restless.

It would be three more days before word came from the Koog family that they did not wish to press charges against Leo and he was freed. Leo showed me a telegram from Mr. Koog's widow expressing her bewilderment over her husband's sudden demise. She had had no idea he was ill, despite the fact that he wrote to her virtually every day. He had been buried in Burnet, but his body had subsequently moved back to his home in Fort Worth.

"He wrote her every day, Leo, and you didn't even know she existed!"

"That's right. I guess it's just as well. Because Koog didn't know everything I did in my spare time, either. If I kick off suddenly, you just stick me in the ground wherever we are, all right? Nobody else needs to be notified. And you can take anything I've got when I'm gone."

"Don't talk like that. We're going to be okay now. What do you want to do first?"

"First, let's check into a good hotel. I need a hot bath and a shave. And a drink. Let's celebrate a little tonight. Then in the morning we'll figure out where to start. I'm not sure what sort of machine we should get."

"Well, I've seen the Phantoscope and the Projectograph here in town and they have one big advantage over the Vitascope."

"What's that?"

"They've got the film on a big spool and they show all the films one right after the other. They never have to stop and change loops; it's just one long strip. Then, when the show's over, you just flip the gears in reverse and it rewinds the film onto the spool. The whole show only lasts about twenty minutes, with no starts and stops. You only need one projector, too."

"Hmm. Maybe we should check that out before we leave town."

That night, we dined royally and Leo wined royally; he was in an effervescent mood and, after we took in a showing of the Phantoscope, he told me he was going off for a bit of hunting. I returned to the hotel and laid on the bed with my hands behind my head, thinking about our future. While the Phantoscope and other projectors of its ilk seemed easier to operate, they seemed to eliminate the need for a lecturer. Would Leo even need me to keep doing the show? I was sure that Leo was fond of me and was appreciative of my efforts to keep our enterprise going. He had not asked me to turn over the fat bankroll to him, apparently impressed by my ability to hang onto money, a talent he was somewhat lacking. But I could not shake the feeling that there was going to be a change in our working relationship. There was no chance we could get the Vitascope license for Texas; Mrs. Koog implied that her sons were going to take over the franchise. So we would have to make a choice from the ever-increasing variety of film projectors and our roles would likely be determined by which one we chose. I slept poorly.

## CHAPTER THIRTEEN

The next morning, Leo and I decided we would take the train back to Austin and began anew there. Houston was already fairly crowded with film machines and we felt we might have a better chance to make a name for ourselves in the state capitol. But first Leo sent off wires to all the film supply companies he could locate in the trade papers. We would have to choose a new projection machine and the market had become flooded with them in the past year. If possible, we would try to choose one that could handle the dozen films we had left, but there were several competing sizes of film fighting it out in the marketplace and it was impossible to know which would win.

We left for Austin just after lunch and discussed strategies for beginning again. How would we secure bookings? What sort of audience would we seek? I confided to Leo that it might not be necessary for me to act as lecturer anymore and that he might not need me any longer.

"Naw, Professor, you're stuck with me. You're good luck. We'll figure things out as we go, but I don't think a one-person company can make it." I was relieved to hear this and began to relax again.

We checked into the Hotel Salge in Austin and it felt good to me to be in familiar territory for the first time in weeks. Not quite a homecoming, but still! In a couple of days, we began to receive catalogues of films and projectors. There was a dizzying array from which to choose. Even Mr. Edison himself was now offering a "projecting Kinetoscope" for which no states rights were sold, but which could be purchased outright. Intense competition among the manufacturers of projecting machines had driven down prices considerably from where they had been only a couple of months before. What to choose, though! We examined literature for the Eidoloscope, the Phantoscope, the Cinematograph, the Biograph, the Magniscope, the Zooscope, the Cinographoscope, the Projectograph, the Centograph, the Kalatechnoscope, the Motograph, the Kinematographe, the Animotiscope, the Panoramographe, the Bioscope, the Kineoptoscope and even more that I cannot recall.

And the films offered for sale ran the gamut from the Edison "actualities" we had used in the past to staged scenes featuring pillow-fighting girls to a scene of the Devil himself performing mystical feats.

We finally placed an order for a Motograph projector and, while waiting for our machine to be delivered, Leo decided we should form ourselves into a company, mainly to add prestige to our efforts. We discussed whether we should rent office space in Austin. What would we call our company? Who would run the office while we travelled? The endless questions and decisions gave me a headache. I just wanted to be back in the show business, amazing grateful crowds and making good money.

We ended up renting a small office above Thos. Goggan & Brother, a seller of pianos and organs at 813 Congress. Thus, we had a steady accompaniment of one-fingered pianists each day as curious shoppers poked at the ivory keyboards downstairs. At the time we took the office, we had to come up with a name for the business. After discussing several ideas, we arrived at a name mutually pleasing to both of us, since it encompassed both of our names and still had a regal, prestigious sound. So it was that Jubal and Leo became the owners of Jubilee Moving Pictures.

Another chunk of our rapidly-dwindling bankroll went for a month-to-month rental of a deserted storefront on East Ninth Street. It had formerly been a gun store run by a man with the euphonious name of Assman. After we painted "Jubilee Theatre" and "Marvelous Moving Pictures" on the front windows, we hung heavy curtains behind the display windows and rented 140 chairs from the funeral parlor two blocks away. While we got a good price on renting the chairs, it was with the understanding that a large funeral might require us to take some or all of our seats back to the owner for a couple of hours. People did not seem to mind standing for what was only a twenty to thirty minute program, the result of our jettisoning the lecture portion and simply showing whatever films we had ganged onto a reel.

At twenty-five cents a seat (or a standing spot), we did very good business for the first few weeks. We began running films at noon and starting again every hour on the hour until eleven o'clock in the evening. Many people who had missed earlier exhibitions of the Vitascope or Eidoloscope or Phantoscope, which only stayed in town a day or two, came to get a first glimpse of the moving pictures. Leo and I took turns running the projector, collecting money and manning the office. I had learned enough now to run the projector almost without thinking, and I never showed upside-down waves again; of course, with the film on a reel, it was difficult to thread it incorrectly. Our projector at this time had no takeup reel, though. The film, after passing by the projector lamp, snaked hypnotically into a large basket until the show was over, when it was rewound onto the reel. We discovered by accident that people would stay to watch the rewinding if we turned on the lamp; the bizarre spectacle of people walking backwards, buildings arising from rubble and two colored men producing whole slices of melon from their mouths was hilarious to our audiences and we found we only needed about fifteen minutes of film, since we could run it first forward and then backward.

After a lucrative period, though, business began to slack off. There seemed to be an attitude of "We've already seen moving pictures, thank you very much." So we were forced to keep investing in new films, which were ten to fifteen dollars each for a 50-foot scene which lasted less than a minute. It was this continuing expense that led us to get into filming scenes of our own.

Leo, who seemed to meet the most interesting people during his excursions into the nightlife of Austin, had met a German named Volz who was a machinist, watchmaker and general tinkerer. Volz had seen our show several times and told Leo it would not be difficult to construct a camera for making moving pictures. He studied the interior workings of the Motoscope and exclaimed how he would use an "intermittent movement like a star wheel." I had no idea what he was talking about, but Leo did, or pretended to, and we agreed to pay Mr. Volz two hundred dollars for the camera.

It was six weeks before Mr. Volz had a finished product. I had ordered some film stock from an import firm, since Edison was monopolizing all of Eastman's output. We ran some test shots from the roof of the theater, pointing the camera toward the Capitol. Leo had mixed up a batch of chemicals in a back room and spent most of an hour developing the test film. We threaded it nervously through the projector and it worked!

We began to take films of local scenes, shooting people strolling along the main streets. We would take the pictures in the morning, develop them in the afternoon and show them that night, after covering the town with handbills proclaiming:

**Come and See Yourself, Your Friends & Your Family**
**In Moving, Living Pictures**
**The Crowning Achievement of This Century**
**Tonight**

This produced great crowds as people packed the hall to try to spot themselves. To encourage attendance, Leo or I would crank the camera long after the film was used up, to be visible to as many passers-by as possible.

After a few weeks, we again noticed a sharp drop-off in attendance. People had grown tired of the moving pictures, or at least our moving pictures. We would have to offer new pictures on a regular basis or else repeat customers would be a thing of the past. So we filmed the local fire company in action, we filmed trains arriving at the station, we filmed the governor riding up the Avenue, we filmed every parade, no matter how small. In short, we became a sort of animated rotogravure section, showing local scenes to local patrons, interspersed with whatever films we could procure from Edison, Lumiere, Biograph or whoever.

It had been months since I had any word with my family. Since the Houston date, our traveling had ceased, except for coming back to Austin. So my parents had no idea where I was. I, on the other hand, had no excuse; I knew exactly where they were. But I told myself it would be embarrassing now to write them after so great a time. How could I explain my partner being arrested? Perhaps when we were on strong footing with the new business, I could write and tell them how prosperous I had become. This decision did not satisfy, but it sufficed. Blanco was never far from my thoughts, though.

After we had filmed every happening in town that we could think of, Leo insisted we think about making a picture that could attract people who had not yet seen a moving picture. "We've got a certain audience that will keep coming as long as we've got something new to show them. But we've got to get those people who think moving pictures are… a novelty or something beneath them. We need to get the women's clubs and the church groups. How can we do that?"

I knew that church groups had indeed hosted moving pictures when they were of an educational, non-objectionable bent. Travel lectures had always been popular, beginning in the magic lantern era and now world travelers could show actual scenes from their treks. I could not think of a way we could finance a trip to China or South America or Africa to bring back a film to show in such arenas.

I found my answer in a magic lantern trade journal (lantern shows were still very much a going concern). An advertisement offered appearances by Elwood Rambeau, who would show slides from the world-famous Oberammergau Passion Play. The play was performed every ten years and Rambeau had apparently acquired views of it during the 1890 season. The advertisement promised 50 scenes of the Passion of Christ, as well as glimpses of the villagers who so reverently played the parts. Rambeau's lecture was said to be a moving and uplifting program, suitable for any age audience.

Excitedly, I shared the idea with Leo. "We could film some Biblical scenes showing the life of Jesus. The church people would love it!"

"Or hate it. Who are you going to find to play Jesus? In Austin, Texas? Most of those church people are going to be up in arms that anyone dared to put Jesus Christ in a peepshow."

"Not if we do it right. We can come up with some costumes, a donkey, some actors. And then we can advertise it as 'The Famous Passion Play.' Everyone will think we imported the film just like the Lumiere ones."

"I don't know, Professor. I don't relish the idea of being crucified myself by a bunch of angry Christians. Seems like it would have to walk a very fine line."

"Leo, come on! Who knows more about the Bible than me? I'll make sure there's not a situation in the picture that can be taken wrong. And I can do the lecture! We just have to find the people to play the parts."

I sat in the hotel and made a list of scene that we would need to include:

1. Manger scene (donkey, sheep, Mary, Joseph, baby[?], shepherds, wise men)
2. Temptation in the desert (Jesus, Devil)
3. Baptism (John the Baptist, Jesus, witnesses, dove)
4. Chasing out the money lenders (Jesus, lenders)
5. Healing the sick (Jesus, blind man, leper [?], dead little girl)
6. Feeding the multitudes (Jesus, multitudes [how?])
7. Walking on water?
8. Palm Sunday (crowd, Jesus, donkey, palm leaves)
9. Last Supper
10. Trial (Jesus, Herod, Pilate, Pharisees)
11. Crucifixion (Jesus, thieves, guards, crowd, three crosses)
12. Resurrection (tomb, stone, angel?)
13. Ascension (no clue how to do this)

It was a daunting list. Where could we get so many people, so many animals, so many costumes? How could we afford the necessary scenery and props?

Leo made a discreet approach to the leader of the local operetta society, in hopes of finding actors who might help us. He was rebuffed, as the leader huffed about the improprieties involved in debasing actors before a toy like the moving picture camera. I ventured forth to a couple of local amateur theatrical troupes, pretending I was interested in joining, but really attempting to find anyone who was willing to go before the camera.

It was ironic that the local townspeople turned out to see our films in hopes of spotting themselves in street scenes, but refused to purposely appear in a "story." There was a certain element which felt that "acting" was a sinful pursuit and that even fictional books were suspect.

I knew virtually no one in Austin; all my time was divided between the office, the theatre and the hotel, where Leo and I had finally sprung for separate rooms. But Leo went out somewhere almost every night. He was bound to know someone in town.

"Don't you have some friends around, Leo? Couldn't some of them help us out? All they'd have to do is wear a costume and stand around. If we put beards on them, nobody will even recognize them."

"I'll ask. What could we afford to give them for doing it? And how long would it take?"

"One day. Maybe two. Depends on where we have to go to shoot the crucifixion scene. Most of the rest we could shoot on the roof of the theater." Our theater building had a large, flat roof and the adjoining, taller building, was constructed from large blocks of white limestone, which I felt would serve as a "timeless" background for some scenes. If we could take our actors just outside the city on some sunny day, we should be able to shoot the processional scene, the baptism and perhaps the crucifixion. I still had no idea how to do the tomb scene or the ascension.

That night, Leo enlisted eight of his drinking buddies and three "ladies" who agreed to appear in our film for a dollar a day and a bottle. Five of the men had beards and could appear suitably "Biblical," while the other three would require crepe beards, which were available in the Sears catalogue for eighty cents each. I dashed off an order for several beards and four bolts of unbleached muslin, which we would use for costumes. I also sent to the Eastman

Company for the raw film stock we would need. While waiting for the supplies to arrive, I asked Leo if he thought any of his chums could play the part of Jesus. "Uh, I don't think so, Professor. They're willing to be in the scenes, but I think they'd feel a little bit superstitious about playing the main part."

This was understandable in those days. Even stage actors did not portray Christ, as it was thought that no mortal could convey the proper "purity" and reverence the part would demand. But it was here that I thought moving pictures actually had the advantage: no spoken words would be necessary. Every person who viewed the film could hear the voice of Jesus in his own imaginary way.

"Why don't you do it, Professor? You know more about the story than any of us do."

"I don't want to do it! I want to guide the person who does. I want to be the… the conductor. The director."

Two weeks later, we had all our supplies, but no Jesus. We had begun transforming the muslin into robes and tunics for the cast and they looked presentable. We shot a camera test on the roof and it looked good; it actually looked authentic!

On a Saturday night in early December, I was sleeping peacefully when the door to my room flew open. I sat up, startled, to see a silhouetted form standing in the doorway, lit only by the gas jets in the hall.

"Come quick, Professor. I have found us a Jesus!"

I quickly dressed and followed Leo downstairs and out onto the Avenue. "What time is it?" I yawned.

"'Bout twelve-thirty, quarter of one. I found this fellow over in Guy Town and I think he looks perfect! He's got long brown hair. Long like Buffalo Bill, you know! And a beard and these dark, piercing eyes." Leo had already got a good start on a snootful, but he was fervent in his description.

"Is he tall?" I asked. I wanted the Jesus character to be physically imposing.

"Uh, I dunno."

*This Is Where I Came In*

"Well, is he taller than you?"

"I don't know!"

"How can you not know how tall he is, Leo? Was he sitting down the whole time?"

Leo stopped walking and looked at me. "No, he was lying down. And if you'll hurry up, he'll still be lying there."

We picked up the pace and soon were in front of one of the Victorian houses which I had finally learned were places where those of such a mind could find whisky, dancing, women, gambling and probably some things I still didn't know about. Under a tree in the front yard, a man lay face down in the dirt, unmoving. Leo knelt beside him, poked him a bit, then grabbed his shoulder and rolled him onto his back. A loud, annoyed groan issued from the body. I leaned closer, since the only illumination was coming from the red lantern on the porch and the moonlight tower several blocks away.

I have rarely been so hopeful, yet so doubtful. In our barn back in Blanco, we once had a pile of barley oats in one corner. Rain had leaked through the roof at some point and the oats had began to ferment and rot. Father asked me to go shovel out the stinking mass and when I pulled the first shovelful out of that pile, a scent attacked me that I had never smelled before or since. Until now.

I tried to breathe through my mouth as I bent close to the man's face. Leo was still holding his shoulders, a fact which finally registered on the man, and he opened his eyes, looked at me and said, "What the hell do you want, you son of a bitch?"

It was the face — if not the voice — of Jesus!

## CHAPTER FOURTEEN

Leo and I half-dragged the limp body back to the hotel and up to Leo's room. We dropped him on the bed where he began to snore right away. We repaired to my room next door to discuss strategy. It was decided that we would try to get him sober and cleaned up in the morning and then make him a business proposition.

Leo and I slept lightly in my room, trying to be alert to any sound from next door, but it was quiet as a tomb. I got up when light began to shine through the window and went down for breakfast, bringing a tray back up for Leo and another for the mystery man. I ventured into Leo's room and poured a cup of black coffee, holding it near the snoring nose of the man. He began to stir a bit and cautiously opened his eyes, which were as red as the lantern by which I had viewed his face last night. He looked around suspiciously, trying to remember by what means he had come to this room, but obviously not finding any answers. "Would you like some coffee?" I asked.

He made a snorting sound and held out a shaky hand. He raised the cup to his lips, spilling a few drops on the bed and on his filthy clothes. We did not speak again until he finished the coffee and motioned for another cup. I refilled the cup, then proffered the tray of food. He turned up his nose in disgust, but finally grabbed a strip of bacon and a biscuit and began to chew, studying me a bit more intently now.

"How are you feeling?" I ventured, cheerfully.

"Poco poco," he said in a hoarse, gruff voice. "I been worse and I been better. Who're you?"

"I'm J.D. Wilkinson. My partner and I brought you here last night. You were in kind of a bad way over in Guy Town."

"Everybody in Guy Town is in a bad way. That's what you go to Guy Town for."

"We've got an unusual business proposition for you. That is, if you're ready to hear it."

He shrugged and continued to eat. I went next door to fetch Leo as I didn't feel quite up to handling delicate negotiations like this alone.

"This is Leo Matula. He and I have a company here in Austin called Jubilee Moving Pictures." Leo extended his right hand and the man gave him a powerful shake.

"I'm Dean. Orvis Dean. What's a moving picture?"

"We'll show you in a little while," said Leo. "Are you from around here?"

"Not hardly. I'm from Ben Bolt." He said that as though we should recognize it, but I had no idea if Ben Bolt was a company, his boss or a location. He saw our puzzled looks and amplified. "Ben Bolt, Texas. Down south in the brush country. I'm a cowboy. Just brought a herd up here to sell and I guess I was trying pretty hard to spend all my earnings last night."

"Did you manage it?" Leo smiled.

"Lemme see." Orvis Dean dug in all his pockets and pulled out a few coins and a crumpled bill. "Aw, hell, no, I'm still flush! Guess I can have some more fun tonight."

"What are your plans, now that your cattle drive is over?"

"Head back south till it's time to bring another herd. Why, you got something better?"

"Indeed we do," I said confidently. "We're making a moving picture right now and we'd like for you to be in it."

"I still don't know what you mean." Breakfast finished, the cowboy sat up on the edge of the bed. "DAMN! I stink!"

"Uh, yessir, you do. Would you like to clean up? There's a barber shop downstairs where you can get a hot bath. And then we can show you what we're talking about. Have you got any other clothes?"

"Somewhere. I got a horse with a roll on it somewhere."

"Well, Leo can lend you something to wear until we find your stuff." Leo pulled out his least favorite suit and a clean shirt and union suit. We got Orvis Dean downstairs and told the barber to give him the works: bath, manicure, massage, but not to cut his hair or his beard.

An hour later, Orvis Dean looked like a new man. He was indeed tall, just about six feet. With clean hair and skin, he looked so much like Jesus to me that I was afraid anyone who saw him would know what we were planning to do.

Orvis followed us down to our theater. We still had a couple of hours before we usually opened for business, so we entered and locked the door behind us. Leo threaded up a reel of film while I explained to Orvis what he was about to see. When the pictures began moving on the screen, he walked up to the front of the room and slapped at the image, as though we were trying to trick him in some way. I showed him the film and the projector light and tried to convey how the image was produced. He seemed impressed and kept his eyes glued to the screen as I talked to him.

Twelve minutes later, the film ended and Leo drew back one side of the heavy curtain, letting some light in from outside.

Orvis leaned back in one of the funeral chairs, looked at me and said, "So you want to make a cowboy picture or something?"

"No, not at all," I said. "We want you to play Jesus in a Bible story."

He stared at me for a moment and then let out a wheezy guffaw. "You boys must have a hell of a sense of humor! I ain't no actor. Wouldn't have the first idea how to begin."

I tried to be reassuring. "You don't have to. I'll direct you every step of the way. All you have to do is wear the robe we've made and stand like I tell you and move where I tell you and look where I say."

"How old are you, boy?"

"Eighteen." I gave myself an extra year and a couple of months.

"And you're the boss?"

"Well, me and Leo are."

Leo nodded. "J.D. is the idea man. He's the one who thought of this and he knows his Bible and if he thinks you're right for the part, so do I."

"I ain't religious."

"Doesn't matter," I said.

"I tend to cuss, even around women."

"Doesn't matter."

"What if I don't like it?"

"You can quit. We should only need a couple of days to film all the scenes."

"What's it pay?"

I glanced at Leo, but he shrugged and held out his hand as though giving me free reign. "Five dollars a day." I saw Orvis's eyes widen and knew I'd scored. "But you've got to be sober while we're filming. And we'll buy your meals and you can stay in Leo's room until we're done."

"You know, I've been to a state fair and several rodeos and even a windmill-greasing or two, but this beats all I ever heard of. I'm in!"

Hallelujah.

## CHAPTER FIFTEEN

We began filming the next day — a Sunday, fittingly enough. We would wait to do the baptism scene until we went to the country and I had decided to omit the temptation scene, since I couldn't figure out a good way to show the devil. Orvis wouldn't be needed for the manger scene. So I decided to start with the scene where Jesus drove the money lenders out of the temple.

This seemed to be a perfect scene for the rooftop, with the stone wall as a background. Leo gathered his disciples and we got everyone wrapped in their muslin robes. We set a couple of wooden tables up and positioned a few cast members around each one. The three women draped themselves around the men, looking properly (I hoped) seductive as temple prostitutes. While Leo looked through the camera lens and directed me, I drew a chalk line on the roof. "Okay, everyone," I said loudly, "You've got to stay inside these lines or else you'll be out of the picture or we won't be able to see your feet. Everybody understand?" I could already see that some of the men were paying excessive attention to the three women, so I assigned some actions to everyone. "Bob, you stand behind this table and act like you want Jim to pay you more than he wants to. And Mabel, you look at Jim like you really hope he comes up with the right money. And you three do the same thing at this table. Delinda, you can stand here, too. You other four men, why don't two of you act like sort of policemen and the other two, you'll come in with Jesus, like you're disciples."

Speaking of Jesus, he was still downstairs putting on his white robe as I rehearsed the troops, but when he came up on the rooftop, there was definitely a moment of silence. "Everyone, this is Orvis Dean. He looks good, don't you think?" There were some dumb nods, but the women looked genuinely afraid or ashamed. Everyone told their names to Orvis and then we went over the movements of the scene again. There would be a few seconds of the money lenders plying their trade. Then Jesus and his disciples would enter the scene. He would behold — sorry, I mean look at — the scene and get increasingly angry, then begin to overturn the tables and frighten the rest of the people.

"Let's try it once before we film it, all right? I'll count one-two-three-go and then we'll start. Everyone ready? One, two, three, GO!"

The action began as I stood next to Leo and the camera. Orvis entered the chalked area, looked around him and then started screaming, "WHAT THE HELL ARE YOU DOING? I'M GONNA HAVETA—"

"Wait, WAIT, STOP!" I yelled. "Orvis, you don't have to holler like that. We're only interested in getting the pictures."

"Yeah," Leo said. "If you do much of that, the cops will turn up here wondering what's going on."

Orvis was apologetic and did a much more reserved rendition of the scene. Leo said he thought it looked good, so we decided to film one. Filming in those days was fairly simple: you pointed your camera at something and started cranking. When it was over, you stopped cranking. There was no zooming in for a close-up, no panning to follow the action. Films were shot as though they were stage plays and you saw the whole stage at all times. For that reason, facial expressions and hand gestures had to be large and grandiose, like stage acting. Only when close-ups became de rigueur did a more reserved style of acting begin to emerge.

So I had the money lenders pleading with both hands while the prospective buyers scratched their chins or made stopping motions. Orvis walked into the scene, looked around and, as I coached him verbally, shook his fist at the sinners, turned over the tables and grabbed a rope and began whipping the offending parties. This part of the scene was a little too realistic for some of the boys, who complained about getting whacked with the knotted rope. But I assured them that we had got the scene and there was no need to do it again.

Moving quickly, we next set up for the healing scene. Since we hadn't come up with any children to be in the film, I decided to have Jesus heal a cripple. Wilbur Haines, one of Leo's buddies, looked to be the most pitiful of the bunch. We had a primitive wooden crutch made from a forked tree branch. I instructed Wilbur on how I wanted him to hold his left leg off the ground as though it was lame. To lengthen the scene, I had some of the other men walk by Wilbur as he stretched out his hands, begging for money.

"Then, Orvis, you'll come in... Orvis? Where is he?" Everyone looked around the rooftop, but he was not in sight. Just as I started for the stairway, he appeared.

"Wait, I'm coming, I'm coming. Just had to go water the pot plants. I'm here now."

As he passed me, I smelled liquor on him. I looked at Leo and made the universal tippling sign, but he waved me on, indicating that we should go ahead and get on with it while we still had good sunshine.

"Okay, Orvis, after the others pass by this crippled beggar, you'll come walking by with some of the disciples and notice Wilbur. Stop and talk to him a minute, then put your hands on his head and say a little prayer. Then, Wilbur, you throw down your crutch and start jumping around on your new leg, acting all excited and grabbing people and telling them about it and such, all right?"

We rehearsed it three or four times, largely due to Wilbur's excessive exuberance after his healing; he kept jumping out of the picture. But we got the shot and I decided to try for the Last Supper scene. We got the money lenders' tables out again and lined them up, then covered them with more of our ever-present muslin. Mabel and another of the women went and got some loaves of bread and fruit and we set the table. We needed twelve disciples for the scene, but besides Orvis, we only had eight men and three women. I decided to put the fake beards on the three women and we used burnt cork to give beards to the three clean-shaven men. But that still only left us with eleven disciples.

"You're gonna have to be one of 'em, Professor," said Leo. "Somebody's sure to notice if we don't have a dozen disciples."

I didn't want to do this, not out of fear, but simply because I felt I could better direct the scene from beside the camera. But there was little choice. I wrapped myself in muslin and applied the burnt cork to my smooth cheeks. I placed myself at the far end of the table so that I could see everyone and so that I would not be near the central figure of Jesus. I told everyone where to sit and we were ready to rehearse when I noticed Orvis was again missing. I ran over to the stairwell and yelled, "ORVIS!"

"Alright, dammit." He came back up the stairs, noticeably unsteady now, but I had little choice but to proceed, since we had no stand-in for Jesus. Fortunately, all he had to do was sit in the center and pass the bread and the wine around the table. We practiced it a few times and then I told Leo to count to three and then start taking the picture. He did so and we began the scene, but a gust of wind whipped the tablecloth up in the front. "Hold it!" Leo commanded. "Everybody freeze like a statue right there." He dashed forward and flipped the cloth down, then started back to the camera and said, "Okay, let's go again," as he began cranking.

Unfortunately, as he walked back to the camera, Orvis fell noiselessly backwards off the wooden crate he'd been sitting on. I didn't hear or see this; the disciples on either side of Orvis saw him going over, but were unsure of whether to mention it or not. It was not until I realized no one was passing the bread that I said, "Stop! What's wrong?"

Orvis was snoozing peacefully behind the table. I decided to stop and take a break for lunch so that we could try to get him back on his feet. Leo made coffee and some of the boys helped walk Orvis around as he drank it. It was all for naught, though; after lunch it got cloudy and windier and Leo said he didn't think there was enough light to shoot. We had to let everyone go home for the day and I was upset that we had only gotten two scenes. I had planned to film everything in two days and now that would be impossible.

I went downstairs to the theater while Leo developed the film we had shot in a makeshift darkroom in the cellar. We were closed since it was Sunday and my mood was getting darker as the day outside turned from afternoon to dusk to dark. Finally Leo came up from the basement and threaded up the projector so we could watch the day's filming. The first two scenes were alright, certainly usable. The third, of course, was only half a scene.

But, every cloud has a silver lining, they say, and that spoiled scene turned out to contain an answer to a problem I had not been able to solve.

My list of scenes included Jesus feeding the multitude and I had not been able to come up with a way to turn a small lunch into a huge amount of food in some way that looked miraculous. But as I watched the Last Supper scene, it hit me! When Leo had stopped filming to fix the tablecloth, all of us had frozen in place. When he began cranking again, there was little change in our positions. But Orvis, who had fallen over backwards while Leo was walking, seemed to disappear instantly from the scene. One moment Jesus was sitting with the disciples (although he was weaving a bit) and then he was gone!

I realized that this was the key to a great many tricks we could do on film, but particularly the miracle feeding scene. All I had to do was have Jesus bless the food and hold out his hands, then freeze. We could then place baskets full of food in the scene and resume filming. As much as I hated to admit it, Orvis had done us a favor. But Leo and I would still have to have a talk with him.

Orvis was big enough and tough enough to make short work of Leo and I both if he wished, but he listened and again promised to shape up tomorrow.

On the following day, we quickly took the Last Supper scene and then I explained to Orvis how we would do the miraculous feeding scene. The women had brought several wicker laundry baskets which we filled with cloth and wadded-up newspaper, then topped off with day-old bread loaves we had got from the bakery and some fish that were at least a day past their prime. As they sat in the sun on the rooftop, their presence became more and more oppressive. But Orvis was sober enough to hold his arms still while we switched the small lunch and the huge feast and Leo said it looked good in the camera.

We did a hurried trial scene, with Orvis standing before Pilate and then Herod. Then, while there was sufficient light, I had Orvis stand right on the edge of the roof, facing us. Leo lowered the camera down so that he was looking up at Orvis. I asked Leo to frame the picture so that he could just see Orvis's feet at the bottom, but not what he was standing on. This gave us a picture of Jesus, hands outstretched, and a nice sky with a few white clouds behind him. I planned to use this as the ascension scene if I couldn't figure out anything else.

That evening, while Leo was running the projector at the theater, I sat in the office and began making notes for the lecture part of the life of Christ program. I would interweave scripture with poetry and maybe even a couple of songs as accompaniment to the dozen scenes we would show from the Bible. I was sure that music would be an effective addition to the program, but I saw no way I could play the piano or organ and do the singing and the lecture, too. We would have to hire another employee to travel with us. After the theater closed, I discussed it with Leo.

"With us owning the film and the machinery already, we can afford it, I think," Leo agreed. "Who are we looking for?"

"I'm not sure. Anyone who can play the piano and is pleasant to work with. I'll put an advertisement in the newspaper tomorrow."

The following day was Tuesday and Leo agreed to open the theater while I took a horse and rode outside of town to find a location for the rest of our scenes. I headed south and found a quiet bend in Onion Creek where we could film the baptism scene. I still had not figured a way to do the walking on water scene and I feared that we would have to leave that one out.

I found a nice smooth dirt road where we could shoot the Palm Sunday scene. But it was December and I didn't know where to get palm branches. We might have to make do with oak or cedar.

And the Crucifixion! It needed to be on a hill somewhere, but I could not find a suitable spot. And how would we make and transport the three large crosses we would need? I was beginning to wish we had waited a couple more weeks to begin filming. I also had no luck finding any sort of cave to use as the site for the Resurrection.

I was discouraged as I rode back to town. I stopped by the Statesman office to place a classified advertisement which said:

> **Wanted for moving picture traveling exhibition: Jovial, talented musician to accompany film and lecture on piano or organ. Must be of good character and able to travel. Apply in person, Jubilee Moving Pictures, 813 Congress Avenue.**

I went back to the theater to relieve Leo. It had been a slow day; we had not added any new films since we'd begun working on the Passion Play and attendance was beginning to suffer as a result. I cranked the films all evening, but my thoughts were on the nagging technical problems that threatened to derail our production. Leo came back for the last show and we talked about what we could film tomorrow.

"We can do the baptism scene, for sure," I said, "although it's going to be pretty cold in that water. And we can do the processional, but we don't have any palm leaves."

"Palm leaves, palm leaves." Leo pulled on one end of his droopy moustache. "I might be able to take care of that. What else do we need?"

"I wish we could do the walking on water scene, but I don't know how. We'd need a boat for the disciples and some way for Jesus to come strolling by on top of the water."

"Don't think I can pull that one off, Professor."

"And we may have to wait to do the cross scene and the tomb scene, 'cause I don't know how or where to do them."

"Just keep thinkin'. You'll get it and we're gonna make a mint off this."

"Okay. I'll see you in the morning. I'm tired of thinking about it tonight."

## CHAPTER SIXTEEN

Wednesday morning was cool, but sunny and our ragged little troupe met at the office and loaded up in three wagons for the trip to Onion Creek. Orvis had obviously had a great deal of fun the night before and his eyeballs were so red I expected blood to spurt from them like tears. As we rode, I told him how we would do the baptism scene, with Horace Eldridge playing John the Baptist, who would dunk Jesus's head under the water for a moment.

"I'm not real sure about this 'un, J.D. I can't swim."

"You won't need to; the water will only be waist deep or so. Horace will dip you back just enough to get your face under and then you'll come right up. You won't be under but a second!"

There is nothing sadder-looking than a sulking Jesus, but that's what I had to endure the rest of the way. We decided to shoot the Palm Sunday scene first, in hopes the water would warm up a little anyway, and Leo produced a surprise — a dozen beautiful green palm branches.

"Where in the world did you find those? In the middle of winter?"

Leo looked at Wilbur and they both laughed. "Let's just say that the lobby of the Driskill Hotel is not looking as fancy today as it did last evening. We sent Bob up to the front desk to ask about a room for the night and while he was asking, me and Wilbur uprooted two potted palms and went out the side door."

I laughed, too. This would look wonderfully authentic. We lined up the cast on one side of the road with their palm branches. Bob unhitched his mule from the last wagon and Orvis climbed aboard. Being a cowboy, Orvis looked a bit too comfortable atop the beast, especially since he straddled the mule's back, revealing that Jesus favored a red union suit for cool mornings in Jerusalem. I convinced him to sit sidesaddle on the mule and instructed the others how to wave their palms and look excited. Leo took the shot and proclaimed it a real doozy.

Baptism time. Horace was not looking forward to this scene, either, since the temperature was about forty-five and he would have to be in the water longer than Orvis. But I assured him we had brought blankets along and we would build a fire by the creek so he and Orvis could warm up afterwards. I didn't even gripe when Horace and Orvis took turns taking a fortifying swig from a bottle one of them produced.

I've often wondered if Matthew, Mark, Luke or John left out some parts of the story in their gospels. This day, I wondered particularly if John the Baptist actually hollered, "God-a-mighty-dammit-to-hell," when he entered the holy baptismal waters. Horace the Reprobate sure did. Leo had the camera right at the water's edge. Horace stood in the waist-deep creek, acting like he was preaching. Then he stopped and looked off to the left and Orvis came into view. He stepped into the water with his back to the camera, thank God, so no lip reader would be able to tell what our Lord had uttered concerning the water temperature. The rest of the cast was laughing hard, but Jesus and John kept their very serious expressions for the rest of the scene. Until, that is, John the Baptist let Jesus slip out of his grip. Orvis plunged under the water and all we could see was arms and legs swinging wildly. He came up, sputtering and cussing to beat the band.

The worst part of it was that we were going to have to take the picture over again. The other men had built a fire and the girls wrapped Horace and Orvis in swaddling clothes and led them to the fire. We had to get Orvis's hair dry enough to shoot again and he was one unhappy cowboy. This time, we rehearsed Horace's movements on the shore and the second time went smoothly. When Orvis came up out the water, he stood, looking quite reverent and wholly sober. Leo shouted for them to freeze where they were and produced his second surprise of the day when he splashed out to the two men and placed a stuffed white dove on Orvis's head. He came back to the camera and cranked a few more feet of film and we had a great scene!

"I got it from Mabel," Leo admitted proudly. "She's got this huge, grotesque hat that had this dead bird on it and I thought it would be a good addition."

"You dog! It's great, Leo! I can't wait to see it on the screen. You didn't happen to think of a way to walk on water, did you?"

"Nope. It don't matter anyway. We don't have a boat to put the boys in. I guess we'll have to lose that scene."

I hated to lose it, but I couldn't think of a way to capture it on film. We took a few brief shots of Orvis praying surrounded by bushes, which could serve as a Garden of Gethsemane scene if I needed it.

On the ride back to Austin, everyone seemed to be in high spirits. Leo and I had one of the girls in our buggy, along with Horace and Jim. Her name was Delinda and she had a pale, sunken-eyed pallor about her which was actually somewhat the fashion at the time. Leo asked her how old she was and she replied that she was seventeen.

"You're only a year older than J.D.," noted Leo.

Delinda aimed those sunken eyes at me and said, "No, I'm about twenty or thirty years older than J.D." She then made a sad little smile and I didn't know what to make of it. Mabel, Delinda and Johnnie Mae had seemed to enjoy being in the moving pictures. They usually appeared tired in the mornings when we started, but they had given their all and done everything I had asked of them. I didn't realize until later in my life that these were women who were acting virtually every waking hour of their lives.

It had gradually dawned on me that the three women were prostitutes, though I had but a cloudy idea of how such business was transacted. I do know that my face reddened with embarrassment and shame when I recalled my first trip to Guy Town over a year ago, after my first meal with Leo and Mabel. That girl who had leaned out the window and offered me dessert? She was one of them, too! How foolish I must have appeared to her… and now to myself. I resolved to learn more about these women without availing myself of their services, for I was curious how a woman, even a fairly attractive woman, could find herself in such a profession. I filed this resolution away in the back of my mind, for I certainly would not ask such questions in front of Leo and the others.

Just south of the river, we saw an outcropping of white limestone and Leo said, "That could be your tomb scene, if it was only bigger."

"Leo, would it be possible to shoot a small stone and make it look big?"

"I guess so… if the lens will focus that close. But how would we make a person look small?"

"Maybe we wouldn't have to. Let's take some of those rocks back with us." We loaded a dozen good-sized chunks of limestone in the buggy and proceeded back to the theater, where we bid the cast goodbye and Leo got started on developing the film. I went down to Bengener & Bro. Hardware and got a stone chisel and hammer and started back to the theater when I remembered that my advertisement was to run in that day's newspaper. It was just after four o'clock in the afternoon, but I climbed the stairs to our office. There was a young lady seated on the top step, but she rose immediately to her feet when she heard me.

"Hello! May I help you, ma'am?"

"I came about your advertisement. For the pianist?"

"Well, you seem to be the only one. Come right in," I said, as I fumbled for the office key. I opened the door and motioned her in.

"Oh, there were several others, but they got tired of waiting. You see, I've been here since nine this morning." She said this not as chastisement, but matter-of-factly. It chastised me nonetheless, though. How could I have forgotten I had asked applicants to apply in person?

"I am so sorry. You must be exhausted. Have you eaten? Please sit down."

She sat primly on the front of the wooden seat and said, "I'm all right, thank you. After the first person left, I considered it a badge of honor to stick it out to the end."

"Well, I cannot apologize enough. Your persistence is admirable. My name is J.D. Wilkinson."

"I am Texana Salyer. How do you do?"

Texana! While I could see nothing particularly Texan about her, I had to admit she was good advertisement for the benefits of living in the Lone Star State. She had black, black hair pulled into a knot on top of her head, brown eyes that looked directly into mine, and she was dressed neat as a pin in a mauve skirt, white shirtwaist and mauve jacket with a black fur collar. Her hat was mauve, too, and I had never really considered the color to be such a much before, but she wore it well.

"My pleasure, Miss Salyer. I'm sorry, is it Miss?"

"Yes, sir."

I leaned back in my chair, struggling to look like an executive officer. "Tell me about yourself, Miss Salyer. I assume you are not from New York?" Oh, what a wit!

"No, sir. I was born in Bastrop, but now I live in Austin with a maiden aunt of mine. I am nineteen years old and have played the piano and organ since I was seven. My father was a Methodist preacher and I grew up playing hymns."

"We have something in common, then. I'm a P.K. too! My father's a Baptist preacher, though."

"Really? How funny that we should both be preacher's kids! My father passed on three years ago. Is yours gone as well?"

"Um, no. He's alive and well. Still preaching. Out in Blanco."

"Blanco. Do you see him often? Is your mother still alive, too?"

This interview was not revealing exactly what I wished for. "I don't see them as often as I wish, of course. Have you ever seen a moving picture, Miss Salyer?"

"No, I have not. I've heard of them, though."

"Well, my partner and I are seeking someone to accompany us on a traveling exhibition of a very special moving picture. There would be a great deal of travel involved. I don't know if that is acceptable to you or not."

"Yes, it is. I love to travel and would love to see more of the world. My aunt is quite healthy and I have only been staying with her until I could find suitable employment."

"I see. Perhaps we could go downstairs to Goggan & Brother and I could hear you play something. Do you have music?"

"No. But I can play for hours without music. I learn songs very quickly."

"Fine, let's go have a listen." Miss Salyer stood up when I did, but the stiff little smile she'd been holding wavered and a frantic look flicked across her face just before she collapsed on the floor.

I leaped around the desk and raised her head and shoulders off the floor. "Miss Salyer! Are you alright?"

Her eyelids fluttered and she looked very embarrassed. "Yes, I'm sorry. I haven't eaten all day and I must be a little weak." She tried to bring back the little smile, but it trembled a bit at the edges. I realized I was staring at her lips and snapped myself back to attention.

"Can you make it downstairs? You must allow me to buy you a meal. This is all my fault." We walked a block and a half to J.B. Billeisen's Restaurant. My companion ate as heartily as any woman I've ever witnessed, but the immediate rejuvenation of her spirit and demeanor was charming to watch. She told me more of her life story, how her mother had died when she was only a child, leaving her as an only child. Texana had grown up helping her father in church work, playing for services and revival meetings since she was barely tall enough to reach the pedals. When her father had died, she had been left virtually penniless and had been forced to look for work. She had moved to Austin to live with her father's sister, and had worked in a candy factory, given piano lessons and tried her hand at store clerking. She still played occasionally for local churches, but had been unable to find any sort of position that made use of her talents.

I was completely charmed by her and hardly felt compelled even to hear her play, but I could not hire her until Leo had met her and added his approval. So I asked her to return in the morning at ten and Leo and I would listen to her. I assured her that it would be difficult for another applicant to impress me to a greater degree than she had with her determination. She gave me that smile again and I could see that she was very pleased.

I called for a hansom cab to take her home to her aunt's house out near the University and bid her farewell. Then I hurried to the theater, where Leo was fuming over having to run things by himself, although the handful of customers could not have caused much problem.

"I think I've found a musician. Her name is Texana Salyer and she —"

"She? I didn't know we were thinking about hiring a woman. Travelling with a woman complicates things."

"How? Three of us couldn't stay in one room anyway. And she's got a similar background to mine; she knows all the hymns and religious songs we could ever need for the film."

"Great. I get to travel with a couple of saints. I'm outnumbered."

"It'll be good for you. Maybe we'll rub off on you." I grinned.

"What's she look like? I probably don't want her rubbing on me at all. Did you say her name was Texana?"

"Yep. We're going to hear her play tomorrow at ten. How did the films turn out?"

"Good. The baptism scene is going to have 'em running down the aisle. When that dove appears, well… it looks like a real miracle."

When we closed the theater, Leo ran the day's films and they did look impressive. Just a few more scenes and we should be able to assemble the finished picture.

## CHAPTER SEVENTEEN

On Thursday morning, I got to the office at nine and was somewhat surprised to see the hammer and chisel I had left the night before. I sketched out a couple of versions of a tomb with a stone to cover the doorway. While I drew, two different men came in to apply for the job. I took their names and addresses, but told them that the position was filled.

Miss Salyer arrived at ten minutes before ten, but Leo didn't show until a few minutes after ten. I introduced Miss Salyer and he was suitably impressed by her appearance. She was all in dove gray today, a color which suited her just as much as mauve.

We trooped down the stairs to the piano store. Miss Salyer seated herself at an upright and began to play Nearer, My God, To Thee. Her playing was confident and she rarely looked down at her fingers, but instead focused on a point somewhere in the air toward the back of the store. As she neared the end of the song, she began to sing, "This all my song shall be, nearer, my God, to Thee. Nearer, My God, to Thee. Nearer to Thee." I was quite ready to propose marriage at that moment! Her voice was a clear, strong alto and she sang with no self-consciousness or shyness. Leo was smiling also. He asked her to play something else and she began Rock of Ages. After the first line, I began to sing harmony with her and it sounded wonderful. Mr. Goggan came out of his office at the rear of the store and stood listening, along with a couple of salesmen and the bookkeeper.

When the song ended, the impromptu audience clapped and complimented us. We repaired back to the upstairs office and discussed terms with the newest member of our company.

Miss Salyer would receive ten dollars a week plus her travel and lodging expenses. She was impressed with this sum, but I was already looking ahead to the time when I could give her a raise, because I thought I had some idea of how much money we could make with our program. I asked her to start on the following Monday. Then we walked over to the theater so that Texana Salyer could get her first look at the moving pictures. She was delighted with them, so much so that I kept digging up new — actually, old — films to show her. We had lost our film of the May Irwin Kiss in the Houston mess, but since it was such a popular scene, we had replaced it with a duped version that was only a bit blurrier than the original. As Texana watched the Kiss, I watched her face; her lips parted slightly and her ebony brows rose as the kiss began. Then her lips closed again, but widened into the smile I was already very fond of. Apparently the idea of kissing was not abhorrent to her.

When she left, I took some of the limestone rocks and began pounding away at them, knocking a good-sized hole in one. I blackened the inside of the hole with some paint and chipped away at another stone until I had a suitable piece for the door covering of the tomb. I showed it to Leo and he thought it might work. We took it up on the roof and I set up the other limestone pieces to form a background, then arranged the little tomb in front. With the camera only a couple of feet away, it looked fairly convincing through the lens. We discussed using a firecracker or something similar to blast the stone away from the opening, but decided that would produce too extreme an effect. Instead, I attached a tiny thread to the stone with beeswax and, at the proper moment, I yanked the stone away from the door of the tomb.

We rushed to develop the film and ran it through the projector. The image of the tomb was slightly blurry, but that actually seemed to make it more realistic. We ran it through several times and learned that when Leo cranked the projector at about half or two-thirds speed, the illusion was even better and the tomb seemed larger and weightier.

Now we needed the manger scene, the walking on water scene, the crucifixion and possibly another version of the ascension and that would be enough for the program, I believed. In the afternoon, Delinda, Mabel and Johnnie Mae came to the office for a meeting I had called. They were more rested than I usually saw them, since we had not needed them for filming that morning.

"Ladies," I began. "We are getting close to the end of this picture and the main scene we need to get is the manger scene. Therefore, I need to decide which of you is going to portray the…uh…Virgin Mary." They exchanged glances.

Mabel said, "Who's got the longest memory?" Johnnie Mae laughed, but Delinda looked very sad. I thought Mabel was too old to play the part, but I was not sure that either of the other two could bring the proper air of reverence to the part.

"How would you feel about it, Delinda? Could you be Mary?" I asked.

Inside those dark, sunken eyes, silver tears glistened, then trickled down the pale cheeks. She shook her head. "I couldn't do it. I'm a Catholic. It…just wouldn't be right." Johnnie Mae patted her on the back and said, "Don't cry, Del. Me or Mabel will do it. You wanna, Mabel?"

Mabel shrugged. "What do you want, J.D.? I'm probably too old, don't you think?"

Thank you, Mabel! "I hadn't thought of that, Mabel. What do you say, Johnnie Mae?"

"Sure, I don't care. Whatever you want."

"All right. I'll send for you when we're ready to film it. Thank you, ladies. Your help has been greatly appreciated." They all headed out and down the stairs, but in a moment I heard footsteps coming up again. Delinda appeared at the door. Her tears had made ugly dark tracks down her cheeks.

"Why are you making this story, J.D.? What's it for?"

I considered. "Well, I think it's a story that a lot of people will want to see. And it might do some good. And I think my father might approve of it."

"Your father?"

"Yes. He's a Baptist preacher and has never been convinced that moving pictures have any good purpose. I'd like to show him different."

"My father threw me out of the house when I was twelve. Said he couldn't afford to feed all of us anymore and since I was the prettiest I should get out and do something about it. I worked in a department store for a year or so. Boys… and men would come in and talk to me and tease me and flirt with me. Just pay attention to me, you know? There I was, surrounded by all these pretty clothes and shoes and jewelry and bows and hats and everything. And I was only making four dollars a week and couldn't buy anything. And then this one man said he would buy me something pretty if I'd have dinner with him and I — I wanted a nice dress so bad and I went and… that was six years ago. Now I can buy pretty things. But I can't take them back to my Papa and say, 'Look, Papa, I made good.' I don't even know if he's still alive and I usually don't even care. If you still care, you're lucky. Thanks for letting me be in your picture. And thanks for treating me with respect, treating me like a lady. I owe you for that, so just let me know if I can do something for you, alright?"

"You don't owe me anything, Delinda. I appreciate your help. We couldn't make this picture without you. I… I hope I didn't offend you by asking you to play Mary."

Her tears were coursing freely now and her voice cracked as she said, "Offend me? It was about the most wonderful thing anyone has every said to me. Once upon a time I had a pure heart. Once I thought I would be a lady. But now —"

I was completely unaccustomed to dealing with a woman's tears; I'm not sure I have ever gotten used to it. But my instincts proved to be right when I circled the desk and held out my arms. Delinda fell into my embrace, sobbing loudly. I hugged her and patted her gently on the back; she smelled of lilac powder and felt so soft and warm that my head was spinning. I don't know why, but I kept saying, "There, there," a phrase I don't believe I had ever uttered prior to this. As her crying slowed and then stopped, she began to cling to me in a way much different from any previous experience of mine. She turned her face toward mine and her lips parted slightly as her eyes closed. She looked ever so much prettier than May Irwin, but I felt it would be ungentlemanly to take advantage of her in such an emotional state. I gave her another pat on the back and then released her from my embrace. "God bless you, Delinda. If I can help you in any way, please let me know."

"You don't like me?"

"Wh–why of course I do. If I didn't care for you, I wouldn't… care." Where was that gift of glib blather when I needed it?

"All right. I'll see you, J.D. You let me know if I can help you, too, right?"

"Yes, I will. Goodbye, Delinda."

She took a handkerchief from her bag and wiped her eyes, then smiled a sad little smile and left the office. I listened to the light tap of her heeled shoes descending the steps and heard the outer door open and close. I sat there in silence, reviewing what had just happened. I was pretty sure this time that she had offered herself to me! To me! But of course I had turned her down. I felt sure that I had done the right thing, but I also felt like I had missed an important opportunity.

While I pondered these things, I heard the lower door open and another set of footsteps coming up. Definitely not one of the ladies, this sounded more like Leo. But he would be at the theater. I waited a moment and was surprised to see a beefy policeman enter the office. He looked around the small office, then focused on me. "Are you the owner of this place, sir?"

"Well, my partner and I rent the space, actually."

"And what sort of business is it you're running, sir?"

"Why, we make and show moving pictures. We have a theater over on Seventh."

"Yes, sir. Well, we've got a problem, sir."

"What's that, officer?"

"The problem is that we don't like whores prancing up and down the Avenue in the broad daylight. And it seems quite a lot of 'em are prancing in here. Why would that be, sir?"

I felt the blood rush to my face, but whether it was anger or shame that forced it there, I could not tell. "Why, we're… we're making a moving picture! I couldn't find any women who wanted to act for the camera. These ladies were agreeable and so we used them in a few scenes. That's all."

"What kind of scenes, sir? Can't think what kind of films you'd make with a bunch of whores."

"Just — story films. Stories of old times, you know? I assure you, officer, they're not playing whores in the films. They're just posing for pictures."

"Posing for pictures, eh?" The nastiest smile imaginable spread across the ruddy face of the policeman, revealing brown teeth that looked like they'd been ground down halfway. "Naked pictures?"

"No, of course not! They are fully clothed at all times. It's a historical picture we're making and I assure you they are well covered. I have done nothing to be ashamed of!"

"Well as that may be, I still don't want to see those tramps on the Avenue in broad daylight. Get me?"

"Yes, you've made your views perfectly clear."

"All right, then. Good day, sir." He was obliged to call me "sir," but it came out with a sneer that let me know he considered me a wet-behind-the-ears pup. He wheeled on his booted heel and clomped down the stairs, leaving me to notice I was perspiring in the chilly office.

I waited a few minutes to calm myself, then locked up the office and headed for the theater. Another skimpy crowd there, indicating that we would be lucky to have any customers at all in a couple of weeks. I stood beside Leo in the back of the room and quietly told him what I'd been doing all afternoon. He smiled as I told him of embracing — but not compromising — Delinda. But when I told him of the visit by the policeman, I could see his jaw clench in the flickering light. He swore a creative oath and asked me what the officer looked like.

"Big. Fat with a red face and a red moustache. Ugly brown teeth."

"Yep. That's Donovan. He's on the take. You should have offered him a few bucks and he probably would have kissed your feet. Damn him! I wish I had been there, Professor. I would have helped him down the stairs."

"What are we going to do? Do you think he'll queer our filming? We only have a couple of scenes to film. I don't want anyone thinking we're running some sort of a — you know, whorehouse — out of our office."

"Don't worry. If we need the girls for anything, I'll go pick them up in a buggy and bring them here, so they don't defile Donovan's angelic streets."

I stood there looking so glum that Leo felt compelled to reassure me. "It's okay, kid. Nothing's going to spoil your film."

"But how are we going to be able to show it around here? He'll know that we used the girls and that will kill us with the religious folk."

"Well, we just won't play it here. I'm ready to hit the road again anyway, aren't you?"

"I guess so. I hate for someone to be blaming me for something I didn't even do, though."

"Live and learn, Professor. Austin will be begging us to play here after we do a few dates around the state. By then, Donovan will have forgotten all about us. Besides, you can't recognize anybody in the film anyhow."

The end of the film trickled through the projector and the bright white rectangle on the screen was unexpectedly bright. "Show's over, folks. Good night, thanks for coming."

One man, apparently a regular, piped up, "Aw, run it backwards, Leo, come on!"

"Not tonight, squire. Mechanical problem. Could take awhile to fix."

The man and his companion left muttering. There was no one waiting outside, so we decided to go ahead and close up for the evening. I slept fitfully that night, rethinking the events of the day.

## CHAPTER EIGHTEEN

The next day, Friday, was Christmas Eve. As I looked through the paper at breakfast, I scanned the advertisements for Christmas candy, cranberries, oranges, blank books for New Year's diaries, and Huyler's candies. I was reminded that this would be my first Christmas away from home… and that I had not written to my family in several months. It was too late now to send anything for Christmas, although I could have afforded to have sent some nice gifts if I'd thought of it sooner.

My mood was not enriched by the advertisement I found on page eight. The Hancock Opera House, scene of the Vitascope debut fourteen months before, proclaimed:

**TONIGHT**
**XMAS MATINEE AND NIGHT**
**Dan Stuart's Veriscope**
Showing life size figures of the memorable
**CORBETT-FITZSIMMONS FIGHT**
At Carson City, March 17 Last
An Exact Reproduction.

**This is an entertainment that children and ladies can attend as well as gentlemen.**
**Matinee prices, 50¢ and 25¢.**
**Night prices, 75¢, 50¢, 25¢.**
**Seats now on sale.**

When Leo came down for breakfast, I showed him the paper and we decided it was useless for us to even open the theater until after Christmas. What moving picture business there was to be had would surely attend the Hancock. In fact, we decided we would attend the evening showing and get a look at the Veriscope.

I spent the morning doing a bit of shopping, buying baskets of fruit and handkerchiefs for Delinda, Mabel and Johnnie Mae, cigars for all the men who had been in the film, and a silver watch fob for Leo, which I had engraved with "Happy Christmas, dear partner Leo, Fraternally, J.D."

During the afternoon, I puzzled over how to film the Crucifixion scene and the manger scene. I had all but given up on the walking on water idea. I stopped by Stokes Lumber to see what sort of boards might be available from which to make three crosses. I supposed we would have to buy the lumber and transport it out to the country. While in the office, Miss Texana Salyer put in an appearance. She delivered a handmade Christmas card in which she thanked Leo and me for hiring her and wishing us a joyful holiday. I noticed that she was once again wearing the mauve ensemble. As we chatted, I realized I had not really told her what sort of film we were making. It occurred to me that I might have done so on purpose, out of feat she would be offended and find our project to be sacrilegious. But when I told her about my attempts to film the life of Jesus, she became very enthusiastic.

"What a wonderful idea! Every person should have to see this film."

"I hope you are right. We've only a couple of scenes yet to film and then you and I will work on the lecture and musical part of the program. I think I've found suitable lumber for the crosses. I suppose we'll have to make a manger, too. I've given up on the walking on water scene, though."

"Really? Oh, why? That would be so inspiring to see!"

"Well, we can't figure out any way to do it and make it look good. I thought about putting a board just under the surface of the creek, but it seems too difficult to work out."

"What a pity. I guess you couldn't do it as they do it on the stage?"

"On the stage? I don't know what you mean."

"Oh, I saw a production of Moby Dick in which they had several scenes of the ship in the ocean."

I sat up in my chair. "How did they do it, then?"

"With long, long pieces of blue cloth. Several pieces of it were stretched loosely across the back of the stage and people in the wings would wave them gently up and down and it made a wonderful illusion of waves on the sea."

"Wonderful! If there's one thing we've got, it's long pieces of muslin. We can dye them a dark color and shoot the scene right on the rooftop. We'll make the front part of a boat out of wood and set it in the middle. Oh, Miss Salyer, thank you for the grand inspiration! You've solved a major problem for us!"

She blushed handsomely and said, "I'm so pleased. I'll certainly be glad to help your production in any way I can. But please, call me Texana. Miss Salyer is so formal."

"Alright, Texana it is. You can call me J.D. if you like."

"What does that stand for?"

"Uh... Jubal Daniel."

"How strong a name! May I call you Daniel? Or Dan?"

"You may call me anything you wish. My mother calls me Daniel, too."

I was strongly tempted to ask Texana to portray Mary in the manger scene. She seemed to have the inner beauty and reverence required. But I was apprehensive that the sight of the Virgin Mary playing the piano along with the film might prove distracting to the audience if they should discover it.

"Would you like to go to the theater tonight, Texana? Leo and I are going to look at the Veriscope, one of our competitors. They're showing a boxing match, but it's supposed to be suitable for women and children as well."

Texana looked surprised at my invitation. "I think not, Daniel. I hate to leave my aunt alone in the evenings, especially on Christmas Eve. I feel I should spend as much time with her as possible before we begin touring with the picture. Thank you kindly for asking, though."

We talked for half an hour about the Passion Play picture and what songs would provide suitable accompaniment. I was determined now that Texana should sing during the presentation; perhaps we could even do a duet.

After she left, I walked to the theater to gather up all the unused muslin and took it to a laundry to be dyed a dark gray. The owner assured me it would be ready on Monday, the 27th.

I met Leo for supper at The English Kitchen and then we proceeded to the Hancock Opera House, site of our first meeting and my first glimpse of the celluloid siren with which I had thrown my lot. The Avenue was very crowded, as shoppers sought their last-minute Christmas purchases. As we walked, I told Leo of Texana's idea for filming Jesus walking on the water. I also told him that I had invited her to join us for the Veriscope exhibition, but she had turned me down.

"She's a beautiful young lady, Professor. But it's going to be hard enough traveling with a woman even without being sweet on her. And it's hardly fair. Maybe I should take one of my lady friends along, as well?"

"Oh, stop it. I just thought she might be curious about our competition. I agree she's very attractive, but I'm not 'sweet' on her." I felt embarrassed in saying this for some reason. I had come perilously close to kissing Delinda the day before and then asked Texana, who I scarcely knew, out for an evening date. What was happening to me all of a sudden?

We sprang for the seventy-five cent seats at the Hancock and went inside. I had been back to the Opera House several times in the past months, but this was the first time another moving picture had been shown since I'd been residing in the capital city. After we found seats, we looked up to the balcony to get a look at the Veriscope. It was not noticeably different from our Motograph, but Leo went up to the balcony to take a closer look and reported back that the Veriscope utilized a wider film than our unit.

When the show began, a lecturer in a tuxedo came out onstage, stirring up a lot of memories for me. This gentleman proceeded to describe the Veriscope or "truth viewer" to us and related some of the history of the bout between Robert Fitzsimmons and James Corbett. The match had been planned for months, but hampered by the fact that boxing was illegal all over the United States. Eventually, however, the fight promoter — Dan Stuart — managed to persuade state officials in Nevada that the match and resulting publicity would be a boon to the state. As the first round began to unreel on the screen, the lecturer gave a blow-by-blow description so we would be sure of what we were seeing.

The image thrown by the Veriscope was larger than any I had seen, and Dan Stuart had made sure that viewers would not be able to forget whose film they were watching. A banner ran along the bottom edge of the ring and bore foot-high letters, proclaiming, "COPYRIGHTED THE VERISCOPE COMPANY 1897."

The fight lasted fourteen rounds. After every four rounds, there was a brief intermission to allow for a reel change on the sole projector and also to provide relief for the viewers, for the "truth viewer" was hard on the eyes, flickering and jumping like a moth on a light bulb. Even so, the audience, which contained a surprising number of women, was vocal and animated in their excited interest in the action. There was a moment in the sixth round when Fitzsimmons took a hard shot and nearly went down and the theater was loud with shouts of encouragement: "Steady, Fitz!" "Hang on in there, Bob!" "Give him some more of that one, Jim!"

Fitzsimmons recovered, of course; we all already knew the outcome of the fight. But it was still an exciting experience to witness Fitzsimmons' blow to Corbett's heart in the fourteenth round which ended the match, although there were rumors that Corbett had been fouled on his way down. Even after the referee raised Fitzsimmons' arm in victory, the film continued, as the defeated and enraged Corbett attempted to get through the crowded ring to give Fitzsimmons a payback punch or two.

There were loud cheers at the conclusion and Leo and I were made well aware of the contrast between the reaction of this crowd and that of our meager audience back at the Jubilee most nights.

On Monday morning, I picked up the dyed muslin and took it to the theater. Leo and I unrolled it on the rooftop and cut it into four long strips, which we would use to simulate waves on the water. Then we cut out the outline of a boat hull from some old packing crates Leo had procured at the depot, and I painted the silhouette to look as seaworthy as I knew how. As I was finishing up, Leo was smoking a cigar over by the front part of the roof. I felt a pebble hit my back and I turned, thinking he was joking around. But he held a finger to his lips, shushing me, and motioned for me to come to where he stood. I walked quietly to the front of the building's roof and Leo pointed down below. I craned my neck over the side and peered down; there stood Officer Donovan, pressing his nose against our front window and shading his eyes with his hands, trying to see if there was anything going one inside.

I looked quizzically at Leo and he made a disgusted face. Donovan tapped on the glass with his nightstick and awaited some response, but eventually gave up and walked back toward the Avenue.

"We're going to have to do something, Professor. He's going to dog us until he gets paid or catches us doing something he can arrest us for."

"Like stealing palm trees, maybe?" I asked innocently.

"If he thought he could pin it on us, he probably would," Leo snarled. "But no, I think we're going to have to grease his palm."

"This is ridiculous! He's supposed to uphold the law! Not break it!"

"Welcome to the big city."

"How much do you think it would take to buy him off? Can we afford it?"

"I don't know. I'll ask around; I'm sure some of the girls would know. Anyway, we should get this filming over and done with so we can hit the road and not have to worry about Donovan anymore."

Our cast showed up just after noon to get into costume and we began to film the water scene. The three women and two of the men and I took our places as wave-makers. I explained to them how we were going to do the scene and we practiced flapping the long cloths energetically to portray stormy waves, then settling down to a peaceful ripple.

Then I coached the other men, who would be behind the boat facade. They were to help rock the boat and look frightened until the waves calmed down.

Finally, I took Orvis through the scene step by step. "First, you'll stand over here," I said, pointing to the right of the rooftop. "The waves will rock the boat for about half a minute. Then, I'll say, 'Go' and you will come walking between the strips of cloth until you get beside the boat. Climb into the boat — Wilbur, Jim, give him a hand into the boat then — and you'll stand up in the boat and stretch out your hands, looking up to heaven. Then the waves will stop, you can sit down in the boat, and all you disciples will look at Jesus with great wonder. Got it?"

Everyone seemed set and Orvis seemed steady as a rock. We ran through the scene twice, adjusting how Orvis could best get in the boat and where he would sit. Then we did it with the camera running and it went smooth as silk. "How did it look, Leo?"

"First rate, Professor. The waves look very good." The three women laughed at this point, and I didn't know why, although they were looking at me. I decided to go on without asking any questions, and we set up the little feeding trough Bob and Jim had made. It was filled with straw and would make a good manger.

Johnnie Mae got into her Mary outfit and I assigned some of the men to stand in for Joseph and the shepherds. We had decided not to try to include the visit of the Wise Men, since their regal costumes were beyond our abilities and budget. So this would be a short scene, without much movement. Mary and Joseph would be by the manger and the shepherds would come into the scene, look into the trough and kneel down to worship the Baby Jesus. We had neither real baby nor doll, but I bundled up the dyed cloth we had used for waves and made a bundle approximately the size and shape of a baby.

We got the picture easily and I thanked everyone for doing such quick work. "All we have left to do is the crucifixion scene and we'll ride out to the country tomorrow providing we have sunny weather. If the sun is out, meet here at nine o'clock. When we're all done filming, we'll have to have a big party, right, Leo?" There were cheers and huzzahs at this and the group began drifting away toward the stairs. Leo and I moved the camera back into the theater and I unlocked the front door so everyone could leave. Delinda opened the door and started out, then gasped and backed into the room again. I turned to see what made her exclaim and saw Donovan in the doorway, smiling his disgusting smile.

"Having a party, are we? Bit early in the day, innit?"

No one seemed willing to speak. Donovan looked immensely pleased with himself, as though he'd caught us all in some terrible crime. He looked around at everyone present, noting the faces of each man and woman. Then he said, "Go on, the rest of you. I've got business with the proprietors. I know where to find the rest of you if I need to." The nine members of our troupe exited quickly, as Donovan held the door open. When the last one was out, he closed the door and smiled at Leo and me.

"I was under the notion you wasn't going to be having any more of your whore parties. Maybe I didn't make myself clear the other day."

"You said you didn't want to see these women on the Avenue," I responded. "We're not on the Avenue now."

"Close enough, boy." Oh, the "sir" was gone now. "I'm having to spend too much of my time keeping an eye on you and your little gang. I don't know what we can do to make things right all around, do you?"

"How much, Officer?" Leo chimed in. "Just name us a price. We don't want any trouble, but we're not doing anything wrong."

"Wrong is in the eye of the beholder, Mister…Matula, is it? When I see something in my territory that bothers me, that's wrong." He walked down the center aisle of the theater, looking casually around. "I think twenty dollars could ease my bother, though."

I glanced at Leo. He nodded at me as if to say, "Pay the man," but I instead said, "Twenty dollars? We haven't got that much cash right now. But we'll run the moving picture show tonight and tomorrow night. How about if you come by on Wednesday morning?"

"Sure, a pair of big tycoons like you don't have twenty between you? I think you like bothering me."

"No, no, we just need a little time. I tell you what, if you'll give us until Wednesday, we'll make it thirty, how's that?" Leo was staring at me like a lunatic, but I looked innocently at Donovan.

"Well, that makes it nicer, dunnit? But don't cross me, boy. I can find cause to run you two in anytime I want. And it would bother me even more if I learned you were talking about this little arrangement to anybody else. I'm a cop. My word carries weight. Am I clear, boy?"

"Yes, sir, and thanks for being patient. We'll have the thirty for you on Wednesday."

Donovan looked at me, then at Leo, considering something in his mind. "Right. I'll see you in two days, then." He moved to the door and left; I could hear him whistling a jolly tune before the door closed.

"Please tell me you don't have some hare-brained plan that's going to get us sent to Huntsville for a long stay," Leo said. "Why didn't you just give him the twenty bucks? We can spare it, can't we?"

"Yes, we can. But I want to teach Officer Donovan a lesson. And while he was talking, I came up with an idea."

Leo groaned, but when I laid it all out, he agreed that it could be a winner. The only thing we had to do right then was paint the window black in the back room, which only took a few minutes. Then we went to dinner.

## CHAPTER NINETEEN

On the following morning, Leo and I hired a wagon and went by the lumberyard for some large two-by-twelve planks. We met the rest of the gang at the theater and began our caravan out to the country for what I hoped would be the last scene of the story. I sat in the back of the wagon, holding the boards steady, and Delinda sat back there with me. On the trip, I told her about our plan for Officer Donovan and she laughingly agreed to participate. She told me that Donovan stopped by the house where she worked on a regular basis to get his weekly graft and that he often tried to get fresh with the girls. She was in such good humor that I felt safe in asking her if she enjoyed the profession she had chosen.

"Most times it's all right. It can get rough if you end up with a crazy drunk. The money's nice, though. Much better than working in a factory or being a servant girl. These early hours are a bit tough on me and Mabel and Johnnie; we usually sleep in the daytime."

"You should get outside more often. You're so pale. My mother would fix you a big plate of food and tell you to go sit in the sun for awhile."

Delinda laughed again. "Don't be silly. Men like a pale complexion. If you're too brown

— or too red — you look like you've been picking cotton all season. So I usually avoid sunlight. I even take arsenic pills to help me stay lily-white."

The more I learned about Delinda, the less I understood.

Once we were well away from the city, we scouted for a suitable place to build three crosses. I preferred them to be on a hill, but it would have to be one suitably secluded; I did not relish explaining why we were crucifying three men in a deserted place. Officer Donovan would have a fine time with that one!

We eventually located a small rise which was sheltered from the dirt road by a heavy growth of cedar and oak. We tied up the horses and carried the supplies through the trees, over a limestone outcropping, down a small valley, and then back up to the top of the hill. From the apex, I looked around in all directions and could see nothing but trees and hills. Even the wagons and horses were hidden, so one of the men went back to guard them.

Wilbur and Leo began digging holes for the three crosses when I had chosen the proper locations. We erected the two outer crosses for the two thieves, but I decided to get a shot of Orvis carrying his cross up the hill. We went back to the valley and everyone got into costume. Then I had Orvis struggle to carry the big cross — which really was pretty heavy — and finally collapse, surrounded by the rest of the crowd. I had not thought out this scene in advance, so I had no Roman soldier costumes. But I had Gilbert, one of Leo's chums, to step in and carry the cross to the top of the hill. It was a small scene, but I thought it would add to our program.

But now there was no way to delay the grand finale any longer. Wilbur and Bob had agreed to play the crucified thieves, so they took their places, standing on the small wooden rung we had nailed about two feet from the ground. I sat on Leo's shoulders and tied their wrists to the crossbeam. We had not come up with a good way to simulate nails in their hands, but the camera would be so far away that I didn't think it would matter. I put a small circle of black paint in the center of each palm of Wilbur and Bob's hands, plus another dot on their bare feet. From thirty or forty feet away, it looked okay.

Orvis had it a bit more difficult, since he had to strip down to the loincloth I had fashioned from the muslin. It was still chilly and I could see the gooseflesh on his arms and legs as I tied him to the cross and painted the dots on him. We had fashioned a crown of thorns from a few thin cedar branches. Again, distance would preserve the illusion they were supposed to present.

It was an odd feeling, though, putting three men up on crosses. And where much of our picture-taking had been marked by humor and a casual atmosphere, the group was noticeably quiet on this day. I stepped back by the camera and directed the rest of the group where to stand around the three crosses. The three women knelt and looked properly mournful at Orvis' feet.

"All right, we're going to begin. Go ahead, Leo. Ladies, look as though you're weeping. Wilbur, Bob, act like you're in pain. Orvis, look around at all the people. Good. Now, look up to the heavens. Like you're searching for something. Yes. Now, Orvis, I want you to make a face, you're really hurting now. Good, good. Now, Orvis, yell out, 'It is finished!' Great, now drop your head down on your chest. Hold it. Hold it. All right, I think that's enough."

We quickly released the men from the crosses. We had done it! Several of the men produced flasks and began an impromptu celebration. Leo and I knocked the crosses apart and put the boards back in the wagon. As we rode back to town, there was a great feeling of happiness in our group and I confess to feeling very content myself, although my work on the project was far from over. I would now have to devise the proper narration to link together the isolated scenes we had filmed. Appropriate music had to be chosen and rehearsed. Dates had to be booked and contracts signed. Travel plans — for three! — remained to be scheduled. No, only a small part of the work was done. The rest would be largely done by me alone. Leo was uninterested in the lecture portion of the show and had never been good at booking or planning ahead. Perhaps Texana could help; I resolved to call on her and see if she could begin work immediately, seeking venues for our production.

Thus lost in thought, I missed much of the ribbing at my expense. None of the men could understand why I would not take a drink, even if it was "just this once, to celebrate." The women teased me also, telling me I should celebrate with them. They began to call me

"Professor," although no one but Leo had ever done so before. They took great delight in this and I finally asked them why it was so amusing to them.

Delinda confided in me that they thought Leo's nickname for me rather ironic; it seems that every bordello was required to have a piano player and this worthy was invariably called "Professor!"

"We know you play the piano, J.D.," taunted Johnnie Mae. "We was just wondering where you got your training?" She and Mabel hooted like owls; they had partaken of more than one flask when offered.

"I'm afraid my story is nothing as exotic as that, ladies. I learned to play in church. Leo started calling me Professor when we were touring with the Vitascope and I took over the lecture responsibilities. That's all. I have never even been in one of the places you're referring to."

"Well, it's high time then, ain't it, Leo?" piped Mabel. "Time the Professor got his diploma, eh?"

Leo grinned, but shook his head. "I doubt you can talk him into it, Mabel. J.D.'s a pretty straight arrow."

"Every arrow needs a quiver, don't it?" screamed Johnnie Mae. Oh, more howls of laughter. "Come on, J.D., let's quiver together!"

I felt my face turn red and hot, but it was not altogether unpleasant to be teased by three women, regardless of their profession.

On Wednesday morning, I walked up and down Congress Avenue until I finally located Donovan, although I pretended not to be looking for him.

"Morning, sir," he nodded. "Thought I might pop around to your place in awhile."

"Uh...fine, Officer," I acted uncomfortable at seeing him. "Why don't you meet me in the alley behind the theater at eleven?"

"In the alley? Why not inside?" His snaky eyes narrowed.

"There's a lady visiting the theater to consider investing in our films. I don't want her to know about this little matter."

"Oh, I see. All right, then. Eleven." He turned and continued walking his beat.

It was just after nine and I dashed back to the office where Leo was waiting. "You go get Delinda and I've got to go get Texana. Meet you at the theater at ten-thirty."

I took a buggy to the home of Texana's aunt. Texana was surprised to see me, but I told her I needed her to come by the theater. "In fact, why don't you bring your aunt? We'll show her some moving pictures so she'll know what sort of business you're going into."

Miss Salyer the elder and Miss Salyer the younger got themselves properly assembled and we drove back to Seventh Street. Leo was not back yet. I unlocked the door and took the ladies inside. I placed three folding chairs close to the front window and invited them to be seated while I made some tea. My hope was that if Donovan saw these two well-dressed women, he would believe my story. While I was in the back room making tea, a rap sounded on the rear door.

"Me, Professor." Leo's voice. I unlocked the door and said hello to Delinda, who was looking more like a fallen woman than I had ever seen her. We quickly ran over the plans and then I gave her thirty dollars in one dollar bills. She folded them in half and then raised her skirt to an alarming height to tuck the bills in her garter. She then repaired to the back doorway of the building across the alley, waiting for Donovan.

Leo went back inside and closed the door, then adjusted the camera so that the lens was right behind a small round hole I had scraped in the black paint on the window. He focused on Delinda and I, then came to the door to tell us all was well.

"All right, Delinda," I said. "This is your big part. All set?"

"Don't worry, J.D. I'm much better at this than playing the Virgin Mary."

"Good, good. Just try to keep him turned this way so the camera will show his face." I scraped a couple of lines in the dirt. "And stay within this space or we'll lose you in the picture. Good luck." I extended my hand for a shake. She laughed and threw her arms around me and kissed my cheek.

"I'll turn in a performance you'll be proud of."

I went back inside and finally took the tea up front to the ladies, who had begun to wonder about me. I apologized, saying I had to help Leo set up some things in the back. I began to tell Texana's aunt about moving pictures, reverting to some of my professorial lecture material. We were sitting in the sunny window when I saw Donovan walk by, nod to us and continue to the end of the block.

I was now extremely nervous, but I kept talking and suggested finally that I run some film for the ladies. I locked the front door, drew the curtains, and put on a reel of film. After it began to roll, I went back to the storeroom, where Leo was already removing the film from the camera.

"How did it go?"

"Beautiful! He was surprised to see Delinda there, but it went off without a hitch. Even better than expected in some ways." While he began mixing chemicals to develop the film, I went back to the Salyers. When the film was over, I escorted them to the carriage and delivered them home. Texana's aunt was effusive over her first exposure to the moving pictures and, although I explained them as simply as I could, she repeatedly said, "Well, I just don't understand all that."

I made hasty farewells to the ladies and rushed back to the theater.

I have waited with anticipation to see many films, but I was nervous as a cat as Leo threaded the new footage into the projector. But it turned out to be everything I had hoped for and more. After we watched it twice, I got a piece of signboard and my trusty black paint and made a title card for our little production.

## CHAPTER TWENTY

Although we continued to open the theater for customers, they were becoming scarcer and scarcer. And because of the plain appearance of our theater, the low price of admission, and the slow turnover of films, the business we did manage to attract was not of the highest caliber. We got laborers, migrant workers, raggedy children… anyone who had a quarter and had precious few other choices for entertainment.

Leo suggested that we either give up the office or the theater for our remaining time in Austin, just as a money-saving effort. If we kept the theater, we could still get a small income from our dwindling audience, but the rent on the office was cheaper and it was virtually a toss-up as to which place we should give up.

We decided to close up the office and operate solely from the theater. I had Texana begin writing letters in her lovely handwriting to churches and religious groups around the state, offering our exclusive film of "The World-Famous Passion Play." I was not going to claim that we had filmed the Oberammergau play in Germany, but if someone received that impression, I would not mind.

I spent several days writing out parts of my narration. Texana brought what music she had for me to look through and we kept out those pieces we thought would be appropriate accompaniment. Leo spliced in black leader film between the different scenes so that it would be easy for him to stop the projector after each scene until my lecture reached the proper point for the next scene.

When we gave up the office, we also lost our privilege of practicing music at the piano store. So Texana and I would rehearse in her aunt's parlor, one of us playing the pump organ while the other sang.

The program began to take shape and we did a few run-throughs in the deserted theater in the mornings, although without musical accompaniment. Replies to our letters were beginning to come in and we began to lay out a tour. We booked a first date in Temple and then developed an itinerary which would include Waco, Hillsboro, Waxahachie, Dallas, Fort Worth and Abilene and then work its way back south. My goal was to get the show perfected, then bring it to Blanco to show my parents. But I decided we would play a seven-week tour and then make further bookings when it was clear we had a guaranteed success.

We had a private showing for all the members of our cast one Thursday night, although Orvis Dean had apparently left town immediately after the crucifixion scene and headed toward Ben Bolt. I was sorry that he had not had a chance to see any of his film appearances, because he looked extremely Biblical. The rest of the group was greatly excited and we had to run the sixteen minutes of film over three times. I did not perform the lecture or musical part of the show, so all they saw was the silent footage, but it clearly had a dramatic impact, even on an audience which was familiar with what was to be shown.

When the men and the three women all left, most in a state of celebratory near-inebriation, I followed them out onto the sidewalk, shaking hands and thanking all the fellows for their participation and hugging the three ladies. They loaded up into a couple of buggies and headed west, back toward Guy Town. I watched the vehicles going away and I could still hear the merry-making voices. I stepped back inside and began to lock the door when I saw a dark form across the street, in the doorway of a harness shop. I could see the periodic red glow of a cigar and I stepped back into the darkened theater, away from the front glass, so I would not be visible to anyone outside.

After a moment, the dark figure stepped out of the doorway and by the light of the moonlight towers I recognized Officer Donovan. He began walking back toward the Avenue, but I was sure we would hear from him soon.

It was in fact the next morning when Donovan came through the door of the Jubilee Theatre. I was going over the travel plans with Leo and Texana and discussing ideas for some handbills and posters we were going to have to get printed. Donovan stood there wordlessly for a moment. Finally I said, "Miss Salyer, would you please go post these invitations for me?"

Texana looked quizzically at me, but arose and took a packet of ten white envelopes from me and left without another word. Donovan smiled his rancid grin and said, "Seemed like quite a party you gents had last night. Sending out invitations for another one? I think there's a bit too much activity going on around here lately. Although I must admit, that 'un that just left is a lot more respectable looking than most of your whores."

"Don't you speak ill of her, you weaselly son of a bitch." I'm not sure whose eyebrows reached higher when I said this, Leo's or Donovan's.

Donovan reached unconsciously for his stick and spat, "What did you call me? I'll have your ass in the clink for that!"

"Maybe. Maybe not." Donovan was not used to people acting blasé in the face of his temper. He paused, unsure, and I continued, "If you're curious about who the invitations are for, it's a special show we're doing for the mayor, the police chief, the editor of the *Statesman*, and a few other dignitaries. We've got some new films to show them. Would you like to take a look? This one's on the house."

"Naw, I don't care about your silly pictures. I care about my money. And if you don't come up with it, you won't be running your films anyway."

"Oh, you'll watch this one, you bribe-taking bastard. Roll the film, Leo. Sit down, Officer. Enjoy the show."

*This Is Where I Came In*

Leo started the projector as I drew the heavy curtains and the show began for our audience of one. First there was a scene of the Austin Fire Department in full gallop toward a conflagration; then came a scene of the shopping crowds a day or two before Christmas on Congress Avenue. Donovan had obviously never seen moving pictures before and his reaction was like most folks'; he was interested in spite of himself.

The third subject on the reel began with a painted title card: "A Hot Tip For The Police." Then there was a scene of my friend Delinda, standing in an alley, looking amazingly whorish, from her stockings with the wide vertical stripes, to her billowing skirt with the lace petticoats peeking out, from the startlingly low-cut bodice to the brazen makeup around her eyes and mouth. While she languished in a doorway, a policeman approached her and spoke sharply to her. Why, it looks like Officer Donovan! The girl speaks to him and wiggles her eyebrows. The policeman smirks lewdly and comes closer. The girl pulls up her skirt and all those petticoats, revealing her shapely legs up to her thigh. She reaches into the top of her stocking and pulls out a wad of bills, then begins to count them out to the policeman. She holds out the money to him and he looks up and down the alley and then pockets the loot. She speaks to him again and he says something in return, then reaches out and squeezes her breast. She looks briefly annoyed and pushes his hand away, but he reaches again for her, this time trying to lift her skirt. She pulls away, almost out of the picture, but the policeman laughs and then leaves the scene. The end of the film passes through the projector and for a moment a rectangle of white light bathes the wall.

I pulled the curtains back, allowing the sun to shine in. Donovan sat still in his chair, staring at the now-blank wall. "So, what do you think, Officer Donovan? Think the mayor and the chief will enjoy these scenes of their fair city? I think they'll be fascinated. Of course we could show them some other films, I suppose. But for that, I think we'd have to be assured that we will never see your face in our place of business again. Oh, and if you're thinking you could take this piece of film with you, well, you're right. But we've got the negative and two more copies of it in the bank vault. So it wouldn't do you any good. Did you enjoy the pictures, Officer? They're just like real life, aren't they? Unfortunately."

Donovan stood up without a word and left the theater. Leo and I exchanged looks; he smiled. I could feel my heart pounding as it always did when I became empowered by the self-confident windbag that dwelt — usually hidden — inside me. I went to the door and watched Donovan walking aimlessly down the street and I wondered what was going through his mind. Of course there were no extra copies of the film in a bank vault. Leo had printed only one, and the negative was in a can in the back room. But the battle had been joined and won.

I cannot claim many "firsts" in the history of the motion picture, my friends. Perhaps you will understand how much pride I have in this one.

## CHAPTER TWENTY-ONE

We retained our lease on the Jubilee Theatre through February of 1898, but it was a month of slow business and final planning for our roadshow, which we had decided to start the first week in March. Our itinerary was complete; we would be showing the Passion Play in five churches and two opera houses. The opera houses were in Dallas and Fort Worth. The smaller towns lacked a performance house of sufficient size, so we would occupy the Presbyterian Church in Temple, Baptist churches in Waco and Hillsboro, a Methodist church in Waxahachie and an Episcopal church in Abilene.

Our weekly plan called for traveling on Sunday or Monday, then papering the town with our beautiful new handbills and posters. I would try to meet with the local pastors on Tuesday or Wednesday so they could encourage their congregations to attend. There was not a great division between denominations at this time; it was not at all uncommon for the Methodists to attend the Baptists' summer revival or for the Presbyterians to hear the Episcopal choir concert. We planned to play Thursday, Friday and Saturday nights, with the possibility of an afternoon performance on Saturday if the population seemed to merit it.

Our posters and handbills were in a beautiful purple ink and had wonderfully ornate lettering proclaiming:

**Come & See**
**The Moving Picture Spectacle**
**The Life of Christ**
**AS PORTRAYED & PHOTOGRAPHED AT THE WORLD-FAMOUS PASSION PLAY**
**A DOZEN INSPIRATIONAL SCENES**
**In Life-Size, Motion Pictures**
**NOT A LANTERN SHOW**
**With Uplifting Musical Accompaniment & Lecture**
**JUBILEE FILMS**
**Brings this exclusive presentation, suitable for all**
**From the smallest child to the most wizened adult**

There was blank space at the bottom to add the date, time and venue to each poster. We were going to ask a fifty-cent admission price, but we could adjust it in each town if it seemed necessary. I suggested we offer a "family rate" which would make it more affordable for large families to attend.

We had packed up the camera and all our secular films, just in case we might need them somewhere along the way. The projector and handbills were all carefully packed in heavy boxes and Leo and I had our dress clothes freshly cleaned and ironed. We had rehearsed the presentation many times, but there was still no way to know how it would actually play before an audience.

On the first Monday in March we picked up Texana and her two small carpetbags in a borrowed wagon, said farewell to her aunt, and rolled down Congress Avenue for what would be the last time for awhile. At the depot, we saw that our equipment was loaded carefully and then joined Texana in the second car for our trip to Temple. She was wearing the mauve dress she had worn the day I met her; it was always my favorite, not just for that reason, but also because I loved the way she pronounced the word "mauve." When I said it, it tended to rhyme with "awe." But Texana had a way of saying it that seemed half "O" and half "AH" and wholly delightful.

We found Temple to be a bustling town and had the wagon driver from the train station drive us around a bit before we went to the boarding house where we had arranged lodging. Texana made notes of the best places for us to post our advertisements as Leo spotted them. I noted how many churches there were and how best to get around to them all.

On Tuesday, Leo and Texana covered the town with paper, while I went to meet pastors of Baptist, Methodist, Pentecostal, Holiness, Presbyterian, Episcopal, Catholic and a few others which have slipped my memory. If anyone knew how preachers acted, looked, and talked, it was me, and I made a good impression on the local clergy, offering them a free advance showing on Wednesday afternoon at the Presbyterian Church.

On Wednesday, Texana played the organ while Leo ran the projector and I did the lecture as we made our debut performance before an audience of ministers, although there were only a dozen present. Some of them came reluctantly; there was a tangible stigma against anything that smacked of "entertainment" or "worldliness." But I had chosen the music and my words carefully and the response was overwhelmingly positive. The Baptist preacher assured me he would bring his whole congregation and several others said the same thing. Leo and I decided we would wait until after Thursday night's performance to decide if a Saturday matinee was in order.

I was restless Wednesday night and did not sleep well. Neither did Leo, although it was probably for a different reason. I had impressed upon him that it was imperative that we lead lives above reproach while showing this film. If any member of our company was spotted drinking or chasing women or dancing, our entire company could be run out of town and publicly denounced from pulpits of all brands. So he was reduced to sipping from a flask in his suitcase, only in the privacy of our room.

We had purchased the railroad tickets for our entire tour and it had left our once-healthy nest egg severely depleted. We had enough to eat and pay for rooms for two, maybe three, weeks, but our future depended on the success of our show.

On Thursday morning, I had meetings with the local newspapers and they agreed to give us a good play, provided, of course, that they enjoyed the show via the free tickets I left for them. I didn't mind this, though, since the Presbyterian Church had done no advertising. Aside from our posted bills, free newspaper reviews would be the only boost we would get.

After lunch on Thursday, I tried to nap, but found it difficult. My speech kept running through my head and I was still finding a word here and there that needed tweaking. Supper was out of the question, all three of us agreed, and we were at the church by five o'clock, two hours before the program was set to begin. Texana would take money for admissions at one door of the Presbyterian sanctuary, while Leo did the same at the other door. This gave me time to pace back and forth in a small room behind the stage platform.

Our screen was made from two white bedsheets nailed to a light wooden frame and hung from the ceiling. We carried the sheets from town to town, but found it simpler to buy the few strips of wood wherever we found ourselves.

At twenty minutes before seven, Leo entered my small pacing room to tell me that, "Every seat is full, Professor. And there's still a line outside both doors. We're going to sell as many more tickets as we can for folks to stand at the back or sit in the aisles." After he left, I went and peeked out the door. It was a safe bet that this church had never been so crowded except maybe on Easter Sunday.

At seven, Texana came back to the little room with a metal strongbox we had purchased to contain admission money. She was struggling because the box was so laden with coins that she could scarcely carry it. We placed the box behind some folding chairs and then we shook hands and wished each other good luck. She went out to take her place at the organ and began playing *Amazing Grace*. After she had played two verses of it, she began to sing in her lilting alto voice: "I once was lost, but now am found; Twas blind, but now I see."

As the song ended, I stepped onto the raised platform at the front of the sanctuary; there seemed to be no place to put another human being in the room and every face looked expectantly and attentively toward me.

"Good evening, friends. I welcome you to this special evening as you have welcomed us to this beautiful city. My name is Jubal Daniel Wilkinson (for a church crowd I decided to pull out my scriptural nomenclature) and my associates in Jubilee Films are delighted to share with you the amazing spectacle you are about to witness."

I began by telling them how the invention of the motion picture had made it possible for the first time for audiences to see realistic scenes from all over the world, life-size and with all the movement of God's active creation.

"And perhaps some of you have seen moving pictures and found them interesting as a curiosity or novelty. But this evening we bring you something new: the moving picture as a tool of evangelism and worship. Join me now as we witness scenes from the life of our Lord and Saviour, Jesus Christ."

All the lights were now extinguished, except for one beside each door at the rear of the auditorium. Texana began to play *Away In A Manger* as I quoted the scripture concerning the birth of Jesus from the Gospel according to Luke. This took several minutes until I reached the point where "the shepherds came and found Mary and the baby, wrapped in a manger." Leo started the projector and the manger scene came on, accompanied by Texana singing *O Come, All Ye Faithful*. There was an audible gasp from the crowd and in the reflected light from the screen, I could see the rapt expressions, the open mouths and the raised eyebrows. After a couple of minutes, the screen went black and I continued speaking of the baptism of Jesus by John the Baptist.

Each portion of the story was accompanied by an appropriate hymn and each scene of the film was buoyed by Texana or I singing another appropriate song. The audience was entirely engrossed in the filmed segments and when something "miraculous" was shown, like the dove appearing on Jesus' head or the food multiplying, murmuring would run through the crowd as they wondered over how such things could occur. The program ran along smoothly and it was over an hour before the crucifixion scene. I could clearly hear women sobbing during the film of this. Finally came the shot of the stone rolling away from the tomb and then the shot of Jesus against a bright sky as Texana and I sang together the grand chorus of *The*

*Holy City*, the song that had so impressed Bess Endicott so long ago. We held the last note out until the screen went black. There was a moment's pause and then came an amazing, swelling wave of applause, peppered with "Hallelujahs" and "Amens" and "Glory to Gods."

The lights came back on gradually and I introduced Texana and Leo and thanked everyone for coming. Then the pastor closed with a lengthy prayer, just to remind everyone that we had indeed been in church, and the program was over.

The great discovery I made that night was that, while people always appreciate good entertainment, they much more appreciate entertainment that affirms what they already believe. The remarks from members of the audience could not have been more effusive. Many women, men and children were in tears as they thanked us for bringing the film. One bald, grey-bearded old man told Texana he was ready to meet his Maker now, because he felt like he had seen the face of Jesus! People milled about as though they did not want the evening to end and I was mostly reminded of our old revival meetings at home, when people would come under the conviction of the Holy Spirit and just start praising and singing. The pastor of the church pumped my hand vigorously and said he had enjoyed it even more the second time.

It was probably close to an hour before the last stragglers left. Leo and Texana and I sat on the front pew and grinned happily at each other.

"You did it, Professor!" said Leo. "I had my doubts, but these folks were about ready to nominate us for sainthood."

"I got a bit teary myself," Texana confessed. "When I heard people crying behind me, I knew we were getting the message across."

I nodded. "That's what makes me the proudest. I enjoyed showing the pictures before, but this one gives people something extra. Like hope. Or faith."

"Or charity," smiled Texana, finishing the quotation from Saint Paul. I got her reference, but Leo looked quizzical.

"Anyway," I said, "Let's go have some dinner. I think I'll sleep better tonight than I did last night." We retrieved the strongbox from the side room and took it back to our hotel, where the three of us sat on a bed and counted the coins and bills. Texana wrote down each amount as we counted and then totaled them up.

"Two hundred sixteen dollars and fifty cents. That's four hundred and thirty-three people packed into that church tonight," she said, impressed.

"We better do that matinee on Saturday," Leo said. "If all those people tonight tell their friends, we're not going to be able to fit the whole town in before we leave."

We walked to a small cafe and ordered the most expensive things on the limited menu. Leo was itching to make a toast, but he whispered that it "feels alien to toast with plain water."

"I'll do it, then," Texana grinned. "To Jubilee Films and our continued success. May this be the smallest crowd we ever have!"

"Amen to that," I seconded. We clinked water glasses and drank.

## CHAPTER TWENTY-TWO

Texana's toast proved to be almost prophetic. We played to a packed church for four more shows in Temple. After our first performance in Waco, we were moved to a large auditorium on the Baylor University campus to accommodate larger crowds, and I could only imagine how my Father would react when I told him his son had packed the hall at the largest Baptist college in the world, not just once, but four times!

By our fourth week, in Waxahachie, we had seen some astonishing reactions to our presentation. In Hillsboro, an elderly woman came to me after the program and told me that she had suffered from painful arthritis in her arms and legs for fifteen years, but that she had been healed from watching the Passion Play. Sometimes people would approach our bedsheet screen and reach out to touch it as if it was some Holy relic. One pastor felt compelled to offer an "invitation" at the close of the program to those who wished to be saved or wanted to rededicate their lives to God. Our first show in a town was always well attended, but the remaining shows were packed to the rafters. Cripples in rolling chairs were pushed in, some people had obviously arisen from a sickbed to attend.

In each town, I made repeated visits to the local bank, exchanging the weighty coins for banknotes. And when the roll of bills got too big, I exchanged smaller bills for larger ones. I saw my first thousand dollar bill in Waco and, by the time we got to Dallas, had acquired a couple more, which I kept in a leather bag that I wore around my neck under my clothes. Texana was sending her entire salary home to her aunt, except for small amounts for incidental purchases. We were eating well, sleeping in the nicest rooms available, and still making more money than any of us had dreamed of.

Texana proved to be the perfect addition to our team. She was almost unshakably cheerful, beautiful to look at, and her lovely voice added a great deal to the effectiveness of the Passion Play. In addition, she was enchanting to be around; she listened to every story I told her as though it was the most interesting thing she had ever heard. She never complained about dusty train rides or less-than-delicious meals we sometimes encountered. I found myself growing fonder of her every day. After we had been on the road for a week, it became clear that the mauve suit and the dove gray suit were the only nice outfits Texana owned. In Dallas, I took her to a woman's shop and bought her two more outfits, one in maroon and the other in emerald green; she was as excited as a child on Christmas morning, and pirouetted before the store mirror, giving me just a fleeting glimpse of her trim ankles.

Awkwardly, I asked, "Do you need…anything else to wear? Any — uh — accessories?"

She giggled at my discomfiture and said that her black stockings would go fine with either new outfit. "And the rest of my 'accessories' are just fine, thank you."

I blushed as I paid for the dresses and a small steamer trunk to carry them in. I arranged for them to be delivered to our hotel and Texana and I strolled along the streets of Dallas. To my great surprise and pleasure, she slipped her hand into the crook of my arm as we crossed the street and it simply remained there once we reached the other side.

Dallas was the second largest city in Texas, exceeded only by Houston. It would have been impossible for me to visit all the churches in town, but I managed to hit the largest in each denomination and we did continue our tradition of offering a free preview showing to all clergymen. The opera house we were playing held nine hundred people and we filled it six times, doing matinees on Thursday, Friday and Saturday. We could have filled it six more times, but we were committed to play Fort Worth, thirty miles away, the following week.

We made the train trip to Fort Worth on Monday and Texana sat beside me on the train. She spoke softly to me, telling me how proud she was to be a part of this show and how much she admired me for coming up with the idea. My heart was so full of things I wanted to say, but I was afraid of being too hasty. I merely told her how glad I was that she had answered my advertisement and that I hoped we could continue our association for a long, long time. She pressed her perfumed handkerchief to her nose because of the smoke from the train, but I glimpse my favorite smile before it was covered by the cloth.

Many of the Dallas pastors had written to their peers in Fort Worth and our appearance was greatly anticipated. Although the Fort Worth Opera House was a bit smaller, holding 640 people, we avoided the temptation to do three shows a day, feeling it would exhaust us completely. So we did two performances on Thursday, both to packed houses. It felt a bit different to do the program in a theater than it did in a church, but there was still a feeling of reverence at each show. Never was there any jeering or noise from the balconies. The theater manager told us it was the best behaved crowd he had ever had.

On Friday afternoon, following the matinee performance, I received a letter from the Presbyterian pastor in Temple. He wrote that the whole city was undergoing a spiritual renewal and that true revival had come upon the land. He also wrote that he knew we had been sent by God to begin this awakening and that he was praying for us in our journeys. But, he cautioned, "be on guard, for the devil hates to see people getting right with God and he will try his worst to interfere with your ministry."

I showed the letter to Texana, but Leo would not have appreciated it. He did not hold with the idea that we were actually ministering to people; he certainly did not fancy himself a minister. But Texana and I shared the belief that, whatever our reasons for beginning this project, it had turned into much more than we could have hoped for. She had worn her new maroon outfit on Thursday and the green one on Friday and she looked extremely appealing.

On Saturday morning, all three of us met for breakfast, but Leo must have felt left out, as

Texana and I looked and talked almost exclusively to each other. Leo was aware of our growing interest in each other, but he seemed mostly amused at the growing torch I was carrying.

Saturday's performances were more of the same, with large and receptive crowds. When the evening show was over, I was meeting and greeting people on the orchestra level, as was Texana. I heard Leo call my name and looked up at the balcony, where he ran the projector. He was leaning over the velvet covered balcony rail and he cupped his hands around his mouth and said, "Can you come up here? This gentlemen is interested in the moving pictures." I nodded and began working my way through the crowd of people in the aisles who were still talking about the film.

When I finally made it to the balcony, Leo was talking to a portly man with slicked-down black hair and a walrus moustache. "J.D., this is Mister… Freulic, is it?"

"That's right," said the man, in a high, scratchy voice. "Jack Freulic. I own a traveling show." He held out a wide hand which I shook.

"Pleasure to meet you, Mister Freulic. I'm J.D. Wilkinson. What can we do for you?"

"Well, this is a mighty interesting machine here. I'd be interested in adding one of these to my show. How hard is it to run?"

"Not hard at all," Leo said. "You just have to learn to thread the film through the projector, trim the arc, and crank at the right speed. 'Course it's more difficult if you make your own films. You have to mix the chemicals and develop the negative and make the print. But it's not too bad."

"Hmm. So you can take these pictures of anything?"

"Well, you need good light. You have to shoot outdoors."

"It's just amazing! I could have sworn I was right there in Jerusalem. What makes the pictures move? I still don't get it."

Leo picked up the end of the film, which was coiled up in the crate on the floor; he had not had a chance to rewind it onto the reel yet. "Look here, see how the picture changes just a tad from frame to frame? You can see it real good here in this part." Mr. Freulic was holding the filmstrip in front of his face, squinting at the images.

"Gentlemen, shall we retire to the office?" Leo and I turned to see Mr. Wagner, the manager of the opera house. He was ready to count the money and divide the cash.

I told him we would be down in a few minutes and Leo added that he thought this audience was the best one yet. As he said this, I turned back to see that Mr. Freulic, trying vainly to see the images on the film, was lighting a match to illuminate the film better.

"NO!" I screamed, and Leo whipped around to see what was going on. Before he could say anything, the film in Freulic's hand burst into flame. Startled, he dropped the strip and it landed smack in the box of loose film. There was a loud WOOSH and a bright orange flame exploded from the crate. Leo and I were both blown off our feet and I got up to see Mr. Freulic's clothes on fire and his arms gesticulating wildly. The velvet curtain which draped the balcony rail now began to burn and people in the lower level of the theater began to scream, "FIRE!" Leo and I tried to grab Mr. Freulic to extinguish the flames, but he was running wild, shrieking and terrified and he twisted jerkily back and forth until he suddenly fell over the balcony rail.

The balcony rail covering was totally consumed in flames in both directions and I watched in horror as the wallpaper and draperies began to burn. It was already very smoky in the balcony and I realized that Leo and I had better find a way to escape. Mr. Wagner had scurried back down the stairway at the first sign of fire, but there were still a few people in the balcony, shoving and pushing toward the exit. I thought about grabbing the projector, but when I turned back, Leo grabbed my arms and said, "Forget it, we've got to go now!" We dashed to the door which led to the fire escape, only to find a chain locked around the handles. Mr. Wagner had told me he had had trouble with young people sneaking in the fire escape during shows; apparently he had found a solution. We started back to the staircase on the other side of the balcony. Several of the theater seats were beginning to smolder and burn.

That's when I heard Texana screaming, "Dan! Leo! Where are you?" Through the smoke I could barely see her; she was standing on the organ bench looking around for us. "Stay there, Texana! I'm coming!" I shouted. It was getting difficult to breathe. I told Leo to try to make it down the stairs with the other people. I stood by the balcony rail. The drape had burned off of it and I touched the rail to see if I could use it to lower myself over the side. The metal was very hot to the touch, but I thought I could stand it for a couple of seconds. I looked below and moved so I was above the empty aisle, then grabbed the hot rail and swung myself over, hanging for a second and then dropping to the floor. I felt a sharp pain flash in my left ankle, but I headed for the stage. The side walls of the theater were now in full flame and the fire was spreading to the proscenium arch and the large curtains on the stage. I could no longer see or hear Texana and my lungs were filling with smoke.

I dropped to the floor and began to crawl, moving as quickly as I could, groping blindly in the grey smoke. I passed a row of seats where Mr. Freulic's now-motionless body still burned. As I crept toward the stage, I was suddenly conscious of the roaring sound of the fire and the screams of people still trapped in the theater. I heard women screaming and children crying, terrified. But it was the sound of men shrieking that scared me the most; it was an unfamiliar sound, the normally deep voices cracking as any trace of bravado was consumed by the flames. Then there was a strange cacophony which I realized was coming from the organ pipes, as heated air escaped them in a ghostly howl.

My groping hands suddenly felt the organ bench. I reached up on top of it but Texana was not there. I screamed out her name, feeling the heat sear my throat like a hot iron. I crawled along the front of the stage, still frantically clawing through the smoky darkness, but finding nothing. My strength was ebbing fast and I could not get a breath of air. I rolled over on my back and saw the arch of flames that had been the proscenium; it was actually quite beautiful. A thought flashed through my mind: I remembered my first glimpse inside the Hancock Opera House in Austin and how I thought it looked like Heaven. And now, I thought, this theater must surely be what Hell is like.

It suddenly seemed very quiet and I knew that I was going to die. I was not afraid, but I was sad that I would not get to see my family, that I would never have a family of my own. I spread my arms out wide in a gesture of surrender and acceptance. But my left hand felt a drop-off — the orchestra pit! I dragged myself over the edge and fell about eight feet to the floor. I knew there was a door from the pit that led to the alley, so I began to crawl with renewed determination toward the left side of the pit. Although it was only about thirty feet across, it seemed to take an eternity before my hand hit a wall. I groped along it and finally found a doorknob. Mr. Wagner had not locked this door, thank God, and I turned the knob and felt a cool rush of air. I hauled myself partway out the door and heard a voice say, "Look, there's one!" A pair of arms grabbed me and dragged me out into the alleyway. I was coughing and choking and I felt consciousness spinning away as my head fell back against the pavement. The last thing I felt was a hand reaching inside my shirt and taking the leather bag from around my neck.

## CHAPTER TWENTY-THREE

I awoke when someone tried to pour water into my mouth. I came to, sputtering and coughing. Several people stood over me and a man proffered a dipper to me again. This time I drank deeply, although it hurt to swallow. I suddenly remembered my money bag and clapped my hand to my chest, but the sick feeling in my stomach told me what I already knew: our money — over four thousand dollars — was gone! I checked my pants pocket and discovered that the gold watch Father had given me had also been taken.

I struggled to get up. "My friends. Where are they? Someone took our money!" The strangers around me were encouraging me to lie down and take it easy, but I pushed my way through them and looked across the street at what remained of the theater. The brick walls were still standing, but the roof had collapsed into the building. Firemen were still playing streams of water across the smoldering rubble, but there was nothing left worth salvaging.

I had no idea what time it was, but it must have been very late at night. We had finished the show by ten and I reckoned it must now be two or three in the morning. But the street was crowded with spectators, police, firemen and neighboring merchants. I made my way around to the far side of the theater, feeling the pain in my ankle at every step, and saw a row of bodies on the sidewalk, over a dozen of them, covered with blankets. A policeman tried to keep me away, but I told him I had to see if my partners were there. I walked along the gruesome display, pulling back the cover from the first face. I first thought the man was a Negro, until I realized my own hands were equally black from the smoke and soot. The first man was a stranger to me, so I moved to the next, then the next, trying to identify the dark faces. The fifth body was that of a young woman, and my heart sank until I looked closely at the features and determined it was not Texana. I continued down the line and my heart stopped when I reached the ninth body. From under the blanket dangled a feminine arm, clad in a mauve sleeve. I began to cry then, and fell to my knees. I moved the blanket away from Texana's face. She looked remarkably peaceful, not at all frightened. I felt such a longing feeling; if only I could have found her in the theater! I would rather have died with her in the smoke than to know she perished alone. I sat there for several minutes before I realized I still knew nothing about Leo.

I looked at the remaining bodies, but none of them were Leo. A fireman told me there were still bodies inside the theater, under debris. I knew one of them had to be Mr. Freulic, since he was also not among those on the sidewalk. The fireman, with a concerned look on his face, suggested I get some medical attention, but I told him I felt fine. He took my arm and said, gently insisting, "Come and sit down, son. You're badly hurt."

Badly hurt? I had perhaps sprained my ankle, but otherwise noticed no ill effects. But a policeman took my other arm and they guided me back across the street, where a pair of doctors was treating others who had survived the fire. One of them looked at me and asked me if I was in pain and I replied, "Only my ankle." He nodded grimly and proffered a flask to me. I told him I didn't drink, but he insisted I take a swallow, so I raised the silver flask to my lips and took a swig. It burned my throat something awful, but it also made me feel suddenly weak and dizzy. I looked at the doctor's rapidly-blurring image and said, "I think I'm going to be sick." That's the last thing I remember.

## CHAPTER TWENTY-FOUR

I awoke in unfamiliar surroundings, a rather spartan room with little more than a bed and bureau. I tried to sit up, but could not move. I looked down to see both hands bandaged all the way up to my elbows. "Hey, someone help me!" I called, but my voice was a whispery squeak. My head fell back on the pillow and I felt panic sweep over me as the memory of the fire returned. I tried moving my feet and the right one at least seemed to be unencumbered, so I banged my right foot against the wall by the bed.

A young woman entered, wearing a long white apron over her clothing. "Oh, you're awake," she said softly. Then she went right out of the room. I started to kick the wall again, but the nurse returned with a man I assumed was a doctor.

"Ah, how are you feeling?" he asked, as he looked into my eyes, then felt my neck.

"Why am I tied down? Where am I?" I squeaked out the questions.

"You were restrained because you were having violent nightmares and we didn't want you to hurt yourself. You've sustained some nasty burns on your hands, broken your left ankle, and done some damage to your throat and lungs from smoke inhalation. And your head, of course, has some burns, too."

I hadn't even noticed that my head was wrapped up. "Am I scarred? Disfigured?"

"I don't believe so. Your hair, your eyebrows, even your eyelashes were singed off and you have some blistering on your scalp. But you're fortunate to be alive. Twenty-six people didn't make it out of the theater, you know."

"Twenty-six! You mean fourteen more bodies had been found since last night?" I croaked.

"Last night? No, sir, it's been three days since the fire. You've been unconscious for a good while."

"Did they find my partner? Leo Matula?"

"There were four men's bodies found that are unidentified. I'm afraid they were burned beyond recognition. All the others are accounted for."

"Texana?"

"Yes, the young lady was identified by a clerk at the hotel. Her aunt arranged for her body to be sent home for burial. We had a bit of a time identifying you. In spite of the fact you were up on the stage all evening, you looked considerably different with no hair and a blackened face. But Mr. Wagner identified you."

"Is he alright?"

"Oh, yes, he made it out in good shape. But the theater, of course, is a total loss, and he did not have sufficient insurance. So I suspect he'll be looking for a new line of work. But, anyway, even when you were identified, no one knew where you were from or how to notify anyone on your behalf. Is there someone I can wire for you? Or telephone?"

The weight of disappointment fell on me then from what seemed a great height. So much for my plans to return home in triumph. So much for my security, for fame and fortune. "No, no one. When can I leave?"

"Well, you'll want to take it easy on that ankle for awhile. The burns will heal in time; I can give you some salve to apply to them. But what's your hurry? You should really rest for awhile."

"I can't afford to stay here. I…I haven't a penny to my name, doctor."

"We never refuse treatment to a patient in need. That's no reason to leave before you're ready."

"I've got to go. I have to find something to do. I — I…" My throat was burning like fire now and what little voice I had was breaking. The doctor patted my shoulder and said, "Just rest. If you want to leave in the morning, I'll fix you a brace on your ankle and you can use a cane to get around."

"My — my clothes. At the hotel."

"Yes, they've sent them over, along with Mr. Matula's things. They're in the bureau and your bag is under the bed."

"Untie me, please."

The doctor nodded to the nurse and she unfastened the long strips of cloth which had bound me. With my bandaged hands I felt the linen wrapped around my head. I asked for a mirror. The doctor considered for a moment, then gave his consent, and the nurse brought a small hand mirror. I peered in the looking glass, trying to recognize the odd person who looked back. Without lashes or brows — and with a bandaged crown — I looked like some non-human freak. My lips were cracked and scabby and there were patches on my nose and forehead that had begun to peel. I thrust the mirror away. "I'd like to be alone, please."

"Would you like something to eat? You must be hungry after several days."

I did feel a deep emptiness in my gut, but had not really attributed it to hunger. I didn't really care if I ate or not, but I said all right.

I downed two bowls of a hearty beef stew and felt better. When I was alone, I eased out of bed and looked in the bureau drawers. I had one shirt and one pair of pants; my other clothes had been at the theater. There were some of Leo's clothes, but nothing else that seemed a part of him, nothing of a personal nature. If he had any pictures or valuables, they must have been on him in the fire and thus were either consumed or stolen like my leather bag had been.

My suitcase and Leo's were under the bed, but there was nothing in either. If I wore the clothes that were in the drawer, there would be no need to even take the grip. That was fine with me. It would be hard enough getting along on a gimpy leg without having to lug along a suitcase.

The next morning, Doctor Harris bound a splint around my ankle and gave me a wooden walking stick. He again tried to convince me to stay for a few more days, but I was determined to get away from the city which had seen all my hopes and dreams turn to ashes. He did give me five dollars and wished me Godspeed. I left after eating breakfast, since I was unsure when my next opportunity to eat might be.

## CHAPTER TWENTY-FIVE

I rode the train all the way to Austin, feeling every bounce and jolt in my ankle. I had to learn to ignore the looks of sympathy, curiosity and disgust from my fellow passengers, but at least I didn't have to answer any questions. By the time I arrived in the capital city, my head was throbbing in conjunction with my ankle. I did not know what the doctor had been giving me to ease my pain, but it was clear that it was wearing off.

It was late night when I entered the station, but I decided to head on out of town. The one thing I did not want was to see my old friend, Officer Donovan, especially since I now had nothing to hold over his head; the film of his bribing had gone up in flames along with all our other filmstrips. And I was afraid he would be emboldened by my weakened state to try to exact his revenge.

So I hobbled unsteadily south along Congress by the light of the moon towers. I came to the bridge across the river and there was not another soul in sight. I crossed the river and started in a general southwest direction until I was sufficiently away from town and lights and people. I found a hedgerow which would afford me some shelter and gently lowered myself to the grassy ground to rest. The pain in my head and ankle were still sharp, but had become so familiar by now that I could almost ignore it.

I awakened a few hours later, when the gray of dawn was beginning to show the landscape around me. I was stiff and achy and I believed I had fever. But I got up and began to make my way along the dirt road. It was probably about two hours later that a farmer offered me a ride as far as Dripping Springs. He asked what had happened to me and I told him a very abbreviated version of the story. He said he had spent most all his money in town buying supplies the day before, but I was welcome to take some cheese and some salt pork. I accepted his offer as my hunger was getting difficult to ignore.

Dripping Springs was the last town before Blanco, still a good twenty miles away. I reckoned if I did not get another ride that I might be able to get there by ten or eleven that night; my pace with the ankle and walking stick was something less than speedy. I found that the best thing for me to do was to keep almost a musical rhythm going in time with my steps: a short, slow step with the bad leg and a fast, long step with the good one. I was humming and sometimes whistling, but I found that I could not sing. My weakened voice and throat could not hold a steady tone, an injury I hoped was not permanent.

I had plenty of time to think about what I could say to my family when I arrived home. I owed them many things and an apology was high on the list. I hoped they would not be too angry, that I had not let them down too much for them to forgive. But I could understand if they had no place for me; I had not fulfilled any of the promises I had made before I left. All I could do was pray as I walked, and even that act felt much more unfamiliar than it should have.

My plans, my plans. I had hoped to return home as the conquering hero, with fame and fortune in my pocket to prove I had made the right decision in leaving home. Instead, I had not a cent in my pocket, not a morsel of food. I had not a clipping, not a single handbill to prove I had performed before thousands of people. The film I had envisioned and guided through to reality and great acclaim? Ashes. Even the negatives and our camera had been in a dressing room at the opera house when the fire claimed them.

I had broken off communication with my family…for no good reason. I had consorted with drunkards, whores, corrupt policemen. I had lied, presented myself under false pretenses. I had taken a sacred story and dragged it through the mud. With every step, the burden on me felt greater and I wondered time and again if I should not just turn around and go…somewhere. Maybe I should take the advice of Job's friends: "Curse God and die." But God hadn't brought this on me. My own decisions had brought me to this inglorious homecoming.

There was no one traveling my way that afternoon and my ankle began to ache unbearably. I wished that I had a pair of crutches so that I wouldn't have to put weight on it at every step. But I kept humming and whistling and stepping along as the sun set ahead of me. I was still probably eight miles away when the sky darkened, but I was in somewhat familiar surroundings at last and believed I could make it from here even in the darkest night.

Fortunately, the night was clear and I could see the path fairly easily. But I began to feel very weak and tired and my body protested with every step. I finally stopped looking ahead and just kept my eyes on the ground, taking one step at a time.

It was when I heard a dog barking nearby that I looked up and saw I was a quarter mile from home. I tried to speed up, but simply could not go any faster. When I at last came to the clearing around our house, the windows were dark; everyone was in bed. I stood for a moment, catching my breath. I yelled, "Hellooooo!" At least I tried to; what came out was a feeble wheeze that could not have been heard ten feet away. So I advanced to the porch, pushed my way up the steps and used my stick to knock on the front door.

Is anything more frightening than an unexpected knock at night? I could only imagine what was going through the minds of the people inside, but I heard a stirring and then saw a lantern approaching through the window by the door.

Father opened the door, Mother half-hidden behind him. He looked askance at me, not recognizing the dirty, bandaged, hairless vision before him for a moment. But then Mother cried, "Daniel!" and I fell into their arms and the tears began all around. Mary, Martha and Paul appeared in the front room then, and they began to cry and hug me as well. Among all the cries of "What happened to you?" and "Where have you been?" and "We were so worried," I was trying to speak my well-rehearsed apology, but my voice was inaudible in such a din.

Finally, relative calm settled in and everyone just looked at me. "Father, Mother," I croaked. "I want to ask your forgiveness—"

Father waved that statement away. "Never mind that. How do you feel? What do you need?"

"Are you hungry, Dan?" asked Mother.

"Yes, ma'am. I could eat something, anything. My head and my ankle hurt something fierce."

"I've got some cornbread and beans and some pie left from supper. Can you make it to the table?"

"Oh, yes, I'll be fine." I stood up and my body finally said, "Enough" and my eyes rolled back in my head and I started to fall.

## CHAPTER TWENTY-SIX

I awoke in the bed I used to sleep in — was it only a year ago? Paul was sitting on the floor watching me. "Hey, little brother," I wheezed.

"What's wrong with your voice? Got a sore throat?"

"Yes. How are you?"

"Good. Hannah got married."

"Really? To who?"

"Sam Griswold. Pa did the wedding. Mama cried. While she played the organ."

"Hmmm. Where are they living?"

"Over with Sam's folks, by Johnson City."

Mother came in the room, with a breakfast of oatmeal, biscuits, bacon, gravy, fried eggs and fresh milk. "I figured you got cheated out of your meal last night, so we'll make up for it this morning." Breakfast in bed was a luxury I had never, ever experienced. I guess Mother was afraid I might keel over and faint again if I tried to make it to the table. "Doctor Crisp is going to stop by directly. Father sent for him this morning."

I ate every bit of food and felt stuffed as a Christmas goose. Then, Mother took the dishes and shooed Paul and the girls outside and told me to rest. I spent the day in bed, drifting in and out of consciousness. Dr. Crisp stopped by and changed my bandages and reset the ankle I had abused so badly. He gave Mother an elixir for pain and it did help, but made me even sleepier, so the day was almost a total loss for me.

When I woke up Saturday morning, I felt considerably stronger and managed to sit out on the porch for most of the morning. Father sat out there, too, working on his sermons for Sunday with his big Bible on his lap as he made notes on small half-sheets of paper. Since the night I arrived, no one had pressed me to tell what happened, although I knew their curiosity must be killing them.

"Did you hear about a big fire in Fort Worth, Father?" I finally asked. He shook his head. "The theater where we were showing our films. It was completely destroyed. You remember Leo? He's dead. And so is Texana, a girl who played the organ for us. Twenty-six people died. I don't know why I didn't."

"I guess your work's not done yet," he said softly.

"I don't know what work I can do anymore. Listen to my voice. I can't sing. I don't know if I can still play or not. I've got no money, no films, no partners." My eyes started to tear up again, and Father patted my knee.

"Take your time, J.D. It doesn't all have to be sorted out right now. Everything will work out when it's supposed to."

I sighed and stared out at the oak and cedar trees.

On Sunday, I felt strong enough to go to church with the family. Word of my homecoming had already spread and I was fretted over by almost everyone present. I sat on our family pew with Mother and the other children. During the hymns, which Father was leading, I had to stand silently, unable to add my voice to the chorus. Mrs. Campbell, a soprano with a spectacularly wide vibrato, offered up a solo rendition of *Down From The Ivory Palaces*.

Then Father stood behind the broad pulpit for the sermon. He opened his Bible, placed his sermon notes alongside it, rested a hand on each side of the pulpit and then stood there in silence for a moment. Then another moment. This was more than a dramatic pause. Finally he picked up the notes and stuck them in the back of his Bible, then begin flipping pages in the Bible until he found the passage he was seeking.

"Folks, I've had a change of subject this morning. I prepared a sermon, but I think the Lord is telling me to do something else. So, I'm going to read my text from the gospel of Luke, chapter 15, starting with verse 11. This is a parable told by Jesus:

> *A certain man had two sons: And the younger of them said to his father, Father, give me the portion of goods that falleth to me. And he divided unto them his living. And not many days after the younger son gathered all together, and took his journey into a far country, and there wasted his substance with riotous living. And when he had spent all, there arose a mighty famine in that land; and he began to be in want. And he went and joined himself to a citizen of that country; and he sent him into his fields to feed swine. And he would fain have filled his belly with the husks that the swine did eat: and no man gave unto him. And when he came to himself, he said, How many hired servants of my father's have bread enough and to spare, and I perish with hunger! I will arise and go to my father, and will say unto him, Father, I have sinned against heaven, and before thee, And am no more worthy to be called thy son: make me as one of thy hired servants. And he arose, and came to his father. But when he was yet a great way off, his father saw him, and had compassion, and ran, and fell on his neck, and kissed him. And the son said unto him, Father, I have sinned against heaven, and in thy sight, and am no more worthy to be called thy son. But the father said to his servants, Bring forth the best robe, and put it on him; and put a ring on his hand, and shoes on his feet; And bring hither the fatted calf, and kill it; and let us eat, and be merry: For this my son was dead, and is alive again; he was lost, and is found. And they began to be merry.*

Father closed his Bible and looked across the congregation and I could see his eyes were welling up. "Folks, I don't know how many times I've read that story. I've always liked it. But I think I understand it a little better now.

"Because, you see, my son was dead, and is alive again. He was lost and now he has been found. And if God our Father is watching and waiting for us the same way I've been watching and waiting for my son, well… I think we're all in good hands. Do you see how much He loves us? I'm just starting to."

And with that, Father said a prayer and the sermon was over. Virtually everyone in the congregation was crying; I certainly was. Father stood at the front of the church to receive anyone who had a decision to make or needed prayer and the tears rolled down his weathered cheeks and I could see how difficult it had been for him, not knowing if I was alive or dead. Mother was playing a hymn, but she was sobbing so much that I could not even recognize what it was supposed to be.

There were many people going to the front to hug Father and to pray. Many of them came to me next and hugged me. This crying and hugging festival must have lasted for twenty minutes or more before people began to leave the church. My head hurt, more from the tears I'd cried than from my injuries. My family rode home from the church feeling more strongly bonded together than at any time I could remember. I regretted causing such pain, but I was incredibly moved by their love and forgiveness and acceptance of me.

The next day, I sat on the front porch with Father and told him everything that had happened. It was not easy to relate the episode of the police arresting Leo or the use of three prostitutes to play the Virgin Mary and other scriptural characters. "I know it sounds terrible, Father. I can't believe it myself now, using fallen women and drunkards to portray the followers of Jesus."

He smiled. "Maybe you're forgetting something, J.D. That's just the kind of people Jesus associated with. Maybe you were being more scriptural than you know."

"I hadn't thought of it that way. You're right. I do wish you could have seen the film, though. People were so moved by it and it really seemed to minister to them."

"I remember the day before you left here, you wondered if moving pictures could be your calling. Maybe it was. You obviously accomplished something wonderful. I'm proud of you for having the idea and seeing it through."

"But why did it have to end so soon? Is my calling done now?"

"I can't answer that for you. You'll know what to do when it's time. I want you to take your time and get your strength back. Maybe your voice will come back. Maybe it won't. I do know this, though: if God was finished with you, you wouldn't have survived the fire. You're not wore out just yet."

I will always remember the rest of 1898 as a period of no smiles for me. I wasn't always sad, but I wasn't ever free enough from the memories of the past year to enjoy much of anything. The burns on my hands and head healed up well and my hair, brows, and lashes grew back. But my voice remained a breathy wheeze and I remained unsure of what I could possibly accomplish with my life. I spent many weeks reading, walking, working some in the garden, and feeling at loose ends with myself. I could not sing or preach. I could not lecture. My list of talents seemed short, but my list of questions seemed endless.

**REEL TWO**

**1905**

*Mike Robertson*

## CHAPTER TWENTY-SEVEN

I hitched my horse to the post in front of the *Austin Statesman* office and walked in to get a copy of the paper. Then I sat out on the covered porch and scanned through the advertisements, looking for a place to stay that would be reasonably priced and clean. I made note of three likely candidates, then mounted my chestnut mare and rode up Congress Avenue toward the Capitol for the first time in five years. I was back in Austin and ready to discover whatever destiny might still be mine to claim.

The last five years had been quiet ones for me. I was now a serious-minded twenty-two-year-old man, with the moustache to prove it. The only traces of the tragic fire that remained with me were a raspy voice (though it was again strong, it retained a hoarse quality that always sounded as though I needed to clear my throat) and a somberness of countenance that was only rarely betrayed.

I had believed in the months after the fire that much of what was good in me had been burned out, melted away by the flames, and that I was largely a hollow shell like the decrepit walls of the gutted opera house. But Father insisted otherwise; he reminded me about the three Hebrew boys — Shadrach, Meshach and Abednego — who were cast into the fiery furnace and yet survived, thanks to the watchcare of God. This event is recorded in the Old Testament book from which came my middle name, the book of Daniel.

For many months after the accident, I behaved much like an invalid. Part of it was because my ankle was slow to heal and I was ordered to stay off it. Another part of it was a general listlessness on my part, which worried my parents enough to become a frequent subject of their prayers.

I filled my days with reading everything I could find. Any newspaper, any book I could borrow from neighbor or church member, anything at all became grist for the mill of my attention. I tried to fill my brain with information, thereby to make the passing of time go more quickly. I also spent many hours playing the organ at home or the piano at church. Mother was very pleased by this and one day intimated that I had now surpassed her — my teacher — in ability. And in the same manner I would read anything that came to hand, I tried to play every piece of music I could find, from carols to concertos. I even tried my hand at some of the "ragged time" music that was becoming popular. I grew to prefer the most challenging pieces. I worked diligently, painstakingly figuring out the fingering sequences that would enable me to more nimbly perform difficult passages. By the time three years had passed, I was a much better accompanist than I had ever dreamed of being, and Mother virtually retired from playing at church, leaving those duties to me. I thus got to accompany soloists of all stripes, learning how to follow a singer, how to enhance the performance of a vocalist of limited skills. For offertories, I would play a verse of a hymn by memory, then improvise variations on the original chords and melody, weaving something new out of something everyone had heard countless times.

After I turned eighteen and my body seemed completely whole, I again became Father's right hand around the farm. He showed me secrets of construction and maintenance, explaining why each step was important. In conjunction with this, he and I built a new barn and a new outhouse. I learned how to grease a windmill, how to tell when the weather was right for hog-killing, how to castrate calves, horses, hogs and sheep.

In the absence of any other clear direction, I reckoned I could best spend my time by learning everything I could about anything at all. I occasionally taught school when the regular teacher was ill or, as in the spring of 1901, when we didn't have a teacher at all. I enjoyed teaching, enjoyed the challenge of finding new ways to help children of various ages grasp ideas that initially seemed totally foreign. The students didn't mind my croaky voice and seemed genuinely excited to learn things their parents had never learned.

During our science studies, the name of Thomas Edison popped up, of course, and I explained how he had devised the phonograph and the moving picture so that sound and light could be recorded and experienced at a later date. I borrowed a phonograph from Alfard Cox and we had no end of delight listening to the stirring Sousa marches, the banjo tunes, the coon songs and the Irish tenors. I regretted that I could not borrow a moving picture machine somewhere, since none of the children had ever seen one. I tried my best to describe it to them, without getting into my personal involvement with the instrument. But how can magic be described? If a picture is worth a thousand words, how many words would be required to do justice to the countless pictures on a reel of film? I could tell by the puzzled expressions on the children's faces that they couldn't really understand what the pictures were like, and their interests moved on to the more tangible phonograph, swapping the blue or black cylinders to hear the same songs over and over.

The moving pictures were still in my mind, though, and I was shocked one day to realize that more than four years had gone by since I had seen one. I had no knowledge of the state of the business at present, although I would occasionally see a mention in an out-of-town paper about some exhibition of one of the many machines vying for public attention.

I had no close friends of my own age during this time. Most of my peers had married or moved away. Bess Endicott had wed a fellow from Wimberley. On the few occasions I saw her, she seemed aloof and I received the distinct implication that she felt I had made a very poor choice when I had left her to chase after those silly moving pictures.

Through my reading, my music, my teaching, my sweat and my countless hours of daydreaming, I began to regain confidence that I indeed had some life yet ahead of me. After I turned twenty-two in February of '03, I discussed with Father my desire to return to Austin and try to find some career that interested me. I believed I could teach piano, perhaps teach school, or maybe even find something in the moving picture line, if such a business still existed. This was nothing like the worried, tearful separation that had transpired six years before; I was older, wiser and perhaps more realistic.

So I arrived back in Austin with my horse and thirty-five dollars I had saved from my school-teaching and from the sale of some livestock I'd raised. Congress Avenue looked not a great deal different from the last time I had seen it. Although there was an occasional automobile to be seen, the Avenue had not yet been paved with red bricks as it would be in a couple of years. The electric streetcar still hummed its way down the middle of the wide street, but the tracks had been extended further to the north to reach the new residences in Hyde Park and the University area.

Austin's dam had been washed away in the flood of 1900, a result of the same storm which virtually destroyed the city of Galveston on the Texas coast. The dam had been rebuilt, though, and the new one promised to be more durable than its predecessor.

The first of the possible rooms for rent had already been taken, but my second choice proved to be just fine. It was a downstairs room with a private entrance in a two-story Victorian house on 19th Street. The owner, a widow named Askew, showed me the small room with a bedstead, washstand, chair and writing desk. She agreed to cook breakfast each morning, but all my other meals would be my own responsibility, although I could use the kitchen if I wished to. I paid her for a month and she proffered a key to my private entrance. She told me that visitors were not allowed, drinking was not allowed, tobacco was not allowed and that she didn't like men who parted their hair in the middle. I parted mine on the left side, so I was well out of that one, and I assured her that I had been "raised right" by my preacher father.

"What church?" she asked.

"Baptist. He's been at the Baptist Church in Blanco for more than 25 years."

Mrs. Askew showed me both of her teeth in a wide grin. "Well, praise the Lord! I'm a Baptist all the way! I was baptized in the Llano River in 1844."

"I'm sure I won't be any worry to you, ma'am."

"What's your business?"

"I don't have one at the moment. I spent some time here in Austin a few years back and decided to come here to try my hand at whatever I can find."

"All righty, then. I'll leave you to your room. I don't have a place for your horse, though."

"That's all right, ma'am. I'm going to board her at the Galloways' stable. Or I might sell her if I find a job close by."

"Might as well. Streetcar stops a block from here, take you anywhere in town, nearly."

"Well, thank you. I'll just unpack my bag and rest a bit if you don't mind."

I placed my clothes in the small closet and some books on the writing desk: my Bible, two Sherlock Holmes novels and a collection of Poe stories. I tipped the water pitcher until the washbowl held a couple of inches of water and rinsed my hands and face of the grime from the day's journey. Then I sat at the desk and read the rest of the newspaper, trying to get some sort of guidance toward a job. There were already a couple of advertisements offering piano and voice lessons, and the only other jobs listed were for delivery boys or salesmen.

I left Mrs. Askew's house and walked the few blocks to the Capitol building. I strolled through the spacious lobby, looking up at the lone star in the dome high overhead. Then I continued out the front door, across the landscaped grounds, and back onto Congress Avenue. I wandered by what had once been the Jubilee Theater; it was now a Chinese restaurant called Joe Wah's. I spent the rest of the daylight hours looking in the store windows and watching the people on the Avenue. All seemed to be going somewhere with a purpose, except for me.

At Sixth Street, I turned right and walked the half-block west to the Hancock Opera House. It looked exactly the same and I paused to read the posters on the building's front, but there was no mention of moving pictures. I strolled back up the Avenue and had my supper at Joe Wah's, looking around the inside of the building where we had shown our films — and where Jesus had performed miracles on the roof. After I finished my chop suey, I hopped aboard one of the electric streetcars and rode it back to 19th Street. I spent the rest of the evening reading in my new lodgings.

## CHAPTER TWENTY-EIGHT

Next morning, I again checked the papers for work, but realized I would have to go out and fend for myself. The city directory was chock full of piano teachers, so I despaired of finding many students for myself. I inquired at several stores and businesses, but found nothing. After lunch, I again went by the Opera House and introduced myself to Manager Walker, who still remembered the Vitascope and the Veriscope, as well as the Jubilee.

"I wondered what ever happened to you fellows," he said. "Went on the road, did you?"

"Yes, sir. We were doing very well until the big fire in Fort Worth."

"Ah, yes. I recall reading about that, but didn't make the connection. You made it out all right, though?"

"Well, you could say that. I had some injuries and my voice won't ever be the same. But my partners were killed. I've been out of the business for the past five years."

"That's a shame. So sorry to hear it."

There was a pause before I changed subjects. "Do you still show moving pictures?"

"Not much. I don't think we've had one in here for a couple of years. Got to be the same old stuff, you know? I guess the novelty wore off. People would much rather see a nice play with fancy costumes and pretty women than a picture of a parade or something. It had its moment, but it's time for something else now, I believe."

"I guess I really hitched my wagon to the wrong horse, then. I thought the pictures were really going to be something. But you haven't showed any in two years?" I sighed.

"Well, I haven't, but they're still around, you know. I mean, there are showings in churches or schools or tents every once in a while."

Relief washed over me and I smiled. "Good. I've missed seeing them."

We made a bit more small talk and I told Mr. Walker where I was staying and that if he needed an accompanist for anything, to please keep me in mind. He agreed that he would, but reminded me that he would soon be closing for the hot summer months. In those days before air conditioning, most theaters remained dark all summer, leaving their audiences to seek summer entertainment in parks, pleasure gardens and tent shows.

For most of a week, I ventured up and down the Avenue and its side streets, trying to find suitable work. Finally, I was hired by Mr. Goggan at the piano store where Leo and I had listened to Texana's audition and above which we had our office. Now I was to be a seller of musical instruments and sheet music. This turned out to be a pleasant and educational job for me; I was able to keep up my piano-playing skills while demonstrating the newest songs available in print. In this way, I was able to stay familiar with all the latest musical trends and my sight-reading abilities improved steadily. If I had only been able to sing those songs with my original voice, I could have sold much more music, but Mr. Goggan was pleased with me nonetheless.

It was a good time to be selling pianos, too, for in the earliest days of the 20th Century, it was almost a necessity for the well-furbished home to feature a music room or sitting room in which the whole family could gather in the evening to sing together. Parties were built around little else besides a piano, a stack of music, and some refreshments. Since I received a commission on the sale of each instrument, I felt fortunate that my recently-dormant gift for smooth talking and authoritative pronouncement was returning, and that I was able to save a few dollars each week, even after sending some money home to Mother and Father and giving a tithe to the First Baptist Church in Austin.

I worked six days a week and attended church — usually twice — on Sunday. But in the evenings, after grabbing a quick meal, I roamed Austin in search of entertainment, especially in the form of moving pictures. There were plenty of weeks when there were no pictures to be found, but on other occasions I got lucky.

In the "variety houses" — a ritzy name for a saloon with entertainment — I discovered that a reel of moving pictures sometimes occupied a spot on the bill. It was fortunate that film was still silent, for these places were always raucous, filled with the sounds of piano, laughter, fighting, flirting and cries for more beer. I usually had to buy a glass of beer, which sat untouched before me as I heard poor singers, watched uncoordinated dancers and tolerated unfunny comedians in hopes I might get to see some film.

The films shown in the variety houses were usually around a minute long and greatly resembled a newspaper comic strip in plot. In one example, a woman is seen trying to light her stove. There is a big puff of smoke and the woman flies out of the top of the frame. Then, after a few seconds, her arms, legs, torso and head fall separately back onto the floor. This was followed by a shot of a grave with a tombstone which bore this poem:

> HERE LIES THE REMAINS
> OF BRIDGET MCKEEN
> WHO STARTED A FIRE
> WITH KEROSENE.

Another film which diverted the attentions of the frolicking men in the saloons was called *The Gay Shoe Clerk*, in which a woman is trying on shoes with the help of a male clerk. As he places a shoe on her foot, the screen is suddenly filled with a close view of her stockinged foot and leg as she draws her skirts up to mid-calf and the hand of the clerk slides brazenly from her heel up toward her calf. The whole scene is again visible when the clerk and the woman kiss. But their bliss is interrupted by the woman's friend, who uses her umbrella to whack the clerk over the head. This one drew whistles and shouts of approval from the tipsy audience for its close-up exhibition of an attractive woman's leg, and for the sight of the clerk and woman kissing. This reminded me, of course, of the May Irwin film which had made such a dramatic impression upon me back in '96.

The rowdies also appreciated the film of a young lady who disrobed while swinging on a trapeze in a theater. I confess I found this one interesting as well, as the woman dropped article after article of clothing while swinging back and forth. She got down to her underthings before the film ran out, but it was something I had never seen before.

I also saw some films in churches and at the YMCA. These were usually travelogue films with lecture by some intrepid soul who had visited Eskimos or Pygmies or Mexican bandits. These were only of moderate interest to me, although I always appreciated the chance to see something I would probably never see in real life. But I paid strict attention to the filming techniques in each presentation, although they were truthfully not much to speak of. In virtually all films of the time, whether of an actual event or an acted-out story, the camera took a shot which corresponded with what you would see on a theater stage. You would see the entire scene and the full bodies of those human beings involved, with never a movement of the camera. On rare occasions, such as in the shoe clerk film, when a close-up suddenly occurred, it was quite startling and it took the audience a moment to adjust.

In the Lutheran Church, I witnessed a filmed Passion Play which was miles ahead of the humble effort Leo and I had assembled years before. There were at least four different Passion Play films available and it was rare for Easter to pass without some church sponsoring a showing. In 1904, I even got to see two competing versions of the gospel story in two different churches during Holy Week. One was filmed against background flats in bright sunlight, which looked especially ludicrous when the shadow of the cross appeared on the "sky" behind it. The other, however, purported to be the actual Oberammergau actors in natural settings and it was well done and very moving.

Occasionally a tent show would come through Austin and show a film, usually a boxing match, but sometimes film of an important event. I sat one afternoon in a tent which had been painted black on the inside to provide a darkened environment for the projector and witnessed film of President McKinley at the Pan-American Exposition, one day before he was assassinated. This gave me chillbumps, to actually see the President of the United States! This was followed by pictures of the funeral cortege for the President and a film that purported to show the execution of the assassin, Leon Czolgosz. I was completely captivated by this film, which began with a panoramic shot of the exterior of Auburn Prison, where Czolgosz was held. Then there was a scene of the fiend in his cell, as wardens entered to escort him to his final reward. The final scene showed Czolgosz being strapped into the electric chair and several witnesses looking on as the current ended his life. The audience, which had cheered heartily at the footage of McKinley, was stunned by the execution scene's graphic realism. They were glad to see justice done, but were sobered at viewing the death of a living being. I concurred with this feeling, but a part of my mind was wondering just how any cameraman had been able to capture this moment. It would be a few years later when I learned that the execution was a reenactment, shot in New Jersey by Edwin Porter for the Edison Company. The oft-repeated adage about "seeing is believing" was taken even more seriously by early moving picture audiences, who believed that "seeing it on the screen means that it really did happen."

The best films available during this period were not to be found in any of the places I have described. Vaudeville — not to be confused with "Variety Theater" — had come to Austin and it had a place for moving pictures on a regular basis. Vaudeville featured "continuous performance" in a clean, nicely-appointed theater, and the program was guaranteed not to offend the most selective viewer. The wonderful thing about continuous performances was that you could enter the theater at any time of day and stay as long as you wished. Most people left when they had seen everything once, but there were always a handful who stayed all day long, taking in the fifteen or twenty acts on the bill three or four times each.

Vaudeville was much nicer than variety theater, and it actually offered more variety than the saloons could proffer. Comedy, song, short plays, acrobats, animal acts, famous people

(I once saw a woman whose sole claim to fame was that she shot her husband.), jugglers, magicians… and sometimes a moving picture!

It was in the vaudeville house where I first saw the films of George Méliès, a French conjurer who began making films as an extension of his stage magic. And what magical films they were! A row of chairs begins to dance! A devil appears in a flash of fire! And a group of people in a large shell are fired out of a gigantic cannon, only to land on the moon! These definitely qualified under my category of things I'd never seen before and I went back to the theater four nights in a row to see A Trip to the Moon. This picture was remarkable not just for the story it told, but for the fact it was made up of several different scenes.

After I had spent a few months hunting out motion pictures wherever they might be found, I began to notice another young man at many of the venues. He was a short little banty-rooster of a fellow, with wiry red hair that resisted his valiant attempts to plaster it to the sides of his head. He dressed in suits of the loudest plaid, invariably wrinkled, with sleeves and legs a good two inches shorter than they should have been. During my third viewing of A Trip to the Moon, I managed to shift my gaze from the screen to locate this round, freckled face a few seats to my right. It was clear that this fellow was — like me — doing more than watching the film; he was studying it.

When the show was over and the audience was filing out, I managed to wind up next to him and I said, "Pretty good film, eh? I liked it better than the North Pole one."

"Oh, no," he replied earnestly. "The North Pole film had that shot of the ladies dressed as stars in the heavens and that gigantic monster who guarded the Pole."

"Well, that's true, but this one has the moon creatures and the shot of the space capsule hitting the Man in the Moon smack in the eye! That's a corker!"

"Yeah. But, hey, did you see that *Life of an American Fireman*? Where you could see that the fireman was thinking about his wife and baby? Wonder how they do that?"

"Sure, I saw that. I see everything." I held out my hand. "I'm J.D. Wilkinson."

The redhead gave me a firm shake. "Kelton Hendricks. I thought I'd seen you around. So you're interested in the flickers, too?"

"More than just about anything. I made one once."

"Really? I have no idea how they make 'em, but I'd sure like to learn."

We went to a cafe and had a late supper while we exchanged life stories. Kelton had been born in Houston, but grew up in Galveston, on the coast of Texas. His father had been a real estate agent and done well in the seaside community as the increasing passion for recreation and leisure made it possible for more people to own beach houses. Mr. Hendricks' prosperity had been wiped out, along with most of Galveston, in the hurricane of 1900 which killed 10,000 people. Kelton's mother and his sister had died in the storm; his father had survived, but the loss of his family and business drove him to commit suicide shortly thereafter. Kelton was thus orphaned at seventeen and went to Houston to seek his future. He tried a variety of odd jobs, working in a saddle shop, a sugar factory, a laundry and a restaurant before he hopped a train to Austin. He was now working in Gammage's bookstore as a clerk and he confessed that he spent virtually every spare cent on moving pictures.

In spite of the tragedy in his past, Kelton was one of the most infallibly cheerful people I've ever known. He listened to my story with interest, growing especially animated when I talked of making a film of my own and traveling with it. When I told him how my venture had ended, his expression got very serious, but a moment later he resumed joking and chattering about moving pictures until the owner of the cafe finally told us he was ready to lock up. We agreed to meet on the next Friday evening, when the Bell Airdome was going to show a new film called The Great Train Robbery. I walked a dozen blocks back to my room feeling exultant at finding someone who understood and shared my obsession.

## CHAPTER TWENTY-NINE

When Friday rolled around, Kelton and I met in front of the Bell and purchased our tickets and climbed the stairs on the side of the Airdome building. In the summer, when indoor theaters closed due to the heat, the Bell was able to offer a night-time program in the relatively cool open air on the roof of a two-story building. Their usual fare consisted of melodramas, minstrel shows and occasional musical revues, but the management had apparently decided to take a chance on a moving picture.

*The Great Train Robbery* was made by the Edison Company, but it bore little resemblance to the half-minute films they had produced in earlier days. This film lasted about ten minutes, although it seemed much, much shorter. We watched as a story unfolded, a tale of a train being held up by armed bandits who blew up the safe as the train moved. They stopped the train, herded the passengers out onto the side of the tracks and even shot one man as he tried to escape. We saw the formation of a posse which chased down the robbers, culminating in a shoot-out in the woods. The puffs of smoke from the pistols were colored reddish-orange. The money was recovered and the film was over — no, wait! Here was a close-up shot of the bandit leader, who raised his pistol, pointed it directly at us and pulled the trigger! Another puff of red smoke and then the screen went black. The audience roared with one accord, demanding that the management "Run it again!" I realized I was on my feet, clapping and yelling along with everyone else; I looked at Kelton and he could only say, "Wow!"

The management, unswayed by our requests, informed us that the film would be shown every twenty minutes and we were cordially invited to see it as many times as we wished, provided we bought a ticket each time. Kelton and I rushed outside and back to the ticket office to catch the film again. Here was something new, all right. This was no fairy tale or comic strip brought to life; this was a glimpse of real and exciting life, of a time not so very long ago. But it was much more exciting than most other films I had seen and I was keen to determine why. During our second viewing, I noticed that the scene on the screen switched rapidly from one location to the other, from the posse to the bandits, faster and faster. Who thought of this? As I've already said, the early motion picture camera was usually employed as though it was in a theater. But this! This film showed things which could never be shown on a stage: fights on a moving train, horseback chases through the woods.

Kelton and I walked up to the Capitol building, talking excitedly about the film we had just seen. I confessed to feeling silly that I had never thought to join consecutive scenes together to tell a story. In our Passion Play, we had shown isolated scenes much like lantern slides, dependent on a lecturer to tie them together. But now it was clear that film could tell a story in a way that no other medium had been able to — by showing the audience what it needed to know.

I had a hard time sleeping that night, inspired as I had not been for several years by the possibilities of the moving pictures. But how could I get back into the show business? It was hard for me to believe that I once had four thousand dollars in my pocket; it was all I could do now to save forty! I would clearly have to take more decisive steps to reach my goal, for it seemed that saving my pennies would only enable me to be a very old showman, not a young one.

Next day, I went to the Odeon, the best vaudeville house in town. I paid my way in as soon as the theater opened at ten-thirty and I stayed there for the next ten hours without taking a break for food. I learned that there were three pianists at the Odeon and each played a four hour shift. The evening player was very good; the afternoon man was adequate, but the morning fellow was nothing much. He seemed much more interested in amusing himself and whatever attractive women might be nearby in the audience, making the silliest faces and wiggling his eyebrows crudely at the ladies. In addition, when a film was shown, he seemed to be able to play only two songs by memory: *Love Me And The World Is Mine* and *Home, Sweet Home*. He would play one of them slowly for a tragic scene, with lots of tremolo on the high notes with his right hand. For chase scenes, he played the same song very rapidly on the lower keys. Sometimes he played the same song as a march, a waltz, a rag. But I also noted that much of the time he wasn't even paying attention to the action on the screen, so intent was he on making goo-goo eyes at some young miss. He glanced at the screen only on occasion and then adjusted one of his two tunes accordingly. His accompaniment for the singing acts on the program — for which he did have to stare hard at the printed music — was often a half-beat behind but not so horrible as to be evident to everyone. It was clear to me that the musician's position at the Odeon was most vulnerable in the morning spot and I mused on how to insinuate myself into it.

On Sunday afternoon, I met Kelton and told him of my plan, enlisting his aid. He was eager to help, especially since he fancied himself an actor and we talked over what he was to say and do in great detail. Since we both had jobs, our plan would have to wait until the following Saturday, but it was on my mind all week long and I was not as good at selling pianos that week as I usually was. When I was not helping a customer, I practiced on the pianos, selecting music that I could use for any sort of film I was likely to encounter.

On Saturday, Kelton came by Mrs. Askew's house, where I put one of my more businesslike suits on him instead of the clownish attire he favored. Then I sent him off on the streetcar for the Odeon. I waited for an hour, then followed.

At the theater, I paid my dime and entered the lobby. I stood there for a few minutes, looking at the posters and handbills. Suddenly, Kelton strode forcefully into the lobby from the theater and headed straight for the manager's office, rapping sharply on the oaken door. The door opened and the distinguished face of L.F. Snider poked out. He took a look at

Kelton's scarlet face and beckoned him inside, then closed the door.

I edged over to the office door, still reading the posters, and heard Kel's voice rising, "He was making obscene faces at my fiancee! She couldn't even concentrate on the stage for his indecent drooling and carrying-on!"

I couldn't make out Mr. Snider's calmer words, but I heard his basso murmur for a moment before Kelton cranked up again. "No, she left in tears! I put her in a cab and then came back in here to demand satisfaction! Just let me take that fellow outside and I shall have it!"

More deep murmuring, although it sounded a bit more concerned now. Then Kelton boomed, "I thought this was a high-class theater, safe for women and children? At the very least, I demand that man be fired!"

I had to fight the impulse to knock on the door right then and inquire, "Are you hiring any musicians?" It wouldn't do to overplay my hand too early. I moved away from the manager's door and went to the other side of the lobby. Presently, the door to Mr. Snider's office opened and he emerged with Kelton, who was peering intently at a piece of yellow paper in his hand.

"I assure you I will deal with this matter, Mr. Hendricks. Thank you for bringing it to my attention." He shook hands with Kel, who then left the theater without looking my way even once. Mr. Snider looked through the curtains toward the front of the theater and made a disgusted grimace. When he turned back to the lobby, he spied me and, re-donning his cordiality, said, "Good morning, sir, may I assist you in some way?"

"Yes, sir, are you Mr. Snider? I'm J.D. Wilkinson and I work up the street at Goggan's Pianos? I'm trying to find a small office where I could give piano lessons and I was told you might have some vacant space upstairs."

"No, I have nothing at the moment, I'm afraid. Sorry." He turned to go back to his office and I saw the thought hit him like a slap in the face. He spun round again. "You play the piano?"

"Yes, sir, ever since I was a child. Are you interested in learning?"

This Is Where I Came In

"No, no, I just… Are you any good? Can you sight-read?"

"I can read just about anything, sir."

"Ever accompany a moving picture?"

Only a small lie: "Yes, sir. I love the pictures. It's quite a challenge to provide appropriate music for every different sort of scene. But I rarely repeat myself. I have over 400 songs committed to memory."

"Four hundred? Jehosophat, I know a sap who only knows two. Would you be interested in working here?"

"Here? Oh, that would be exciting! But I'd have to leave the piano store. What does your position pay?"

"Twenty a week to start. Then we'll see. And that's for only four hours a day, so you could still teach your lessons or find a part-time job."

"All right. That sounds good to me. When would I start?"

"How about right now?" Mr. Snider motioned for me to follow him and he pushed through the curtain and started down the aisle. The piano player was blissfully unaware of his approach, being preoccupied with winking at a woman who was breast-feeding a baby in the front row. Thus it was a complete surprise when Mr. Snider grabbed the buffoon by his hair and pulled him off the stool. The act onstage, an acrobatic trio called Bennett, Smudge and Bennett, paused in their antics as the attention of the whole audience shifted to the right side of the theater. Mr Snider dragged the hapless Romeo up the aisle, pausing only to kick him in the seat of the pants every few steps. The crowd applauded, enjoying this unscheduled comedic interlude.

I seated myself at the piano, looking quickly at the score on the music stand. It was simple patterns of ascending chords, designed to go along with the acrobats' performance. All I had to do was play the steadily rising chords, keeping an eye on the stage, until the leader of the gymnastic trio gave a flourish with his arms; thereupon I hit a major chord of fanfare. When they finished their turn, I played them off with something I improvised, while flipping through the stack of music before me. Luckily, the next act was a monologist, who only required entrance and exit music. During his speaking, I looked over the music left in the stack. A few numbers looked challenging, but I was mainly looking forward to the moving picture spot on the program, which arrived a few acts later.

The reel of film lasted about twelve minutes and contained four different short films. I kept my eyes glued to the screen, having no need to look down at my hands, and tried to accompany every scene, every movement, with appropriate music. It was exhilarating work because I had not seen any of the films in advance and had to stay on my toes to match the action. When the screen went black and the lights came up on the stage again, there was a smattering of applause for the films; I chose to believe that part of it was for me. Cracking my knuckles, I glanced toward the lobby and saw Mr. Snider's face framed by the maroon curtains. He gave no sign, but withdrew to the lobby.

I played the two and a half hours left in the first shift and only stopped when I got a tap on the shoulder from pianist number two, who whispered, "What happened to Max?"

"I guess he got canned."

"Not surprised. I'm Phil. Scoot."

"I'm J.D. See you later."

I went back to the lobby and found Mr. Snider. "Good job, son. Be here every morning at ten. Except for Sunday, of course." He reached in his pocket and counted out four dollars. "See you Monday morning."

I strolled out onto the Avenue, blinking at the bright sunlight, and began walking north. I had only gone a few steps before a red-headed gorilla jumped onto my back. "You were in there long enough! You must have gotten the job!"

"Sure did. You are a good actor! How'd you get your face to turn red like that?"

"Held my breath. It's easy." He jumped off my back, but he was more full of energy and joy than even I was. He took three steps, then leaped up and grabbed the frame of a store awning, swinging his feet back over his head. He hung there for a second, then released his grip and fell to the sidewalk, but when he hit the ground, he rolled smoothly into a somersault.

I didn't have the heart to mention he was performing these hijinks in the suit I had loaned him. So I applauded and said, "You should have been onstage with Bennett, Smudge and Bennett. I had no idea you were an acrobat."

"Naw, I just try to keep fit. Let's go eat. We should have had lunch two hours ago."

"Okay; it's on me, though. Thanks for helping me get the job. I owe you one."

## CHAPTER THIRTY

And so began my true education in the world of the show business. Every morning would find me in place at the piano as the parade of variety acts began. I had the best seat in the house and, being able to learn music quickly, I was able to keep my eyes on the stage most of the time. This allowed me not only to accompany the live acts more closely, but to sample the full range of talents that made up vaudeville. The bill changed every week, so I was able to see a great many performers a dozen or more times each. I soon came to notice how the comedians could change a line or a word — or sometimes just the inflection of their voice — and provoke a great laugh where only a snicker had been before. I saw how singers could move their bodies and arms in ways that made it seem they were truly feeling sorrow or love or patriotism for the first time, when in fact they did it several times a day. I learned the importance of pacing, how a dramatic singer should not follow a knockabout comedy troupe. This and much more I learned in front of the stage, but I learned just as much when I began to spend time backstage after my shift.

In the small, cramped dressing rooms, comics tried out new jokes, read the trade publications and chased all the women on the program. These women had the habit of lounging about in the skimpiest attire, seemingly unmindful of the sheer square footage of skin they were exhibiting to the likes of me. I was accepted into this community, not as a "star" but as a kindred soul working with whatever talent I could muster to better myself.

I learned the slang of the vaudevillian. I understood that "two-sheeting" meant loitering outside the theater in front of the posters advertising the acts. I began to read *The Billboard* courtesy of the performers, who seemed to know every person listed in these papers. I learned that a dirty collar could be whitened with chalk when you didn't have time (or money) to have it laundered.

I also became very skilled at playing for motion pictures. The first time I saw a film was always challenging. But by the end of the week, I truly accompanied the story. For every sideways glance the pretty girl made, I had a fillip of the keys to fit it. For every sneaky footstep of the villain, I provided minor chords to build the suspense. I discovered a great deal of satisfaction in devoting myself to this work, which neither of the other two pianists seemed as concerned with as I. This also kept me from being distracted by the women in the audience, many of whom really did like to sit near the piano to breastfeed their babes, apparently for some lullaby-like effects on the tots.

There was plenty enough distraction on the stage. It was not uncommon by the middle of the week for me to get a big wink from a dancing girl, or a kiss blown at me from behind a Japanese fan or twirling umbrella. The girls loved to do this because of the crimson flush it invariably brought to my cheeks.

I was also trying to get Kelton employed in some capacity. After a couple of months, I asked Mr. Snider about hiring my friend to be trained as a projectionist. I introduced Mr. Snider to Kelton, hoping he would not remember Kel's acting performance which secured my job for me. But Mr. Snider peered intently at Kelton's face for a moment, then said, "I know you! You were the one who complained about the —" Then he looked at me and grinned. "Well, lucky for you that J.D. was up to the task. I guess I can't complain about your tactics. I understand you want to run the projector?"

"Yessir," said Kelton. "I can help out any way you like, Mr. Snider."

"Well, you can take tickets, change the posters, sweep up the theater, clean the lavatories as well as learning how to show the pictures."

Kelton's face only fell a little. He was in show business at last!

Through the rest of '03 and into 1904, we learned all we could about the theater and about the moving pictures. One morning before the theater opened, Kelton invited me up the ladder to the projection box. It was a good thing neither of us was particularly stout, because the opening to the booth was only about sixteen inches square. The tiny room was lined with tin, which mainly insured that the hapless projectionist would be roasted alive in case of fire, but the rest of the theater might be spared. There had been some improvements in projecting machines since last I had operated one; the calcium arcs burned brighter and steadier, producing a better image onscreen. And the annoying flicker which had given many people headaches in the early days had been greatly diminished. The Odeon's projector still had no take-up reel, though. A cloth hamper caught the coils of film, which Kelton then had to rewind with another device made for that purpose. He also had to run the magic lantern, showing the slides which introduced the acts, instructed patrons to remove their hats or to be patient while the film was fixed.

Each week we studied the new crop of films, noting which companies produced which kind of stories. I began keeping a list of the production companies, along with their addresses, not really knowing why or how I could use this information.

After my fourth month at the Odeon, I was given the middle shift, from 12:30 to 4:30 p.m. Phil, whose place I took, was not happy about it, but Mr. Snider had been told by several customers that my playing made the show better. And no, I didn't put anyone up to saying that! It was simply that I had found another niche where I fit comfortably, soaking up the endless variety on the stage before me while my playing grew ever more expressive and complementary. I had continued working part-time at the piano store while I played the morning shift, but my promotion to afternoons included a raise in pay that enabled me to offer Mr. Goggan my resignation.

One of the great pleasures of working in the Odeon was the chance to see talented people my own age and younger, some of whom would go on to great things. In late 1904, the bill was enlivened by an acrobat act called the Three Keatons. Joe Keaton and his wife Myra were skilled performers; Joe could kick your hat right off your head while standing a foot in front of you, while Myra played the saxophone and caused Joe to endure all sorts of falls and spills onstage. The surprise in their act, though, was their son, who was called Buster. He was nine years old when I saw him, but he had been in the family act since the age of three and was now a seasoned, though small, professional.

Buster and his father seemed intent on sending each other to the hospital during their act. Buster would swing a basketball on a rope, letting the tether out slowly until it was cutting a circle of twelve feet or more. While he did this, Joe would be facing a mirror, his face lathered and a huge straight razor in his hand. As he squinted into the mirror, raising the blade to his neck, the whirling basketball got closer and closer to the back of his head, drawing shrieks and laughter from the audience. Finally, the ball would hit Joe a loud whack on the side of the head and shaving cream would fly everywhere. He would turn to see Buster standing innocently by with the deadpan expression that would earn him a fortune in a few years. Joe would then grab Buster by the back of his jacket and fling him headlong into the backdrop and Buster would slide headfirst down to the floor, never changing his expression. The crowds loved the Keatons, although the local authorities sometimes charged that little Buster was being mistreated. More than once, he had been forced to remove his shirt before a judge, only to reveal that there wasn't even a bruise on him. For Joe had taught him how to take a fall without even feeling it.

Kelton, of course, was enthralled with the Keatons, and begged Joe to teach him everything he knew. Joe was not about to give away all his trade secrets, but as long as Kelton fetched him a bucket of beer after the show, he was willing to share a few things. Kelton, however, bore the bruises from his "lessons" for a couple of weeks after the Three Keatons hit the road again.

In the years since the fire, I had not formed a close friendship with anyone until Kelton came along and I had not realized how much I had missed such a friendship. Whenever we were away from the theater, we were usually together, talking about the films we'd played at the Odeon or comparing the various vaudeville acts with each other.

In the summer of 1905, Father wrote to tell me he had been invited to preach the Sunday sermon at the annual Confederate Veterans' Reunion at Camp Ben McCulloch. This event was held a few miles outside of Austin, so I arranged to meet my family for a camping trip. The camp was on Onion Creek and I enjoyed swimming with Paul, swinging from ropes in the tall trees to drop into the cool, clear water. There were always special attractions at Camp Ben: sideshows, plays, musicals and — in '05 — a new way of seeing moving pictures. At one end of the midway was a tent with banners and signboards advertising Hale's World Tours. I parted with a dime just to see what was inside the tent. I was admitted to find a full-size replica of a train car. I boarded the car along with my fellow passengers and took a seat halfway from the front of the car. When the car was full, the lights dimmed and the sound of a moving train was heard from somewhere nearby. The car began to rock rhythmically and I could feel air blowing by the open window by my seat. Then, at the front of the car, a screen lit up and a moving picture began to play, showing a view of the Rocky Mountains as they would appear from the front of a moving train. Combined with the rocking of the car, the sound effects, and the rushing air, the illusion was nearly perfect, and the passengers exclaimed with delight at the scenes of snow-capped mountains and deep river chasms. I found myself leaning when the train went into a curve and I grinned at how easily my mind had been fooled into thinking we were really moving. After a few minutes, the picture changed and we were traveling into Paris, the Eiffel Tower plainly visible. Twenty minutes went by, with scenes from various countries around the world. It will be difficult for the modern reader to appreciate how novel this presentation was, especially since it was unlikely that anyone in that ersatz railcar would ever cross the ocean; this was as close to seeing the world as most of us would ever get. And it was enough! When we got off the car, everyone was chattering about seeing the pyramids, the Alps, or the New York City skyline. As everyone else exited the tent, I looked around to find the projection equipment. It was actually located behind the screen, the first time I ever experienced the phenomenon of rear projection. I chatted up the projectionist while he prepared for the next group of passengers, but he was less than friendly, so I took my leave.

I convinced my father and mother to try Hale's Tours, so they could at last see what a moving picture was like. They were both enthused by the experience, but then I had to try to explain that most pictures were not shown in a mock train car, that most films told a story rather than simply showing scenic vistas passing by. My parents nodded, but I'm sure they still had no real grasp of what I was talking about.

I heard Father preach on Sunday morning under the tabernacle at the camp. He did a good job and I was proud to see him receive so many compliments afterwards. That afternoon, there was a lecture by another preacher, a Reverend Thomas Dixon, who had just written his second novel about the South in the aftermath of the Civil War. It was called *The Clansman* and he referred to it many times in his lecture as a romance of the Reconstruction. His speech, however, was full of anger toward the black race, calling them sub-human animals. I looked at my father's face while Dixon spoke and I could see the tight jaw and stern expression. Many others in the crowd were in vocal agreement with all that Dixon said and his fiery style of rhetoric drew thunderous applause and shouts when he finished.

Back at our campsite, I asked Father how a minister could express such hateful sentiments. He sighed deeply and I suddenly saw the weight of years on him. "J.D., I'll tell you the truth; the only thing bad about Christianity is Christians. Reverend Dixon may have been a successful preacher, but he's a poor example of a follower of Christ. I don't recall Jesus ever condemning an entire race. In fact, the only people He ever condemned were the religious leaders. That ought to tell you something."

For the rest of the evening, Father was in a depressed mood, the exhilaration of his own sermon crushed by the hate and venom of Thomas Dixon's speech.

## CHAPTER THIRTY-ONE

By the end of 1905, I was the evening pianist at the Odeon, having proved myself to Mr. Snider's great satisfaction. I was rarely ill, always prepared and invariably attentive to what was happening on the stage. I didn't drink or smoke, I always showed up early for work and did my best. I had tried to make myself indispensable to Mr. Snider and succeeded well. Working every evening meant that I had to miss some of the other entertainments which played Austin in the evening, but I knew we were getting most of the best acts right in the Odeon; I didn't miss hanging around in the variety houses with drunks and rowdies.

In February of 1906, I turned twenty-five. I had saved almost 200 dollars by living frugally, and I had hopes that I might eventually afford to buy a camera and projector. But my plans were changed in April when Mr. Snider beckoned me into his office one afternoon before my shift began.

"Sit down, J.D.," he said, indicating a curved-back wooden chair by his desk. I settled myself with a vague feeling of unease; I was sure I had been doing well, so I couldn't imagine the reason for this conference.

"J.D., I'm thinking about starting something new and I'd like your advice."

"Yes, sir, I'll be happy to help."

"You see, it's about these moving pictures. I didn't like them that much when I first started running them here. But I think they're getting better. Don't you?"

"Oh, yes! They've come a long way since those early fifty-footers. They're telling real stories now."

"Exactly. But it's more than that. They're dependable. A reel of film never gets sick or gives a half-way performance. You can run 'em fifty times and they never complain. In the beginning, I used them in the closing slot, just to let people know the show was over, but they're staying around to watch them now. They are becoming an attraction on their own."

"I've always liked them, Mr. Snider. You know that." I still had no idea where this was going.

"Here's what I'm considering, J.D. You know where Johnson's Livery used to be, a couple of blocks north on Congress?"

"Yes."

"Well, I'm thinking about renting that building and putting in some seats and showing nothing but moving pictures… all day long! What do you think?"

"You know, Mr. Snider, my partner and I used to do that around on Seventh Street. We started out okay, but people got tired of it after awhile. Films are expensive, too."

"Yes, but there are enough companies turning out pictures now that we can rent new pictures every single week. There are already several of these up north and they're doing well. They drop the ticket price so that anyone can afford to get in, show them thirty minutes worth of film and then bring a new crowd in. Don't you think people would pay a nickel to see a thousand feet of film?"

"A nickel? How are you going to make any money off that?"

"Oh, it can work. Look, first of all, if we have fewer than 200 seats, we don't have to buy a theater license from the city. So we put in 199 chairs, fill 'em up at a nickel each and turn the place over every thirty minutes from ten in the morning until ten at night. That's a possible take of almost 240 dollars a day. We can rent films for fifty a week, the building's only forty a month. Some of these northern guys call them Nickel Odeons. Nickel Theaters, get it?"

"Well, I know I'd be a regular attendee. If that's what you wanted to know."

"No, that's not it. What I want to know is if you want to run it for me. Play the piano when you want and hire someone to play it when you don't. A pianist, projectionist and ticket-seller should be able to run things. I'll pay you fifty a week and all I want to do is count the money at the end of the week. We'll make it a little jewel of a theater with continuous flickers. Hey! Let's call it the Jewel Theater! What do you think?"

I was again amazed at how my destiny seemed entwined with those long ribbons of cellulose nitrate. I tried to focus my thoughts on what the negative side of Mr. Snider's offer might be, but I couldn't really see one. I would have to give up seeing the vaudeville acts, but they were never my primary interest anyway.

"How much do you think it will take to set up the theater?" I asked.

"I think a thousand dollars will cover it. Projector, chairs, some remodeling of the front of the building."

"Instead of me just being an employee, how about if I invest in the theater? I've got a couple hundred dollars…"

Mr. Snider paused to consider this offer. "Hmm. Tell you what. I'll give you twenty-five percent of the business. In return, your salary will only be twenty-five a week, plus your share of the profits. Deal?"

"Yes SIR!" We shook hands on it; that was the extent of our contract with each other. I went into the theater to play my shift, but for once my mind was not completely on the stage. I was part owner of a jewel!

## CHAPTER THIRTY-TWO

Five weeks later, the Jewel Theater opened for business on a Saturday morning. I stood in front of the narrow storefront, appraising the impression the new business might make on passers-by. We had knocked out the front wall, building a new wall ten feet in from the sidewalk. This gave us a covered entrance and lots of wall space for posters and handbills. In the center of the new wall was a small, glassed-in ticket booth. To the left of the booth was the entrance door; to the right, the exit. Every open space had been whitewashed, even the pressed tin ceiling above the entry. On all the walls were colorful placards advertising the newest films from the Biograph Company. Above the ticket booth, a circular hole had been cut in the wall, through which the tulip-shaped horn of a phonograph poked. A Sousa march was playing on the phonograph, manned by the Jewel's official projectionist, one Kelton Hendricks. In the ticket booth sat a young lady named Delphine Shelton, who had responded to our ad in the Statesman. She was watching me make my last-minute inspections while she nervously fingered the yellow strip of tickets she was ready to sell.

"Alright, Delphine. I guess we're ready." I opened the entrance door and waited for the first customer to step up and buy a ticket. Because Congress Avenue was such a busy thoroughfare, we had taken advantage of the weeks of remodeling to make sure everyone knew that something new was coming.

A man and woman stopped at the booth, paid for tickets and entered. I bowed and said, "Welcome to the Jewel, folks. Enjoy the show." I then took the tickets Delphine had just sold to the couple and dropped them into a wooden box with a slot on top.

I looked back to the outside, but there were no other customers waiting. Kelton poked his head down from a hole leading to the projection box and raised his eyebrows at me. "Yes, go ahead, Kelton. We might as well not keep them waiting." The red head disappeared and in a moment the lights went down and the films began to flicker on the screen. In a moment, several other people bought tickets, but the first showing was seen by only seventeen people total. When the reel was over, Kelton put up a lantern slide which read, "One moment, please, while we rewind the film." No one left the theater until the film began again; then, as the film reached the spot at which they entered the theater, each customer got up to leave.

The morning attendance was sparse and discouraging, but at noon we had a sudden rush of people on their lunch break, including large groups of women. The noon and 12:30 shows were almost full and I began to cheer up a bit. The afternoon crowds were better than the morning had been, and the evening houses were again almost full. I brought up the house lights at ten o'clock and thanked the remaining customers for coming. Then it was time to count the gate.

Delphine had sold 863 tickets, for a total of $43.15. Not earth-shaking, but not bad for the first day's business. We had Sunday off, then started up again Monday morning. When Delphine took her lunch break, I sold tickets. When Kelton took his, I ran the projector. I had no break for meals, but stole a bite of a sandwich when I had a free moment. We had some repeat customers on Monday, along with many new ones during the lunch break. But I began to worry that running the same films for a whole week might severely deplete the audience by the final day or two. I discussed this with Mr. Snider. He was still using a reel of film as an act at the Odeon, and we decided to switch halfway through the week. I made new signs for the front of the theater: "PROGRAM CHANGES TWICE WEEKLY." Since the Odeon mainly showed Edison films, this gave us some much-needed variety.

The Jewel proved to be fairly successful, but after two months, Mr. Snider and I decided to seek sources for more films so that we could change programs even more frequently. Film exchanges were a relatively new idea, but several of them had sprung up and were competing with each other, lowering prices, offering more new pictures. By fall of 1906, we were changing films daily. That sounds like a lot of change, but in fact we saw many, many of the same customers every single day! They didn't care much what they saw, as long as it was something different and new. Salesgirls would eat a quick lunch and then pop in for a half-hour of motion pictures before returning to work. Even the first show of the morning drew respectable attendance, as the newly-initiated fans of the pictures wanted to be among the first to see the day's new releases.

Mr. Snider, in his weekly counting of the money, was very pleased at the growth of the little theater. And our success aroused envy in others around Austin. In November, another nickelodeon opened on Congress, followed by another, then another. By spring of 1907, there were eight nickelodeon theaters on Congress Avenue, within three blocks, all of them changing their film programs every day. This meant that a person could see three or four hours of new films every day, if he was so inclined.

Obviously, this led to a great hunger for new films, for films that would attract more audience than the films down the street. Movie companies formed overnight and theater managers like myself were besieged by catalogs, magazines, flyers and personal visits from film company representatives, each promising the very best films at the very least cost.

As the first nickelodeon in Austin, we were in a good position to take our pick of the crop. Our program schedule eventually came down to this:

Monday: Pathé<br>
Tuesday: Biograph<br>
Wednesday: Essanay<br>
Thursday: Triangle<br>
Friday: Edison<br>
Saturday: Biograph

Through exclusive agreements, then, we would be the first to show new Biographs on Tuesday, or new Edisons on Friday.

One afternoon, I was taking tickets inside the door when I noticed a young woman standing outside. Every time someone bought a ticket and opened the door, I could see her craning her neck to get a glimpse of what was inside the theater. When I had a moment, I stepped outside by the ticket office. I had on my managerial suit and the young woman must have thought I was going to admonish her to move along. She turned and started away, but I called to her. "Miss? May I be of some assistance?"

She turned to face me and I was first conscious of her emerald green eyes. I could not remember ever having known anyone with eyes quite that color and I was staring at them so intently that I scarcely heard her say, "No, sir. I was only passing by."

I forced my gaze from her eyes and realized that her face was equally remarkable. She was tan, with flawless skin and brown hair pulled up under her hat. Her clothes were obviously patched, but clean and neat. "Do you like the moving pictures?"

Her eyes flicked away from mine. "I…I've never seen one. I was just curious."

"Well, you're certainly welcome to come in and take a look. Our theater is neat and clean and you'll have a pleasant experience, I assure you."

"I'd like to, really, sir, but — I really need to be going along now."

I realized that this woman had not even the nickel required to gain admittance. Nickelodeons had proven a great boon to the lower economic class, bringing entertainment into affordable reach for the first time. Almost anyone could come up with five cents, and the pictures didn't discriminate; the illiterate, the immigrant, the factory worker, the child — all could follow the action on the screen, regardless of their native tongue or ability to read.

But this young lady couldn't afford it, had never been able to afford it. I bowed slightly and said, "Ma'am, I am the manager of this theater for one reason. I believe that moving pictures are magical and that everyone should have the chance to see them. It would be an honor to give you your first glimpse of this miracle." I reached with one hand for the door and realized that Delphine was watching this playlet with great fascination.

The woman hesitated, but I bowed again and opened the door. She stepped timidly by me and I guided her to a seat in the darkened theater. "Stay as long as you wish," I whispered. "Enjoy the show."

I returned to the front door to resume taking tickets. Delphine looked at me with a smirking grin and I felt a flush of color in my face. Delphine and Kelton were constantly talking to each other in their spare time and had gone out for sodas on a few occasions. But I had not been seriously attracted to a woman since Texana's death, which by now was almost a decade ago. I had certainly thought about the fair sex on many occasions, but I had scant opportunity to meet anyone, since I was spending more than sixty hours a week at the Jewel. I was still trying to attend church on Sundays, but most women my age who attended were either married or had already been consigned to the "old maid" category. Kelton and I had ventured west of the Avenue on a few occasions, visiting some of the sporting houses in Guytown. My presence there was solely to study the pianists and learn from them the latest rags and other songs. Kelton, on the other hand, came away from these trips poorer but seemingly happier. He had tried once or twice to convince me to take a girl upstairs for awhile, but I was still determined to keep myself chaste until I found a woman to marry. Once he saw my resolution on this point, he ceased from tempting me and merely enjoyed himself upstairs while I was furthering my musical education downstairs. He also was not averse to having a drink now and again, but he never seemed to drink to excess. Again, he knew how I felt about this issue, and we agreed to mind our own business regarding such matters.

"No need to make that face, Delphine. I'm only trying to do a good deed."

"Of course, Mr. Wilkinson." She continued to smile.

I tried to act indignant, but couldn't really pull it off. I was in a very odd mood, feeling a burst of rejuvenation that I had not experienced in a long time. I continued taking tickets in a jolly manner, heartily greeting patrons with glee. I took over the ticket booth while Delphine went to supper, then relieved Kelton in the projection box. When I climbed down from the box, I looked to see if the young woman was still there, but the seat to which I had guided her was occupied by a fat, sweaty man in a derby. "Ah, well," I thought. "Perhaps she had a good time anyway."

The rest of the evening was routine. At ten-thirty, Kelton killed the projector and brought up the house lights for the last few stragglers. I was ready with a broom and garbage pail to clean up between the rows of chairs and straighten them for the next day. I was surprised when I saw the lovely lady, now perched in the middle of the front row. She had been in the theater for more than six hours, seeing the same reel of film perhaps a dozen times, but she still looked expectantly at the screen, hoping for more. She finally tore her gaze from the screen when she realized I was standing next to her.

"I had no idea you were still here. Did you enjoy the films?"

"Oh, yes, sir! It's the most wonderful thing I ever seen. I never thought I would get to see places like those mountains or that place with the long boats on the little…uh… waterways. Where was that from?"

"Venice," I said. The film of the gondoliers had been introduced by a title card, but it was apparent now that this girl could not read. "Venice. In Italy."

"I moved up front when I saw an empty spot. Was that alright?"

"Certainly. First come, first served. I'm glad you had a good time." I saw Kelton at the back of the theater; he pulled his watch from his vest pocket and pointedly checked the time. "I'm sorry, but we're closing for the evening now."

"What time is it?" Those green eyes looked right through me.

"It's… ten-forty."

"WHAT! Ten-forty? Oh, dear, I've got to go right now." She jumped up from her seat and started up the aisle. "Oh, but thank you so very much, sir. I'm so glad I got to see the pictures."

"W-Wait. May I get you a cab? Or walk you home?"

"No, sir," she said, a bit too forcefully, I thought.

"Oh. Well. Come again, Miss…?"

"Brown. I'm Miss Brown." She extended her hand in a worn green glove.

"Miss Brown, I'm delighted. I'm J.D. Wilkinson. Please come again, won't you?"

She shook my hand briefly, but we were now outside under the awning. She looked up and down the darkened street, as though unsure of where to go. "Are you sure I can't get a cab for you?"

"No, sir. You've done plenty for me today. Thank you again. Good night." She started south down the Avenue at a quick clip, almost trotting. There were few people on the street this late and I watched her until the darkness swallowed her up. Kelton appeared behind me. "Come on, J.D., let's go get us a dope."

"I don't think I need a Coca-Cola this late at night, Kel. I think I'm going on home to bed."

"Aw, come on! Let's go over to Rosie's for a little bit. Just to relax from a long day."

"Not tonight. You go ahead." I turned off the electric lights and locked the front doors, then walked the dozen blocks north to Mrs. Askew's. But sleep was hard to come by that night.

## CHAPTER THIRTY-THREE

Two weeks passed without Miss Brown making a repeat appearance. I became quieter, brooding over what I could have done or said differently. I was returning from the bank after taking over a bag of nickels, when I saw her standing in front of the theater, looking at the posters.

"Hello!" I burst. "So nice to see you again!"

"Oh, hello," she said. "Is there different pictures today?"

"Yes, ma'am, we change the program every day. I think you'll like what we have today. A new Biograph, a western, with lots of cowboys and Indians. Very exciting."

"That sounds good." I moved to open the door, but Miss Brown moved instead to the ticket booth, where she reached into a tiny coin purse and extracted a nickel. I had watched a great many people slide their coins across the counter to Delphine, but never had I seen anyone look so regal doing it. Miss Brown looked like a Queen bestowing a knighthood on some worthy hero. She looked at the ticket Delphine handed her, as though it might have some magical quality about it, but then surrendered it to me as I opened the door for her. She wore a different outfit from before, but it was in a similarly faded and worn condition. As she brushed by me, I found myself leaning closer, breathing in a clean scent — not of perfume — but of soap and sheer womanliness. I escorted her right to the front row; it was morning and the theater was not crowded, so she could sit in her favorite seat. "Miss Brown," I started. But those green eyes were already fixed on the screen where an eagle had swooped down to carry off a crying baby. Further conversation was obviously pointless, so I made my way back to the outer alcove. Delphine looked at me, but said nothing.

It was only about three hours later that Miss Brown emerged. I had half expected her to stay until closing again, but she apparently was determined not to spend all day in the theater. We chatted for a few moments about the films on the program. Then I asked if she would like to step across the Avenue for an ice cream soda. She looked surprised, but said yes. I whirled and told Delphine to keep an eye on things and that I would be back shortly. Delphine looked shocked; I had never left the theater in the afternoon before.

Miss Brown and I strolled to the corner, then crossed over to the ice cream parlor. She asked for a strawberry soda and I had a Coca-Cola. We sat at a small marble table and I asked her what her first name was.

"It's Melva," she said. "I hate it." I had to admit it was not a name I would have chosen for her.

"Well, mine is no prize, either. My first name is Jubal. Jubal Daniel Wilkinson."

"That's a strong-sounding name. Jubal. I never knew anyone named that."

"Neither have I. Perhaps we should both change our names to something we like better. What would you choose?"

"I like Evangeline. Or Katherine."

"Evangeline is a lovely name. I'd rather be David… or John. Something normal."

There was a pause while we both sipped our drinks. "Miss Brown, do you live here in Austin?"

She took a long pull on her straw before answering. "South of town. Across the river."

"Really? Do you work in town? What do you do?"

Another pause. I realized I should slow down. "I'm sorry if I seem overly inquisitive. I'll mind my own business, all right?"

"It's all right. I don't work anywhere right now. I've been looking for a job."

"Perhaps I could help y—" I saw again that I was pressing too hard. "I'm sorry. I seem to be prattling away like a fool."

Melva took a sip of her soda, leaving a small pink moustache before her pink tongue peeked out to whisk it away. "What's wrong with your voice?"

"I was in a fire back in the late nineties. Inhaled a lot of smoke. Ever since, my voice has been like this. Pity, really, as I used to love to sing."

She took another sip. No expression of sympathy or concern, no request for further information. It was refreshing not to have to go into the details of the fire, but it was also a bit disconcerting; I hoped desperately to appear interesting to her and it didn't seem that I was succeeding. The conversation lagged a bit while I thought of something appropriate to say. "Are you from Texas?" I queried, since it was the best I could think of.

"Yes."

That was all. I was bewildered. "Miss Brown. Again, I ask your forgiveness, but I'm not trying to pry. It's just that I am legitimately interested in — in learning more about you. When you accepted my invitation for refreshment, I naturally assumed that you might…uh…be interested in a similar way. Have I misunderstood you?"

"What is it you want, Mr. Williamson?"

"It's Wilkinson. I only wa — I mean, you were so — I thought perhaps that I…"

The green eyes twinkled at my discombobulation. She leaned toward me and said, "What? What is it, Mr. Wilkinson? Do you want to kiss me?"

If I had been flustered before, I progressed now to being fully flabbergasted and I'm afraid my mouth gaped open for a good five seconds. I was grateful that I hadn't had a mouthful of Coke when my jaw became unhinged. I could not form a coherent thought, let alone a witty rejoinder.

"Well, do you?" she said, cocking her eyebrow. "Haven't you even thought about it?"

I felt as though every person in the soda shop was staring at my crimson face, but I gathered vast stores of courage and whispered, "I have thought of little else for the past two weeks, Miss Brown."

"Perhaps you should call me by my first name. If we're going to be close friends."

Equanimity was gradually returning to me. "I would prefer to call you Evangeline. May I do so?"

Her laughter trilled up a musical scale I wished I could play on the piano. "Yes, you may. I'd like that. Now, where would you like to kiss me?"

The first answer in my mind was… well, never mind. The second one was "in front of a church full of friends and relatives." But it was my third choice that I actually voiced. "Any place. Every place. Any time. All the time."

For the first time, I thought I detected a spark in those emerald orbs, a spark with my name on it. And if she wanted my name to be Williamson, so be it!

"What time is it now?" she asked.

I was surprised to find that we had been sitting there almost an hour. "Oh, my goodness. I really should get back to the theater. I have to relieve Delphine, and then Kelton. Would you like to come back with me? Then, after they've returned, perhaps we could go for a stroll. Have dinner."

"I really should get on about my business. But, let's see. This is Friday. Maybe we could meet for lunch on Sunday. Do you have to work Sunday?"

"No, no, that would be perfect! May I call for you at home? I can get a carriage."

"No. I'll meet you. If it's nice, you could bring a picnic lunch."

"Wonderful. I'll meet you…where?"

She thought for a moment. "How about in front of the Capitol? We could picnic on the grounds there. At noon?"

"Done!" We left the soda shop and walked to the corner. She said she was going to go on home and she extended her gloved hand to me. I clasped it gently and told her I would see her on Sunday. Then she leaned close and whispered, "Think about me, all right?" And her lips briefly touched my cheek. She turned and started away. I was conscious of a cool wet spot on my cheek and the faint scent of strawberries. And I noticed that my heart was beating, something I hadn't noticed for years.

## CHAPTER THIRTY-FOUR

It would be no exaggeration to say that I was virtually useless on Saturday. I had told Kelton about my soda date and the upcoming picnic, and he was happy for me as only a good friend could be. I had no doubt that he had passed the news to Delphine as well, for she wore that smirk all day.

I woke up very early Sunday morning and decided to attend an early church service. I sat in the pew and silently, selfishly prayed for myself, that I would say and do the right things and that I would not be a nervous fool. Afterwards, I stopped by Del Rubio's Cafe and bought a fried chicken, some beans, a loaf of fresh bread, a wedge of cheese and a small container of fresh strawberries. At the drugstore I purchased a wicker hamper to hold all the food, plus two bottles of ginger ale.

I was on the steps of the Capitol at twenty till noon, trying unsuccessfully not to pace. I was still dressed up for church and tried hard to look casual but elegant. Just as the bell on St. Michael's began to strike the hour, I saw her coming from the east side of the grounds. She didn't pick up her pace when she saw me, but kept strolling at a calm rate. I picked up the basket and started toward her. We met in the shade of an enormous oak and decided that it was a fine spot to settle. I spread a tablecloth on the grass as Melva began to extract the articles from the basket, offering some kind word of appreciation over each item. I nibbled on a drumstick, but it was only a pretense; food could not provide the nourishment I was enjoying from gazing into the emerald eyes of this lovely woman. I was eager to get past the meal and on to more exceptional pursuits, but Melva took her time eating and actually evidenced quite a hearty appetite.

Finally, after the last strawberry was eaten, giving her lips almost more redness than I could bear to behold, we packed the vestiges of the meal back into the basket and began to stroll down Congress Avenue, her hand in the crook of my arm. We looked in store windows, watched people passing by, even took a short ride on the streetcar. All too quickly the afternoon passed and it was almost five o'clock. Again I dared to ask if I could see her safely home and again she said no, thank you.

"At least let me get a cab for you. We've walked so much today!"

"No, thank you, Daniel. Not today."

Back at the Capitol, we stood under the tree where we had eaten and I thanked her for coming. "This has been the best day I've had in years."

"I'm glad," she said. "I had a nice time, too."

I stood there, fresh out of chit-chat, but content to look at Melva's face. She looked back at me for a long time with a bemused expression and then softly said, "Put your arms around me."

I complied. She felt so comfortable in my embrace. I was conscious of her hands pressing against my back, and of her breasts pressing against my chest. Our faces were mere inches apart and I searched her eyes for something I could not name. "Go ahead," she whispered. "I want you to." She closed her eyes and leaned her head back slightly.

I was sorry I had waited so long. I had no idea that her lips would feel so soft against mine, that the sound of her breathing in my ear would give me chill bumps. May Irwin had laughed during her kiss; I understood that impulse now, but I also wanted to cry, to shout, to sing until my dead voice regained its former glory. I actually felt, in a spot right between my eyebrows, a swirling, dizzy sensation, and I opened my eyes to make sure I didn't fall. When I did, I was lost in those green pools again. "Couldn't we have started this at noon instead of waiting until five?"

"Next time we'll start earlier. Good-bye." She kissed me again, then walked away. I died and went straight to Heaven.

## CHAPTER THIRTY-FIVE

I began my work week with a feeling of euphoria and was forced to tell Kelton and Delphine about my Sunday afternoon. But my giddiness was tempered by the knowledge that I had no way to contact Melva and no idea when she might be back. Kelton said it was strange that she was so secretive about her home, but I preferred to view it as being cautious.

Fortunately, I did not have to wait very long. On Tuesday night, Melva materialized in front of the theater just after eight o'clock. I was excited to see her, but restrained myself from making a spectacle on the street. She looked a bit tired, but smiled a beautiful smile at me. I ushered her into the theater and to a seat down front. I whispered in her ear, "I've missed you. I couldn't wait to see you again." She smiled again and lightly stroked my cheek. "I'll let you watch the pictures. See you in a while."

At ten-thirty, I introduced Melva to Kelton and Delphine and we all went to Joe Wah's for a late supper. Melva was quiet at first, but soon joined in the conversation when it turned to moving pictures. Kelton talked of how much he liked the Western stories, while I liked the "trick" films by Melies and others, in which fantastic things happened to ordinary people or everyday objects. Delphine didn't care for the pictures very much, but Melva said she liked seeing foreign countries and the comedy stories. She asked if we really changed films every single day.

"Every day," Kelton replied. "I don't think I could stand it otherwise."

Melva pondered. "So many stories! Who makes up all those stories?"

There was a silence; none of us knew the answer. In my years of loving the motion picture, I had seen hundreds of pictures of every kind. The films which recorded actual events required no story. But the westerns, fantasy films, love stories and illustrated jokes had to be created by someone. In my own brief experience making films, I had used Biblical stories, and I had seen short films based on much-edited Shakespearean plays. But many others seemed not to be based on existing material. "I don't know who comes up with them," I said. "But I'm going to find out. I'll ask some of the film distributors next week."

Conversation turned to other topics then. Melva continued to avoid talking about herself. I began to notice how masterful she was at shifting attention from a personal question about her to another subject, usually without anyone noticing. I was alert to this ploy, however, since she had performed it on me in the past. When Delphine innocently asked where she was from, Melva deftly answered that she was from a small town in south Texas that nobody had ever heard of and where in the world did Delphine get that pretty brooch she wore around her throat? With just that much ease, Delphine was diverted and lured into chasing a different conversational rabbit.

At the end of our meal, it was nearly midnight and Melva became very restless.

Kelton spoke up. "Let's get a hansom and take the ladies home, J.D."

The green eyes swiveled toward me and I said, "I've got to get on home, Kel. Got a long day tomorrow. Besides, I think Melva already has transportation planned." Kelton looked at Melva and she nodded her assent.

"Yes, thank you, though. I've had a lovely evening, but I do need to run along home. I do hope we can do this again," she said, rising to her feet. She shook hands with Delphine and Kelton and I dropped some money on the table to cover our food. We walked back to the theater and stood under the now-dark marquee.

"Thank you for helping me at the restaurant, Daniel. I'm not trying to be mysterious, really I'm not."

"I'm glad to help you in any way, Melva. I suppose I just don't understand things completely right now."

"I know. I'm sorry. I — this is all very different for me. I just have to do things as I see fit right now."

"All right. I'll gladly put up with most anything as long as I can spend time with you."

"You're sweet." She stepped closer to me and I took her in my arms for another kiss. I again felt the intoxicating dizziness between my eyes as her gloved hand touched the back of my neck, holding me to her longer than I would have attempted on my own. "You're very nice to me," she whispered. "I want to repay your kindness. And I will. Just be patient with me, all right?"

As though I could have refused her anything. We kissed again and I hugged her tightly to me, trying to memorize the feel of a soft, womanly body pressed against me. Then she was gone.

On Monday, I sent letters to Biograph and the Edison Company, inquiring where their stories came from and whether they accepted them from people outside their companies. For most of the week, I tried to keep busy enough to not ask myself the questions that surfaced in my mind when I was at rest. I was falling in love with Melva Brown, about whom I knew next to nothing. I had never known anyone as reluctant to talk about herself and I could not decide whether this was a bad sign or not. The one thing I was sure of was that it felt immensely comforting to recall the kisses, the walks, seeing my twin reflections in her green eyes.

On Thursday, I received a letter from the Biograph Company, informing that they did indeed accept stories — they were apparently called "scenarios" in the trade — and that they would pay twenty-five dollars for any that they used. I talked to Kelton about this, but he wasn't all that interested, saying that he didn't really know any good stories. For the rest of the day, as I carried out my duties, my mind was considering and discarding one story after another. Finally, I began to consider stories from the Bible, but I had the idea of putting them in modern settings. I ran through the sixty-six books of the Bible in my head, rejecting many stories as being impossible to film, unless Georges Melies somehow could make a whale swallow a man or part the Red Sea. I considered the story of Elijah, one of the Old Testament prophets. The episode that I most vividly recalled from Sunday School studies of Elijah involved a group of children who made fun of Elijah because he was bald-headed. Elijah, being of the same humorless and sour demeanor as many of the Christians I had known, talked God into sending a bear out of the woods to eat up the mocking children. The lesson I learned from this scripture was that one should never make fun of a bald-headed preacher; otherwise, it seemed to fall under the heading of those "mysterious ways" in which God was known to move.

Seeking to modernize the story, I sat in my room that night, scratching on a piece of paper, crossing out words, starting over again and staring at the ceiling. Finally, I wrote a page-long story of a man who is taking home a large box. Inside the box is a bear costume which he has rented for a costume party. As he walks along a street, a group of children laugh and point as he struggles against a strong wind which threatens to send him and his package tumbling. The man makes it to his house, fuming about the rude children. Then he gets the idea to don the bear suit and creep back down the alley, jumping out from behind a fence and sending the children scattering and screaming. He pulls the bear head off and laughs and slaps his thigh as the film ends.

There it was. Certainly not an epic, but it did bring a smile to me as I visualized it on the screen. I had certainly run far worse subjects on the Jewel's screen. On the next day, I crossed the Avenue to an employment agency.

"May I serve you, sir?" inquired a severe-looking woman behind a desk.

"Yes, ma'am, I wish to hire a typewriter for a short time."

"What sort of girl did you have in mind, sir?"

"Um, it doesn't matter. I just need someone to typewrite a story I've written in longhand.

It's only a page. Oh, and I need a cover letter to go with it, I suppose."

"I see. Follow me, please." She led me to a closed door behind her desk and we entered another room which contained over a dozen women of various shapes and sizes. "Ladies, this gentleman needs a typewriter for an hour." The women fell into a single line and looked me over. I had not anticipated being called upon to select a typewriter as though she was part of a box of assorted chocolates. I was quite discomfited by the pleading glances of the women; some looked coquettishly at me, others attempted to be stern and business-like. I looked quickly down the row and selected the one who seemed the most needy, a mousy little thing in a black suit. "She'll do nicely," I said. My selection stepped forward as the other women dropped back into their chairs. The severe woman and I stepped back out to the office, followed by the little lady. The older woman glanced at a card and said, "This is Miss Wallace."

"How do you do, Miss Wallace? My name is Wilkinson."

Miss Wallace nodded her head at me, grinning shyly. The older woman spoke again. "Mr. Wilkinson, do you have a machine for Miss Wallace to use?"

"No, ma'am. Should I have?"

"Some employers who hire our lady typewriters have their own machines. If not, we can rent a machine to you for Miss Wallace to use."

"Fine. It shouldn't take long."

I left the agency, followed by the tiny Miss Wallace, who never spoke a word to me. She lugged the typing machine until I took it from her. We crossed to the theater and went into the small office.

"Now, Miss Wallace, here is the story I need to have you typewrite for me. I also need a letter to go with it. Do you take dictation?" She nodded. "Very well. It should be, uh, 'To whom it may concern, Enclosed is a sto' — no, change that — 'enclosed is a scenario for your consideration.'"

Half an hour later, Miss Wallace left, taking her machine and payment for her services. She never spoke a word and I didn't know if she was mute or shy. But the letter and scenario

*This Is Where I Came In*

looked professional, I thought, and I mailed it straightaway.

On Sunday, Melva and I met again for another picnic on the Capitol grounds. Then we took a streetcar down to the river, where I bought two excursion tickets on the Austin Queen. We enjoyed a long cruise on the boat and found a place to sit out of sight of the other passengers. There we spent much more time looking at each other than at the scenery along the riverbank, exchanging kiss after kiss in broad daylight. I had to hold my tongue to keep from blurting out some proclamation of everlasting love, but I was certainly feeling it in my heart. Melva even began to open up a bit, telling me that she lived with her mother across the river.

"What about your father?" I asked.

"I don't know where he is. He left us when I was very small and we haven't heard from him since."

"You poor dear," I said, pulling her close to me. "It must have been very difficult for you. Thank you for telling me, though. I feel closer to you somehow... though I didn't think that was possible."

She kissed me again, so tenderly and sweetly that I wanted to take her away immediately to some fairy castle where she would be forever free of care and worry. Instead, we sat quietly, holding hands and feeling the sunlight on our faces.

"I wrote a story for the moving pictures," I ventured.

"You did? How wonderful. Tell me what it was about."

I recited my simple plot as she smiled and nodded at each detail. "I think that will make a lovely film. What happens now?"

"That's the end. That's all."

"No, I mean, what do you do with your story to make it into a moving picture?"

"Oh, well, I mailed it off to the Biograph Company a couple of days ago. We'll see if they like it. I'm not getting my hopes up," I said.

A little furrow appeared between Melva's eyes as she frowned. "You should get your hopes up. Hopes are wonderful things. Many's the day when all I had to keep me going was hope. I had about given up hoping for some things. But now, when some of my hopes are coming true, I keep finding new things to hope for." She grasped both my hands and looked straight into my eyes. "You have every right to hope, Dan. It don't cost no money. And can't nobody take it away. Except yourself."

I was touched by her encouragement, even as I was conscious of how she had lapsed into a backwoods, country way of expressing it. She seemed to know what I was thinking, though, and added, "I know, I know. I didn't say that just right. I try so hard to say everything correctly, but sometimes it just slows down my thinking and I just can't take the time to make it sound pretty."

"Melva, everything you say is music to my ears. Don't worry about trying to impress me. I care for you very deeply. And I'm fond of you just the way you are." A trace of tears glittered in her eyes before they closed and she leaned toward me for another kiss. We rode the rest of the way in silence.

After the boat docked, I stopped by a flower cart and bought a bouquet of spring flowers and presented it to Melva. "Posies for you, madame. They look like weeds compared to you, my dear Evangeline." Outside of a revival service, I have never seen anyone so happy yet tearful.

"No one has ever given me flowers before. Thank you. I — I'll miss you until next time."

"Perhaps it won't always be so long between our encounters," I smiled. "I could grow accustomed to seeing you every day."

We made our farewells and she crossed the bridge over the Colorado as the shadows began to lengthen. I had often thought of following her, but my conscience would not let me. Still, part of me was going along with her; of that I was certain.

## CHAPTER THIRTY-SIX

On the following Wednesday, I was flipping through the mid-afternoon mail, when I came to the white envelope bearing the Biograph logo in the corner. I was accustomed to receiving bills from them for film rentals, but this was a smaller, thinner missive. I nervously tore open the envelope and pulled a folded piece of stationery out of it. When I unfolded it, a rectangle of cream-colored paper fell to the floor. I picked it up and saw it was a check, made out to me, for twenty-five dollars! I read the letter, which was short and to the point:

Dear Mr. Wilkinson,
Received your scenario. Liked it. Check enclosed. Send more.
Yours,
E.J. Dougherty

I dashed out of my office and entered the darkened theater, climbing up the ladder to the projection box. "Kelton! Kelton!" I whispered loudly.

My red-headed chum was cranking away at the projector, but glanced down at me for a second. "What is it? What's wrong?"

"Nothing's wrong. Biograph bought my story! It's going to be a picture!"

Kel stopped cranking and looked at me, his mouth agape. "Congratulations, old man! We must celebrate. That's the best news I've —" He stopped speaking due to the howling that had arisen in the theater due to the stopping of the picture. "Oops. There we go," he grinned, as he resumed turning the little handle. "Almost melted the film. Anyhow, I'm proud of you, J.D."

"Thanks. I'll talk to you later."

I showed the check and the letter to Delphine and she was also congratulatory. But I wished for some way to tell my sweetheart that one of my hopes had come through. Since I had no idea when I would be seeing her, I instead channelled my thoughts toward thinking of other story ideas. After the Jewel closed that night, Kel and I went out for dinner and then over to Guy Town. I bought his dinner, but his recreation was strictly on his own dime. I listened to Antoine, the pianist at Miss Sarah's, as he ripped through the latest rags and some other tunes he called "strides." I studied his movements as his left hand alternated between hitting bass notes and chords, while his right hand reeled out a twisting melody, full of trills and flourishes. I put a dollar in the cigar box atop the piano and he said, "Thank you kindly, Mister Wilkinson, but you don't gotta pay for no music. You's welcome here."

"I know, Antoine. But I got some good news today and I wanted to share my good fortune. Thanks for the lesson." He smiled and continued playing, never missing a beat. When Kelton came downstairs, we walked back to the Avenue and took the streetcar north to our abodes. I got undressed, but sat in my bed with the gaslight on, writing down ideas for more stories.

I got my Bible from the bureau and flipped through it, hoping that some name or passage would suumon up a story I could use. I settled on the story of Jacob seeking a wife, from the book of Genesis. Jacob spotted Rachel and worked seven years for her father to earn her as his wife. At the end of the seven years, Rachel's father instead gave his eldest daughter, Leah, saying it would not be right for Rachel to marry before her big sister. So Jacob worked another seven years to win Rachel.

I retained only a small part of this story, devising a plot in which a shabby young man answers an advertisement placed by a wealthy man seeking a suitor for his daughter. The young man gets all cleaned up and appears at the address in the ad, where his knock is answered by a beautiful young woman who shows him into the study of the rich man. As the beautiful girl stands by his chair, the rich man examines the young man, asking him questions and sizing up his worthiness. Finally, he nods his assent and rises to shake the hand of the very excited young man. At that moment, the beautiful girl opens a door and in comes a hideously ugly woman who promptly showers the young man with kisses as he realizes he has bargained for the wrong daughter.

I wrote up this story, along with two others, and again hired the reticent Miss Wallace next day to typewrite them. After they were mailed, I went about my business at the theater. After selling one story to Biograph, I began to study even more closely the films which ran each day in the Jewel. I was pleased to know that my story would become a film, but I was well aware that my achievement would be mostly unheralded. Films of that time did not even give the names of the actors, much less the director or writer. Still, I would know.

The weekend arrived before I again saw Melva. She was very pleased when I told her my news and asked when the film would be showing at the Jewel. I had to confess I had no idea how long such things took.

"You should show your story for a whole week. I think people would be impressed to know that a local man is writing for the moving pictures," she said.

"Oh, I don't want to make too much of it," I demurred. "It will still only play for a day. Will you come to see it?"

"I'll surely try, Dan. What day of the week would it be?"

"Well, Biographs are always on Tuesdays. But I usually get advance notice of the film titles which will be coming. So I will try to let you know in advance. It would mean a great deal to me for you to be here to see it. You must! You're my inspiration."

Melva and I continued our strange courtship, seizing whatever precious moments she could share with me. Each time we kissed, she seemed more passionate and I found myself wondering what might happen if we had some private spot for a rendezvous. But as it was, I could certainly not take her to my room in Miss Askew's house. And Melva expressed not the slightest tendency toward taking me to wherever it was that she lived. She did finally confide in me that she was born in Lufkin, but that she hadn't been there since she was a small child. Other than that, I knew precious little about her. I did not ask her age, feeling that would be ungentlemanly. But I estimated that she was about twenty-two, four or five years younger than I.

More than a week went by after I had sent the three stories to Biograph, and I had begun to doubt that they had been accepted. But after twelve days, another Biograph envelope arrived, with a check for 75 dollars and another brief letter saying, "Keep them coming!"

I cashed the check and went to Scarborough's department store, stopping in the ladies' section: unfamiliar territory to me. A young lady asked if she could help me.

"Yes, please, I want to buy a nice dress. As a gift."

"Certainly, sir. Do you know the lady's size?"

"Um, no. But she's this tall," I demonstrated with my hand.

"All right. Is she thin or stout?"

"Thin. Her waist is about this size," I held my hands apart, making an oval the size of her slender waist. Then I blushed as I realized what I was doing. "At least I think it's about like this."

"I'm sure we can fit her, sir. What sort of dress were you thinking of?"

We spent half an hour looking at various materials, styles and sizes. I eventually picked a deep maroon skirt and waist made of velvet and trimmed with black brocade. I asked the girl to recommend a hat to go with it and she sold me an enormous thing with a large maroon bow. "What else would be good?" I asked.

"Well, sir, you could add a purse. Or some jewelry. Stockings. Perfume."

"No, no perfume. Maybe some jewelry."

I looked at the jewelry selection, eventually settling for an ivory cameo brooch. I had the hat boxed and the dress was wrapped, with the jewelry pinned to it. I took it back to my office, where it sat for several days until my Evangeline again appeared.

She was excited that more stories had been sold and I told her I had a gift for her in appreciation of her encouragement and affection. She looked almost afraid, saying she wasn't used to getting presents, but then began to query me as to what it could be.

"Open the rectangular box first," I said. She exclaimed over the pretty paper and the satin ribbon as she carefully and slowly removed the wrapping, trying not to tear anything. When she removed the lid of the box and saw the maroon dress, she let out a little cry, then looked at me wonderingly. Her fingers gently touched the velvet, tracing along the brocade and gliding across the golden brooch. Then she removed the dress from the box, holding it before her.

"It looks so beautiful! How did you know my size?"

"I just guessed. Do you like it?"

"No. I love it! It's the most beautiful thing I've ever seen and you should not have spent your money on me, you silly thing." Before she could get more emotional, I handed her the hat box and she repeated the opening ritual, squealing with delight over the bonnet.

"I'll leave you alone here in the office if you'd like to try it on," I ventured. "Just lock the door behind me. I'll be outside." She nodded and I went out into the sunshine, feeling very happy and good. It was probably ten minutes later when the door to the theater opened and Melva's face peeked out.

"Do you want to see?"

"Of course I do. Step out here in the light."

She pushed the door wide and swept into the bright afternoon. I wished I was a painter when I saw her, for she was surely the most beautiful sight in the world, a beautiful woman who at last had some beautiful new clothes to wear, along with a beautiful expression of perfect joy on her perfect face. She twirled about, revealing her ankles as she showed me all sides of her. The dress fit her as though it had been custom-made to her body. And the hat only drew attention to the pretty visage underneath it. I knew at that moment that I was in love with this woman and that I would do whatever it took to make her mine. She hugged me strongly, thanking me over and over, until I finally told her to go on inside and watch the films; passers-by were beginning to notice our public display.

She stayed until the theater closed. We then went with Kel and Delphine to get a bite to eat. After the meal, we walked back along the Avenue and said farewell to Kelton and Delphine. Melva reminded me that her other clothes were still in my office, so I unlocked the door to the darkened theater and we entered. I closed the door, locking it from the inside and reached out for Melva's hand, guiding her through the pitch black lobby to the door of the office, where I fumbled in the dark for the lock. Once inside, I turned on the light, but Melva reached out and turned it off again. Then she reached for me and we fell into a series of caresses and kisses that had me reeling. After a few moments, she turned on the light and said she had better put her old clothes on before she started home.

"Oh, all right," I said, reaching for the doorknob. "I'll wait for you outside."

"No. Stay."

I turned to look at her as she began unbuttoning the black buttons on the front of the maroon dress. Her white chemise was revealed underneath and I could see the gentle swelling of her breasts at the low neckline. With a shrug, the jacket was off and her shoulders and arms were bare. Then, she loosened the long skirt and let it fall to the floor. She stood there in stockings, corset and chemise, looking at me with the most remarkable, unashamed gaze.

"Do you love me, Daniel?" she asked.

"Yes. Yes, I do."

"Have you ever been with a woman like this before?"

"No. I haven't."

"Well, then, Daniel, it would be an honor to give you your first glimpse of this miracle," she smiled, quoting the overblown prose I had spouted on the first day she came to my theater. She came toward me, reaching for the buttons on my vest, then guided me gently with a word here, a touch there, a sigh or a kiss here… or even there, or there. And when at last I had given my all to her, she hugged and kissed me and told me that she loved me and ran her fingers through my hair and held me until my heartbeat slowed to almost normal.

## CHAPTER THIRTY-SEVEN

A month later, I had sold several more stories to the Biograph. They had accepted everything I had sent, with the exception of two stories which were returned to me. I sold one of the stories to Triangle and the other to Essanay. I felt it was good to have more than one source for my work and having access to three studios made me feel even more confident.

At the end of the month, Melva and I sat in the theater, holding hands expectantly as the new reel of Biographs began to run. First on the reel was my story, now titled *The Bear Suit*. I was gratified to hear the laughs of the audience at the antics onscreen. Whoever had directed the picture had done some creative shots which improved the story, including a close-up of several of the screaming children's faces when the bear jumped out at them. We sat through the reel two more times, not just because of my handiwork, but also because the darkness made it pleasantly possible to hold hands.

Kelton was enthusiastic about the films also, encouraging me to keep up the good work. I had just about run out of Bible stories to adapt, but I had discovered that if I observed people, listened to their tales, and used my memory of events in my own life, I could come up with situations which could be adapted for filming. I submitted my first Western scenario, a fast-paced tale called *Rats On The Range*, which was snapped up by Biograph; westerns were becoming extremely popular and I was gratified that Biograph was taking most of my output. The films issued by Biograph seemed to have a bit more care taken in their production, which drew larger audiences. At this period in the nickelodeon era, films were not advertised by name, but by company. When the posters outside proclaimed "New Biograph Feature Today" there was a measurable increase in tickets sold.

The motion picture was a growing success, but as far as anyone knew, they had become all that they would ever be. I never heard a customer say, "If only the films were two hours long!" or "Why can't we hear them while we see them?" Films were films and the public was plenty glad to have them, judging by the ever-increasing number of theaters and film studios. There was no sense that we were "missing" anything or that what we were watching was primitive. They were little slices of life, whether real life or reel life, and most folks couldn't get enough of them.

Between my income as manager and part-owner of the Jewel and my income from writing scenarios, I was able to save a goodly sum of money each month. In the back of my mind, I'm sure, were thoughts of proposing marriage to Melva, but I restrained such emotions as hasty and told myself there was plenty of time.

I had other things to consider, as well. Mr. Dougherty of the Biograph had invited me, in one of his brief notes accompanying a paycheck, to come out and take a look around the studio, to watch the films being made. This was an offer I found very tempting, especially since his letter implied that a job offer was a real possibility. But I had doubts about pulling up stakes and leaving Texas, leaving Melva, leaving Kelton and the Jewel. Kelton said I would be crazy not to take the job if it would get me into the business of making pictures instead of just showing them. He was also eager to have a friend in the film business so that he could get his foot in the door as a comic actor in the pictures.

I did not immediately tell Melva about the quandary I was weighing. She was beginning to be more open with me, telling me that she would have me to her home sometime soon, while warning me that it was nothing fancy. She said she had spoken of me to her mother and that her mother looked forward to meeting me.

"Wonderful," I said. "I'm equally enthused at the thought of meeting the woman who gave birth to you."

"Well… We will do it, Dan. I'm not quite ready yet."

I was eminently ready to introduce Melva to my own parents, but they seldom traveled and I was at the theater every day except Sunday. I had written to them frequently, however, and Mother was especially curious about the girl about whom I gushed in my letters. She added that she hoped I knew that she had always prayed I would find the right young lady and that I should be patient to see if this was the one.

Near the end of summer, Melva and I sat in my office on a Sunday afternoon. We had just experienced another "miracle," as we had come to refer to our coition. "Someday," I smiled, "I want to find out what this feels like on something softer than a desk."

She smiled wanly as she buttoned up her shirtwaist, obviously thinking about something else. "Dan… there's something I want to ask you."

"Yes, my darling Evangeline, ask me for the world and it is yours."

"No, no, it's not a request. It's just a question. But I'm afraid it will change the way you feel about me."

A curious weight fluttered in my stomach, but I smiled and said, "Nothing can change my feelings for you. Surely you must know that by now."

"I want to believe you. But I'm afraid."

"Evangeline, my father often preaches about Agape love, unconditional love. That's what I feel for you." I tried to maintain my smile, but the right corner of my mouth was twitching spastically.

"Dan. You are so good to me. I can't do very much for you in return. But I must tell you what is inside of me."

I leaned back against the desk, half-sitting on the oaken top where we had writhed moments before. "Go ahead. I'm listening."

"Well, I — I know I've had many secrets from you. I was so fearful of scaring you away, but now I care too much to keep the secrets. Dan, I am a mother. I have two children. A girl and a boy. Amelia is six and Garland is four."

I let her words sink into my brain, but they refused to register. "But… but how can you? I mean, did you —?"

"I was married. To a bad man. He was horrible to me and to the children. So I left him."

"So you… you're divorced?"

"No. I could never afford to divorce him legally. I had nothing, not a penny when I left him. I had to go home to my mother. And she had not much more than nothing herself. So in the eyes of the law, I guess we're still married."

"How long ago did you leave?" I asked.

"Two years ago. He lives in San Marcos, but he shows up every now and then. He still thinks I will take him back." Tears began to trail down her cheeks as she continued. "He still comes around, Dan, and he still hits me and he still makes me… But it's not like it is with us, Dan. It's not loving and tender and sweet." She could not continue because she was sobbing so hard. I embraced her and tried to console her, but I was stunned at the enormity of her secrets. And I also felt a rage at the thought that anyone could mistreat this dear, sweet girl.

"It's alright, Evangeline. It doesn't change anything. I know how hard it was for you to tell me this and I'm deeply moved by your trust in me." She merely cried all the more and I had little recourse but to wait for the tears to subside in their own good time. Finally, she sat, red-eyed and drained, her hair coming loose from her chignon. She looked at me sadly, apologetically.

"Will you ever want to see me again?"

To my surprise, tears now clouded my own vision. "Oh, can't you see that I love you? Don't you know you're in my head every second you're not in my arms?" We hugged some more and she dabbed at my eyes with her already soggy handkerchief. "You're going to have to come up with something more horrible than that to get rid of me, Melva."

She pressed her finger against my lips. "Shhhh. Don't ever say that again. Melva is dead. I am your Evangeline."

That evening, I rented a carriage and took my Evangeline home for the first time. We crossed the river and then turned east, into a shabby neighborhood of houses that seemed to have been made from scraps of lumber and scavenged odds and ends. She directed me to a tiny house at the end of a narrow dirt road. It was surrounded by weeds and thistles a yard high and the whole structure seemed to lean a few inches toward the river. But there were a few flowers in a cracked pot on the porch and the house itself seemed clean and neat. Evangeline looked at me unashamed, relieved to be done with the secrets and unafraid of the truth.

"May I come in and meet your family?" I asked.

"No, not yet, Daniel. It wouldn't be fair to surprise them like that. We'll have dinner one evening soon. When I can have everything properly prepared."

"I'd like that."

I held her hand and helped her from the carriage. I was conscious of some of the neighbors' peering out their front doors at the unusual sight of a new carriage and horse delivering a passenger to this neighborhood. Evangeline alighted regally from the carriage and whispered, "I want to kiss you, but I don't want to do it with everyone watching."

"I understand. You can owe me that kiss until next time. I'll be happy to come and pick you up whenever you want to come to the theater."

"Oh, don't be silly. Your place is at your job. I can get there easily enough. You can bring me home, though." At the front porch, she extended her hand and I did an exaggerated bow and kissed it. By the time I crossed the river again, heading north up the Avenue, the moonlight towers had come on and I realized with a start that it had been eleven years since I first entered the city of Austin under that artificial moonlight. A flood of memories and faces raced through my mind: Bess Endicott, Mr. Koog, Leo Matula, Texana, Officer Donovan, Orvis Dean,

Mother and Father, Kelton, Delphine. And my Evangeline. How much tragedy there was in the world, I thought. I wondered again about my purpose in life. Was it plausible that I was put on earth to bring a bit of joy into the life of a lovely but lonely young woman? I decided to proceed as though it was.

## CHAPTER THIRTY-EIGHT

Mr. Snider stood with me in front of the Jewel as we looked down Congress Avenue to the half-dozen other nickelodeons within two blocks. "I wonder if I might have shot myself in the foot, J.D. Daytime crowds at the Odeon are way down. The evening crowd is still pretty good, but it seems like vaudeville is losing ground to these flickers."

"Oh, but you're a trendsetter, Mr. Snider. This seems to be the wave of the future. I wish we had more than 199 seats in the Jewel; I believe we could sell twice as many seats every day."

Mr. Snider remained taciturn as he examined the patrons who entered the Jewel. "Well, it's a big change, I suppose. You're drawing a different crowd from what I'm getting. Evenings, I get the upper crust of the town, with the ladies all dressed up and the men in their best suits. But look there! Wetbacks, children, servant class people… I guess they couldn't keep up with anything very complicated."

"It's democracy in action," I replied. "For the first time, the average poor working fellow can actually afford some entertainment. It's a shame it took so long to give it to him."

"Yes, too bad. Well, I shouldn't complain. Just hate to see things change, you see? Maybe we should open another nickelodeon. There seems to be no limit to how many can prosper right here on the Avenue. See you later, J.D."

I was somewhat relieved to see Mr. Snider go. One of my scenarios was showing that day, a melodramatic romance which the Biograph Company had titled *Poorhouse to Palace*. I was eager to see it, but I had not told Mr. Snider of my burgeoning career as a writer, even though I was selling two or three stories a week now.

I stood at the back of the small theater and watched the end of a newsreel before my film came on. It was always interesting to see how the films differed from the pictures in my head when I wrote them. This one featured an attractive girl with long curls whom I was sure I had seen before in other Biograph films. I had no idea who she was, but she was enormously appealing as the poor urchin who was plucked from poverty by a wealthy young man through an accidental encounter. I knew the story was effective when I heard a few women in the audience quietly sniffling over the happy ending.

Late that evening, only an hour before closing, Evangeline came to the theater and I was delighted to see her and to sit beside her as we watched my story twice. When the lights came on, she looked at me with shining eyes and said, "I like that story very much. Did you think of me when you wrote it?"

"Of course I did. But I think of you all the time."

We helped straighten the chairs and sweep out the theater while Kelton and Delphine finished their closing tasks. Then Evangeline and I repaired to my office for another frenzied session of lovemaking. She was enticingly forward at such times, a fact much appreciated by such a novice as myself. She taught me what to do that would be pleasing to her, as well as to myself, and I was an eager pupil. When we were once again presentable, she said, "Would you come to supper at my home on Sunday evening?"

"With pleasure. When should I arrive?"

"Supper time, of course. Whenever you get hungry." Though I offered several times, she refused to let me bring anything, insisting that she would take care of everything.

I went to church that Sunday morning, ate lunch alone, then took a stroll along the Avenue. I still felt the need to take something to supper and finally decided that a bouquet might be a worthy addition to the meal. By five o'clock, I could wait no longer; I picked up the rented surrey and headed south across the river. In the daylight, the neighborhood looked dustier and shabbier than it had on my evening visits. Raggedy children playing in the street stopped and looked at me as I passed; their expressions bespoke a dull curiosity. They wondered what I was doing in their world, but there was no resentment or even envy, only a brief stirring of interest at the break in their routine.

I was dressed in my best suit, having freshly bathed and shaved. I tethered the horse to a leaning post and walked up to the porch of Evangeline's house. I knocked gently on the door and heard scurrying within and Evangeline's voice in a loud whisper: "All right, there he is. Please behave!"

Then she opened the door, beaming her smile at me with extra candlepower. "Come in, Mr. Wilkinson." She was wearing the dress I had bought and she looked beautiful.

Formality was the order of the day, was it? "Good evening, Miss Brown. So lovely to see you." I bowed and kissed her hand. She took my arm and guided me into the house.

It was rather dim inside. There was only one window in the front room and the lower half of it had been painted over. Curtains made of flour sacks covered the top half. A coal-oil lamp sat in the middle of the dining table and a few candles were scattered around the room. The table had four mismatched chairs; an apple box had been turned on end to provide a fifth seat. There was little other furniture in the room. A pile of neatly folded quilts in one corner indicated that someone slept on the floor in this room. There was not a book or a framed picture to be seen, but some colored magazine pages had been tacked on the walls to add some color. A fireplace against the north wall held a small fire, though the day was not cold; an iron pot, bubbling with a stew that smelled delicious, hung above the flame. The poverty evident in this room was heart-breaking to me; I had thought the preacher's family in Blanco were poor, but we seemed like Croesus compared to this. But the house was clean and the floor had obviously been scrubbed until the worn wood shone. My eyes completed the circuit of the room and came back to Evangeline. Her right hand was in the crook of my left arm, but her other arm indicated the two children next to her. "Mr. Wilkinson, this is my daughter, Amelia, and my son, Garland." Two lovely, green-eyed children stared at me as though expecting me to burst into flame at any moment. The girl looked to be about six and the boy three or maybe four years old. I bowed to the little girl.

"A pleasure to meet you, Miss Amelia," I said, lightly kissing her hand. I then held out my hand to Garland, who thought it very funny that I shook his hand vigorously up and down, causing his body to shake with laughter. "I'm delighted to meet both of you. I knew you would be fine folks since you have such a fine mother." Their eyes darted to Evangeline, then back to me. Neither had spoken a word.

"What's wrong with you two?" their mother asked. "You've been chattering away all day and now you act like the cat's got your tongue."

"Yes, Amelia, I was looking forward to talking with you. That's why I brought you this bouquet," I said, holding out the bundle of violets and pansies. I saw immediately that I had made points with both mother and daughter; Amelia's mouth dropped open and she exclaimed, "Oh, thank you, thank you. They're real pretty!" Garland was excited by this transaction, but I realized he was going to feel left out unless I made a similar gesture toward him. I wished I had brought some candy or coins or something, but the thought had not occurred to me earlier.

"Garland, my horse outside is waiting patiently for a reward. Would you like to give him some sugar?"

"'Kay. Can I have some, too?"

"Garland." His mother's voice.

"It's alright, Miss Brown. I have a few extra cubes for my helper. We'll only be a moment." Garland took my hand and we went out to the surrey, where he somewhat skittishly held a cube of sugar on his palm for the big horse to eat. He giggled when the horse's lips nuzzled his hand and had to do it again. "Here's one for you," I said, holding out a cube to him. To my surprise and delight, he did not reach to take it, but leaned over and gobbled it from my fingers just like the horse had done.

We returned to the porch, where Evangeline and Amelia watched. An older woman came out of the house and Evangeline introduced her as "my mother, Mrs. Pitts." I repeated my bow and hand-kiss, then looked more closely at the woman. She did not have the green eyes of her daughter and grandchildren, and if she had ever been beautiful, time and care had eroded it like a river over a muddy bed. She wore a lacework of wrinkles on her face and a worried look in her brown eyes. Her hair was an even mix of black and gray and it was pulled back in a severe bun that only made her look older.

"Howdy do," she nodded to me.

"My pleasure," I responded. "Thank you so much for having me to supper. It smells wonderful."

"It ain't much. We don't get much company, so there ain't no fancy cookin'."

"Mrs. Pitts, I'm a country boy from Blanco, Texas. I'd rather have a crawdad than a lobster any day." A couple of the wrinkles around her mouth turned up a little.

"Well, come on in. It's about as ready as it's gonna get. We better eat it 'fore I have to th'ow it to the hogs."

We sat around the table and Garland clambered atop the apple crate. Everyone reached to hold hands with those on either side; Evangeline held my left hand and Amelia was on my right.

"Would you say the blessing, Mr. Wilkinson?" asked Mrs. Pitts.

"Yes, ma'am." I was only a bit rusty on my public praying, but I managed to cover all the basics. Mrs. Pitts and Evangeline then hopped up and began bringing food to the table. There was a rich, thick beef stew, full of vegetables and wonderfully seasoned. To go with it, there was hot cornbread and red beans with bacon in them. Mustard greens and sliced tomatoes completed the meal. It was my first homemade meal in many months and I savored every mouthful, finally protesting loudly that the ladies were obviously trying to kill me and that, while I couldn't imagine a more pleasant way to go, they would have to roll me through the door and I wasn't sure I could still fit.

Mrs. Pitts said little through the meal, but took note of what I ate and what I had to say about it. She received each compliment with a bit more belief than the previous one and I intuited that she had been very nervous about this "theater manager feller" coming to criticize her cooking. But it was truly the best meal I had ingested in ages. I was in trouble when Mrs. Pitts brought in a rhubarb pie, since I was already stuffed, but I managed somehow to dispose of a piece.

As the women — even little Amelia — carried the dishes out to the kitchen, Mrs. Pitts murmured, "Well, he's got a good appetite, anyway." I played with Garland until the dishes were done and then we all repaired to the front porch, where we sat and talked quietly. Garland showed me how he could turn a somersault and Amelia made up a story about the man in the moon. Finally, when the stars were visible overhead, Mrs. Pitts said, "Come on, young'uns. Time for bed."

The children told me good night and I thanked them for their hospitality. I assumed Mrs. Pitts would put them to bed and then return, but she said, "Good night, Mr. Wilkinson. Hope you got enough to eat."

I quickly stood up and effusively thanked her for the meal. "I never had a finer supper, ma'am." She nodded and went inside.

"The children will sleep in the bedroom with Mama," Evangeline said. "We can go back and sit at the table if you like. I'm getting chilly out here."

Back inside, the door to the kitchen and the door to the bedroom were both closed, furnishing us with a semblance of privacy. We sat at the table and held hands.

"Well, did I pass the inspection?" I smiled.

"Oh, yes. She would have told you if you hadn't. And the children clearly think you're really something."

"Good. I like them, too."

We kissed a few times over the table, but I was leery of proceeding further. After another hour or so, we said our goodbyes and I rode back toward the Capitol.

## CHAPTER THIRTY-NINE

While Kelton was still my closest friend, the nature of our friendship had changed, due to the circumstances of our work. I was now his boss, although I never tried to order him around. But the activity which originally brought us together, going to see pictures, was now our business and we rarely had time for much socializing outside the theater. We occasionally went to eat after the theater closed, and once or twice a month we would visit Guy Town so I could listen to music and he could dally with the girl of his choice. But we never had the long discussions and soul-bearing sessions which had meant so much to me in the past. He did tell me that he was thinking of marrying Delphine and wondered what I thought about that. I encouraged him to be sure of his feelings for her and then to do what his heart said was right.

"I guess I'd have to give up coming to Guy Town," he mused. "But why eat out when the kitchen at home is always open?" He nudged me in the ribs, but I thought it a crude thing to say. I was having my own mixed emotions about the sexual activities of Evangeline and myself. My lifelong determination to wait until I was married? It had crumbled. And here I was, involved with a woman, a mother of two! And though my parents would have been aghast if I was seeing a divorced woman, how would they react to know this woman was apparently still married? I had never told Kelton or anyone else about Evangeline's past, but how long could I keep such large secrets?

The next time I saw Evangeline, I told her my idea. "I want to pay for your divorce," I said. "I feel guilty about what we're doing, you being married and all. I have enough money. Please let me do this so you'll be free of this man." She readily agreed and we consulted a lawyer the following day. He drew up the papers for forty dollars and said he would notify me when it was finalized. The divorce decree bore Melva's real name, of course, and I noticed that she could not sign the paper, but made a simple "X" mark.

About two weeks later, on a Sunday evening, I had again had supper at Evangeline's house. I had brought a doll for Amelia and some tin soldiers for Garland and they had each hugged me in gratitude. I had racked my brain to think of a suitable present for Mrs. Pitts, rejecting books, anything to eat (which might be seen as a complaint about her cooking), anything to wear. Instead, I bought a Kodak Brownie camera and asked her if she would like some family photographs. She readily agreed and I snapped pictures of the children in front of the house, on the porch, sitting on the horse, and standing with Evangeline and Mrs. Pitts. While there was still enough sunlight, I took a couple of Evangeline standing by a scrub oak, her hand resting on the trunk. I got as close as I dared, about six feet away, and hoped the shot would remain in focus. "I'll send this film off tomorrow," I said, "and bring the pictures next time I come."

Mrs. Pitts was almost excited, and mentioned several times how nice it would be to have photographs of the children. We had another good meal and another enjoyable session on the porch, being entertained by the children. I even ventured to sing a song in my raspy voice, the first time I'd tried in years. It was nothing great, but it felt good to me.

Later, after the others had gone to bed, Evangeline and I sat at the table, talking and touching. She kissed me passionately, then moved over onto my lap, holding me close to her. I hugged her and whispered in her ear that I loved her. She repeated the words to me and added, "We'll have to be very quiet." I had not intended for anything else to happen, but she kissed me on the neck before sliding down to the floor, kneeling between my knees. She began to unbutton my britches, looking up at me in the dim lamplight and I thought again how lovely she was.

Her hand began to work its way inside my pants and my eyes started to close. Just then the front door burst open and a large, roaring man stood there, wild-eyed. He was a huge, bear-like brute, with several days growth of beard and I could smell the liquor on him from several feet away. He was screaming, "You're not gonna divorce me! I'll kill you first!"

Evangeline had jumped to her feet and headed toward him, crying, "Sam, no! Please leave!" I got to my feet, trying to quickly button my pants, but this action caught the eye of the man.

"Oh, had your pants down, huh? I see what's going on here now!" He backhanded Evangeline across the face and she hit the wall, sliding down to a sitting position. He advanced toward me as I finished fastening my britches. I was bringing my arms up when the first blow struck the side of my head. He was using his arms like clubs, not punching, but swinging them wildly. As I reached for the place he had struck me, his other arm hit me in the face and I smelled and tasted blood. Evangeline was screaming and crying and now the bedroom door was open and the children were hysterically shouting, "Daddy, don't do it!" and "Daddy, stop!" Mrs. Pitts was trying to pull them back inside the bedroom, but having a hard time of it. I raised my arms, trying to cover my head, but the blows continued to rain down on me. The man kept ranting, "You don't get rid of me, you whore! You're mine! Mine! I'll kill your little boyfriend here, too!" I did not doubt him at that moment. Evangeline had struggled to her feet, but she was limping as she came toward the man, grabbing at the back of his shirt and begging him to stop. He turned and grabbed her hair, pushing her toward me. "You wanna kiss him now? Go on! Teach your kids how to do it!" He then shoved her face into mine and I saw my blood on her cheek.

The chorus of screams was deafening and my mind was racing even though time seemed to be moving in slow motion. I saw that the man still held Evangeline by her hair and he was drawing back his fist to strike her. That's when I hit his nose with everything I had. Blood spurted on the three of us, but the man seemed to react — not with pain — but with anger that I had dared to strike him. He roared like a deranged lion and dropped Evangeline to the floor. At that moment I dived on him, seeking to pin his arms to his sides. We fell back on the table, then onto the floor, but I kept my grip around his body. "Take the children! Go! Run!" I yelled, as the man struggled, and the women dragged the screaming children out the front door. The man kept trying to regain his footing, but I saw my only hope in keeping him down. I repeatedly knocked his feet from under him so that he could not stand. We rolled around on the floor, almost into the fireplace, while he continued to call me vile names and to scream obscenities. Then he began to yell, "She's my wife! She's my wife!"

"Well, she's gone," I said. He stopped struggling and looked around, realizing that I spoke the truth. I released my aching arms and he jumped to his feet, running to the door to look out. But in the dark he could not tell which direction the others had gone. Residents from nearby houses stood out in their yards and some of the neighbor men stood in the street near Evangeline's. One man had a shotgun and most had a club, an axe or some sort of tool. The man with the shotgun said, "Sam, get your sorry ass out of here or I swear to God, I'll shoot you."

Sam spit on the ground and uttered another obscenity, but when the unmistakable sound of a gun being cocked was heard, he decided to take his leave. He walked unsteadily to a horse, climbed on and rode off, swearing at me, at Evangeline and at the whole neighborhood.

"You alright, mister?" asked the shotgun man. "You don't look so good." I protested that I was fine, but the man led me across the street to his house, where I learned his name was Benny McGee. His wife washed my face and hands with a cool washrag. I could see that my hands had numerous scratches from Sam's fingernails. "That Sam Pitts is a worthless dog. I shoulda shot him, just to put him out of our misery."

My head was aching and my mind was foggy, but I said, "Sam Pitts? His name's not Brown?"

"Naw, he's a Pitts. He growed up right there where you was, but he wasn't never any good, especially after his daddy run off."

"But... why does Eva— why does Melva live with his mother?"

"They just get along, I guess. His mama just give up on him a long time ago. Ever'body keeps thinkin' he's gonna wind up in jail or dead, but he just keeps poppin' up like a bad penny."

A boy appeared at the front door. "Mr. Wilkinson?" he said.

"Yes?"

"Ahm, Miss Brown said to tell you that she's okay and the children's sleepin' and they're all at a friend's house and she'll talk to you tomorrow. Oh, and she said this is yours." He held out the Brownie camera. I thanked the McGees for their help and walked across the street to the surrey. There were still a few people out in their yards and I was aware that they watched me as I drove past, whispering behind their hands.

## CHAPTER FORTY

I awoke the next morning hurting in a hundred places. Every inch of my head seemed tender and the small scratches on my hands and face burned. I sat on the edge of the bed, feeling the aches and pains all over and I felt tears come to my eyes. It was a helpless, violated feeling that I had never experienced before. I didn't really want to go to work that day, but there was no telephone in Mrs. Askew's house and I had no way to let Kelton or Delphine know I was not well. I looked in the mirror over the washstand; to my surprise, I didn't really look too bad. My nose was still very sore, but it had not been broken. There were a few small scratches on my face, but nothing very obvious.

I got myself cleaned up as well as I could and took the streetcar downtown. Kelton was waiting at the front door for me to open up, but I didn't tell him about the events of the previous evening. Delphine arrived shortly afterward, and I told them I was not feeling well and that I would be in my office if I was needed for anything.

I sat at the desk and pondered what courses of action were open to me. I first thought of going to the police until reason kicked in. What would I tell the police? That I was caught in a compromising situation with a woman? By her husband? If he had killed me, they probably would have let him go with a sympathetic pat on the back for being the poor, cuckolded innocent.

But what else was I to do? Track down the brute and — and what? I was more than certain that I could never beat him in a fair fight, and I was fairly sure that I could not shoot him or in some other way inflict damage on him.

I mostly wanted to take Evangeline away somewhere peaceful and calm, where she could know happiness and the children could be free from worry and fear. But thoughts of Evangeline brought even more questions to mind. Why had she introduced Mrs. Pitts as her mother? At this point, I didn't know if her name was really Brown or Pitts or something wholly different. Why did she feel unable to trust me with information like this?

I sorted through the mail, glancing through some film catalogues. My head was beginning to ache badly, so I went down to the pharmacy for some medication. While there, I dropped off the roll of film from the crushed Brownie. Mrs. Pitts would still want those photographs, I was sure.

Back at the office, my head still pounded. I had hoped that Evangeline would come by to assure me that she and the children were safe. A visit would likely be the only way she could notify me, I thought, as I remembered she was unable to write. By mid-afternoon, I felt sick to my stomach and I told Kelton and Delphine to cover for me.

I went home and went to bed, sleeping fitfully. I ate no supper, having little appetite and no energy to go get something to eat. Mostly, I laid in bed, staring up at the ceiling, wondering what could happen next.

On Tuesday, I felt better and was able to carry out my duties as usual. I spent the morning getting caught up on correspondence, ordering films and preparing the bank deposit. In the afternoon, things were quiet enough that I decided to hire a horse and go check on Evangeline. I coaxed the horse into a trot once we were out of the main section of the Avenue and crossed the river, following the dusty road I had come to know well.

When I arrived at the house, the front door was closed. I knocked softly and waited, then knocked more loudly. There was no response. I leaned close to the door and heard no sound within. I stood for a moment, then reached to try the doorknob. It turned easily and the front door swung inward with a creak. I stepped inside, letting my eyes get accustomed to the dark interior of the house. The room was bare. The table and chairs were gone. The pot from the fireplace was missing. Even the magazine pictures had been taken off the walls. My stomach began to heave and I crossed to the bedroom door.

I had never seen the bedroom and now there was nothing in it to see, just a small, stuffy room with not a stick of furniture nor any sign it had ever been inhabited. I walked into the kitchen, but it was also bare, the cupboard yawning open to show no dishes or cups. The back door opened to a tiny back yard with a clothesline and an outhouse which stood open.

The house was bereft of any sign that a living soul had ever lived there. I looked back in the front room, determined to find some remnant, some trace of the woman I loved. But even the ashes had been removed from the fireplace. I stood in the center of the room and turned around and around, but there was nothing to be seen.

I walked across the street and knocked at the door of Mr. McGee. He was not there, but his wife was. "Mrs. McGee, excuse me, ma'am, but do you know where the folks across the street went?"

"Nope. They come back yesterday with a old, rickety cart and loaded up ever'thing. Said they was moving to another town, but I didn't hear 'em say which 'un."

"I have to find them, it's very important! Look, if you hear anything, or if anyone around here knows anything, could you let me know? I work at the Jewel Theater on Congress? I've got to find them."

She nodded, but didn't seem overly interested in knowing where the family had gone or in letting me know about it. I mounted the horse and rode up the street, stopping to ask several people if they knew the whereabouts of their former neighbors, but no one did. The day before, I would not have believed that my spirit could sink any lower. But as I crossed the river — for the last time? — I discovered new depths, deeper and colder than any I had experienced before.

## CHAPTER FORTY-ONE

For the next few weeks, I stumbled through life blindly, not caring much about my appearance or my business. Kelton grew alarmed at my glum demeanor and tried his best to cheer me up, but I was not interested in cheering up. My mood was not helped on the day the envelope from Kodak arrived, containing twelve pictures of Evangeline and the children. I wept again as I looked at her lovely smile, at the eyes that beckoned me into the photograph. I pulled open a drawer of the desk, dropped the stack of pictures in, and slammed it shut. But after perhaps two minutes of staring at the wall, I pulled the drawer open and looked at them again.

I wrote a few scenarios, more than one of which featured a huge, burly man trying to carry away a small, attractive woman. In my stories, however, the hero always arrived in time to save her. The stories were melodramatic, but such was the order of the day in the moving picture business, and Kalem, Biograph and Edison snapped them up.

As I had so many times in my life, I found myself searching for my purpose, for a reason to go on, for a clear sign of what I should do. I got my sign courtesy of two envelopes that arrived on my desk the same day. The first was a plain white envelope with no return address, but the postmark was from New Orleans. I tore open the envelope and pulled out a single sheet of paper covered with a childish scrawl in pencil.

> Dear Daniel
> My cousin is righting down what I want to say because I caint right myself. I am so so sorry to leave town without talking to you but I did what seem right to me after Sam came and everthing got so wrong. I no you want me to come back there but I cant do no more harm to you I care to much about you it is not right you shoud suffer from my trubles. I really do love you and no you love me to but you dezerv better then me. Please dont try to find me just go and get on with your life and find a real lady like you ott to have. Sam cant find us ether and We will be ok dont worry about us. Goodbye now just goodbye. She is crying now while she say this mister. love from Evannjuline thats Melva if you dont no.

After I read the letter a second time, I folded it, replaced it in the envelope and dropped it into the drawer where the pictures of Evangeline, Amelia and Garland were. A mixture of relief and pain washed over me, relief at knowing she was safe and pain from the reminder of how much I missed her. It was a hollow, empty feeling and a voice in my head warned me never to try to fill that spot again, that I had done a poor damn job of it every time I'd tried and it was best to stop pushing on that door.

I reached for the second envelope, one that I recognized from the Biograph Company. In it was a check for fifty dollars and another letter from Mr. Dougherty. He wrote, "Two more good ones! I'm getting tired of mailing these checks to you. Why don't you come and collect them in person? I know we can keep you busy here." I got up from the desk, left the office, went out on the Avenue and walked down to the Odeon to see Mr. Snider. I told him what was on my mind. He tried to talk me out of it, but I told him the signs were clear and I was going to follow them.

When I left his office, I had a check in my pocket for my twenty-five percent of the Jewel, plus the current salary and profits owed me. I stopped by the bank and cashed it; I also withdrew all my savings and closed my account. The teller, Mr. Baldwin, asked if I was going somewhere.

"Yes, sir. I'm leaving Austin. Leaving Texas, in fact. I won't be bringing you those bags of nickels anymore, either."

"Well, we'll miss seeing you, Mr. Wilkinson. Where is it you're going?"

"You've been to the pictures, haven't you, Mr. Baldwin?"

"Oh, sure, every chance I get."

"Well, I'm going where those pictures are made. I'm going to see if I can make some of my own, maybe. I'll be right there in the thick of where they make all those cowboy pictures and comedies and romances."

"Where is that?"

"Why, the moving picture capitol of the world, Mr. Baldwin. Fort Lee, New Jersey."

## CHAPTER FORTY-TWO

I sat in my Pullman compartment, watching the countryside roll by. I had spent two nights on the train and had one more before I would roll into New York City. I had never left the state of Texas before and I was curious to see what other states looked like, but so far they all could have been different parts of Texas. Some of the country looked like the Piney Woods of East Texas, while others looked like the Hill Country I had grown up in.

Kelton had been shocked that I was leaving, but he made me promise that if I ever needed someone to do acrobatic things in a picture, I would let him know. I had written my parents from the depot in Austin before my train departed, telling them that I was taking a new step and that I would let them know when I had a new address. I was actually thankful that they didn't have a telephone; it would have been difficult to hear their reactions to my moving so far away.

In my two days on the train, I had jotted down as many ideas for scenarios as I could come up with, wanting to be prepared when I reached the city. I was fairly solvent, thanks to my savings and the money from my portion of the Jewel, and the Pullman compartment had proven to be a most enjoyable way to travel.

I awoke on the fourth day of my journey and raised the window shade. I could see incredibly tall buildings in the distance and my heart leaped at the thought of being in New York City. I quickly dressed and packed my bags. The porter brought breakfast and put away the bed, leaving me a comfortable window seat in which to enjoy my last meal on the train.

As we rolled into the city, my eyes were filled with the sheer size of it. Austin, Dallas, even Houston paled in comparison. I resisted the urge to see the sights and instead hailed a cab, giving the address of the Biograph Company on Fourteenth Street. I went inside and asked for Mr. Dougherty. I introduced myself and he laughed as he shook my hand. "So you did decide to come pick up your checks in person, hey? Good, good! Come on in, there's hardly anyone here. Everyone's out filming today."

I declined Mr. Dougherty's offer of a drink, but sat and talked for half an hour. He asked where I was staying and I told him I did not know, that I had come directly from the station. He picked up a telephone on his desk and called the Astor Hotel, telling them to hold a room for me. "Nothing much to be done around here today, but be here in the morning and you'll see all hell break loose. What are your plans? Are you going to stay in New York?"

"I don't really have a plan. I've sold scenarios to several of the film companies here and I'm hoping to get permanent employment with one of them."

His eyebrows raised. "I didn't know you were writing for anyone else."

"Usually, it was a script that you had already rejected. But I thought it best to have more than one iron in the fire."

"Hmm. Well, I'm sure we can keep you busy right here. I'll talk to the boss. In the meantime, why don't you go check into the hotel and rest awhile? I'll come by and take you to dinner someplace nice, maybe bring a couple of the gang with me. What do you say?"

"I say thank you, that would be fine." I shook his hand and went out to find a cab waiting for me. In a few minutes, we stopped in front of a beautiful hotel. I was impressed, but I knew I would have to find more sensible lodging if I did not wish to deplete my savings too quickly. I checked in and received my key to a room on the twelfth floor. I had never been in a twelve-story building and I was relieved that there was an elevator in the lobby. A young man in a red costume welcomed me to the hotel and recommended some sights and restaurants in the city as we rode slowly upward.

The room was lovely, full of overstuffed leather furniture and greenery, ornate carpeting and a sturdy bed. I unpacked my bags, washed my face and looked out the window. The distance to the street below was dizzying. I opened the window and listened to the sounds of the huge metropolis as I gazed at the buildings stretching far, far into the distance. Then I sat at the desk and wrote to my parents on the hotel's elegant stationery, telling them where I was staying. I decided to change my clothes before dinner and then thought I might as well avail myself of the large bathtub in the suite. After a hot bath, I felt comfortable, but sleepy, so I laid on the bed, intending to rest my eyes for a moment.

I was awakened by a rap on the door. I stumbled back into consciousness and opened the door to find Mr. Dougherty in a cheery mood. "Ready to go?" he asked, although it was obvious I was not, since I had only my drawers on.

"Uh, just a moment," I said. "I fell asleep. Must have been more tired than I thought."

"Sure, sure. Get your duds on and we'll go have something swell at Delmonico's. The girls'll love that."

"Girls?"

"Yeah, I brought along a couple of kids who are in one of the pictures we're working on. Real cuties. You'll love 'em."

"Oh. All right. I'm just… okay, never mind."

I quickly dressed and we rode down to the lobby while Mr. Dougherty told me about the films Biograph was currently preparing. "Tomorrow, we'll take you out to watch one of the crews filming. Maybe you can pick up a few pointers. We've got a new guy directing; he was an actor — not a very good one — and he's written some scenarios for us, too, but I think he might make a good director. Name's Larry Griffith. Oh, hell, that's not right, it's David

Griffith! He was using Larry as his acting name."

We arrived in the lobby and I was introduced to two attractive young women, Victoria Wilson and Monique LaFleur. Victoria was a somewhat stout brunette with a pretty face and curly hair, but her teeth were spaced far apart and she covered her mouth quickly whenever she smiled or laughed. Monique had black, straight hair and full, pouty lips, which she had painted a shocking red. A fake beauty mark had been pencilled onto her cheek and she tried hard to affect a French accent, but I seriously doubted that she had been any closer to Paris than I had been. Still, the girls were talkative and friendly and asked me plenty of questions over dinner about Texas and about managing a nickelodeon. Victoria had appeared in a half-dozen Biograph stories, usually in background crowds, but she had recently had her first chance to "act" by portraying an orphan girl whose dog was stolen. Monique had only been in one film, having just entered the moving picture field two weeks before. She had been cast, predictably, as a seductive French girl in a saloon scene, and apparently felt that her niche was in playing Parisian paramours. Neither girl had any previous acting experience, but Mr. Dougherty said they both photographed well and they were learning quickly.

"Besides, most Broadway actresses wouldn't be caught dead in a moving picture. They think it's beneath 'em. But some of our gang are okay, aren't they, girls?"

The girls nodded in agreement. "Florence is really good," said Victoria.

"Who's Florence?" I queried.

"You know the girl with the long curls that's in a lot of the melodramas?"

"Oh, the Biograph girl? Sure, I've seen her. I didn't know her name, though."

"That's right. We don't want anybody to know her name. If the whole world knows that Florence Lawrence is the Biograph girl, she's liable to ask for a bigger salary. And hell, she's making fifty dollars a week as it is. You girls forget you heard that, hear?"

I could see that visions of dollar signs were dancing in the girls' eyes as they envisioned what they could do with fifty dollars each week. We finished our meal and walked back to the hotel. Mr. Daugherty and the girls tried to entice me to go to a show with them, but I pleaded fatigue and retired to my room, promising to see them in the morning. I sat on the bed in my room, looking out at the seemingly infinite number of lights I could see shining.

Next morning, I was at the Biograph office by eight o'clock and met several other members of the company. David Griffith turned out to be a tall, lanky fellow with an aquiline nose and an exceedingly dramatic way of speaking. When I introduced myself as J.D. Wilkinson, he asked, "And what, pray tell, do those initials stand for?"

"Well… Jubal Daniel. They're both Biblical names and —"

"Of course they are. You're named after a musician and a prophet. What do people call you?"

"Most call me J.D. Some call me Dan…or Daniel."

"Hmm. Pity to waste such a splendid moniker. I shall call you Jubal." In his parlance, it came out "Joooobal."

Monique stage-whispered to me, "Tell him you'll call him 'Wark' if he does."

"Wark?" I said.

"Yes, that's my middle name. David Wark Griffith. It's a family name and I am not ashamed of it, Monique. Although you must be ashamed of your real name, whatever that may be." Monique blushed a vivid pink and the rest of the crew laughed, obviously aware of her pretense.

"This is Billy Bitzer, our cameraman," Mr. Daugherty said, indicating a portly man with a red face, who chewed on an unlit cigar.

"Pleased to meet you," grunted Bitzer as he shook my hand.

"J.D. is the guy that wrote The Bear Suit and Drums Along the Brazos and, well, a bunch of other stuff for us. I'm trying to talk him into joining us permanently, but he's also sold stuff to Kalem and Triangle and other companies."

"Philistines," sniffed Griffith. "Biograph is making the finest films in the world."

"I tend to agree," I said. "But Meliés is doing some nice things as well."

"All trickery, all smokepots and costumes. His stories lack drama. They're fine for children or as a curiosity." For a fellow who had only directed one film, Griffith was certainly sold on his own abilities. I decided to hold my tongue and observe. The crew walked over to Biograph's new studio, where I saw for the first time the banks of greenish Cooper-Hewitt lights which made it possible to film indoors. No longer did Griffith and company have to wait for a sunny day or endure gusty winds in what was supposed to be a quaint drawing room. "Controlling the environment is crucial," he confided in me. "Billy can shoot anything I ask him for, but these lights make it possible to set up a shot with the most flattering lighting and not have to worry about the sun going behind a cloud."

The crew was shooting a scene in a living room involving a father, mother and two young girls. Griffith carried a one-page story which he glanced at occasionally, but it seemed to be only a rough sketch to him and he set about fleshing it out.

"Now, Victoria, you find the note from the kidnapper in the morning mail. You will read it, then react with shock and dismay." Griffith then proceeded to act out the part for Victoria, calling her attention to the motion of his hands and the way his eyes darted about. Victoria, playing the part of one of the young daughters, tried to duplicate Griffith's actions as he observed her. He made some corrections and suggested other things for her to do, then asked Billy Bitzer if he was ready.

"Yes, sir." Bitzer sighted into a brass tube mounted on the side of his camera and shifted the box a fraction of an inch to the left.

"Very well, then, let's begin." Bitzer began to crank the handle on the camera and I heard the whirring of the film through the gate. "Now, Victoria, sort through the mail. Good, good. Open the letter. Read it. Move your head. Now, you are shocked. Frightened! You don't know where to turn. Look all around! Where is your father, your mother? You must tell them! But you feel faint! You almost fall. Now look at the letter again. Now exit. Fine. Stop, Billy." Griffith's stentorian voice had guided Victoria through every action and every emotion and he was satisfied with the scene. He then brought in the father and mother and other daughter to play the scene where Victoria delivers the fateful letter. For each shot, he carefully described their movements, usually acting them out himself, then he watched as they rehearsed the scene several times. Then he would shoot it once or sometimes twice.

I was fascinated as Griffith guided his actors through every motion and emotion, playing them like I would play a hymn on the organ, building to dramatic peaks, then dropping away to a delicate pianissimo. I had been fairly confident that I could direct films, but Griffith's sure hand made me doubt my own abilities.

However, I was to subsequently find out that David Wark Griffith was one of a kind. In the following days, I visited the other studios to which I had sold scenarios. I quickly discovered that most of the men making pictures operated on a much more attainable level. One fellow's "direction" consisted of saying, "Start!" and "Stop!" to the cameraman, who recorded the bumbling and confusion of the cast as they tried to figure out what they should be doing. The nadir of this newly-born skill was probably exhibited by the director at the Imperial Moving Picture Manufacturing Company.

## CHAPTER FORTY-THREE

I had sold only one script to Imperial, a rather feeble melodrama which had been rejected by Biograph, Edison and all my regular patrons. Since it only cost me a stamp to try another company, I finally reached sufficiently low in the barrel to scrape against Imperial. They bought the scenario — for a mere twelve dollars — and made a wretched split-reel story from it that made the Passion Play Leo and I had made look like Ben Hur. I was too embarrassed to even tell my friends that I had written this pile of celluloid, but I decided to drop by their studio, mainly to make a clean sweep of all those who had purchased my work.

Imperial was housed in a rundown brownstone six blocks east of Biograph. The eight steps down from the sidewalk I had to descend to enter the office seemed a fitting metaphor for the drop in quality evidenced by all the Imperial films I had seen. A bald man sat reading Frank Leslie's Illustrated Weekly in a collarless shirt with enormous sweat stains under the arms. Without looking up, he growled, "Yeah? Whadaya want?"

"I'm looking for Mr. VanLandingham."

One fuzzy eyebrow buckled upward and a bloodshot grey eye rolled in my direction.

"Yeah? Who're you?"

"I'm John Winkler," I said, for the first time in my life. You see, Kelton had convinced me that I should use a different pen name with each company. Biograph, who had bought my first scenario and many subsequent ones, knew me by my real name. The Edison Company knew me as James Watson. Kalem wrote their checks to Jim Wilson.

"Who? What do you want?"

"I'm John Winkler," I repeated. "I sold you a scenario a few months back. It was called *The Lady and the Robber*?"

"Oh, right. I'm VanLandingham. What are you doing here?"

"Well, I'm in New York looking at the film business. I've been making the rounds of all the companies, seeing how they do things…"

VanLandingham turned a page in his newspaper and said, "Buzz and the gang are up on the roof, cranking out another masterpiece, if you wanna go take a look."

"Oh, fine. Thanks." I waited for further instructions, but it became clear that none were forthcoming. So I looked around until I found a staircase. I climbed five full flights before arriving on the roof of the brownstone. There I found six people. The four men were smoking cigars while the two women talked, their heads close together. Near one edge of the roof was a camera on a tripod. Opposite it was a flimsy, three-sided set which seemed intended to portray a sitting room. A threadbare couch, an overstuffed armchair, a potted palm and a grandfather clock were placed in front of the poorly painted backdrop. A door was painted onto one wall; a window and a hanging landscape were painted on the middle section. On the third panel, another door was denoted by a rectangle of white paint. As a set, it rivaled the worst I had ever seen in vaudeville.

The six people looked at me; no one spoke to me, so I introduced myself. "Hello. I'm John Winkler. Uh, I wrote a scenario for this company a while back. Mr. VanLandingham said I could come up and take a look. I hope I'm not interrupting."

"Aw, hell, you're not interrupting anything but a bull session," said a stocky fellow in a bowler. "I'm Buzz Vernon. I crank the box while these hooligans pull the monkeyshines." He indicated the other with a jerk of his thumb as he extended his hand.

A handsome young fellow stepped up to greet me. "I'm Wallace Flatt. Nice to meet you. I'm in this picture, but I usually work downstairs. Duping films." I shook his hand, then turned to see an older gent, dressed in a butler's outfit. He looked fairly convincing as an English manservant, but the illusion was spoiled when he opened his mouth and I was given my first glimpse of the Bronx.

"Hey, howyadoon? I'm Bertie Hansen. Where ya from?"

"Texas. My first trip to New York."

Bertie clapped me on the shoulder. "Well, you made it to the big town now, Johnny-boy! Ya need any advice about what to see or do, lemme know, you got it?"

"Yes, thanks."

"Here, meet the girls. Lorna, Agnes, meet Johnny-boy!" Lorna was dark-haired and stout and looked at me as though I was a new item on the menu and she was feeling like a snack. She was wearing a maid's uniform and performed a clumsy curtsy as I clasped her hand. Agnes was a thin, timid-looking girl with frizzy light brown hair and large, liquid eyes. She was wearing a long blue velvet dress and was apparently playing the lady of the house.

That accounted for five-sixths of the group; the last was a forty-ish Irish man with red hair going gray and a straw boater on his head. He stepped up only when I had met everyone else and snapped, "I am Henry Harmon. I am the director. This is my picture. You're welcome to watch if you can stay out of the way." He didn't extend his hand, but wheeled and returned to a chair placed next to the camera. "Come on, let's get back to it. Van's gonna can us all if we don't finish this thing."

Henry Harmon had an ego comparable to D.W. Griffith's; unfortunately, he had absolutely no talent to back it up. My experience watching Griffith direct had made me wonder if I could perform such a task, but watching Harmon convinced me that a monkey could do no worse. His approach was original — and it was destined to remain unique, since no sane person would ever use it again.

Harmon told the four actors where to stand for the scene and then told Buzz to begin cranking the camera. I was watching the actors when I was startled by Harmon's shout of "Three! Three!" I turned to see what he was doing, but he was watching the actors intently. Then he shouted, "One! No, one!" I looked back at the actors and saw that Agnes was crying and making pleading motions with her hands.

"Four! Four!" came the cry, and Agnes showed an expression of surprise. I realized that Harmon had boiled down the whole of acting to a half-dozen or so emotions and actions, assigned a number to each, and simply shouted them to get the reaction he wanted. He abruptly stopped the scene and yelled, "Dammit, Aggie, I said 'Four' and you gave me a 'Two' instead! Can't you keep it straight? Four, FOUR!"

"I'm sorry, Henry. I got mixed up." She was embarrassed at being corrected in front of everyone else, and I felt sorry for her. At the same time, I wanted to kick Henry Harmon in the pants. I watched awhile longer, then retreated down the stairs to find Mr. VanLandingham, who had finished his newspaper and was now trimming his fingernails with a huge pair of scissors.

"Find 'em?" he said.

"Yes, I did."

"Learn anything?" He stopped clipping and looked at me.

"I'm not sure I could learn anything from Mr. Harmon. His methods are... odd."

"Odd? Hell, he's an idiot. But he's all I got. Why, you think you can do better?"

"Mr. VanLandingham, I could take a blind cameraman and a handful of Kewpie dolls and get a better performance on film than he can."

"So you say. Ever done it?"

"Well, I did direct a Biblical drama a few years ago. It came out pretty well. But I left the picture business for awhile, and when I got back into it, it was as a writer."

Snip. The scissors went back to work on Mr. VanLandingham's thumbnail. "Other words, you haven't done any directing since — what? — the Vitascope days?"

"Yes, sir, I guess that's true. But I'm confident I can put a good story together. How did Mr. Harmon get the job directing?"

"He was developing film down in the basement. When Billings left, Henry volunteered. He's done thirty one-reelers so far."

"Is he getting better?"

For the first time, I saw the unsightly smile of Lucas VanLandingham. It was a grin without joy, without mirth, but he apparently felt it made him look pleasant. "Hell, no, he's not getting better. He's sure getting harder to live with, though. He thinks he's God's gift to the show business. I don't give a damn about that; I just need a reel a week that I can sell a few dozen copies of. Henry's sales are dropping off."

"Look, Mr. VanLandingham, I ran a nickelodeon in Texas. I know what people want to see. I know that the Imperial name doesn't sell a ticket in Austin unless there's a reel of something else playing that day. I'd like the chance to write a scenario and then see it through the filming stage."

The scissors went back into the desk drawer and Mr. VanLandingham pulled out a pencil and began digging in his ear with the blunt end. "Winkler, I'm not interested in changing the world. Some of our pictures play just as well if you run 'em backward. As long as they sell, I'm a happy clam. All I ask is that they be made on time…cheap…and mostly in focus. What did I pay you for your script?"

"Twelve dollars."

"Okay, here's the deal: I give you twelve for your next story and…say, eighteen for directing it. That's thirty dollars a week to start. If you take more than six days to shoot it, I'll dock your pay. Wanna try it?"

"All right. When do I start?"

"Well, unless you want to go upstairs and fire Henry, you better wait until Monday. Have a story ready and be here by eight."

I agreed to these terms and left the office before Mr. Vanlandingham could proceed further with his grooming rituals. In the following five days, I spent additional time watching Griffith work on his latest Biograph and trying to come up with a good story idea.

## CHAPTER FORTY-FOUR

When I again entered the dingy sprawl of Imperial on Monday, I had a single page scenario in my hand. It was called *The Watchful Women* and dealt with a pair of old maids who constantly eavesdropped on events which occurred on their front steps, especially when a young man would bid his sweetheart goodnight on the stoop. VanLandingham took the script, laid it on his desk unread, and gave me a tour of the premises.

In the basement was a filthy laboratory for developing and printing films, with huge drying racks and deep vats of smelly chemicals. The floor above had a rudimentary business office. The second floor was taken up with several battered tables which sagged under the weight of hundreds of film cans and reels. I recognized Wallace Flatt as one of four men at work on strips of film. He grinned when he saw me and waved me over. "Hallo! Glad to see you back. Looking forward to working with you."

"Thanks. What's that you're working on?"

"This? Oh, it's the new Pathé film. Getting it ready to duplicate."

"What do you mean? What do you have to do to get it ready?"

"Look here, I'll show you." He held a strip of film up to the light coming in through the windows which lined the front of the second floor. Handing me a jeweler's loupe, he said, "See the rooster on the mantelpiece?"

"Yes. The Pathé logo."

"Right! Well, I've got to paint it out of each frame so we can sell copies of it."

I may have mentioned earlier that the concept of copyright was somewhat hazy in the early period of moving pictures. Companies did their best to protect their films, and many had resorted to placing their company logo somewhere in each scene. While this was not terribly noticeable in indoor scenes, it could become bizarre when an outdoor scene featured a tree, a picnic spread, and a picture company logo planted in the ground like an odd plant. I thought Mr. VanLandingham might be embarrassed at Wallace's willingness to spill the beans so quickly, but he grinned his sharky smile and said, "Wally's the best I ever had at erasing trademarks. I can sell forty or fifty dupes of this and make a damn nice profit."

"I see." I can't pretend that I was highly offended by this activity. What did I know about copyright? In later years I would grow increasingly possessive about film rights, but such rights had not been clearly defined by law in 1908.

On the third floor were racks of costumes, every one seemingly past its prime, but still usable according to the Imperial standard. And finally, on the roof, the three-sided set of stage flats, waiting to be used for…for my directorial debut.

After we returned to the office, Mr. VanLandingham quickly scanned the scenario I had brought. "Okay, what's it gonna take to put this on celluloid?"

"Well, I thought that one set could be the front stoop of an apartment building and another could be the drawing room of th—"

"Another? We've never used two sets on a picture yet and we're not going to start now. You can use the drawing room set Henry left from last week. And if you've got to have a stoop, you can shoot out in front of the building."

Wishing to appear agreeable, I did not quibble with this compromise.

"Okay, how many bodies? Two old ladies, one young one, three or four fellows. That it?"

I nodded.

"I don't know about the old broads," he continued. "You'll have to make up some young ones or go find 'em yourself. You can use Wallace and some of the lab guys for the other parts. Maybe play one yourself?"

"Um, well, what are we allowed to spend for actors? If they come from outside, I mean?"

"Try to get 'em for a buck a day, but you can go to two if you have to."

"W—Where can I find actresses?"

"Jesus Christ! Are you gonna direct this picture or do I have to do it all? You've got until Friday to put a reel of something in a can. Do it!" VanLandingham turned, clearly dismissing me and I went outside to sit on the stoop for awhile.

Here I was, in New York for less than two weeks, knowing no one, and now having to dig up a cast. For the rest of the day, I visited theatrical agencies in the Broadway area, but every agent sneered at me. One told me, "What legitimate actress is going to appear in your lousy flickers? No self-respecting theatrical will risk their career for a couple days work."

I was discouraged when I made my way toward the hotel that evening, having struck out at every turn. I asked for my key at the front desk and climbed the stairs to my room, where I sat on the bed staring at the Currier & Ives print on the wall, mulling over my options. It didn't take long. I was going to have to make two old women out of two young ones.

I sat there on the bed, motionless. But all of a sudden my shoulders began to shake and I started laughing out loud. I crossed over to the dresser and took two of the Lucifer matches out of the brass cup. They were normally used to light the gas jet, but I had a different purpose in mind. I lit the matches, letting the thin sticks blacken and shrivel, then blew out the flame. When the burnt matchsticks had cooled, I used them to trace wrinkles across my forehead, around my eyes and mouth. I pulled the crocheted bedspread off the bed and draped it over my head like a scarf. Then I stood before the mirror on the washstand and made scowling faces. I could scarcely keep scowling because I was so amused by the sight in the looking glass — a hideous old crone. The grotesque illusion was marred by two things: first, I needed a wig; and second, I was probably going to have to shave my moustache.

## CHAPTER FORTY-FIVE

Next morning, I removed the underbrush beneath my nose and walked to the Imperial building, where I collared Mr. VanLandingham. I launched into a spirited spiel, tapping into my reserve supply of blarney and soft soap, in an effort to convince him to play one of the old gossiping women with me. At first he was adamantly opposed, but I somehow convinced him that we could sell more copies of this story than any other film in Imperial's short, inglorious history. Money was always the prime motivator with VanLandingham and he perked up when I told him I would forfeit my salary if we didn't sell at least seventy-five copies of the film. We shook hands on it and then went up to the second floor where Mr. VanLandingham foraged through a trunk full of ratty wigs until he found two white ones that would serve. There was a small makeup kit in the costume room and I drew lines on his face, then on my own. I had hired Agnes to play the girl in the film and she helped apply beauty marks and rouge to our faces. The men who worked in the building began to pop in and out of the costume room, bursting into laughter as they saw us, then leaving to fetch a coworker to share in the laughs.

We found a couple of dowager dresses; mine fit fairly well, but Mr. VanLandingham's could not be buttoned up in the back, so he could not turn his back to the camera. We went up to the roof, where the rest of the cast waited. I described the first scene to them, then waited while Buzz set up the camera, looking through the ground glass lens to frame the shot and adjust the focus.

For three days we cavorted on the rooftop, having a grand time. Mr. VanLandingham was already in his dress by the time I got to work on the second and third days; the acting bug seemed to have bit him rather deeply. In the evening, Buzz and I watched the film from the day before and we found ourselves laughing all over again at the absurd activities on screen.

After three days, we had filmed everything I could think of to do with the brief scenario. I stood beside Buzz while he spliced the various scenes together. Finally, we shot a title card, painted by a German sign painter across the street: The Watchful Women. On Saturday, Aggie, Wally, Buzz, Mr. VanLandingham and I sat in the darkened room and watched my first one-reeler. Aggie and Wally laughed a great deal. Buzz laughed, too, but since he had seen the footage several times, his laughs weren't quite as hearty. I experienced that curiously naked feeling of allowing other people to see what formerly existed only in my head. But when I looked at Mr. VanLandingham, I saw the wicked smile and I could have sworn I heard the sound of cash registers.

*The Watchful Women* sold one hundred and fourteen copies, almost twice as many as the previous best-selling Imperial film. It ended the directing-by-numbers career of Henry Harmon and gave a great boost to mine. I was now Lucas VanLandingham's golden boy and he paid me well. We embarked on a series of films and I was given free reign to devise or adapt the stories of my choice. I acquired the right to read the scripts submitted to Imperial; at first, they were ninety-nine percent awful, but, as my films began to reach the marketplace, the quality of the scripts improved. I soon settled into a routine of filming one script from another writer, one of my own, and one adapted — swiped — from another source. As far as I know, Imperial was the first company to film *The Taming of the Shrew* — in one reel, no less! They weren't all great, by any means, but they all made money. Every one of them.

I kept in touch with David Griffith and we sometimes met on weekends to go to a theater, sometimes seeing our own films, sometimes seeing those of our competitors. Whichever, we critiqued every picture over a fine meal, arguing how a story could have been more effective or whether an audience could understand a particular point of editing. I also ran into Griffith occasionally in New Jersey, where virtually all of the New York film companies went to shoot outdoor scenes for Westerns or other stories that weren't set in the city.

It was a fun time, and I felt as though I had the Midas touch. Oh, I knew my films weren't as good as Griffith's, but they weren't as bad as most of the others available. But Griffith was a once-in-a-lifetime sort of talent; he found ways to convey emotion, suspense and action that had literally never existed before, inventing a new way to tell a story.

I suppose we could have rocked along forever in this idyllic little business. But, as usually happens when money is being made, someone decided they should get more money than anyone else. In this case, that person was the Wizard of Menlo Park. Thomas Edison, in an attempt to gain control of the entire motion picture business, formed the Motion Pictures Patent Company. The members of this group included almost everyone who owned a patent related in some way to the pictures. They contended that no one could use a motion picture camera unless they were a member of the group and paid a royalty for every foot of film. If Edison truly believed this would eliminate his competition, he was sorely mistaken. Instead, a group of outlaws sprang up, defying the Patent Company while continuing to make films.

Now, which group would you expect Lucas VanLandingham to join? I can still hear the echo of the epithet he spat when he learned of the conditions for joining the Patents group. He swore that that "light bulb blowing sonofabitch" could wait till hell froze over before he'd get a penny in tribute from Lucas VanLandingham.

Thus began my career as an outlaw. On countless mornings, the ragtag Imperial crew took the ferry to New Jersey, where we did most of our outdoor shooting. The difference from previous trips was that we now added a new employee, Herman Switzer, whose sole responsibility was to lookout for detectives hired by Edison and the Patents group. When one of these shamuses was spotted, I would throw a blanket over our camera and Wally — our fastest runner — would dash into the woods with it. This was no idle practice, since the detectives had been known to put a bullet through a camera, effectively ending the usefulness of that machine and ruining the day's filming. Mr. VanLandingham purchased a Gaumont camera, which we packed along on location. The Gaumont was almost worthless for taking moving pictures, frequently jamming and causing the film to buckle and jump right out of the gate, but it worked on a different principle from the Edison patents and hence did not infringe on them. When a stranger confronted us and demanded to know what we were doing, I could show him the Gaumont and get a brief respite from harassment.

The nickelodeon craze was in full swing and showed no signs of slowing down. At Imperial, I was regularly grinding out two reels every week. We worked six long days most weeks, although there were times when we even had to film on Sunday, due to a bad batch of film or excessive interference from the Patents Company goons.

It was an astonishing time to be alive. Any kernel of a story idea that popped into my head would soon find its way onto film. Being responsible for two reels of film a week educates a fellow in short order. Some weeks we came close to Art; other weeks we had to hold our noses until the film was canned.

## CHAPTER FORTY-SIX

In 1910, I sent a telegram to Kelton Hendricks, telling him I needed a redheaded comic actor who dressed in ridiculous clothing and acted like a monkey. He arrived almost before his letter of acceptance got back to me. I arranged a room for Kelton in the hotel where I lived; as he gazed out the window at the metropolis, I told him that my name was now John Winkler. He nodded, then turned and looked hard at me. "What am I supposed to do, uh, John? Do you have some ideas?"

"Not at the moment, Kel. But when the time comes, so will the ideas. Meanwhile, let's go see the city." I had spent many of my Sundays becoming familiar with New York and I shared my knowledge with Kelton. We climbed up to the torch on the Statue of Liberty, whooping and laughing as we looked over the railing at the ground far below. The Lady had not yet begun to turn green and I remember the coppery shine of the gigantic arm below us.

We saw George M. Cohan on Broadway and were lucky enough to find the Three Keatons playing the Palace. We went back to talk to Joe, Myra and Buster, who was now in his teens, but still taking an amazing amount of rough-housing from his father in the act.

On Monday morning, though, I introduced Kelton to the rest of our troupe and we started on a new story. I let Kelton watch the first day, explaining how the actors had to stay within the chalked lines on the roof or else be out of the frame. In the afternoon, he sidled up to me self-consciously and I could tell he wanted to say something. "What is it, Kel? Got an idea?"

"Well, I'm not sure. What if the guy on the ladder gets his foot stuck in the paint bucket? And then the ladder starts to sway and it tips over and he goes with it… except the top of the ladder hits right there at the window and he tumbles right out of it. Would that be funny?"

"It sounds funny to me. But I'm not sure Bertie is going to want to take a tumble like that."

"I can do it! Let me do it, John!" Kelton was vibrating with excitement; he had waited for years for this moment.

"If you do it, Kel, I'm going to have to reshoot the previous scene where Bertie came in to paint the room. I don't know. I'd sure like to have that shot, though." I paced a moment, then decided to splurge and give Kelton his chance. After he eyed the scene and tipped the ladder to measure the distance to the window, he placed the ladder where he thought it should go and chalk-marked the floor around the legs of the ladder. Then he put on the costume Bertie had worn, climbed the ladder and looked at me, somewhat less confidently than before.

"Alright, everyone, let's try it," I said. "Ready, Buzzy? Okay, begin… good… okay… ready when you are, Kel." The ladder swayed, righted again, then tipped toward the window. As the ladder fell, Kelton flew right through the window and the rest of the cast cheered and applauded. I was about to tell Buzz to stop cranking when one of Kelton's hands gripped the windowsill; then the other hand appeared and then the goofy face of my best friend was framed in the window, smiling the smile of one who has triumphed over dire fate. "Hold that pose, Kel. Wally! Drop the window!" Behind the flat, Wally released the window so that it came down on Kelton's fingers. His face made a priceless expression of pain and his wide mouth opened in a big yowl. He pulled his hands out of the window and promptly dropped out of sight.

Everyone was laughing and clapping and I was exhilarated by the comical scene that had grown so easily from a simple idea. Kelton emerged from behind the flats, grinning and rubbing his sore fingers, but his pain was forgotten as the other cast members slapped his back and praised his comedic talents.

In the ensuing months, Kelton and I began to concoct more and more comedies. He was too odd-looking to successfully play a dramatic part, but he was perfect for laughs. Imperial Films began to find a larger and larger audience and we were beginning to receive letters from people all over the country who wanted to know the names of various members in our troupe, especially Kelton and Agnes. Mr. VanLandingham, knowing that fame for his stars would cost him more money, refused to release the names of any actors, instructing the secretaries to refer to Kelton as "Imperial Ike" and to Agnes as "That Imperial Ingenue."

There was a great deal of money to be made, supplying fodder to the thousands of nickelodeons that now dotted the country. Rare indeed was the town which had no flickers showing. Imperial was gaining some prestige, not on the level of Biograph or Vitagraph, but not the company of last resort it had formerly been. VanLandingham, although a boorish and thrifty man, treated me well, and I was able to build up quite a good nest egg. This time, though, I kept most of it in a bank instead of in a grouch bag around my neck. I sent money home on several occasions, but Father always sent it back, adding that they were doing fine but they appreciated the gesture.

Living in New York City held more temptation than Austin could have imagined, but I focused so intently on my work that I had little time or desire for anything else. Kelton, however, soon knew every bar, every bordello, every bookie in town. He was making more money than he ever had before, but it burned a large hole in his pocket and he often hit me up for a twenty to buy a drink for his latest and loveliest friend. He had maintained contact with Delphine for awhile, but now he never spoke of her and the relationship seemed to have ended.

As the moving picture found a larger and larger audience, we began to attract more actors from the legitimate stage. And a never-ending string of young women came by the Imperial office, usually after trying two or three other companies, seeking to audition for the flickers.

Many of these applicants were young, beautiful and eager for acceptance, a risky combination in the City. Kelton, Wally, Buzz and some of the other guys felt as though a buffet was being served and tried their best to be present when VanLandingham and I held auditions. I maintained my distance, remaining professional and frequently cautioning the young ladies about the dangers inherent in being an actress. Even back in 1910 there were men who made films of young women being disrobed and debauched. But young ears hear what they want to hear, I suppose, and I doubt many of them were swayed by my cautionary tales.

The winters in New York were difficult for me. I had rarely seen snow in Texas, and hardly ever more than an inch or two on the ground. Now I was faced with bitter cold and great drifts of snow and I thought I would never be warm again. One day we were filming a chase in New Jersey and I stood most of the day in shin-high snow, directing the cast, yearning for Texas and sun and warmth. But the only heat was from the Patents Company; even on that snowy day, a detective trailed us and interrupted the filming to demand that we show him the inside of our camera so he could determine if we were violating the Edison patents. Instead, Buzzy and I showed him the Colt revolvers we wore inside our long overcoats and offered to show him how they worked. He cursed and said he'd be back, but we changed locations frequently to avoid further confrontation.

Mr. VanLandingham, with dollars signs dancing in his eyes, was eager to increase Imperial's production schedule. This could not be done with our present crew, so he instructed me to look around for another cameraman and director. I began to study other companies' product and I found that the films of the Eldorado Film Company were photographed well, better than most others. Eldorado was based in Philadelphia and I wrote a letter to the company, politely inquiring who their cameraman was. I received a terse reply which said that Eldorado did not release names of its employees. I could scarcely quibble about this, since Imperial had a similar policy. VanLandingham hired a detective of his own to travel to Philly to find out the name of the cameraman. Four days later, the detective returned with the knowledge we sought, and I wrote a letter to one Leonard Magnum, care of the Vantage Hotel in Philadelphia.

Dear Mr. Magnum,

Please allow me to introduce myself. I am John Winkler, director of Imperial Films in New York City. Our company is growing at a rapid rate and I am looking for a qualified camera operator to build a second production unit. I have seen your work in several Eldorado pictures and believe you are more than qualified for this job. I would like the opportunity to speak with you about this position. Naturally, I am aware that discretion is necessary. So, if you are interested in merely discussing this job, I would be happy to meet with you at the place of your choosing, perhaps on a Sunday afternoon? Please advise me of your wishes in this matter.

I received an answer in three days that Mr. Magnum was indeed interested in talking and would be coming to New York in two weeks. We arranged for him to come by the Imperial building on Sunday at two o'clock and I told Mr. VanLandingham I would interview the prospective employee. He was amenable, ready to do anything that I told him would increase film production.

So, on the designated Sunday, I had lunch, then walked to the office, unlocked the front door and seated myself behind VanLandingham's oaken desk. Promptly at two, the door opened and a bald man with spectacles walked in, wearing a nice overcoat and impeccably dressed. I stood and held out my hand. "Mr. Magnum? I'm John Winkler. Pleased to meet you."

But Magnum only stared at me. My hand remained outstretched, waiting. But it began to shake when Mr. Magnum, in a quavering voice, said, "Professor?"

## CHAPTER FORTY-SEVEN

"Leo?" I shouted. "Is it you?"

"Yes, J.D. Yes, it is!" We both began to cry as we embraced. I looked more carefully at his face and could now see the vestiges of the Leopold Matula I once knew. The moustache was gone, along with most of the hair, and the glasses changed his appearance, but it was truly my old friend! We both talked at the same time, trying to pour out more than was possible. Finally we sat down and caught our breath.

"Leo, how is this possible?" I began. "I thought you were dead!"

"I thought the same thing about you. What happened to you?"

For the first time in years, I relived the night of the fire in Fort Worth. I told Leo how I had jumped off the balcony, breaking my ankle, and crawled to the the front of the theater, looking for Texana. I told of falling into the pit, eventually reaching the outside, unable to find Texana. His mouth tightened as I told him about passing out as someone stole our money and my father's watch.

"God damn that person," he spat. "J.D., when the fire began to spread, I headed for the stairs. Got knocked down in the rush and trampled on. By the time I got to the lobby, the smoke was heavy and the heat was unbearable. I was looking for Texana, too, but when I tried to get into the theater, it was all in flame. I noticed my clothes were beginning to smolder and I dropped to the floor and began crawling toward the front door. Something fell across my legs, a drapery or something and suddenly I was on fire. I finally found the door and made it outside, where some folks threw a wet blanket over me and put out the flames. I must have blacked out then and that's the last I knew until I woke up in a hospital. I had some pretty bad burns on my legs and back…and on my left arm, see? But I was lucky to be alive.

"I laid in that bed for around three weeks. On the second or third day, a young policeman came to see me. He said they wanted me to help them identify one of the victims of the fire. I was barely able to talk, from the smoke and all, but I said I'd try. Then the cop said, 'Do you know the owner of this watch?' and he showed me this." Leo pulled from his vest pocket the watch my father had given me, more than fourteen years before. "Well, I got sorta shook up then, and I told him yes, I knew the owner. He was my best friend. And he said that you had been killed." Leo and I were both crying now, as I held Father's watch in my fingers, feeling the intricate molding.

"I asked him about Texana and he told me she was gone, too," Leo continued. "It was quite a setback. The cop said they would take care of everything, but he left the watch with me. They kept me pretty full of morphine for a few days and then I had to think about what to do with myself. But…but why would that cop tell me you were dead, J.D.?"

"I don't get it either, Leo. If he stole my watch, why would he turn around and give it to you? It doesn't make sense."

We sat in silence for a few moments. Then Leo told me how he'd gone to Houston, trying to find a job in the picture business. He ended up working for a photographer, where he learned a great deal about lighting, lenses and composition. He had gradually made his way east as the picture business grew and bought a German camera, with which he started filming parades, military exercises, public ceremonies and the like. Some of these he was able to sell to the various newsreel companies and he soon was able to support himself as a cameraman.

He had been with Eldorado for three years and was ready for a change, since Philadelphia had only a small film industry. His desire to leave was only intensified when he learned who I was, so we spent the afternoon talking — not about his new position, but catching up on the details of the last twelve years. It was astonishing that we had found each other again, after presuming the other to be dead for so long.

As the light outside the windows turned gray and the office darkened, Leo said, "You know… we could start up our own company again."

The same idea had been brewing in my mind. I felt little compunction to remain loyal to Mr. VanLandingham. It would be nice to start over with just Leo and myself. I felt sure Kelton would join us, which would be helpful because of his increasing popularity and recognition. I only had one suggestion.

"Leo, can we go somewhere that's warm?"

## CHAPTER FORTY-EIGHT

I could smell Hollywood before I could see it. In 1911, the town was still surrounded by orange groves and dirt roads. The open cab I had hired came to a stop in front of the Hollywood Hotel, a rambling two-story affair. I had arrived in Los Angeles by train that morning and quickly decided that the City of Angels would be too distracting for a home base. Hollywood was eight miles away, but the difference was remarkable. It was a clean little town with neat rows of houses and the scent of oranges hung in the air. The driver of the cab informed me that the ocean was only a few miles west. "And if you go the other direction, you've got mountains, you've got desert. It's all right here, mister."

I was impressed. What a wealth of locations were at hand here! From snow to sand to surf to sidewalk, any sort of film could be made close by. I cannot claim prescience here. Centaur Films already had an office in Hollywood, but the paint was still fresh on their windows.

When Leo and Kelton and I agreed to start our own company, we first thought of moving back to Texas. But Griffith, who had made a brief trip to California to make a film, suggested we at least consider the Los Angeles area. I had come as the advance team to see if it was a workable location.

I checked into the Hollywood Hotel and got settled in my room. The following morning I hired a car and drove around Hollywood in every direction. I found mansions which would make ideal film settings, craggy hillocks which could hide all manner of cowboys and outlaws, a beautiful blue ocean with wide and sandy beaches. Ideas for scenarios began to fill my head and I didn't even bother driving out to the desert or the mountains. I simply drove, feeling the sun on my face and the cooling breeze, gazing at the first palm trees I had ever seen — not in a pot, anyway. Texas had lots of sunshine, too, but I had never felt weather like this. Clear skies, clean air, warm sun, cool breeze…and California was a long way from the Patents Company and its goons. I was not the first to fall in love with Southern California and I would certainly not be the last.

Leo had asked me if I wanted to call our new company Jubilee again. I told him no; there were too many unpleasant memories connected with that name. Instead, I suggested Phoenix Films. He smiled. "Oh, I get it. Rising from the ashes, eh? Okay, fine with me."

Kelton had agreed to join our company. I offered him a partnership, but he didn't have any money to invest, since he had been a contract player at Imperial. He merely asked for a raise from what he was getting and if I could come up with a better name for him than Imperial Ike. "And I'd like my name to be shown on the screen. Like in a play, you know? Why shouldn't the audience know who the actors are?"

I didn't have a good answer for him. VanLandingham had always preached that increased recognition of actors would lead to increased salaries and increased headaches. But I couldn't imagine Kelton giving me problems on either account. "Fine, Kel. Do you want to be Kelton Hendricks?"

"I don't think so. Let me think on that one. I want something folks'll remember."

I found a barn on Cahuenga Street (a dirt road) and arranged to rent it from its owner for a year. I engaged a carpenter to put some small office in the upper part of the loft and to build a large, open stage out behind it. We would be doing almost all our filming outdoors until we had built up enough capital to buy some studio lights. Between the outdoor stage and the myriad outdoor settings available, though, I did not feel handicapped by this limitation. I wired Leo and Kelton to buy their train tickets and come join me.

I was standing in the middle of the dirt street, watching a sign painter put the finishing touches on the brilliant red Phoenix Films logo on the front of the converted barn. I was thinking about how to find actors. I also needed a business manager, since I did not relish the idea of trying to keep the books while I was the sole director of the company.

But I had to be ready with a script and a cast by the time Leo and Kelton arrived. I spent evenings in the hotel, scribbling out ideas. During the days I visited local businesses, introducing myself and looking for interesting-looking people who might be interested in being in the pictures. The experience of being in a moving picture did not have the allure it would have in another year or two. Most people viewed my inquiry as though I was trying to talk them into some sort of nuisance. "What, spend a whole day outside play-acting? I'd be embarrassed!"

I was eager to use the rolling streets of Hollywood in a chase. There were very few autos around and the streets were clear most of the time. I finally decided that our first film should be a cops and robbers comedy. Kelton would be the kooky leader of the police force and we could end with a wild chase down those streets.

Leo and Kelton arrived together on the Chief and I picked them up. I had decided to buy a large touring car, since I figured we would need it in getting from location to location, so I was sitting in a big yellow Pierce-Arrow when they emerged from the station. After loading them and their luggage, I drove them through Los Angeles and along the coastline. Kelton, who had grown up on the coast in Galveston, was not so interested in the scenery as he was in telling me his ideas about a new name for himself.

"How about Kenneth Hampton?"

"Ugh. How about Imperial Ike?"

"Konnie Karlson?"

"Nope."

"Keith Happy?"

"You can't be serious."

"Aw, it'd be great! A comedian with the last name Happy?"

"Keep going."

He did. He didn't seem to be reading from a list, but he seemed to have a million names stored away somewhere. Leo was merely enjoying the ride and the fresh air; he had heard the list on the train. My own attention was beginning to lag, when Kelton finally suggested, "Kelly Green?"

"Hmm. Now that one I like. Kelly Green. What do you think, Leo?"

"Fine with me."

And so Phoenix Films began shooting the first Kelly Green and His Boys In Blue story. We built a small set for the interior of the police station on the deck behind the barn. Otherwise, every scene was shot on the streets of Hollywood. Leo would stand at the bottom of the hill, slowly undercranking the camera as two autos came careening down. When projected at a normal speed, the cars seemed to be traveling at incredibly dangerous rates of speed. When a car turned suddenly, spilling Kelton out in a somersault, it was quite amusing.

It is useful to remember that the aspects of the pictures which became clichés were all once brand spanking new. There was a first time for a pie fight, for a damsel tied to the tracks, for a fat man to slip on a banana peel. Such ideas delighted audiences at the time and a laughing audience is hard to argue with.

Kelton, Leo and I all lived at the Hollywood Hotel for several months, until we began to see sufficient returns from some of our early reels. The Kelly Green films proved to be very popular with audiences and we turned out two of them each month. For our other two films, we tried whatever ideas occurred to us: westerns, costume dramas, love stories, tales swiped from classic literature. I felth immense freedom at being in California and away from the charming Lucas VanLandingham, who had not taken my departure gracefully.

We drew our actors mostly from inexperienced locals who hung around when we were filming on the streets. A pretty girl or a hefty man who enjoyed watching the antics of Kelly Green and His Boys In Blue could usually be tempted into service by the offer of ten dollars a day. That's how we found Gus Alonzo, a 350-pound giant with the disposition of a puppy. As he watched Kelton's antics, Gus's whole body shook with a contagious laugh. He was surprised when I asked if he was interested in being in the pictures, having no acting experience. But when we put a large moustache on him and put him between Kelton and the crook he was chasing, the humorous value increased immediately.

Thanks to the presence of our company and a small handful of others, Southern California was soon becoming known as a center of picture-making. There were plenty of real cowboys around who could do trick riding or rope anything you asked them to. Their normal working clothes spared us the expense of costuming them and they were always happy to pick up ten bucks for a day's work.

As the picture business around Hollywood began to grow, people started showing up on our doorstep each morning. This was actually a blessing; it saved much of my time because I didn't have to go out searching for cast members. A little before eight each morning I could step outside the office, survey the forty or fifty people there and say, "Okay, I'll need six pirates today and a large lady who doesn't mind getting dirty." Then I'd simply point out the ones I liked and take them back inside for costuming and makeup. It was a valuable pool of talent, virtually all of which had never acted before.

A lack of acting experience was not the handicap you might think. The director's role was to elicit the desired performance from each actor and I had several tools at my disposal. Since all film was silent, the director could talk continuously through the scene, telling the actor exactly when to look up, when to be frightened, when to jump up and run. Sometimes this was difficult; another scene might be filming on the opposite side of the scenery, while carpenters were building sets for another scene. Hence developed the use of the megaphone. For quiet, intimate scenes, I used a small one, less than a foot long. For scenes on the street involving several people, I used one almost four feet long.

Another tool was music. Actors, especially women actors, responded well to music played during their scenes. If crying was called for, a pump organ or a violin would began playing Hearts and Flowers or something similar as I spoke gently to the woman, telling of the tragic things she was enduring. Seldom did I fail to get the weepy reaction needed for the film.

Since actors did not have to deliver lines, scripts were frequently little more than an idea or a setting on which we could hang a series of gags and stunts. For comedy, broad gestures were still the norm. Guz Alonzo became the master of what we called the "slow burn," in which he would go from happiness to insane rage in about 15 seconds.

In dramatic stories, a more naturalistic style of acting was coming into vogue. D.W. Griffith was the leader in this trend, and everyone else followed along. Dramatic actors were more difficult to find and required more careful coaching than did comics.

A new profession also started around this time. Some mornings I would look over the crowd of hopefuls in front of the studio and ask if anyone could jump off a cliff or slide down a telephone pole or be dragged behind an automobile. I never had trouble finding volunteers. Many of the cowboys were game for anything and the majority of the first group of what became known as "stunt men" came from their ranks.

Phoenix Films was prospering and so was Hollywood. The locals, first bewildered by the new industry, grew to like and accept the presence of this manic group. And why not? If you owned an impressive-looking house, you were certain to be offered a handsome sum to allow a few scenes to be taken in front of it. However, some citizens grew to resent the constant presence of film people on the streets, especially when the Boys In Blue were competing with the Keystone Kops and other similar casts in doing spectacular chase scenes down residential streets. In fact, it was the Hollywood locals who first coined the term "movies," although they used it to refer to the people in film rather than the films themselves.

It was not uncommon to read ads in the paper like: "Room to let, clean, furnished. 18 dollars a month. No animals, colored or movies." Nor was it unusual to be in a restaurant and be asked, "Hey, are you fellows movies?"

Kelton was certainly a movie. Once the public had a name — Kelly Green — to attach to the face on the screen, a connection was formed more powerful than anyone could have foreseen. It was not uncommon for a whole bag of mail to arrive for Kelly Green each day. We were forced to hire a handful of secretaries to answer it.

Kelton began to be recognized, occasionally at first, but soon it was an all-too-frequent experience. Never the most handsome of men, he was amazed and delighted when lovely young women would approach him and gaze fawningly at him. With his name recognition, though, other studios began to seek him out, blatantly trying to take him from Phoenix. From his initial start as a ten-dollar-a-day player, Kelton was soon earning a hundred a day. Not long after, he would get twice that.

As would happen with many others who achieved stardom in films, Kelton began to believe his own fan mail. The first evidence of this came on a picture called Kelly's Belles, when a gag called for him to do a tumble down the side of a hill. I was explaining the set-up to him when he nodded and said, "Fine, J.D. Just get it the first take. I'm not doing it again."

"What do you mean? What if we don't get it the first time?"

"I mean I'm not going to do it more than once. I'm tired of taking all the hits and getting all the bruises."

"But that's what you're paid for, Kel! That's what you wanted to do ever since the day I met you!"

"Still. It's my hide and I'm looking out for it. Get it the first take or you're out of luck." He turned and walked away.

That was when I knew we would eventually come to a parting of the ways. Kelton's conduct became more and more haughty, and he expressed dissatisfaction with virtually every aspect of every film, from the casting to the story line, from his costume to the hours we had to work. I was first puzzled, then saddened by this turn of events, but I could no longer reason with Kelton. Someone else had his ear and was filling it with "should'ves, would'ves and could'ves." Other cast members began to dislike him; he was apt to scream at them when a take was over if they had not played the scene to his liking. Leo and I had many discussions at the end of the day. We couldn't include Kel in these talks, since he disappeared after the last scene of the day and went off with a new bunch of friends.

This same scenario was being repeated in other studios. Any performer who caught the public's attention became the object of bidding wars and campaigns to steal him away. I'm sure Gus VanLandingham was somewhere laughing and saying, "I told you so."

## CHAPTER FORTY-NINE

I was pleased when D.W. Griffith came to town in 1911. He made an initial trip out, during the harsh New York winter, and then decided to move permanently when he made his break from Biograph. He was beyond question the most talented director working and had been very successful at Biograph, but he was desirous of making longer stories, while the studio merely wanted more of what he had been giving them. He made a four-reeler called Judith of Bethulia, a spectacular costume drama, but grew weary fighting the studio for every cent.

We had dinner together on his second night in California. As he sipped his wine, Griffith told me about his next project. "I'm going to tell the story of the War between the States, Jubal. The true story, the whole story. I don't know how long it's going to be, but probably as long as a night at the theater. My grandfather was in the War, you know. He told me many stories."

"As long as a night at the theater? How do you know an audience will sit still for three hours or more? And will the story really take that long to tell?"

"Probably. It will show how the War affected two families. And for the first time, people will see how the South suffered in the aftermath of the defeat."

"What's it going to be called?"

"*The Clansman*. It is based on a book by the Reverend Thomas Dixon. Are you familiar with it?"

I had read Dixon's book when it was published several years before. And I had heard him speak at the Confederate Reunion where my father preached. Dixon's book was full of hate, especially for the Negro. I sat in silence for a few seconds until Griffith looked up at me and said, "Don't worry, dear boy, I'm only going to put the truth on the screen. As a Southerner, I know you will like it."

I was not so sure, but Griffith began to describe how he was going to shoot battle scenes with hundreds of soldiers, and how the film would resemble the photographs of Matthew Brady. It was hard for me to get very enthusiastic in describing my own one- and two-reelers after hearing his plans for this epic.

Two months later, Kelton informed me that he had received an offer of a thousand dollars a week from a rival studio and that I'd better come up with a similar offer if I expected to keep him. "Your present contract has ten more months on it, Kelton. If you want to negotiate an extension for that, I'm more than willing, but I don't think we can match a thousand a week."

"That contract can be broken. My lawyer says it's full of holes." He stood there, staring at me belligerently.

"What the hell has happened to you, Kelton?"

"I've made you a ton of money, J.D. I'm only looking out for myself."

I opened the large drawer in my desk and found Kelton's contract with Phoenix Films. "If you're not interested in fulfilling this contract you signed with me, then I'm not going to hold you to it." I tore the contract into halves, then fourths.

"Fine," he said. "I'll see you around." He stood, held out his hand for a shake, then walked out. Leo was hanging around the outer office and he poked his head in the door.

"Did he leave? Never mind, I can see that he did." He entered and sat in the seat Kelton had warmed. "What are we gonna do, J.D.? The Kelly Greens are the most popular things we do."

"I don't know, Leo. Did I do the wrong thing?"

"Aw, no. He was becoming impossible to work with. But he's sure gonna be tough to replace."

We ended up making several Boys In Blue comedies without their famous leader. They did okay, but not nearly as well as the ones which featured Kelton. Our other films continued to do reasonable business, and we were still doing alright, since we were saving a lot of money which had been going to appease Kelton's ego. We had built up a cast of character actors who were versatile and dependable and we began to give them each larger parts in other stories. But I was beginning to feel stale after several years of cranking out a film a week. I was lonely, too.

Any day of the week, I could step out in front of the studio and examine a bevy of young women who had heard the siren call to California. Some of them were extremely beautiful; it would become routine for the prize in many beauty pageants to include a trip to Hollywood for an audition. In the group outside my door, there were always several who had come to the Coast, had a cursory "audition," caught the fever, but never secured a role. Some were stranded there, having no funds to go back home, and were forced to take jobs in stores and offices while still trying to break into the picture business. This adds up to desperation and I grew accustomed to that hopeful-yet-haunted look in the eyes of pretty girls who believed I could give their life purpose by casting them in a silly comedy and who therefore were willing to do whatever it took to get that part.

I am not bragging when I relate that I never took advantage of any of these women. There were great temptations, yes, and there were some women outside my front door who did go on to be stars. But on my desk in a gold frame was the photograph I had taken of Melva/Evangeline. She looked content and happy. But her picture was a reminder to me that I had not done well when I opened my heart.

So I worked. When I was not on a set, I was viewing rushes or reading scenario ideas or casting the next picture. In rare moments away from the studio, I ate meals in restaurants — I could not remember my last home-cooked meal — and went to theaters to see the films of other studios. Leo finally convinced me that we deserved and needed a vacation. So I closed the studio for two weeks and he and I took the train to San Francisco. The city was still recovering from the tragic earthquake in 1906, but the progress was remarkable. Films of the quake's aftermath had run in every nickelodeon in the country and it was impressive to see the determination of this unique city in making its own rise from the ashes.

For two weeks, we tried not to think about the movies. We ate well, read a lot, rode the cable cars, took ferry cruises. And we thought about the movies, of course. Our livelihood could not easily be shunted from our conversation; after all, it was the very reason Leo and I had hooked up in the first place. Leo asked me if I believed we were meant to be partners.

"I don't know. I do believe everything happens for a reason. But I'm not sure if God has an interest in the picture business or not."

"Are you getting itchy to do a big feature like Griffith?"

"No, not really. I'm happy if we just keep making films that make people laugh or forget their troubles for a little while. I don't have any big message to deliver."

"That's good," said my old friend. "Because you know Griffith is going to fall on his face with this one, don't you? I heard he's already used up all his financing and hardly had a shot to show for it."

"I've heard it, too. But he's always known what he was doing, Leo. It's hard to argue with his choices in the past, isn't it?"

"Everybody comes to the end of their lucky streak, Professor. Let's just ride ours for as long as we can."

I agreed. But I was concerned enough to send a telegram to Griffith. In his reply, he asked me to come visit him when I returned to Hollywood, promising that *The Clansman* was going to be a spectacular achievement unparalleled in the history of film. Oh, yes, by the way, would I be interested in investing in it?

That didn't sound promising. Griffith had come to California with hefty backing to begin his new company and so far had produced nothing in the way of finished films. Where was all that money gone? I did not care to invest in a project that seemed unlikely to ever reach the screen.

## CHAPTER FIFTY

I was on the set, coaxing a performance from a boxer dog named Buttons when a telegram arrived. I called for a break, then tore open the yellow envelope. It was a letter from my sister Martha, informing me that Father had died suddenly, apparently of a heart attack. He had gone to bed as usual one night and never awakened. Mother had been strong and in control, using their new telephone to call one of the church deacons who came and helped with the body. Martha said she knew there was no way I could make it home in time for the funeral, but asked if there was anything I wanted them to do for the service.

I wanted so much to talk to Father then! I wanted to ask him if Heaven was as he pictured it and if there really were golden streets… and did he enjoy his life? I wired Martha and said I couldn't think of anything to add to the funeral service. I sent them all my love and I included some comforting words for Mother, but I didn't feel very eloquent. The finest man I had ever known was gone.

A few evenings later, I was surprised to get a visit from D.W. Griffith. He greeted me effusively in that wonderful voice and inquired as to my welfare. I told him about my father's death and he seemed genuinely sympathetic; family ties were very important, he said, and I should always honor my father's memory. We made some additional small talk before he came to the point.

"Jubal, I come to you in need. I cannot meet the payroll. Every penny I had has been put into this film and I have nothing else to give. My backers are afraid. They think I should close up shop and cut the losses now. But the footage we're getting is magnificent! I just need some friends to share my resolve. This would be an investment, of course, not just a gift."

"David… can I see some footage? I'm not doubting you, I just want to see what I'm putting my money into."

"Of course, dear boy. Let's go to my place right now."

We rode in Griffith's car to his studio, where some sort of work went on twenty-four hours a day. He roused a projectionist and showed me some of the battle scenes. I was stunned; what looked like thousands of Confederate soldiers were shown fighting thousands of Union troops, all dressed authentically down to the buttons on their tunics. There were explosions like I had never seen in a film, shots of cannon fire, shots of hundreds of bodies lying dead on the battlefield. It was amazing stuff, convincing in every detail. If I hadn't known better, I would have believed it was actual documentary footage from a time when no such thing existed.

At the end of the reel, the lights came up and Griffith looked my way without saying a word. "How much do you need?" I asked.

"I need at least two thousand to pay the extras and to buy more film. Most of the leading players have been working without salary; they believe in the picture."

Although the scenes I watched had no plot as such, being random shots of battle, they were filled with such power that I had to believe in the picture as well. "I'll have to visit the bank in the morning. I can let you have six thousand dollars. I'll bring it by as soon as the bank opens."

Griffith's face brightened. "Wonderful! Thank you, Jubal. You're a true friend." We shook hands and then he drove me back to the hotel. I dreamed that night that I was a Rebel soldier.

## CHAPTER FIFTY-ONE

Months later, Griffith had finished *The Clansman* and its premiere was scheduled for February 8, 1915, at Clunes Auditorium in Los Angeles. I had heard from several other people in the film business that they had been approached by Griffith for money just like I had. Most had given it; the film community in California was small enough to have a sense of family to it and Griffith was nothing if not self-assured. But it was clear that he had called in every favor from every acquaintance and that, if *The Clansman* was not a huge success, he would likely lose everything he owned. I was fearful for him, yet I found myself admiring his dedication to his dream. I had fallen into a routine, cranking out formula pictures week after week, with little thought of "advancing the art," a phrase Griffith was wont to use. I resolved to put more of myself into the films I directed.

The premiere night was spectacular. The huge Clunes Auditorium was full of curious viewers, eager to see what new thing D.W. Griffith had wrought. I was seated directly behind Lillian Gish, who was frequently cited as the finest actress in films. I chatted with her a bit and she called my attention to the presence of several dozen old men. "See? That entire row is former Confederate soldiers. Mr. Griffith invited every veteran he could find in the area." Some of the old men wore their gray jackets proudly, even if they could no longer be buttoned.

Silent movies were never truly silent. Every theater had some sort of musical accompaniment, even if it was only a piano or — in the cheapest variation — a phonograph. But on this night, I watched as musician after musician slipped into the orchestra pit until it looked like a symphony was to be performed. Little did I know.

At the appointed moment, the orchestra erupted into a fanfare that gave me chills because of its grandeur and power. Simultaneously, the title of *The Clansman* appeared on the red curtains, even as they slowly opened to reveal the huge screen. I looked down at my Father's watch to check the time. When I was able to look at it again, more than three hours had passed.

I had not been so transfixed and amazed by a film since the first night I saw Edison's Vitascope back in Austin in 1896. *The Clansman* engrossed the audience from the first frame and held its attention for reel after reel. After reel. The soaring orchestral accompaniment was inspirational, and I felt my emotions were simply another instrument being played by Griffith, the master conductor.

There were scenes of such impact that I realized the row of seats in which I sat was being shaken by the sobs of men, an experience I have not had before or since, except in a church service. As the proud South fell in defeat and then suffered at the hands of the carpetbaggers and reformers, there was no doubting where Griffith's sympathies were.

There were also scenes when I wanted to crawl under my seat from embarrassment. Dozens and dozens of white actors, in blackface, mugging and eating fried chicken and watermelon, playing newly-elected Southern senators who hated to wear shoes, but loved to drink whisky, even on the floor of the Senate. This was what I had feared after reading Thomas Dixon's book; he believed the Negro to be subhuman. My discomfort was shared by many in that huge theater. And the heroes of the film, who ride in to rescue the desperate people? None other than the white-robed Ku Klux Klan, a secret society who had long since disappeared.

Even so, the story of the film drew me in and kept my attention through the very last reel.

When it was over, there was a tumultuous ovation. Griffith appeared on the stage, looking very small, and basked in the applause, triumphant once again.

Griffith took *The Clansman* back east to high acclaim from most everyone, although colored groups picketed the film and tried to have it stopped. I believe it was after the second premiere when Thomas Dixon encouraged Griffith to change the name of the film. You are probably more familiar with its second identity, *The Birth Of a Nation*. The film began to play in roadshows around the country and drew huge crowds and huge protests everywhere it went. Audiences lined up to pay the unheard-of price of two dollars a seat for this film, at a time when you could see a movie for a dime anywhere in America.

I had continued to work on my own films, trying to inject them with more quality, but I found it increasingly difficult. If I came up with something that would make the story more powerful, it invariably made it run too long. I began thinking about doing longer features. Many of the trade papers believed that feature films were the future of the business. I decided to take some time off and make a trip back to Texas to see my Mother and the rest of my family. I left Leo in charge with a couple of scripts to make with our young directors. I went back to the place of my birth.

## CHAPTER FIFTY-TWO

The town of Blanco now had its own movie theater! Other than that, not much had changed around the town square. Little about my home had changed, either, except that I realized with a shock that my Mother was growing old. Her hair had turned completely gray and she had developed a small tremor. But we had a wonderful visit. She told me that Father had been proud of me and had wanted me to have his Bible. The book was old and frayed; Father had written notes on almost every page in his tiny, neat handwriting. By each scripture was a notation telling when he had used that verse in a sermon. I turned to the passage in the gospel of Luke, the story of the Prodigal Son. Next to the verses was a date in 1898 — the Sunday after I stumbled home broke and broken from the fire. It was almost a diary of the life of this man who had been such a devoted servant of God.

I was introduced to all my nieces and nephews, most of whom I had never seen before. We had large family meals, including a picnic by the creek, and I felt the pressures of Hollywood slip off my shoulders. I spent two lazy weeks at home, then got back on a train. I was heading back to work, but first I planned to make a stop in Fort Worth. *The Birth Of a Nation* was to play there on the weekend and I decided to stay over a couple of days so that I might see it again, with a Southern audience, and judge whether it was as powerful as I had previously thought.

Fort Worth had changed much more than Blanco, of course. The city now had skyscrapers and paved streets and automobiles. And movie theaters! The opera houses of the past had given way to the newer theaters, bearing names like the Palace, the Egyptian and the Fiesta. I strolled around the downtown area for hours, going into a few theaters to watch a reel or two of films and to see what the places were like inside.

*The Birth Of a Nation* was to play at a large movie house called the Rialto, an ornate venue with rococo furnishings of gilded plaster and lush carpets. I studied the posters outside, beautiful color lithographs praising Birth as the greatest achievement in the history of film. It was still two days before the film would open. I bought a ticket and went inside to look over the theater. It was a beautiful lobby, full of rich maroons and gold, warm and inviting. I stepped into the large auditorium where a film of John Bunny, the beloved comedian, was playing to good reaction from the audience. I watched for a few minutes, but I had already seen the film, so I mostly took note of how the people in the theater behaved. Most of my film viewing in California was in private screenings and I missed watching pictures without an audience; reactions were always magnified and the experience seemed much more enjoyable in a crowd.

I observed for a few minutes, then decided to go back to the hotel. In the lobby, I looked for the restroom, finding it down a short corridor from the lobby. My intentions were changed, however, when I passed an oak door with gold lettering on it: Arthur J. Donovan, Manager.

I stopped still and felt my heart leap even as my stomach sank. Arthur Donovan had been the name of the crooked policeman in Austin who had caused Leo and I so much trouble. Surely it could not be the same man. I stood before the door, feeling a great sense of fear which I could not shake. I wanted badly to open the door to see the face of this Arthur J. Donovan, but I was afraid of what I might see. I returned to the lobby and paced for awhile, unsure of what to do. I hoped that the manager might make an appearance when the film ended, so I waited for a half-hour near the front doors. But the films simply started over without a break and I never saw the proprietor.

I went back to my hotel and had an unrestful night. Donovan was a name I had not given much thought to in many years. I had never considered where he might have gone after leaving Austin. I told myself that Arthur Donovan was not an uncommon name, that in the state of Texas there could be several men with the same name.

Next morning I went to the offices of the *Fort Worth Telegram*. I asked in the morgue room to see the clipping file for Arthur Donovan or the Rialto Theater. There was no file for Donovan, but there was a small one for the Rialto. I sat at a table and examined the handful of clippings. There was a lengthy one on the opening of the Rialto in 1909, with lengthy descriptions of the new theater's interior and furnishings. The fourth paragraph began:

> Proprietor Arthur J. Donovan says the Rialto will show only the finest pictures. Mr. Donovan is a veteran of the motion picture business in Fort Worth, opening his first nickelodeon in 1905. Prior to that date, he operated a vaudeville house on Commerce Street, where he also exhibited moving pictures. Mr. Donovan was also a decorated member of the Fort Worth Police Department for three years from 1898 until 1901. He received special commendation from the City for heroism after the tragic fire which consumed the Fort Worth Opera House and claimed twenty-six lives.
>
> Mr. Donovan left the police force when a small inheritance gave him the capital to open his first theater. The moving picture craze was a boom time for him and he had six nickelodeons operating within the city at one point. The splendid new Rialto will be the focus of his attention now, Mr. Donovan assures, and he promises that his new theater will show films of only the highest quality.

There was much more, but I found myself trembling. Donovan had been there the night of the fire! The night I was robbed of four thousand dollars, my watch, my voice…and a beautiful young woman. I returned the clipping to the file and left the newspaper office, walking aimlessly as thoughts tumbled through my head. Donovan had been a Fort Worth cop and had helped during the fire. Another policeman had shown Leo my watch as evidence that I was dead. I had lost four thousand dollars. Donovan had received an "inheritance" which started him in the theater business. I felt feverish, as though my head was going to explode, and I went back to my room, where I tried to sort out the pieces of this puzzle. I could not eat anything all day; my stomach was tossing furiously.

I returned to the Rialto, determined to get a look at Donovan, but he never made an appearance. I asked the ticket seller if Mr. Donovan was around. She said he had been, but that he was very busy getting ready for the premiere of *Birth Of A Nation* tomorrow night and was gone to see to some last-minute details.

I fell asleep surprisingly quickly that night, but my eyes popped open in the middle of the night. I groped for my watch and turned on the lamp to see that it was 3:20 in the morning. I could not go back to sleep, but tossed helplessly back and forth. At six I went downstairs to find coffee and a newspaper. On the front page of the paper was an article concerning the local chapter of the National Association for the Advancement of Colored People and their efforts to block the showing of Griffith's film. Several other Negro organizations supported the boycott and promised to protest the opening of a film they claimed was "injurious to the image of the Negro people."

I manage to get some breakfast down, but I was already feeling exhausted by 8:00 a.m. due to my lack of sleep. I walked the six blocks to the Rialto. Protestors were already in evidence and the group grew throughout the morning. Several hundred Negroes and perhaps a hundred whites stood before the Rialto, shouting and waving placards. I watched them and wondered what Griffith would have to say about this. I felt sure he would be aghast that the colored public would find fault with his portrayal of the Reconstruction. He had used a white character as the leader of the Negroes in the film, a role which was based on Thaddeus Stevens. But this crowd seemed unlikely to be appeased by such a tactic. They were demanding that the film not be shown. The demonstration was doubly ironic, since most of the protestors could not sit inside the theater anyway; colored audiences were consigned to the balcony, as was the case in most Southern theaters at the time.

Around noon, the street was packed with people and the police were struggling to maintain peace. Tempers were flaring as the protestors tried to dodge rocks, epithets and the occasional billy club. Then I heard a black woman scream. I looked around and saw several in the crowd pointing down the street and when I turned to see what had aroused them, I saw a sickening sight; sixty men on horseback, clad in gleaming white robes, with white hoods obscuring their faces. Even their horses were draped in white. Many of them bore a red cross over the breast and some carried long, thin wooden crosses. The sight of them seemed to whip the black protestors into a fervor and many of them began to scream and shout.

I wondered if D.W. Griffith had ever foreseen that his epic film would bring about the rebirth of this secret society of hate-mongers. The Ku Klux Klan had been a dead issue for many years, but now that *Birth Of A Nation* had painted the hooded horsemen as heroes, there was new interest in such groups. When I saw the looks of terror on the faces of the Negroes in the crowd, I wanted to weep. The marching horses were nearly to the theater when the Klansmen began shouting and waving their crosses. Pandemonium broke out as the first wave of white uniforms met the crowd. One black man produced a pistol, but he never got the chance to fire it. A Klansman shot him in the head and now the panicky crowd became a riotous mob.

Most people merely wanted to escape; a few wanted to stay and fight. In the end, many were trampled — by human and horse. I saw a Klansman draw back his cross to strike a black woman in the crowd; I lunged, leaping wildly to intercept the swing. The cross hit my elbow with a loud "thwack" and snapped in two. The hooded head swung to face me and I found myself looking into two eyes filled with such hatred that it saddened and sickened me. He reached inside his tunic with one hand and I knew he would shoot me without a second thought. I slapped his horse's hindquarters as hard as I could; the horse, surrounded by a frenzied mob, was already terrified and reared up, tumbling the Klansman off backwards. He fell into the crowd and sank beneath the wave of humanity. I did not see him surface.

The police were swinging their clubs wildly, accomplishing little except feeding the panic of the crowd. Eventually, the surge of people began to move eastward and break apart. I found myself running, trying to avoid stepping on those who had fallen. When I reached the corner, I looked back and saw the Klansmen who were still on their horses rallying and retreating to the west. It was over. Only the devastation remained. As the first ambulances arrived, I headed back to my hotel. I took a long, hot bath, conscious of many bruises and scrapes I had garnered. I thought back over what I had seen and it evoked an incredible sadness in me. How could people hate so much? How could a person belong to a group based on such hatred?

## CHAPTER FIFTY-THREE

The showing of *Birth* went on as scheduled that night, although a phalanx of police fronted the theater. I forced myself to enter and soon was sucked into the world Griffith had formed; the man could tell a story! Billy Bitzer's photography was the best in the business and the audience cycled through every emotion during the three hours. As the film ended, there was thunderous applause, pierced by a few boos.

When I reached the lobby, I glanced toward the manager's office. There stood Arthur Donovan. His reddish hair was mostly gray now, but his ruddy complexion had deepened and he had gained some weight since his days walking a beat in Austin. He was watching the crowd file out and he had a dour look on his face, as though expecting a fight to break out any moment. I avoided his glance and went on out to the sidewalk. But I was aware of something which made me feel ashamed; I realized I was as capable of hatred as a Ku Klux Klansman.

I stood in front of the theater, watching. The crowd broke into little groups and drifted away. I could see Donovan inside the lobby, instructing a group of ushers. When they dispersed to do his bidding, he walked down the corridor toward his office. I slipped back into the lobby. One usher was near the ticket booth, chatting to the young woman inside, and he said, "Theater's closed, sir. Did you forget something?"

"No, thank you. I need to see Mr. Donovan for a moment." I didn't break stride, but said this as I moved intently through the lobby. When I reaced the door of the office, I did not knock. I opened the door and saw Donovan seated behind a large desk. Stacks of dollars covered the top of the desk; he was counting the evening's take and it was a good one. He looked up to see who dared to intrude in his sanctuary.

"Yes? What do you want?"

I stood silent for a moment. What did I want?

"Do you recognize me, Mr. Donovan?" His rheumy eyes widened as he examined me. "Think back. I made a movie about you."

He sneered. "Ah, yes. I remember you. What do you want?"

"I want to know what you did the night of the fire. I want to know where you got the money to open your own theater. I want to know about this watch," I said, holding up Father's timepiece.

Donovan opened a drawer, pulled out a revolver and laid it on top of the desk. "You can go to hell."

"No, thanks," I said. "Already been there. Tell me what happened."

He smiled. "I don't have to tell you a thing. I shoulda pushed you back in that building. You should be grateful I didn't. I saved your life."

"You took everything I had."

"That's what you say. I was merely helping people get out of a terrible fire. I'm a hero. I got the medal to prove it."

"Who'd you steal that from? Come on, Donovan, I just want to know why. I can understand the money. I can even understand you stealing my watch. But why return it to Leo?"

He showed those tiny yellow teeth. "That was my favorite part. I wanted you and your buddy to suffer for what you done to me. I saw 'em taking him away and I found out where they went. I sent in another cop friend of mine with the watch. I wanted your pal to think you was dead. I figured I could bust up your little partnership."

"You evil bastard. You went to a lot of trouble to settle the score, didn't you? If I hadn't been there myself, I'd suspect you of starting the fire, too."

"Ah, no. That was Mister… Freulic, I believe the name was?" My blood ran cold; how could he have known the name of the man who struck the fatal match?

"So that's it? You had that man come in to burn our film? You sent a man in to die, along with two dozen others, to settle your little feud with me?"

"I didn't say that. I'm sure Jack Freulic didn't expect things to get so out of hand. Who could have known that stuff would go up so quickly?"

I felt like the world had turned upside down. I was stunned to feel the weight of this man's hatred for me and to discover the depths to which he would go to satisfy it. The revolver was in his hand now, pointing at me. "So did you come here wanting your money back, then? Here, put some in your pockets. Go on, take as much as you want."

I realized now how Donovan had decided this confrontation would end. A thief breaks in while the theater manager counts the money. The thief tries to steal the cash. The thief is shot before he can escape.

"You know what, Donovan? I didn't track you down. I wasn't looking for you. Despite your insane acts seventeen years ago, I'm still in the movie business. You didn't stop me. I own a piece of the film you're showing here right now. D.W. Griffith is a friend of mine. I own Phoenix Films and Leo is still my partner. Your schemes failed. You're a failed human being. Oh, you've gotten fat and prosperous — on my money — but deep down you're still the slimy cop who's shaking down anybody with two nickels to rub together." His smile was gone and his jaw clenched.

"Pick up that money."

"No. It's got blood all over it."

"Pick it up, I said. I will shoot you. Don't doubt that I will. And if you don't put the money in your pockets, I'll just do it for you…when you can't argue about it anymore."

I reached down to the desktop and picked up thick stacks of bills in each hand; there were hundreds and hundreds of them. I threw them at Donovan's face, a cloud of green, fluttering butterflies, and dived around the right side of the desk. I heard the report of the pistol, but I grabbed the telephone and crashed it into the side of Donovan's head. He fell out of his chair and dropped the gun. I picked it up and stood for a moment, breathing hard, trying to figure out what to do next. There was a door behind Donovan's desk, what I assumed to be a closet, and I decided to put him in there until I could escape. But when I opened the door, I was startled by a ghost.

A white robe hung in the closet, topped by a white hood, its empty eyes dark and dead. The whiteness of the robe was broken only by the scarlet cross on the chest and by a few drops of dried blood on the sleeve, souvenirs of the day's riot in the street. I closed the door and leaned against it. Donovan was getting to his feet at the end of the desk.

At that moment, I felt tired, sad and alone. Donovan looked at me with rage in his eyes. I raised the gun and shot him in the middle of his forehead.

## CHAPTER FIFTY-FOUR

That was pretty much the end of my career in the movies. There was a quick trial. Because I could afford to hire a good lawyer and I insisted on entering a plea of guilty, I was sentenced to life in prison. I entered the state penitentiary in Huntsville on October 15, 1915, the same day that the Supreme Court ruled against the Patents Trust for their unfair practices against the independent film companies.

Life in prison was not that difficult for me. I accepted my fate as being exactly what I deserved and I was willing to pay the price. In every way I tried to be a model prisoner. I eventually ran the prison library and read every book in it. I became the chaplain's assistant, helping prepare for chapel services and playing the organ. I wrote letters for fellow inmates who could not read or write. I was never in a fight, never broke a rule. Oh, yes, I also ran the projector whenever we were fortunate enough to get to see a movie.

I had numerous opportunities for parole and my record seemed to warrant it, but every time I faced the parole board, they asked me if I was sorry for what I had done. My answer was always negative. I truly believed that the world without Arthur Donovan was a better place than the world with him in it. Parole boards like remorse; I had none and never tried to fake it. I was prepared to spend the rest of my days paying for the choice I had made.

My family, of course, was aghast, and I was thankful my father did not have to see me behind bars. Mother visited me, but only twice; she died in 1918, during the influenza epidemic that swept the country. My sisters and brothers wrote to me for awhile, but their letters became less frequent and eventually ceased.

Leo kept in touch for the rest of his life. He tried to keep the studio going, but eventually sold everything and went to work for Goldwyn. He lived just long enough to see the premiere of Al Jolson in The Jazz Singer in 1927. We joked about how no one would ever believe the story line of that film; the son of a religious leader running away to enter show business? Preposterous!

Leo didn't think that sound would catch on. Actually, most people who had been in the movie business didn't see the need for sound. We had finally found a medium which could be understood by people anywhere in the world; why botch it up by adding spoken language? Leo's last letter was full of reminiscence about the time when we met and when we toured with our Passion Play. "I just wonder where we would be now if that fire hadn't started. Or if we had just paid Donovan his bribe and never tried to do anything else."

I wrote him back that it was useless to speculate about things we could not change. But he never got that letter. His wife Evelyn, whom Leo had married in 1917, wrote to me that Leo had died on the set of a Harry Langdon film, of an apparent heart attack.

You've probably heard of what happened to Kelly Green, the former Kelton Hendricks. He was the first film star to fall victim to a drug problem and his morphine overdose was front page news all over the world.

I heard a few times from D. W. Griffith. He was shocked at my fate, but sent words of encouragement. He would eventually be all but forgotten by Hollywood, the town he had done so much to build up. He died, mostly alone and unremembered, alcoholic and unemployed. But those who had invested money in *The Birth Of A Nation* reaped incredible benefits.

The film played for years, at the highest prices. No one is sure how much money it made. All I know is that the six thousand dollars I put in were returned almost a hundred-fold. Through my lawyer, I directed the saving and investment of those funds; I took a great loss in 1929 when the Crash happened, but I still had a good-sized fortune thanks to time and interest.

In 1959, I was informed that I was to be released, having served forty-four years. I sat on my bunk, looking around at the cell that had been my world for all those years. There were stacks of books I had ordered; I gave these to the prison library. The cartons of cigarettes which functioned as currency in the pen — I never smoked them — were distributed to my friends. The only thing I took with me, in the pocket of the suit the prison furnished me, was a fading picture of a green-eyed girl leaning against a tree.

I stepped out into a world I no longer knew, with a few dollars in my pocket, but with almost a million dollars in a bank in Austin. I had briefly considered moving back to Blanco, but eventually rejected the idea. The only relative I had there was a great-nephew, one of Paul's grandchildren, who lived on the old family homestead. But there was nothing left for me there.

Instead, I returned to Austin. I purchased a small house in the area that used to be Guy Town. It was now a residential district with no sign of its wild past. From there I could walk to Congress Avenue to the State Theater or the Paramount. I also spent a lot of time at the old Hancock Opera House, which was now the Capitol Theater. I go to the movies and to the library almost every day. I go to church every Sunday. They don't know my past; I like to think they would forgive it.

I was seventy-seven when I got out of prison. I lived quietly and made few friends. That's why it was such a surprise when I got the call from this Kevin fellow this week, in 1965. He had tracked me down, which must have been some task, considering all the various names I used. He's an English fellow and he's interested in silent film. He wants to interview me. I talked to him on the telephone and told him I wasn't sure how much my eighty-three-year-old brain could recall, but he was welcome to it.

He told me that a bunch of old Imperial films had been found in a basement in North

Dakota, titles like *The Watchful Women*. I told him that had been the first film I directed and wrote for Imperial and he got very excited. I asked him if he'd ever seen a picture called *The Bear Suit* and he said yes! Seems that the Eastman House has a print of it. He asked me why I mentioned *The Bear Suit* and I told him it was the first scenario I ever sold. This got him even more excited and he said he would be flying to Austin next week to interview me — on film! He told me how rare it was to find someone who was making movies as far back as 1907. I kind of laughed and told him I went even further back than that. I thought he was going to have a heart attack when I told him about the Passion Play. He said he couldn't wait to meet me and to please be thinking about all the early films I could remember.

Remembering is a skill that comes easily to me. Forty-four years in the pen gives you plenty of time for introspection. Plenty of time for asking yourself questions and waiting until an answer comes. I'm looking forward to this fellow coming to ask me his own questions. Maybe he'll ask if I consider my life to be a failure? I don't, you know. I'm proud of what I accomplished. Oh, sure, there were other things I'd like to have done. I always wanted to have children…and I've always wondered if perhaps Evangeline might have been carrying my child when she went away.

But I have felt love and loss and fear and rage — all the colors in the paintbox, I reckon.

I have loved two women.

I have hated one man.

I have had absolutely nothing and I have had everything I wanted.

I have been through hell and I am looking forward to heaven.

And even now, when I ease my creaking body back on my pillow and try to find restful sleep, I frequently see those flickering images. I still see May Irwin kissing John Rice and it still makes me smile. Sometimes I see the images of white-robed Klansmen, riding along to save the day, with Wagner playing in the background. Or I see the great train robber pointing his gun right at me and I wait for the soundless "bang."

Who could have guessed, back in 1896, that the moving picture would become so important? I still have a hard time calling them "movies." To me, they'll always be the pictures… moving pictures.

But, you know, moving pictures really don't move at all. It's just one still picture after another that gives the illusion of movement.

That's how I view life, as a bunch of moments frozen in time. They go flickering and clattering by, bringing us laughter, terror, love and pain.

Then the film trails out through the gate and there is only the light.

It's all about the light.

*Mike Robertson*

## About the Author

Mike Robertson is a pastor, speaker and writer. This is his first novel. He previously published a collection of essays, *Shiny Spots In The Rust*. He lives just outside of Austin in the town of Dripping Springs, Texas. He is married to Lisa and they have one daughter, Lindsey.

Mike Robertson